ONE SUMMER'S NIGHT

"I will pursue you, Laurel Carrington," Dane said in his deliberate manner, "with every ounce of my being. The sun won't rise or set on a single day that I won't make my intentions known. Don't look at me with fear in those big eyes of yours."

"I'm not afraid of you," she replied.

"I won't do anything that you don't want me to do."

"I know you won't," she retorted. "I won't let you."

"But you do want me to kiss you. And you're mistaken if I'm not serious. I told you before, there is a connection between us I've never experienced before. And you felt it, too. I see it in your eyes. . . ."

Other Avon Contemporary Romances by
Mary Alice Kruesi

SECOND STAR TO THE RIGHT

One Summer's Night

Mary Alice Kruesi

AVON BOOKS ◆ NEW YORK

To Elizabeth Potter Kruesi
"Nana"
for years of magic

AVON BOOKS, INC.
An Imprint of HarperCollins*Publishers*
10 East 53rd Street
New York, New York 10022-5299

Copyright © 2000 by Mary Alice Kruesi
Inside cover author photo by Michael L. Abramson
Published by arrangement with the author
Library of Congress Catalog Card Number: 99-96444
ISBN: 0-380-81433-1
www.harpercollins.com

First Avon Books Printing: April 2000

AVON TRADEMARK REG. U.S. PAT. OFF. AND IN OTHER COUNTRIES, MARCA REGISTRADA, HECHO EN U.S.A.

Printed in the U.S.A.

WCD   10   9   8   7   6   5   4   3   2   1

Prologue

It was a night for magic and miracles. The soft, bluish light of the moon lingered on the purple mountain peaks, and above, stars flickered and filmy clouds drifted along the Milky Way like sailing vessels at full mast.

Maybelle Starr sat at her broad, wooden desk and stared out her open window. It was a crisp night, and in the distance where the woods met the open fields she could see the twinkling of countless tiny, brilliant lights. They were dancing, and as she watched them a wistful expression flitted across her face and unbidden memories waltzed in her mind.

A great white owl hooted in the distance, breaking her reverie.

"Yes, yes, Omni, I know," Maybelle said with a shake of her silvery head. Tapping a quill pen against her lips, she shifted her gaze to the calendar on her desk and reached out to finger its worn, dog-eared pages. She had long, graceful fingers with short, oval, unpolished nails, but her gaze caught the wrinkling of the pale skin against fragile bones and the faint hue of brown freckles—age spots, humans called them.

Twenty-one years have passed, she thought with a sigh overflowing with memories and hopes. At long last! Maybelle glanced again at the calender, at May 16 circled in scarlet, then again at the full moon that hovered low—expectantly—over the mountain peaks.

"It is time," she said aloud to the owl, to the moon, to the stars, to the dancing white lights. Taking a deep

breath, she smoothed out the letter on the desk with determined strokes and signed her name with a flourish.
Folding the thick parchment paper into thirds, she tucked
the letter into an envelope and affixed a stamp. Then, in
a sudden, impulsive move, Maybelle closed her eyes
tight, whispered a fervent wish, and kissed the letter.

One

The moon was full and shone in the sky like a resplendent queen smiling upon her subjects below. A gentle breeze stirred the air, carrying with it the many sweet scents from the flowers that were blooming at Longfield Gardens. Laurel Carrington always walked home through the winding parks. Usually she took her time to linger with the flowers and plants she adored. But tonight she pushed on at a steady pace, conscious that a tight-lipped Colin was tapping his foot at the door. When she passed the rose garden, however, her steps slowed involuntarily, she couldn't help herself. Her passion for roses was her one indulgence and after all, it was her birthday.

Pausing at the black wrought iron fence that bordered the hybrid tea roses, Laurel breathed in the night air and thought it wouldn't be too long now till the roses were in bloom and filling the air with their intoxicating scent. Ever since she could remember she was locked under the spell of roses. It was as though a thorn was stuck deep in her heart since birth, and each time she saw one she felt a small, exquisite prick of awe. Only one person in the world loved roses more than she—her father.

Yet why, whenever she caught the scent of a rose, did she think of her mother?

She gave in to the urge and leaned heavily against the fence. Another birthday and still her mother had not tried to reach her. Twenty-one birthdays of silence. Her father hadn't even wished her a happy birthday. Not that she'd expected it, but, like a silly child, she hoped. She hated this sentimentality that lurked deep within her to spring out at such things as birthdays, Christmas, and other holidays. Her father said it was an inner weakness to be cast out. She'd tried, she really had. But such things as remembered birthdays or gaily wrapped presents, or wishes on a star still mattered to her. That's why she hated birthdays. Every year they came around and every year the longing surfaced and it was a reminder of her character flaw.

So this year, her twenty-first, she'd taken pride in the fact that she'd almost forgotten it entirely.

She ran her hand through her head of cropped, blond curls and thought how pathetic it was to feel that a birthday was special. So she was twenty-one, she told herself. Big deal. Today she became an adult in the eyes of the world. Tomorrow she would graduate from college. She should be elated. Up to this point, her life had progressed in an orderly manner. Yet just when she should have been basking in her father's praise, disaster had struck.

She hadn't been accepted into graduate school. It was cocky to apply to only one, but she'd been so sure of her success. Now, all her carefully laid plans to become a biogenetic engineer had collapsed like a house of cards. She felt lost and adrift. She wouldn't admit this to anyone, but on her twenty-first birthday, she didn't know what steps to take. If only she had some sign, a signal of what she should do.

A sudden gust rose up. It was an unusually warm, gentle air that seemingly swirled around her head to caress her face and from somewhere in the distance she heard the high, musical sound of bells, or perhaps wind chimes. She closed her eyes and caught the sweet scent of mountain laurel and freshly mowed grass and moisture in the air, and for a fleeting moment she was transported to a familiar place in her heart where she felt young and carefree. A place visited only in her dreams.

Opening them again, she saw the familiar, orderly gardens of Longfield with their neatly trimmed roses, the spotless curved walkways, and the straight little signs directing a weary visitor which way to turn. In the distance, a church bell tolled the hour.

Nine o'clock! She really had to rout out these lapses into sentimental gushes, she thought to herself. Colin's face flashed in her mind and she frowned, pushing away from the fence and straightening with a look of stubborn determination that her fellows in the Longfield labs would have recognized immediately. With a firm tread, she took the familiar path once again.

Within minutes she was on the block she had lived on for as long as she could remember. It was a stately, suburban block, lined with tall oaks, elms, and maples that had been planted generations earlier and lovingly tended. Wilmington, Delaware, was a town that prided itself on its historical homes and spectacular gardens. Great or small, each house was a gem. Her father had brought her here when he was recruited to work at the famous Longfield Gardens as a young man, and he had single-handedly raised her and his career over the past twenty-one years, becoming in that time a renowned curator.

Coming up to their front door, she thought how their house was rather like her father, Arthur Carrington. It was a stuffy old Victorian solidly constructed of wood and stone yet surprising with moments of grace. She opened the door to find the house shadowy with the heavy velvet drapes drawn. She'd expected Colin and her father to be hovering at the door.

"Hello?" she called out loudly. When there was no answer she called again, "Hello, anybody home?"

How odd the house was so quiet, she thought to herself. Then her heart began to flutter with excitement. From deep inside an old, childlike wonder escaped: Could her father at last be throwing her a party? It would explain Colin's eagerness to get her home, and his worry that she was late. Twenty-one years was a long time to wait, but better late than never. With slow steps she moved from the foyer into the living room, her heart beating harder with each footfall. At any second she was expecting the lights to flash on and a dozen or so people to jump up from behind sofas and chairs and yell, "Surprise!"

But no one did. She tried to ignore the ripple of disappointment and searched the dining room, the kitchen, and library, moving through the rooms slowly. God help her, but she really was hoping someone would jump out and wish her a happy birthday.

But no one did.

A noise outside in the garden drew her through the kitchen, where no special dinner was simmering on the stove and no festively decorated cake was resting on the counter, to the porch where she saw her father and Colin bent over a rosebush engaged in a heated discussion.

There they were, two peas in a pod, with their suit coats slung over their arms, their ties loosened at the collar and their short hair gleaming in the blue moonlight, Arthur's with a silvery glint, Colin's white blond. They were undoubtedly discussing some theory, oblivious to the world outside them or the people that inhabited it.

She laughed at her own disappointment, telling herself that she didn't really want a party anyway. She silently returned to the house to the front hall table where the day's mail was stashed in a basket. Picking up the basket of mail, she sifted through the stack. There were a number of white and pastel-colored envelopes, no doubt cards from friends and family sending best wishes, a few bills, a magazine . . .

Nothing from Cornell University. Laurel slumped onto the hall bench and her hands rested dejectedly over the stack of letters. The one surprise she did hope for on her birthday was a long, white, hopefully thick envelope from Cornell's graduate program so she could show her father she was a success after all.

"Well, look who's finally home!"

She glanced up sharply to see her father standing in the foyer, a cup and saucer held in his long, elegant fingers. British born, he had always appeared stiff and out of place when compared to the fathers of other local girls. When other children were tossing softballs in the yard or going on family picnics, she and her father were pruning rosebushes or hiking through prairies.

"Hello, Dad," she replied with a reluctant smile.

Laurel saw her father's eyes dart quickly to the stack of letters then rise again, question shining in the bright blue.

Crimson scorched her cheeks as Laurel understood the question. She lowered her eyes and shook her head no.

"I see. Well . . ." He cleared his throat and looked discomfited. Laurel knew him too well for him to hide the disappointment in his eyes before he shook it away. "We shouldn't let that get us down in the dumps," he pushed on amiably. "It's your birthday, after all. May it be a very happy one. Come here, and give your old dad a kiss."

He couldn't know what those few words meant to her. She hurried to comply and when she squeezed tight, he muttered, "Good, good," while patting her back stiffly with one hand and balancing his tea cup with the other. She stepped back quickly, knowing these physical shows of affection always made her father uncomfortable.

"Thank you for remembering."

"You know how absentminded I am about such things. Colin's the one to thank. He's still out back. Shall I tell him you're here? He's been pacing about like a young buck. He's even brought champagne!" His tone implied he couldn't imagine why.

Laurel shrugged her shoulder. "Sure, that'll be fine. But before we celebrate, I've bad news. I've finished the series of slides." She licked her lips and looked away. "The results were negative."

She sneaked a look at his face. It had fallen in disappointment and she wished, with all her heart, she could do something to change it.

"Why don't you get Colin and the champagne? I'm just going to finish going through my mail first, if you don't mind."

"Very good. I'll just go tell Colin you're home."

Leaning against the smooth wood of the bench, she

turned to the stack of mail with ho-hum enthusiasm. The first card opened was a graduation card, the next a birthday card, then another. So much the same, she thought, just like every day of her life. The next letter, however, gave her pause. It was different that the others in that the large, irregular-size envelope was made of a heavy parchment and the elegant script was penned with an artistic flourish. The return address read only: Fallingstar, Vermont.

"I don't know anyone in Vermont," she muttered to herself. Her curiosity piqued, she pried open the envelope, careful not to destroy the lovely, thick red wax seal stamped with the design of a star. A sudden breeze rose up to kiss her cheeks as she opened the letter. A laugh escaped her lips. Laurel attributed the scented breeze to the open window in the foyer. The laughter she couldn't explain.

The paper was of the same thick, roughened parchment and, bringing it to her nose, she caught the distinct scent of mountain laurel. More curious than ever, she smoothed the paper and began to read.

My dear Laurel, (May I call you Laurel?)

Warmest wishes from me to you. I sincerely hope this letter arrives to find you well. You may be curious as to why I, a stranger, am writing to you. But, you see, I am not such a stranger!

I saw your paintings when you exhibited at the Delaware Art Fair some years back and they left an indelible impression upon me. I remember thinking, "Such talent, such potential for one so young!" Sadly, I have not seen other exhibits of yours since then, although I've tried to keep abreast. You see what a fan I am of your painting?

Laurel looked up and blinked in a stunned manner after reading the first page. She tried to recall when she'd exhibited those early landscapes. Why, it must've been five or six years ago, back when she was sixteen and still dreamed of being a painter. That was her one and only show, but it was memorable. She'd sold every painting, a remarkable feat for any artist. She could still remember vividly the flush of excitement and accomplishment she'd felt at this triumph.

Even so, her father had discouraged her from continuing her art, claiming that it was a nice hobby but should not take her away from her more serious pursuits in science. Immediately after the show he'd offered her a job as an illustrator for his books and the Longfield catalogues. The painstakingly detailed drawings left little time for her oil paints. In time, her desire to become an artist was tucked away with so many of her other "childish" inclinations.

But this woman claimed to have seen her work—and admired it! Who was this woman? Laurel flipped to the third page. The letter was signed in a large, elaborate script: Maybelle Starr.

Laurel's breath hitched as her hands stilled in disbelief. *The* Maybelle Starr? It seemed impossible that the world-renowned artist would be writing, much less complimenting her art. Why would the famous recluse take notice of her? This was crazy. Laurel dove back into the letter, her hands trembling slightly.

I have reached a point of decision in my life, as I believe you have as well. Sadly, my eyesight is failing and I find I can no longer paint as I once could. I've been searching for an artist willing to serve as my apprentice and, hopefully, train to be my eventual successor. Please believe me when I say that not just any talented painter can elicit the magic necessary to create a painting about the world of fae. It requires imagination, a unique sense of color, and a certain something I cannot put to words. I saw that something in your work. Now I am left to wonder, to hope, that you might consider visiting me at my home and studio—as my guest—to discuss the possibilities?

I know this must appear as a sudden invitation,

but I have been considering this for a very, very long time. Unfortunately, my eyesight worsens at an alarming rate and suddenly, time is of the essence. Thus, I would very much appreciate a timely reply.

Remember, my dear Laurel Carrington: Do what your heart—and your instincts—command and you will not be disappointed!

> *I eagerly await your reply,*
> *Maybelle Starr*

Laurel's breath stilled on her lips. The letter lay in her limp hands as she tried to make sense of it. With swirls and loops scribbled in ink, Maybelle Starr had taken her world and turned it upside down. Why, she still remembered the thrill she and all her girlfriends felt as young girls reading Maybelle Starr's tender books and poring over her glorious drawings of fairies. Maybelle Starr took the sweet paintings of Cecily Mary Barker and Tasha Tudor to a new level, hinting at a mysticism, even a sensuality that went way beyond a young girl's imagination. When looking at an enchanting fairy painting by Maybelle Starr, Laurel could almost believe that fairies existed.

Almost.

Laurel leaned her head back. To entertain such an invitation would be senseless, frivolous, even ridiculous. It would be something her mother might've done, and Lord knew she'd spent a lifetime endeavoring never to be like the awful, nameless woman who had abandoned her after her birth.

Yet now it felt to her that this letter had whisked away her father's warnings as the sweet breeze had swept away her sadness moments ago. In these few words this woman, this Maybelle Starr, had given voice to her most secret dream: to paint, to really paint in vivid colors and broad strokes, not the tight, clean, orderly black lines of her illustrations.

It was too much to deal with all at once. She could feel herself getting carried away and took steps to bring herself back under control.

"Look who's finally decided to come home," Colin called out as he entered the front hall.

"At last," she replied, lifting her face to receive his quick kiss. She quickly folded the letter and tucked it into her pocket.

"Happy birthday, love," he said near her ear. Then turning to face her father, he said more loudly, "You certainly have a beautiful daughter."

"As she's been beautiful for each of her twenty-one years. Let's move into the other room, where I can open this fine bottle of champagne and offer a proper toast. It's legal now," he said with a wink to Colin. "Time marches on and we're none of us getting any younger."

She shot a surreptitious glance at the two men. There was the sparkle of a secret in their eyes and a little too much animation in their tone. Those two were up to something.

Laurel patted the parchment envelope in her pocket, then wrapped her slender arms around herself as she followed them into the library.

Her father beamed as he saw them standing together, then clasping his hands like a man before a feast he said, "Before we open this excellent bottle that Colin brought for the occasion, why don't I leave the two of you alone for a few moments. I have a few things I must tend to and . . ." He cleared his throat as that light twinkled again in his eyes. "Who knows? We might have something else to celebrate tonight."

Laurel opened her mouth to protest his leaving but a thousand excuses died on her lips as she watched the door close. Laurel slowly turned to face Colin with a sense of dread as he approached with a steady step and in his eyes she saw a pompous certainty rather than what she'd always imagined would be a suitor's nervous anxiety. When he took her hands, his own hands did not tremble as hers did.

"I think you know what I want to ask you," he began with confidence. "We've dated for three years. I've not been with anyone else in all that time, nor have I wanted to be. And during those years I've made no secret of how much I admire you, and how much our relationship has meant to me. We are compatible, we share the same interests. You are the perfect choice to share my life. And at last, the time seems right. You're twenty-one, you've finished college. I've been waiting for this moment, for this day, for a long time." He straightened his shoulders and said with the solemnity of a preacher making a grand pronouncement, "Laurel, I want you to be my wife."

Laurel opened her mouth but no words came out. Her mind was whirling with indecision. There were a number of strong reasons why she should accept his proposal, and she analyzed them as she had her data an hour ago.

He was a handsome enough man, elegant in style and manner like her father. He was extremely bright, thus increasing the likelihood that they would have intelligent offspring. And he was a rising star in his field. His future was assured, a quality she wanted in a husband. And finally, she was fond of him. Perhaps this was all there was to love? It made sense for her to marry Colin.

But suddenly reason and common sense were choking her. Perhaps Maybelle Starr's letter prompted this surge, but suddenly she saw her life as neatly organized as the grid of her father's gardens and she wasn't ready yet to fall into line.

Her hand groped for Maybelle Starr's letter in her pocket and she was oddly reassured to feel the heavy parchment against her fingertips. *Do what your heart— and your instincts—command and you will not be disappointed.*

"Well, Laurel?"

Her rambling reasoning quieted and, acting on instinct, one word slipped out.

"No."

"What?" He appeared slapped.

Something in his tone roused her ire. Maybe the hint of superiority, or the implication that he expected her to meekly say yes. She dropped his hands and clasped her own tightly.

"I'm sorry, Colin, but the answer is no."

"But Laurel, I've always assumed . . . You've given every indication that . . ." His face mottled and he blurted out, "Even your father expects that we marry!"

She paced the floor trying to gather her wits and her temper. "You and my father are ready for me to marry, but I'm not ready for me to marry!" Stopping, she swung around to face him. "You say you care about me? You find me the perfect choice for a life's partner? For heaven's sake, Colin, you talk about me as though I were one of your genetic specimens! What about love? Passion? Don't you feel these things for me as well?"

Colin seemed thunderstruck. "But . . . of course I do," he stammered. "That goes without saying."

"It shouldn't! I want to hear the words. You never speak those words to me. You never make me feel those words. Every girl wants to hear that when a man proposes marriage."

"I didn't think you were the sentimental type."

That hurt, and she didn't even know why. "Well, I am! Maybe I didn't know just how much I was until this very moment. But I know now and I also know, Colin, that I cannot marry a man who doesn't love me."

"I can't help but notice there's no talk of love on your side either!" Looking into his gray eyes, she thought they looked like maelstroms.

Something in her face must have alerted him because he drew himself up, closing his eyes tight and taking a deep, shuddering breath. When he opened them again, his eyes looked like calm seas. "I'm sorry for raising my voice, Laurel. I don't think you know how deeply you've hurt me."

"Oh Colin," she said, feeling a rush of guilt. "I'm very fond of you, I may even love you. I . . . I don't know. I just need some more time. I'm not saying I'll never marry you. I'm just saying not now."

"Are you quite sure? It's not as if you have all that many options at the moment."

Her cheeks flamed but before she could reply there was a brisk knock on the door and her father entered.

"I'm not disturbing anything?" he asked, his brows rose in expectation.

Colin squared his shoulders and his lips pinched. "Nothing at all. I'm sorry, but I've got to be going. I'll see you at the graduation, that is . . ." He turned stiffly to face Laurel. "If you still want me there?"

"Of course I do, Colin."

She expected a smile, or at the least a softening of his rigid expression, but she'd underestimated the depth of his hurt. He only nodded, blank faced, then turned to walk briskly from the room.

"Will someone explain to me what's going on?" her father asked, his brows raised and eyes wide.

"Don't you think I should be asking you that question?"

His expression altered. "I know that Colin asked me for your hand in marriage. It was the proper thing to do and I respect him for it. And I gave my blessing. You know how I feel about the young man."

"But do you know how I feel about him, Father?"

He appeared stunned. "Why, yes, I thought I did."

"How could you know? We never discussed it. We rarely discuss anything of importance to me. I suddenly realize, Father, that you know very little about me. And what's even more amazing is that I know as little about myself. Isn't that a heck of a thing to discover at twenty-one years of age?"

"What did you tell Colin?"

"I told him I couldn't marry him."

Arthur's chin dropped. "How could you refuse him?"

"Are you're implying that it's only logical that because we've dated for years I should spend the rest of my life with him?"

"Yes, confound it!"

"What about love, father? Doesn't that enter the equation?"

"Love alone won't build a marriage. Too often passion and . . . lust cloud reason, and before you know it all you'll have left is desolation and despair. I don't want that for you, Laurel. Care, compassion, concern—these are the building blocks of a solid marriage. Colin is a good man, a man with a future. He'll take care of you."

"I don't want anyone to take care of me! Not even you. Don't you understand that?"

"You're being unrealistic!" he exploded.

"Whenever I do something I want to do rather than what you want me to do you tell me I'm being unrealistic," she fired back.

He visibly pulled himself together, unaccustomed to her fighting back. "Let's be sensible and talk this through," he began again. "Sit down, please."

"I don't want to sit down." She set her jaw and began to pace the floor, filled with a heady new sense of rebellion. It felt great.

"Then if you'll excuse me, I will. I'm not as young as you." He made a show of settling into his favorite armchair, crossing his legs, and settling comfortably in the cushions. Laurel crossed her arms and readied herself.

"You're at a crossroads," Arthur began, sounding every bit the patronizing parent. "You're graduating from college tomorrow and your future looms large. The way I see it, you have three choices." He held up his fingers. "One is to marry. Let's just table that decision for now. Two is to go to graduate school to pursue your career in biogenetics. But we both know that option hasn't panned out. Third is to come work full time at Longfield."

He cleared his throat. "I was going to discuss this tomorrow after your graduation, but I'm offering you a full-time position at Longfield. You can continue as my assistant and as an illustrator for the catalogues. The terms are fair, if not generous. And best of all, you and Colin can continue to work together." His lips twitched with amusement and he added, "Which makes option one and three a combined deal, as it were. So. There you are!" He clasped his hands together on his folded knee, obviously pleased with *his* plan for *her* future.

For a moment Laurel felt like a bird that had just been put into a cage. Her heart began fluttering wildly, fearing the closing of the gate that would lock her in forever. Her hand fumbled by her side and felt the crinkled lump of Maybelle Starr's letter. With a flash of inspiration, Laurel saw an escape. Her hand darted to her pocket and she pulled out the letter, brandishing it in the air with triumph.

"I have another option!"

Arthur raised his brows with suspicion and asked, "What option is that?"

"I received a letter today from Maybelle Starr," she began, her voice betraying her with its ringing excitement. She moved quickly forward, opening the letter. "It's the most remarkable thing. She saw my art exhibit." When he looked perplexed she added, "Remember when I showed my paintings at the Delaware Exhibit? You *don't*?" She frowned but pushed on. "Well, this woman remembered them. You won't believe it, but she's invited me to come to her studio in Vermont to be her apprentice."

He rose from his chair to tower over her. "You can't be serious! What nonsense is this? An artist's apprentice? You? Who is this woman, anyway?"

"Maybelle Starr. She's a world-famous artist. She illustrates books and has collections of her own. She paints . . ." Laurel hesitated, knowing her father would scorn anything even remotely associated with fantasy.

"Paints what? Abstracts? Landscapes?"

She exhaled heavily. "Fairies."

The color rose in his face as he stared in shock. Then he blurted out, "Ridiculous. Outrageous! This is no option, this is caprice!"

"It is not! It's real. And I want to do it."

He slammed his fists in his pockets. "You're just like your mother!" he blurted out.

Laurel's color paled. All her life, the worst thing that her father could say to her was that she was like her mother. To be compared to her, the indulgent, heartless creature who abandoned father and child, never to be seen from again, was cruel and painful. A slap to the face would have hurt less. Far less.

"I am not!" she fired back, but she couldn't stop the tears that flash flooded her eyes. Hastily she wiped them away. "I'm nothing like her. I've done everything you've asked of me all of my life and just because I want to do something for myself you throw that at me? That is so unfair."

Arthur bent his head and took a deep, calming breath. "I know and I'm sorry," he said in a low, tremulous voice. "I shouldn't have said that. It's just that when I see you act so impulsively I lose my head. Surely you see the futility of an artist's life? It's a fine enough hobby, but not a career."

She raked the short curls of her hair and held a clump close to her neck. "You may be right. I don't know. I only know I need some time to myself. Away from Colin—and you." When his face fell and he sat back into his chair, she came to his side and sat on his knee, the way she used to when she was a little girl. Resting her cheek against his chest, she spoke softly.

"Please try to understand, Dad. I'm not happy. I know I'm not like my mother. But I can't keep trying to be you, either. And I can't yet be Colin's wife. Don't you see? I woke up this morning realizing that I was twenty-one years old and I only know who I am not. I don't even know what I'm good at."

"You're very good in horticultural science."

"But not good enough. I have to face the facts." Her voice trembled and she tried to collect herself before she gave way to the loathsome tears. She was comforted by his gentle patting on her shoulder.

"I want to go to this studio in Vermont. It's different and new. It will give me a chance to explore myself and what I really want. I might even find out that I'm good at painting. Is that so crazy? It seems to me to be a very rational step at this point in my life."

Arthur's eyes were sad as he reached up to touch one

of her short blond curls with his fingers. She saw again that pain in his eyes that came from somewhere deep inside.

"When you were arguing with me, I saw a flash of something in you that reminded me very much of your mother."

"I have a terrible temper . . ."

He smiled gently, not with reproach. "Not so very terrible." He rubbed his jaw then said in a slow manner, as though the words were being dragged from his mouth, "I suppose it wouldn't be a bad thing if you were to take a little time for yourself."

"No, it wouldn't," she replied, gaining heart.

"And painting is a fine enough hobby."

"Umm-hmmm," she replied, letting this comment slip by without debate.

"Just a summer madness, eh? A final fling—before you settle down." His patting ceased, followed a moment later by a brief but heartfelt hug. "I'll miss you."

"Thank you, Dad," she said, leaning forward to kiss his cheek. She knew in her heart it was so much more than a fling. Inside, joy and excitement bubbled in her veins, bringing her to her feet. She was giddy with the realization of her first impulsive act. An initial listening to instincts.

And her instincts told her to fly!

Two

Driving to Vermont, Laurel felt in her heart that she was flying. She'd never been on an adventure of her own choosing before. In typical fashion, she'd planned each minute detail of the journey carefully. She was flying solo. She'd never done anything so impulsive, so daring in all her life!

Two states to the south, Colin and her father were no doubt wagering just how long it would be before she came running back home. But as she drove toward Vermont and put more miles between them, she couldn't help but feel that her brief respite was in fact more of an escape.

By late afternoon she'd crossed the border into the Green Mountains. The wheels rolled beneath her but she felt the hum in her veins. Once off the highway, she opened her window and breathed in the sweet mountain air and tapped her fingers in time to the music on the radio. It was a perfect day! The sun shone in a cloudless sky upon an intense spring-green grass that spread out over acres of rolling hills and mountains, a veritable feast for scores of black and white cows standing in the fields.

Raising her sights, she marveled at the dreamlike quality of the soft, hazy green of leaf buds that encircled the trees like jade clouds. Spring was further behind this far north and she was glad not to have missed it. It seemed poetic to be experiencing a rebirth within herself as the earth sprang to life outside.

After another hour of winding two-lane roads she spotted a small green sign that announced—to anyone paying close attention—the town of Wallingford in bright white letters. With excitement bubbling, Laurel set aside the road map and pulled out the second letter she'd received from Maybelle Starr. In it she'd written of her absolute joy about Laurel's decision to visit Fallingstar, and she had included travel directions that were as strange as they were precise. Her father had taken one look at them and rolled his eyes in dismay. Apparently, the reclusive artist didn't pay heed to the usual road signs, markers, or buildings. She had her own unique manner of seeing the world.

Follow the main road from town until you come to a wide, spreading hay pasture bordered with a crumbling stone wall and a lovely stretch of marsh marigolds. You'll recognize it by the ancient spreading oak tree smack in the center of it, alone and proud as only a tree can be. You'll know it when you see it. Turn left after you pass that field, then left again when you reach a patch of rhubarb that thrives near an old cellar hole.

What kind of directions were these? Laurel chewed her lip and squinted her eyes out the window, slowing to a crawl in search of any road markers. But there were none. She had to still be on Town Route Nine, hadn't she? Continuing onward was an act of faith.

Then she saw it, an open, rolling hayfield and right dab in the middle of it, standing proud against a cloudless sky, was the most magnificent oak tree she'd ever seen. Turning left, sure enough she spied a wide patch of rhubarb with its thick fanlike leaves spread wide over bright red stalks and she believed without a doubt that a cellar hole was under there somewhere. Turning left again, she veered off the paved town road onto a private, narrow gravel one.

Laurel slowed to a stop. There was no proud gate with the name Fallingstar emblazoned upon it. There was no gate at all to hint that this was the estate of the world-famous artist. Only a tilting metal mailbox at the end of the road indicated that there was even a house somewhere beyond in that wilderness. She bent to check her directions, such as they were.

Now you'll enter a tunnel of leaves that marks the entrance to Fallingstar. Welcome, dear Laurel!

Looking up, Laurel saw that the branches of the thick border of trees were so close they touched and formed a seemingly impenetrable tunnel. It looked as though it was the passage to a strange, even foreboding, world filled with trolls under bridges and elves and other supernatural creatures she'd seen in Maybelle Starr's books. Taking a deep breath, she fired her engine and pushed on.

The car whined as it made its way up, up, up the twisting gravel road that traversed the mountain in a slow, steady escalation. Part of the way up she ambled along a smallish brook with clear water that gushed madly downhill over smooth white rocks. The higher up she went, the more dense and dark the woods became, and though it was beautiful she wasn't sure she liked it here where the wild and untamed governed. Just when she thought she'd have no choice but to back the car down miles of precipitous road, the trees cleared and she broke through the darkness to a lovely clearing of land perched high on the mountain ledge. It didn't seem possible that such a place could suddenly appear so high up—but here it was.

Laurel stepped from the car and stood in the clearing a moment, stretching her legs and fanning the long khaki skirt that clung to her legs. The air was cool and sweet this high up in the world and she breathed it in deeply. Looking off into the distance her breath caught in her throat to see just how high she'd come.

This peak was higher than most of the other mountains in the area. The pointed tips of other mountain peaks poked through the thick, low-lying clouds like mystical islands. Above, the sky was exploding in pinks and purples as the sun began its descent. Laurel felt for the first time in years a palpable yearning to paint. The air, the scene, the mood—it was no wonder Maybelle Starr painted the enchanting world of fae.

Eager to meet her hostess, she turned her head from left to right in search of someone, some greeting, but no one came.

"Hello!" she called out. Only the cry of a bird in a distant tree replied. Her brow furrowed and, searching the horizon, she saw what looked like a break in the solid hedge. Drawing nearer, she discovered a small shrubbery gate and through it, a narrow pathway of stone and wild thyme. As her foot brushed by, the ground-cover's scent filled the air.

She turned a curve and her breath caught in her throat with wonder. Stretched out before her, far out to where the woods began again, was the most delightful garden she'd ever seen. It rolled and cascaded with riotous glee down slopes and around curves. Yet it was perfection in symmetry with winding walks bordered by neatly clipped shrubs, trees, and countless flower and herb beds.

Banked against the wall of the mountain, seemingly carved out of the mountain itself, nestled a low, spreading house of wood and stone with wide, mullion windows to catch the southern sun's rays. A thick roof of grass sloped low and hung like crocheted lace over the eaves.

She laughed out loud because standing on it, with ears perked, was a dwarf, long-haired angora goat munching away as free as you please. The little house was obviously inhabited as the crooked stovepipes on either side puffed blue-black spirals of smoke. Most eye-catching of all, however, were the fairies.

Everywhere she looked—sculpted onto stepping stones and rock, etched on metal windchimes, carved from wood, and painted on murals, were fairies drawn in the unique style of Maybelle Starr. There was no doubt whose house this was and her heart beat faster at the thought that she would be staying at this utterly beguiling place. Excitement quickened her step to the massive front door of solid oak carved with an intricate woodland scene of toadstools, ferns and, of course, sprites. She knocked three times, but no one answered.

She didn't mind having to wait since she it meant she could explore the garden. She liked being alone, was accustomed to it. Walking along the laurel-hedged pathway she stopped occasionally to bend and study more closely a rare genus of plant that she'd only read about in books. It was like being a child walking through a candy store. Here was a wondrous collection of ancient species of herbs and flowers! Her father would be enraptured. This was clearly the garden of a master. Lost in her fascination with the garden, she was caught by surprise to hear the high whinny of a horse approaching.

Jolting her head up from a polyanthus shrub, she saw a figure, a man, emerge from the thick green wall of woods at the far edge of the plateau. He was too far off to see clearly in the deepening dusk, but she could tell he was tall and broad shouldered, a giant of a man, who walked with a bold, comfortable swagger through the tall grass of the clearing. His attention was on the spirited, broad-boned, white horse he led, pulling a small cart. She stood still, breathless, waiting. She knew the moment he spotted her because his long stride came to an abrupt stop, jerking the lead in his hand and causing the horse to shake its long, flowing mane and whinny in complaint.

They stood facing each other for a long time as ripples of tension flowed in the air between them. He wore a wide-brimmed hat slouched low over his face so she could not see his eyes but she sensed they were glaring at her with suspicion, for his body stood rigid in his high, muddy boots. Everything about him, from his shadowy features, his hulking size, the tautness of his shoulders beneath the worn, tattered suede jacket appeared threatening. When the stranger moved forward again directly toward her, her breath hitched. She took two steps back, then stopped as an innate stubbornness clicked in.

I belong here. I am invited, she told herself with the straightening of her shoulders and the lifting of her chin.

She hawked his every step as he drew nearer. He took his time about it, but never for a moment did his head turn as he marched straight toward her. He stopped only long enough to tether the horse at a post, his movements too deliberate for ease. He offered a few long strokes to soothe the restless animal. She noticed that his hands were enormous, tanned and streaked with dirt. Then he was coming toward her again and she felt as though the earth rumbled each time his foot hit the ground.

"We don't welcome strangers here," he said before he even came to a stop.

She swallowed hard and looked up into the dark eyes in the shadow of the wide-brimmed hat. He was intimidating, and common sense told her to turn and walk away as fast as she could. But she remembered the gentleness with which he'd soothed his horse.

"I may be a stranger," she replied. "But I am an invited one. My name is Laurel Carrington, and if this is Fallingstar, then I believe I'm expected by Maybelle Starr."

There was a pause, then he reached up to whisk off his hat in a clumsy attempt at good manners.

"This is Fallingstar, Miss Carrington," he said in a rich baritone that rumbled from deep inside his chest. "And you're expected."

It was polite enough, though begrudgingly said. Laurel stared up into the face of this mountainous man and mustered her resolve. It wasn't his size alone, but his presence that filled the space before her. He was all angles and sharp planes with a broad, tanned forehead, high chiseled cheekbones, and a strong, proud nose. His jaw was like squared granite and his long arms and legs were as strong and solid as tree trunks. He wore his hair long to the neck and it was as wild and unkempt as field grass. But it was the same dark, rich color of the earth that streaked his hands, clutched tightly now around his hat.

He appeared to be in his late twenties but his dark eyes were lined at the edges and had the wariness of an old man hardened with years of experience. A simple man. A laborer, probably someone local hired to chop wood. No one to bother with.

"Is Ms. Starr here?" she asked in a crisp manner.

He studied her a moment with his dark, piercing eyes, then stuck his hands in his pocket and replied in a Vermont drawl. "Yep."

"I knocked on the door of the house, well at least I think that is her house, but no one answered."

"She's not there."

"Oh? Do you mean that's not her house? I should have known better. It is such a queer little place and she's such a famous artist."

"That'll be her house." He spoke plainly with his eyes square on her. If this was a card game, with each phrase he upped the ante.

"Oh? I see. Well," Laurel stammered, feeling a blush color her cheeks. "Then she *is* home?"

"Nope."

"But you just said she was."

"I said she's here. Somewhere."

"Well," she said, nettled. "Do you know when she'll be back?"

"Nope."

Laurel pinched her lips. He was being deliberately obstinate, the mule. "She *will* be back tonight, I assume?" she said as politely as she could through clenched teeth.

A teasing smile twitched at his lips. "One never knows."

"What does that mean? Is she coming back or not? I don't think that's a difficult question to answer." *Not even for you.*

"It is if you knew Maybelle Starr."

"But it's late!" Laurel blurted out at last, exasperated. "It's dark!"

"Yep. Almost."

"Well, she has to be back soon," Laurel said in a decisive manner, clasping her hands together in a tight clinch. She was speaking more to herself than to the imbecile before her. "She's expecting me, after all."

"Maybelle loves the night as much, maybe even more, than the day. Some nights she stays out till dawn."

Laurel's eyes widened as her vision of a prim recluse of an artist fizzled in her mind, replaced by the image of a wild and restless old woman who wore crooked red lipstick, had frizzled hair and danced all night in bars. Maybelle Starr, the famous artist of sweet and lovely fairies was *that* kind of artist? What had she gotten herself into?

"That's great, just great," she said, bringing her fingertips to her throbbing temples. "So what am I supposed to do while she's out dancing? I can't stay out here all night. There are wild animals wandering around. Bears and wolves and, and . . . who knows what else? And I'm exhausted. I've been driving all day and I'd kill for a nice cool glass of water."

"There's a nice inn back in Wallingford," he said without a hint of concern in his voice. "You could drive there, spend the night. Then, if you want my advice, you should go on back home to wherever you came from. It's best that way."

So, the village idiot can speak in complete sentences, she thought with a frown.

"I see. And you know what's best, I suppose?" He paused to lazily rub his jaw and she thought she'd scream in frustration if he answered *yep.*

"Maybe."

Her eyes narrowed as she scrutinized the tall, rugged man before her who seemed to be enjoying this game of cat and mouse. "Just who are you, anyway?"

"Dane."

She waited for more but after another long pause it was clear nothing more was forthcoming. "Dane . . . ?" She raised her brows with her voice.

"Just Dane."

A stubborn mule, she thought to herself. She drew herself up and said with ringing sarcasm, "Well excuse me, *Just Dane,* but I'm not inclined to take your advice. I'm an invited guest of Maybelle Starr and I've traveled a long way to get here. The last thing I intend to do is turn around and go back home to Delaware. And since you are obviously not as well informed as you pretend to be, I'm not just passing through. I'll be spending a long time here. The entire summer, in fact, if not longer."

"That'll be long enough," he said in a low growl.

Now it was his turn to draw himself up from his lanky slouch. Like a bear rising from hibernation, his broad chest swelled and his dark eyes burned with the fire of indignation.

"I know who you are and where you've come from, Miss Laurel Carrington," he said without a trace of his earlier drawl. "And I also know that you've been especially invited here to work with Maybelle Starr on this notion of hers to find herself an apprentice. I also know that people like you find her and her house and the way she does things *queer,* as you put it, and will no doubt laugh and mock what she holds most dear. Most people don't matter to Maybelle Starr and she can laugh right back at them. But I suspect, for whatever reason, that you might be different, and I don't want to see her get hurt."

"You think I've come all this way to hurt her?"

"I don't know why you've come, Miss Carrington. And I don't really care. But I do care about Maybelle Starr. She is a good, kind, and loving woman who means a great deal to me. So if you have any idea that this is just some summer camp for laughs and good times then turn around right now. We don't need your kind here."

He glared at her in warning, then flopped his hat back on his head, turned heel and walked back to his white horse with such force the heels of his boots gouged deep half moons in the gravel.

Laurel watched his back aghast. *Your kind?* She'd never been so insulted in all her life. That this common woodcutter would dare to verbally cut her into little pieces infuriated her. She wanted to hurl something at him and flexed her fingers, searching for something to put in them. She spun on her heel and stomped back to the front door of the strange berm house and with desperation knocked hard on the front door. When no one answered, she looked around with exasperation. There was no sign of life, save for that stubborn man untethering his horse and the small goat chewing grass and looking at her dispassionately. Without much choice, she rested her bottom on a tilting sculpted toadstool by the door, grateful that at least it wasn't another darn pointy winged fairy.

As the sky deepened around her, she dropped her chin in her palm, tapped her foot and fumed, shooting mental arrows into the back of one mule of a man as he led his white horse down the mountain road. Above on the roof, the goat shook its head, ringing the bell around his neck, and bleated a loud, piteous, "Baaaaah."

"My feelings exactly," she retorted, settling her chin in her palm.

Maybelle Starr hurried home through the woods. Her slender arms were overflowing with a wide array of wildflowers picked especially for Laurel Carrington's arrival: buttery-colored cowslip; coltsfoot, with its leafless stalks crowned by heads like miniature sunflowers; the delicate blue blossoms of violets; pure white trilliums; and a few solomon's seals with their sweet bell blossoms.

She wanted to wreath her young guest in flowers, giving her a homecoming fit for a princess. Her bare feet sped along the well-trod path with single-minded purpose. Tempted though she was, she didn't slow when she heard the high-pitched whispers in the trees, or when two fawns crossed her path for a visit—not even when she spied a yellow-eyed may apple hiding beneath its parasol leaves. Laurel Carrington was due to arrive at any moment and she wanted everything to be in the ready. All had to be dazzling, she thought, picking up her pace as she approached the light of the clearing just ahead.

Just as she was about to step out from the dense foliage she heard raised voices in the garden, voices that sounded tense and angry to her sensitive ears. She stopped short at the edge of the clearing and cocked her head to listen more carefully. First she heard a low, masculine voice that she recognized, followed by a high, feminine one she did not. Scuttling back a few steps she hid herself behind a broad maple trunk and peered out from the shadows.

Even with her failing eyesight she could readily pick out Dane with his good, strong back and his imposing height, standing in his usual wide-legged stance. And dwarfed beside him stood another figure—a slight, willowy shape so thin it seemed a gust of wind could pick her up like a dandelion puff and carry her across the mountains.

"Laurel . . ." she said in a whisper, her fingers tightening against the coarse bark. Behind her she heard the name echoed in the trees.

Maybelle cradled the flowers closer to her breast and squeezed her eyes tight with ecstasy. Laurel! She tiptoed from her hiding place closer to the edge of the clearing, desperately trying to make out the young woman's features with her shadowy eyesight. She *tsked* in frustration. It was hard to see in the dusk. Perhaps if she squinted . . . Oh, how thin she was! Didn't he feed her? And how rigidly she stood with her arms clenched about herself like steel bands. She couldn't quite see her eyes but . . .

Maybelle gasped in horror. Her hair! How short her hair was. Why, even Dane's hair was longer than hers!

She could have stood for hours just drinking in the sight of Laurel Carrington but the dusk was deepening and already the figures were but wispy shadows. And from the sounds of it, those two young ones were fighting. She pursed her lips as Dane stalked off and began leading the horse down the mountain in an angry gait. A moment later, Laurel was slumping on a stool beside the door.

Not a propitious start, Maybelle thought. "Well, we'll just have to change things, won't we?" she said aloud. From deep in the woods she heard the faint, tittering sound of laughter.

Three

Laurel thought she saw a sudden movement, a faint flash of light just in the far corner of her eye. She jerked her head but there was nothing there. A few yards away, fireflies were skimming the rain barrel. Would this day never end, she wondered, suppressing a groan. She was exhausted from a day's travel, hungry, and eager for a friendly face. Now she was seeing things. Maybelle Starr, where are you?

Searching the horizon she caught sight of a woman's figure walking in a smooth, floating gait from the forest with her arms overflowing with what looked to Laurel like wildflowers. She walked with a proud, regal carriage and wore a long, white gauzy dress that seemed to flow from her slender shoulders to the hem, which dragged along the high grasses of the open meadow. Bathed in the blue twilight she seemed to glow with an other-worldly quality.

This woman, she knew, was Maybelle Starr.

Laurel slowly rose to a stand, unconsciously straightening her skirt and smoothing her windblown hair.

"You must be my young guest," the older woman said in a melodic voice while gracefully extending her hand.

Laurel smiled and reached out to take the small hand into her own. At the touch there was a surge of warmth and good will that immediately set Laurel at ease. Maybelle was a dainty woman, smaller than herself by inches, and Laurel was only five foot four. Her hair was the color of spun silver and wound in a tight skein around her head. Most arresting, however, were her eyes. Under finely arched brows her large eyes were the palest green, an odd color that reminded her of dragonfly wings. Eyes so opaque that Laurel decided it must be the blindness that was overtaking her that gave her eyes that luminescence. Yet they sparkled with delight as she stepped forward, smiling.

"I'm Laurel Carrington, yes. Pleased to meet you, Miss Starr."

"Oh, we'll have none of that between us. Where I come from it is considered bad manners to use the last name when speaking. I am simply Maybelle. And you are my dear Laurel. But you came so soon! How clever of you to find your way without trouble."

"Your directions were unusual but clear. I might not have found my way so readily without them."

"Really! How wonderful. Most people complain about them. They take a few wrong turns or enter into some mishap in the woods. It is such a long way up and the road is iffy. And so you see, I have very few guests."

While she talked her eyes roamed Laurel's face as though she were capturing every detail. Laurel supposed it was an artist's way. "I hope my being early isn't an inconvenience."

"You've caught me by surprise, 'tis all. No matter. I love surprises! And look, I have one for you. See what treasures I've found for you during my walk in the woods!"

Laurel glanced down to take in the armful of flowers. "You picked all those wildflowers for me? It must have taken hours and hours."

"Oh fiddleheads," she said with a light laugh. "I have my sources."

Laurel's head turned to take in the vast gardens with numerous flower heads bursting through the soil. A profusion of daffodils bordered the woodlands. "There are so many flowers right here that are beautiful. You shouldn't have gone to any trouble just for me."

"They are beautiful, aren't they? But only *wild*flowers would do for your welcome, of course. Protocol is protocol, after all. Here, for you." She plucked a stem and tucked it behind Laurel's ear, stroking Laurel's short hair once with a tender expression. "That's better," she said. "Come, let's put them in water quickly. They're so thirsty. Follow me."

She turned and led the way to the house with an easy familiarity, as though Laurel had lived here for a long time already.

Stepping inside, Laurel felt that she had. It was a cozy, welcoming house of several small, low-ceilinged rooms that led from one to another like a rabbit's warren. Dark, roughly hewn ceiling beams contrasted with freshly painted white walls and the hand-crocheted white lace at the windows. It was a simple room with a simple charm. Everything appeared chosen for warmth and comfort in a harsh climate. An enormous fireplace dominated the room, braced on either side by tall stacks of chopped wood and a collection of cast-iron tools and pans with long handles.

It was also the room of a busy woman. Beside a lumpy, worn easy chair in the corner was a large wicker sewing basket. Fresh flowers graced all the tables. A spinning wheel sat near the window to catch the morning light, and circles of bright, multicolored hand-braided rugs covered the plank wood floors like stepping stones. On cold winter days, she could imagine skipping bare foot from rug to rug.

Following Maybelle to the kitchen, however, it was clear this was the heart of the home. It was as large as the front room, with the same white walls and dark wood trim. Stepping in, she was enveloped in the enticing scent of baked bread, cinnamon, and that delectable scent of something sweet from the oven. Sure enough, cooling on the counter were three round yellow cakes. Laurel's mouth began to water and her stomach begged.

An enormous, positively ancient black stove with its long necked pipe snaking to the wall was the focal point of the kitchen. It was an old war horse, standing on four legs, ready for more battles. Hanging on the wall around it were several shiny bright copper pots and pans, and beside it was another tall stack of chopped wood. Best of all, there was a bump-out greenhouse filled with spring seedlings leaning toward the glass. Laurel thought it was by far the most beguiling country kitchen she'd ever seen.

"Forgive the mess," Maybelle said by way of apology for the clutter of batter bowls and flour. She hurried to the sink to set the flowers in water. "I hate doing dishes, but then again, I hate a messy kitchen, so I do what I must. This afternoon I was just in the middle of baking when I saw how high the sun was and rushed out to pick the flowers before you came. And well, in the woods I lost track of time. That happens to me when I'm concentrating."

Laurel smiled, understanding that situation completely.

Always in motion, Maybelle began pumping the long handle of a red metal water pump. Laurel was stunned to see water flow through to the old porcelain sink and it slowly dawned on her that there was no running water to the house. Taking a quick look around the room, she noticed that there were no electric fixtures or sockets in the wall—not even a refrigerator. She'd read that Maybelle Starr lived a simple life, but she hadn't expected simple to mean primitive.

"There, that's better," Maybelle said, carrying a crock full of wildflowers to the table. "I can arrange them later, but now it's getting dark. I must get dinner started and a few lamps lit or we'll be scurrying about like mice, which might be fun, but let's not tonight. I'm sure you're very tired after your long journey and anxious for a meal and bed. You are hungry, Laurel, aren't you?"

Laurel was still digesting the fact that they'd be lighting oil lamps. She nodded, and her stomach growled on cue.

"Then I'll hurry. Do you mind going about the house and lighting a few lamps while I start dinner?"

Before she could utter a sound, matches were thrust in her hand and she was left to wander the strange house in search of oil lamps. She didn't have a clue how to light an oil lamp, but on removing the hand-painted shade, the long wick made it fairly simple. A flick of the match and suddenly a soft glow emanated from the glass globe. By the time she returned to the kitchen, soft lights glimmered cheerily in the warren of rooms and the oven was warm with a fire burning in its belly.

The house was even more cozy in the evening, if such a thing was possible. Maybelle's pots bubbled on the stove and soon she served a delicious vegetable stew with big chunks of cheese, hearty brown bread, and butter served in hand-carved molds.

As the candles flickered low and the bowls emptied, their somewhat stilted conversation gradually shifted from general comments about her schooling to more personal topics. The words were not as important as what was understood nonverbally. Through eye signals, tone of voice, manner of speech, Laurel discovered that she really liked Maybelle. Relief flooded her, and she felt the long day's journey weigh heavily on her lids. By the time they'd finished the dessert of sponge cake served with fresh berries and cream, their safe chatter wound down and Maybelle led her exhausted guest to her room.

"I don't know why you're so hot and bothered. What can one girl do?"

Dane looked at his younger sister, slouched on the sofa with a beer in one hand and casting a fishing rod with neat flicks of the wrist with the other.

"If she's anything like you, she can cause a lot of trouble."

Daphne snorted and took a long swallow of her beer. "Even if she does, Maybelle can handle it."

He shook his head and walked across the cramped, messy kitchen of the farmhouse they shared to pull out his pouch of tobacco and pipe from a bureau drawer. "I don't know. At one time, sure, I would've agreed with you. Hell, Maybelle took care of all of us." While he spoke he shook the tobacco into the bowl of the pipe and tamped it down. "But with her eyesight going, she seems more fragile. Vulnerable." He lit the match and brought it to his pipe, taking long puffs. When he had it lit, he smoked a bit in thought before saying, "It worries me. She's always done well enough alone. Insists on being alone. But if she needs anyone to help her now, she needs someone she can trust. Someone she knows."

"Oh no, don't go lookin' at me with those sorry eyes of yours," Daphne cried out, shifting her weight to face him. She was wearing a baggy pair of white overalls to cover a sunny yellow T-shirt that clung tight to her voluptuous body. "No way I'm moving back in with her. I like my own space, to come and go as I please. I can't go waiting on anyone or have anybody waiting on me or wondering where I am or what I'm doing. If I get the urge"—she paused to whistle and make a zippy movement with her hand—"I'm outta here. And Maybelle's just like me. She doesn't like anybody spying on her, either. She took me in as a child and we had five fine years together, but both of us are happier living on our own. You know that's true. Me and Maybelle like things just the way they are. She keeps an eye on me and I keep an eye on her."

She smiled and cast her rod in his direction. "And now that you're back from your travels, you keep an eye on everyone. Besides, it's all done. Maybelle went and found someone to stay on the mountain with her all on her own. That Laurel girl."

Dane saw again in his mind the wisplike girl with her strange, tilting eyes the color of moss. Maybelle would say she had the fairy in her eyes and in this case, he'd believe her. There was something come-hither about them that stirred him, even as they disturbed him. He didn't trust those eyes, or how they made him feel. Better that she leave them all in peace and go back where she came from.

"I don't like that Maybelle's chosen some stranger. And especially not this Laurel Carrington."

Daphne stopped casting the fishing rod to scrutinize her brother. He was staring out the window up the mountain, where Maybelle's house was hidden in the woods. His massive brow was furrowed with worry.

"Give her a chance, Dane. You've only just met her."

"I know her type. Opinionated, self-centered. Right brain."

"Oh yes, the wise world traveler speaks," she replied with a roll of her eyes. "One glance and you've got her pegged."

He turned to face her, not goaded by her tease. "Precisely. I've traveled from east to west and met people of all economic backgrounds, ethnic groups, religious beliefs, and cultures, and I'm telling you, little sister, no matter what color the skin, how many degrees, or how many dollars in the bank, a person's core is either good or rotten. And most of them are rotten. So when you find someone who's good, you protect her and treasure her. And Maybelle Starr is pure goodness."

Daphne cast her line with a sharp flick that indicated her annoyance. "Maybelle's got her other side too, which you've always been blind to. She's a trickster, a meddler, a first-class scamp." She took a jaunty swallow while her eyes sparkled with the devil. "She's my kinda woman. She's also a frustrated matchmaker and we're her pet projects. So if she's got some pretty young thing up there at the house, I'd be workin' way down in the barn, if I were you. It's fishin' season and Maybelle's bringing out the lure." Her eyes raked him with mock intensity. "She's got her eye on one big, mean ol' bass in particular."

"She knows better," he replied, rankled by her obvious show of casting her line and drawing in a big one. He'd been caught once before by a crafty angler and he'd never be caught again. "Besides, it's you that has them boys hollering outside your window like cats on the scent."

Now it was her turn to frown as she tugged her overalls higher over her voluptuous chest. "Silly asses, all of 'em. I can handle them boys. And if they start carrying on this summer like they did last I'll just have to whip 'em again." A cocky smile tugged at her full, sensuous lips. "And I can do it, you know I can. Besides, they're just sniffin' for some honey, but I told them outright that they can buy my honey at the market like everybody else 'cause that's the only kind of honey I'm giving out."

Dane looked at his sister with undisguised affection. Wild Daphne, with her fiery-colored hair to match her temperament. He couldn't blame the fellas for flocking around her. She was a beauty, same as their mother had been. He'd had to bloody more than a few noses ever since she came to puberty. With her overly endowed body and her cupid's bow lips, every male in the vicinity had blood boiling for Daphne. Not that she cared. It was odd how she was as cold as ice in that way. She was a free spirit who played poker with the guys, but when it came to relationships, Daphne backed off. Maybelle told him that Daphne was like one of the bees she raised—sweet as honey when she wants to be, but with a stinger poised and ready. Maybelle had also advised Dane to leave her be and not to try and make her fit into the mold of the other ladies in town.

Still, he worried about her and what was to become of her. She'd led an odd childhood, first raised by their miserable excuse for a father, and then by Maybelle with her peculiar beliefs and ways. It was no wonder Daphne felt more at home alone in the woods than with lots of folks she didn't fit in with.

"Well," he said with a tone of resignation, "I guess we'll just have to keep a close eye on what goes on up there." He exhaled a long plume of smoke. "We don't want any talk."

Daphne's brows gathered as she wagged a finger at him. "Ah, so that's the burr on your butt. You're worried that something's going to happen and bring folks back investigating."

He scowled and bit down on his pipe. "Yes, I'm worried. Maybelle came under a lot of suspicion when Ma disappeared. There's still talk."

"Idle gossip." She flicked her wrist and the cast the lure across the room.

The air thickened between them as Dane puffed at his pipe. "Foolish, loose tongues. The things they say. Ma was wicked sick. She went into the woods to die."

"Except she wasn't found."

He puffed. "It happens."

"And Pa?"

He bit down on the pipe and said through clenched teeth, "I don't know what happened to him and I don't care. He's no father of mine, as he reminded me enough times in my life. Besides, he's too much the cunning rat to have gotten lost in the woods. He knows these parts better than anyone besides me. I know because he could find most of my hiding places back when I was a boy to drag me out and lay the stick. If I were a betting man I'd bet Joe Flannery just took off somewhere. He set it up so people would think he got lost in the woods just so he could collect his insurance."

Just talking about Joe Flannery riled Daphne. "Dad's dead," she fired back. "That's just stupid."

Dane winced as though stung. Being called stupid or dumb in any way cut deeply.

Daphne ran her hand through her long snarled hair, cursing when she tugged on a knot. "Damn, I'm sorry, Dane," she rushed, but the hated words floated in the air between them. "I shouldn't of said that. I just got fired up because, well, it doesn't make sense that Pa wanted to collect on his insurance. He's dead, everyone knows that."

After a pause to cool down, Dane leaned back in his chair and said calmly, "Joe's body was never found. I'm just saying it takes seven years to declare a missing man legally dead." He took a long puff on his pipe. "And it's seven years this July."

"What are you saying?" Daphne sat straight on the sofa, swinging her legs around as she confronted him. "Do you think he's going to rise from the dead to collect his money?"

Dane drew on his pipe and blew out a long stream of Os. Daphne was either naive or blind to the reality that her father might still be alive. Dane was neither.

"A hundred thousand dollars is a lot of money to a man like him. When that policy comes due in July, I wouldn't be a bit surprised if we started seeing ghosts."

Daphne froze for a moment in thought, then in a sudden fury she frowned and tossed her fishing rod on the floor. She took a fierce swig from her beer. "You're just still mad at him, is all," she said, refusing to accept the possibility that her father might return. "You always hated him. Hell, who didn't? No, no, no . . . He's gone for good, and good riddance."

"Maybe. But no matter." He caught her gaze and held it firm through the haze of smoke. "I'm here now," he said in a low voice that held a strong current of reassurance. "And you never have to worry about him or anyone else ever hurting you."

"I don't need you to protect me!" she said with her chin out like a knife blade. "I don't need anyone. I can take care of myself."

It hurt Dane to watch as she brought her knees up to her chest to hug them, the same way she did as a child when Joe was drunk and screaming obscenities and started in at beating him again. Dane took it then because he was just a boy, and because he wanted Joe to take out his anger on him rather than Daphne. He knew he could stand it—had to. It was the only way he knew how to protect his sister.

But he wasn't a boy any longer. Joe Flannery had better not come back, he swore to himself. Not alive, anyway.

Higher up on the mountain, Laurel rested her head on the soft, downy pillow, yet could not fall asleep. Turning on her back, she stared around the small room she would call her own for the next few months. It was so different from her room at home. That one was modern with sleek furnishings and high-tech equipment. This was a room designed for a young girl, all whimsy and charm. The bed she slept in was snug with crisp linen sheets embroidered with blue moons and gold stars and wrapped like a gift with yards of tulle draped around the four posts. Across the pastel-colored, hand-crocheted rug she'd unpacked her clothes into a tall, maple armoire gloriously painted with woodland animals dancing together under smiling stars. They glowed in the moonlight that flowed in through the lace curtains. It was a room she'd dreamed of having as a child, and she wondered what lucky child had slept here.

Laurel yawned with exhaustion. This place was charming but so *foreign.* She wasn't sure she could survive three months here, where the living went beyond simple and veered into primitive. As cozy and tasteful as the house was, it had no heat other than wood stoves and no running water other than what pumped in the kitchen. The brook outside the house with its frigid fresh mountain water kept food cool in the summer. There would be no television, no CD music, no computers, fax machines, or any gadget that she so carelessly plugged in to that magic in the wall called electricity.

And there was no toilet. She'd have to use an outhouse!

She smothered a groan against the pillow. What was she doing here? *I should get up in the morning and go home,* she thought, clutching her pillow tight. Life in Wilmington was predictable. Normal. If she returned she had a sensible job and a stable, daily ritual in which she felt secure. Heck, she had a toilet.

If she stayed . . . There was so much new here. So much expected of her.

Outside her window she heard the distinctive hooting of an owl from the open window. It sounded very near. Again the owl hooted, seven low hoots, and its ancient song was soothing in its melancholy way. A breeze ruffled the lace at the windows, and looking up, she thought the moonlight sparkled with a fine, silver dust.

So much new here. So much expected of her. Her own words played again in her mind. They were true. Yet, she sensed that a whole new world was ready for her—here—if only she was willing. When she'd asked Maybelle why she didn't have any modern conveniences, she'd replied that she needed to stay as close to nature as possible to hear and see its joy. The modern world, she explained, could be too distracting with all its noise and clutter. Thus, she chose to live in her simple world.

And Laurel longed to experience that world. She wouldn't go home, she decided. There was too much at stake to scurry back to the security of the familiar. Come what may in the crazy realm of Maybelle Starr, she'd face it.

The owl hooted again, beckoning.

"Good night, Omni," she whispered, surprised at the name that fell from her lips. Now why did she think his name was Omni? she wondered, turning on her side and closing her eyes. She rested her cheek against the soft pillow, inhaling the overpowering scent of mountain laurel. It was a sweet, strangely familiar scent, one that came to her frequently throughout her life and always left her with a feeling of security and love. It was pervasive here.

Drifting to sleep, she felt like the little girl who must have slept in this room. Not a frightened child fearful of the mysteries of the night; not at all. Rather, a child filled with wonder.

Outside Laurel's room, Maybelle stood with one hand on the closed door and the other against her heart. Her eyes were closed and a smile hovered at her lips. Did she like the room, she wondered? Laurel couldn't know that with every embroidered stitch, with every hooked loop in the rug, with each star and fairy lovingly painted on the ceiling, Maybelle had thought of her. Every night for twenty-one years she'd come into this room and thought of her. Each morning for more than two decades she stood at the window and waited for Laurel's arrival. It was magic and miracles that had brought her to this house, to this room that was prepared just for her—at last.

"Welcome home, dear Laurel," she whispered as tears flooded her eyes. "My own sweet daughter."

Four

The moonbeam eventually changed to a sunbeam that washed her face and pried open her eyelids. Laurel yawned and stretched, bewildered and not quite certain of where she was. It took a moment for her to recollect that she was at Fallingstar and that this delightful, small room was now hers.

How sluggish she felt, like she was Rip Van Winkle and had fallen asleep in the mountains for a hundred years. Her dreams had been more vivid last night, too, and for the first time, she could almost see through the veil that always clouded her dreams. *It must be the mountain air,* she thought. There was a lassitude, a stretching, yawning kind of laziness that waged war with her eagerness to rise and meet her first day at Fallingstar.

But rise she must, she told herself, dutifully tossing back her luscious down blanket. What time could it be, she wondered, searching for an alarm clock, a wall clock—any kind of timepiece. Oddly, there wasn't a one. Even her wristwatch seemed to have been misplaced. It had to be late, she decided. Daylight bathed the little room with a golden light and already the beam was warm, hinting at unseasonable afternoon temperatures. Maybelle had already been in to fill a large, floral porcelain pitcher with fresh water, and beside the matching bowl she'd lain out a bar of homemade scented soap, a small linen towel, and a vase of wildflowers.

Pretty, Laurel thought, but what she really longed for was a pounding, hot shower to wash away the road's travel. She glanced at the claw-footed tub beside the fireplace with longing, realizing it would probably take twenty buckets of water hauled by hand and heated on the stove to fill it. Baths would be a luxury here.

But a bath was not her top priority at the moment. There was no way she could avoid the outhouse any longer. Maybelle had told her that the small door in her room led directly to the outhouse outdoors. With a muffled groan, she opened it and stepped outside. The warm morning sun was already high and her ears were pierced with the screeching of the crickets and countless other insects—an army of which she was sure were amassing in the dark bowels of the outhouse, just waiting for her. The small gray wooden structure was perched on a slight rise of ground beside the house. It looked clean and neat enough.

"Ready or not, here I come," she muttered as she tiptoed across the dewy stepping-stone path. The door creaked loudly on rusted hinges and cautiously peering in, she was relieved to find the little box was spotless. No spider webs lurked in the corners and light flowed in through the crescent moon window. Nonetheless she wasn't convinced some animal wouldn't nip at her bottom once she sat down, and vowed then and there she would neither eat nor drink after dark during her stay at Fallingstar.

After she dressed, she followed the scents of freshly baking bread to the kitchen. Standing at the door, she saw Maybelle dressed in another of her unusual, medieval-looking dresses, busily stirring batter with a wooden spoon while steam whistled from the teakettle behind her on the wood-burning stove. Her movements were quick and graceful, like those of the bright yellow bird in the cage near the greenhouse window. It chirped brightly in response to Maybelle's prompts and together they sang an odd morning song that was as poignant as it was lovely.

"Good morning, Maybelle."

Maybelle's face brightened on seeing her, and again

Laurel felt as though her gaze was swallowing her whole.

"There you are, sleepy head! It's almost good afternoon. Not to fret. The mountain air does that to newcomers. It's as though all the hustle and bustle of the city has to leach out from the system. Often it takes guests days and days to catch up on lost sleep. Amor and I've been waiting patiently for you to wake up."

Laurel glanced for a clock but again, found none. She was always one to glance at the time. "I apologize for sleeping so late. And on my first day. There isn't a clock of any kind in my room and I can't seem to find my watch. I haven't a clue what time it is. That's not quite the impression I wanted to set. Please, Maybelle, wake me early tomorrow and I'll get right up."

"Doesn't matter to me in the least when you wake up in the morning or when you fall asleep at night. Your time is your own. And I don't keep timepieces at Fallingstar. The sun and the moon do their job well enough. As for your watch, well," she rolled her eyes and offered a slight shrug of her delicate shoulders, "things have a way of disappearing and turning up again here. I'm sure you'll find your watch. And I make it a rule never to disturb one's sleep. Who knows what dreams might be interrupted? Though I'll wager the birds won't be so cordial every morning. They chatter about so loudly it's a wonder you didn't hear them." She turned toward the petite yellow bird in the cage. "No offense, Amor."

The bird began chirping, cocking its head and looking at Laurel with an uncanny awareness in its bright, shiny black eyes. She could almost swear the bird was talking to her.

"Well, in that case, good day to you, Amor, whatever time it is," she said in good humor. Then, taking in its distinctive black cap and wings, she said, "I thought goldfinches were wild."

Maybelle's face turned wistful. "They are, yes. But Amor was hurt years ago and must stay in his cage. But he is content in his cage as I am. And we are the best of friends, aren't we?"

The goldfinch hopped with animation from perch to perch.

"As we shall be." Maybelle's eyes were glowing as she brought her gaze to rest on Laurel.

Laurel smiled and nodded, feeling equally certain. "Speaking of birds, there was the most amazing owl outside my window last night. He sounded very near."

"That would have been Omni."

Laurel looked sharply up. "What did you call it?"

"Omni. That's his name," she replied matter-of-factly, adding flour to her batter.

Laurel swallowed hard. How did she know its name? Maybelle *must* have mentioned it to her, she reasoned.

"Do you name all the animals around here?"

"Of course not! They have their own names. They simply tell me."

Laurel released a drowsy breath, letting that comment pass without discussion. First she needed a cup of coffee for fortification. Her eyes began searching out a coffee maker, or a percolator, or at the very least, a jar of instant coffee.

"I've made breakfast," the older woman said, indicating the table set for one. "Berries, pancakes, and dark maple syrup I tap from my own trees. It's almost ready, so do sit down and make yourself comfortable."

"Please don't go to any trouble on my account. I don't usually eat breakfast. Just a cup of coffee and I'll get right to work." Her head pounded in dismay when she didn't see a pot or smell the cherished heady aroma. "Do you have any coffee?" she almost begged.

"That poison? I've made you some lovely herbal tea and a breakfast that will stick to your ribs during your day. Now, don't wrinkle your nose. Do try my tea. I make it myself from a special blend. Mustn't be stuck in old thinking, and who knows? You may like it."

Laurel slumped into her designated chair beside the seedling-filled greenhouse window and watched with horror as Maybelle poured her a steaming red concoction into her cup. *Red*, she thought with dismay, her stomach turning and her brain aching for a specific brown liquid with an aroma she craved. Sniffing the brew she asked petulantly, "What's in it?"

"Oh, a little of this and a little of that. I made a blend especially for you."

Laurel gingerly picked up the thin porcelain cup and after a final, suspicious glance, slowly tried one quick sip. It was sweet and mild. Harmless enough, she hoped. Not that it made up for the solid jolt of java she craved, but for lack of anything else, Laurel drank it thirstily while Maybelle watched with a satisfied grin.

"It's good, thank you," Laurel said, trying to remember her manners.

"I know it is." Maybelle's gaze wandered to Laurel's hair. "Poor darling," she asked with a voice laced with pity. "I simply must ask. What on earth happened to your hair? Was there an accident? Were you ill?"

Laurel's hand shot to head. "My hair? No! What's wrong with it?"

"There's so little of it! It should have grown long by now, to your waist at the very least."

She looked at Maybelle's hair, which was wound in multiple braids and looped again and again like a thick skein of yarn at the nape of her neck. Her hair must be as long as Rapunzel's, she thought.

"My hair's always been short," she replied, tugging a curl at the neck a bit self-consciously. "My father cut it when I was little, probably because it was easier to comb. I used to make the worst fuss when he brushed it so I can't blame him. Anyway, it's so easy I just got used to it, I suppose, and have always kept it short." She saw what could only be pique and pity in Maybelle's eyes and with a twinge of stubbornness added, "I like it short."

"Let it grow now, Laurel," Maybelle replied with gentle urging. "Long and free—as it was meant to grow. I'll teach you to braid it and do all sorts of lovely things to keep it out of your face. Where I come from a woman's hair is her crowning glory."

"Where I come from, short hair is quick and easy to manage. That suits me fine."

Maybelle pulled out one of the jeweled hairpins from her marvelous braids. "A small gift. May I?" When Laurel nodded with hesitance, Maybelle gently pinned back a fallen lock of Laurel's hair.

"You have such lovely hair, Laurel, like spun gold. Never put a shears to it, at least not while you're here at Fallingstar. It will, how shall I put it? Cut off your inspiration."

Laurel laughed shortly. "I can't see where the length of my hair would make any difference."

"There are things you can't always see at face value. You have to believe in what you don't readily see."

"My first lesson," Laurel muttered under her breath. She watched as her teacher flipped pancakes onto a platter with the ease of a short-order cook. The pancakes soared in the air, turned and landed on the platter with uncanny grace. Dressed in her buttery-yellow, flowing, gauzy gown and with her silvery hair wound around her head, Maybelle seemed in sync with the old fashioned country kitchen, the seedlings in the greenhouse window, and the wilderness of the mountains outside. Looking at her own tan shorts, tank top and strappy sandals fit for a resort, Laurel felt out of place at Fallingstar.

Maybelle sailed over to the table and served a tall pile of pancakes while Laurel looked on with dread.

"Please, not so many. I could never . . ."

"Fiddleheads," she said, nudging the plate of pancakes closer to Laurel. "You're as thin as a cattail and you'll need energy to work hard every day." As though she'd heard her thoughts, Maybelle continued in earnest, "We live a simple lifestyle at Fallingstar and it is demanding on one's strength and commitment. This is not a place for the faint of heart, though I like to think Fallingstar is a place for the young at heart. So eat a hardy morning meal, and eat again whenever you are hungry throughout the day. Eat to your comfort point—neither too full or too little. Listen to your body and it will let you know its needs, just as the wind speaks to you with news of a storm. We'll fatten you up a bit, firm up your muscles and let the mountains work their magic. Soon you'll be blooming as fresh and pink as a May flower."

Laurel pinched her lips tight, refraining from telling her hostess in no uncertain terms that that she wasn't a child and preferred to eat meals at precisely seven, noon and six. This was her apprenticeship, she told herself, and instead, she nodded politely and reminded herself again that while she was here she was going to try to shift gears to fit in. Even if the gears were grinding at the moment.

"I may have had a slow start this morning," Laurel said in way of explanation. "But I'm actually a hard worker. I'm ready and eager to start right in. Can we talk a bit about how we'll start the apprenticeship?" she asked, picking up her fork and staring at the mound of pancakes.

"Of course." Maybelle slipped down in a chair beside her at the table and clasped her hands neatly together in her lap, looking at her expectantly.

Laurel held the fork and stared back at her, waiting. When it became apparent that the older woman wasn't going to say anything more, she elaborated.

"Well, for starters, it would help if you let me know what to do."

"Do nothing. Do everything!"

Laurel closed her slack jaw and placed the fork back down on the table. "Certainly you must have some plan?" At Maybelle's blank expression, Laurel pushed on. "A schedule you want me to follow?"

Maybelle smiled sweetly, eyes wide.

"Do you have a suggestion?"

"Well," she began in all seriousness, tapping her chin. "If I were you, I'd wander around a bit. Explore the garden, hike down the road and back, anything you wish to get a feel of the place."

"But not all day, Maybelle. I don't want to waste your time. I should start working, don't you think? After all, I can walk around during my breaks."

"Breaks?" she asked, uncomprehending.

"Free time."

"But all your time is free, my dear."

Laurel cocked her head, unsure whether Maybelle was teasing her or not. The expression on her face was sincere, so Laurel decided to try a new tack.

"Perhaps you could tell me what—specifically—you'd like me to do?"

"Eat your breakfast."

Laurel sighed in defeat and obligingly picked up her fork and faced the seemingly insurmountable stack. "And then?"

"You could go to the woods. That's where the heart of Fallingstar lies. Don't ask me where to go—specifically," she hastened to add even as the question formed on Laurel's lips. "It's your adventure. Open your eyes and your ears. Smell the flowers. You'll come to know the fairies through your senses first, you know."

The fork stopped at Laurel's mouth. "You're speaking metaphorically, of course."

"I'm speaking about entering the woods and the heart of nature."

"Maybelle," she said, resting the fork again on the plate. "Really, when you talk like that I don't understand."

"Not all things are meant to be understood."

Laurel took a deep breath, thought better than to debate this one either, then quietly looked down at what looked like the Leaning Tower of Pancakes. She picked up her fork again and forced herself to eat a bite. Her eyes widened, then drifted closed in ecstasy. The pancakes were as light as clouds and the dark, thick syrup exploded in her mouth with the rich flavor of maple.

"Oh, unfair," she groaned with delight. "These are heaven. No one could not devour them." She took another bite, then another, surprising herself by making short work of the stack of pancakes.

Maybelle poured her a second cup of tea, beaming.

"Aren't you eating?" she asked between bites.

"Goodness, I've eaten hours ago. But I'll share a cup of tea."

When Laurel reached for the pot beside her to pour out a cup, Maybelle said with some alarm, "No, no, that

pot of tea is just for you. I've my own blend, over here."
She was already on the move toward the counter. "I'll
pour my own cup."

"While you do that, let me get my notes. I've tried to
prepare and maybe if we chat awhile, I'll be able to
understand what you want me to do. Hold on, I'll be
right back." She hurried to her bedroom to fetch her
briefcase. When she returned, she was pleased to see
Maybelle sipping her tea at the table. It was a rare moment when the woman sat still.

"I've done some research before I came," she said,
joining Maybelle at the table and pulling out files from
her briefcase.

"Research?" Maybelle replied, her brows arched high
with surprise.

"Yes. I always try to be well prepared," she replied
with pride. Her research capabilities had served her well
all her life "I know you're the expert, but I didn't know
anything about fairies and I thought I'd better bone up
before I tried to paint them. I started with fairy tales."

Maybelle appeared astonished. "You had to do research on fairy tales? Why, didn't your father read them
to you as a child?"

"Dad?" A short laugh escaped. "No! If you knew him
you'd see the humor in that statement."

Maybelle's brows furrowed as she tapped her tight
lips.

"His idea of bedtime reading was *The Language of
Flowers* and Darwin's adventure on the *Beagle*," Laurel
continued matter-of-factly. "I picked up some fairy tales
on my own one way or another, they're pretty hard to
avoid. But I never actually read them. Or anything about
fairies per se. Other than your work, of course," she
hurried to add, not wanting to offend. "But your paintings were, well, different. Not the least childish. I don't
know why they appealed to me so much. I can remember
sitting in the garden, high in the branches of the weeping
willow just turning the pages of your books. Your fairies
weren't cute little flying women like Tinkerbell or the
Flower Fairies. They were so real, so mysterious. They

touched a chord," she said in a soft, faraway voice. "I think I wanted to believe they were real." Then, because Maybelle reacted with a seeming heartfelt relief, she added, "But of course, I was a child."

"But isn't that the point, Laurel? You were a child. Children are spontaneous and open, eager to believe."

"*Naive* is the word that comes to mind."

"Oh no, dear. *Wise* is a better word. Children listen to their instincts. They know that another world exists and revel in it. Watch a child at play and you will see joy and creativity. The darlings are always chatting with the Other World. It is adults who label that world *imaginary*. The secret is to try to see the world as a child again, Laurel."

"Is that another lesson?" She immediately regretted the sarcasm in her voice. She looked up and saw Maybelle studying her with her fine brow arched.

"If you insist on that term, then yes."

Laurel fingered stacks of research notebooks as though they were a lifeline to her own world of concrete thought. It was too easy to fall into the trap of fantasy, especially here, high in the mountains where the guru of fantasy land was spoon-feeding her philosophies with her pancakes.

"Let me show you something," Laurel said with deliberation, pulling papers out of her briefcase. Seeing her notes and charts grounded her. Soon, the table was piled high with papers filled with her feathery script. "I started with an Internet search, narrowed the search down, then prowled the libraries. I have to admit I was amazed. I had no idea how much there was to learn about fairies, in so many different cultures. Even the name is complex."

"Really?" Maybelle replied, but Laurel missed the sarcasm in Maybelle's voice.

She shuffled through stacks of papers, pulling out one and reading it. "It says here the term *Faerie* comes from the Latin *fatum*, or fate. Presumably because in more primitive times the people believed they had some control over human destiny."

Maybelle *tsked* with disdain. "A little meddling, perhaps, but what's the harm with that? Just a bit of fun, is all. Hardly what I'd call controlling destiny. Only humans like to exercise control over everything they encounter."

"Oookaaay," Laurel said with a roll of the eyes, returning to her pages of copious notes. "It says here that in France a fairy was called *fée*, and in England, *fae*. But in old England the Anglo-Saxons called an individual fairy an *elf*." She looked up and scratched her head. "You see, that's when I started getting a bit confused because I'd always thought an elf was some little man in the woods. Sort of like a leprechaun."

"They live in Ireland, dear," Maybelle said after a quick sip of tea. Setting her cup down she reached out to gently remove the papers full of notes from Laurel's hands and set them on aside on the table. "It's quite complicated," she explained. "Yet very simple, too. Don't get confused with human interpretations. Try instead to think of the basic four elements: earth, water, fire, and air. Then think of energy manifestations of these elementals—and there you are. Fairies!"

She appeared delighted with her explanation, as though Laurel should have understood it all instantly.

Laurel understood none of it. "That's much too vague. I can't paint energy. I need details and explanations. For example, what is the difference between gnomes, sprites, nixies, and pixies? There are dozens of different names, a bewildering number of creatures in all shapes, sizes, customs, habitats, and histories. I'm trying to get them all straight. If I could just come up with a single term or even a theory that unites them all."

Maybelle looked at her with an expression of pity. "Do you *need* to organize them into a single term or theory?"

"But of course. Or else how can I ever reason it out?"

"You can't. Reason will close your mind. What you think you understand puts parameters around what simply *is*. Don't be afraid. Open your mind, Laurel dear. Toss away all those research papers. When you walk in the woods let your soul flow out and nature flow in. Let them blend together and fuse into one. Only then can you truly understand."

Her father's warnings against nonsense and fantasy triggered in her mind and Laurel sat back, shaking her head. "No, that's just not my way of learning. I need to classify the fairies to study them."

Maybelle laughed lightly. "Careful, dear. The fairies won't have it! They're tricksy creatures and will delight in confounding your expectations. As soon as you categorize one, it will change. Shape-shift into another, just for spite."

Laurel paused, unsure of what she was hearing. "You talk about them as if they're real," she said in a soft voice.

"But of course they are."

Laurel felt her curiosity shrivel inside. This was too weird for comfort and she didn't know whether to laugh or pack up and go home.

Seeing her expression, Maybelle laughed lightly again and reached across the table to tap her hand. "Now don't put on such a sour face. It's really not difficult to understand."

"You're not making this any easier. I don't understand what you're talking about half the time."

Maybelle's face softened. "Or you don't choose to understand. Ah dear, I'm worried about you. You really are stuck in the mire, aren't you? How shall I ever pull you out?"

Laurel pulled away and shuffled her papers back into the briefcase, feeling hurt. "You think I'm stuck in mire simply because I don't believe?" She shook her head. "I don't think this is going to work if you expect me to believe. Skill with a paintbrush is one thing. Faith is quite another. Besides, I'd hate to think of what people would say about me if I went around saying I believed in fairies."

A frown flickered across Maybelle's face. "You're quite right. Faith is not at all the same thing as skill."

Then with a haughty sniff she added, "And we certainly don't care what people say!"

This isn't going very well at all, Laurel thought with dismay. She looked at the unfinished pancakes on her plate and felt her stomach turn.

Outdoors, a rooster crowed, sending Maybelle back to her feet. "My stars, the day is flying by! We can't sit and dilly-dally any longer, can we? There's always so much to be done."

"But Maybelle," Laurel called out to the petite form fleeing from the room. "What did you want me to do today?"

Maybelle paused in the hall to turn and face her.

"Anything that strikes your fancy put down on paper and we'll discuss them tonight. Is that all right with you?"

She simply nodded.

"Good. Then off with you. Anything and everything at Fallingstar is yours to explore. Have fun! And remember, no worries! I must be off now. We'll meet here for tea when the sun moves to the west." With a quick wave of her hand, she hurried down the hall, grabbed her straw hat and gardening basket from the iron hooks by the door, then scurried out.

Laurel released a pent-up sigh and leaned forward on the table to shake her head in her palm. To her left, the goldfinch chirped with animation in the cage.

"No worries, she says? Tell me, Amor," she said as she watched the diminutive woman through the window, her long garments flowing in the gentle morning breeze as she made a beeline for the gardens. "Just what have I gotten myself into?"

Dane's favorite time of the day was early morning, when the rising sun burned off the low-lying fog and dew sparkled fresh on the vibrant green of the mountains. The world felt brand new in the early hours before work and responsibilities and the fatigue they rendered stooped the shoulders and the spirit. When he was a boy, the hours just after dawn and before chores were his favorite time to play in the woods. He'd never felt lonely or sad in the imaginary world he'd created for himself in the forest, and the memory of that one-time joy still lingered in his heart.

His work day started in the cool, shadowy barn with the heady scents of newly piled hay and animals. Unlike most people he'd met in his life, his farm animals were steady and loyal. Elsie, his great Jersey cow, waited patiently every morning to deliver her sweet milk. The pair of Fjord horses with their long flowing manes and stocky build were happiest when they were pulling carts full of wood or hitched to a plow. Like him, they felt a fierce pride at putting on the harness and completing an honest day's work. The chickens were a messy lot, but they delivered their day's supply of eggs, even if they did squabble.

Hard work was the lifestyle of a farm, and there was never any shortage of it, especially in the spring, when it was planting time. Chores evolved as summer days grew longer, then again in fall with the plowing and ripe harvests. Work in the fields, however, was not the same as work in the gardens. They grew their own at Fallingstar, as they liked to say, providing for their table. He tilled and planted, and Maybelle tended. But the flower gardens weren't considered work by either of them. The flowers and herbs were pleasure.

He was on his way there now, his long legs taking strides up the mountain road that led from the barn to the terraced gardens. He'd be there by eleven as usual, just in time to meet Maybelle. She'd offer him a cup of iced tea, a warm smile, and a slice of whatever it was she was baking. That was always the highlight of his day, and he picked up the speed just thinking of her mouth-watering cakes.

He whistled as he passed through the surrounding hedge that hid the house and garden, rounded the curve, then stopped short. The music choked in his throat. The woman in the garden wasn't Maybelle. This woman wasn't wearing a flowing dress but trendy shorts and sandals. This woman wasn't bent over the flower bed;

this woman was lazily sitting in an Adirondack chair, curled over a sketch pad. She seemed engrossed in her work, so much so that she didn't hear him enter the enclosed garden. The thought that he could leave now, unnoticed, was tempting. He'd spent a lifetime escaping the notice of smart city women like Laurel Carrington. Except that he had his day's work cut out for him and he'd be damned if he let a prissy thing like her interrupt his schedule.

There was no avoiding her, he decided, resigned to his fate, though his lip curled in distaste at the thought of having to spend the rest of his morning—his summer—in her proximity. All the music he'd felt in his heart died in a squeak of disappointment as he moved forward.

Laurel felt him approach before hearing him. A warning sense tingled down her spine and, turning, she saw the towering figure of Dane approach in his swaggering gait. *Dear God,* she thought with dismay as he pulled out shovels, hoes, and forks. It looked like he was going to be here a long time. He was probably Maybelle's hired hand.

She rubbed her eyes under her flop hat. How was she going to concentrate with his sulking, glowering presence hovering about? She couldn't imagine what she'd done to make him hate her so—or perhaps it was just everyone he hated. Yes, she could imagine that. Only a gentle earth mother like Maybelle Starr could tolerate a surly man like him.

From under his broad-brimmed hat his eyes raked her like a plow as he approached, barely nodding and grunting some form of polite greeting. His feelings at finding her here couldn't have been more clearly expressed than if he'd written her a treatise.

"Good morning," she replied with precise diction. Someone here would be polite, she decided.

He didn't reply right away. With an arrogance that put her teeth on edge, his gaze moved from her to her sketch pad. She fought the urge to cover her drawing of the dianthus with her palm. She wouldn't cower, she swore to herself, sitting straighter in her chair. She might have been uncertain of her skills with oil paint, but she was confident of her talent with charcoal. To press the point, she deliberately raised the sketch pad to improve his view.

To her surprise, he didn't make a snide comment but studied her drawing in earnest.

"You've got it wrong."

She released a short laugh. "Oh really?"

"Either you want to get it right or you don't."

Laurel saw a flash of intelligence in his eyes that clashed with his pose of ignorance. "I thought I had gotten it right."

"Not quite," he replied with an authority that nettled. "What you drew is the deltoides variety. The glaucus has a bluish-gray foliage. It's the most common, so I'm not surprised. But you can't assume everything in nature is the same." He picked up the delicate stem and held it in his large palm. "See there," he said, pointing a long finger.

She couldn't quite believe she was on the receiving end of a lecture from a farm hand on a subject she was so well versed in. When she squinted he stepped closer, bending low to better her inspection. His nearness was overpowering, clouding her vision of the small flower head that lay in his callused hand. His clothes smelled of wood and hay, an enticing scent, even stirring. She cleared her throat and bent closer to focus her attention.

"You see, Miss Carrington, you can't always judge something at first glance. You have to take the time to study it without jumping to conclusions." He straightened and took a step back. "A miss is as good as a mile."

Her cheeks flamed, having understood the subtlety of his lecture. Not only had she missed the telling detail of the plant, but she committed the greater error of assuming the man was ignorant by virtue of his clothing.

"Your point is well taken," she replied, swallowing her pride.

His eyes sparked with surprise at her honest response,

then smoldered with curiosity as he studied her with the thoroughness he'd just described.

"Where did you learn so much about plants?" she asked, turning her face upward.

His eyes grew guarded. "Do you mean where did I go to school?"

She lifted a shoulder. "I suppose I do."

He twirled the stem of the flower in his fingers but his eyes turned hard. "Rutland High School," he answered deliberately.

This time, she didn't fall for the obvious. His response was far too learned. "I doubt you learned details like that in high school."

"Miss Carrington, you don't learn details like that in any school at any level. No book can teach someone to observe. It's just something you teach yourself. And I'll let you in on a little secret. Nothing in Maybelle's garden is ordinary. She collects the extraordinary. So keep your eyes open for the small things."

He almost smiled then, just a faint curving of the lips and a spark in his dark eyes, and held out the flower for her to take.

Laurel hesitatingly reached out to take the flower from his hand. In contrast, her own hand appeared as small and delicate as the flower itself. Her wrists were as thin as stems and her almond-shaped nails were polished a soft pink. She saw her hands as he did, uncallused, unaccustomed to the soil, unable to endure a hard day's work. Coupling them over the offensive sketch, she realized with another pang that he also found them wanting in talent.

"The sketches are good," he surprised her by saying. "Very good. Your talent is obvious and you've captured the spirit of the plant and made it seem real. I guess I can see why Maybelle selected you."

The compliment was begrudgingly given, and thus all the more sweet. She could imagine what it took for him to offer it. Before she could thank him he turned away and went straight to his tools, picking up a huge burlap bag and hoisting it over his shoulder as though it weighed only a few pounds.

She watched him walk away to the far end of the garden, whistling a tune that was carried by the wind. She took a deep breath and exhaled heavily as he disappeared around a tall hedge. Gathering her notebook, she decided to take Maybelle's advice and just walk around a bit to better acquaint herself with the place.

For nothing was as it seemed at Fallingstar.

Five

For the several weeks before her voyage to Fallingstar, Laurel had been filled with the business of finishing up her research project, firming up her plans with Maybelle, getting a cleaning woman for her father, reassuring Colin of her affection, and packing up her belongings for the summer. She didn't have time to worry about why Maybelle had chosen her for such an honor, or whether she had the talent to fulfill the expectations. Or so she told herself. In her heart she knew it was total avoidance. On that first morning, Maybelle had asked her about faith. In truth, just getting in the car and driving to Fallingstar represented a huge leap of faith for her.

She thought of this when her eyes opened on her second morning at Fallingstar. Lying in bed as dawn broke the night and the birds called out their greeting to the new day, Laurel wondered what had happened to the faith she'd once had in herself. Not too long ago she would have described herself as a motivated, focused, confident young woman. One who was sure of what she wanted and how she was going to get it. In the past few months, however, it seemed as though the stars had shifted and fate had predetermined that she would fail.

Surely if she applied herself diligently she would change this course and succeed. She just had to work harder, she was sure that was the answer. Hadn't her father always told her so? Walking around and looking at flowers might be fine for a day of inspiration, but

Laurel was certain that what she needed to do now was to set up her easel and get to work.

She released a long sigh, feeling clear headed. *There is no problem that a little common sense and determination can't solve*, she told herself, dragging herself from her comfortable bed. Outside her window the eastern sky was as red as her tea and again, fog lay low in the valley. It was a beautiful morning, but most important, it was early. No more sleeping in for her. She'd show Maybelle—and Dane—her mettle. She dressed quickly and followed the sound of clanging metal to the kitchen.

"Good morning!" she called out, pleased to see Maybelle's expression of surprise. "You were right about those birds."

"Chatty, aren't they?" Maybelle replied with a delighted smile. She was busy loading logs of wood into the stove. "I think they just love to hear themselves talk, same as some humans do."

Laurel was amused by the way Maybelle often referred to "humans" as a separate species. She helped load wood into the stove and learned how to pump water into the sink. Maybelle welcomed her help gratefully, and it occurred to Laurel that her life alone at Fallingstar might not just be lonely for the older woman, but physically exhausting. She resolved to try and learn as many chores as possible to alleviate some of the strain.

After another hearty breakfast of cheese omelets with sautéed fiddleheads—and the ever-present red tea—Laurel was ready once again to broach the subject of her apprenticeship. But before she could ask a single question, Maybelle leaned over the sink to peer out through the glass.

"Aha! I see your day is about to begin. You'd best finish your breakfast and gather your gear. I see Dane coming up to the door."

"What's *he* doing here?"

"I've asked him to take you a short ways into the woods. There's no better guide, I can promise you."

"Him?" Her mouth grimaced and she bit back a comment. *God save me,* she thought to herself. *He's likely to lead me into the woods and leave me there.* "I thought perhaps you might go with me."

"Oh no, I can't, I'm sorry to say. My eyesight is failing me, as you know. I wouldn't want to lead you anywhere unsafe. Best to let Dane introduce you to the woods. He knows them as well as the back of his hand."

Laurel wondered how this wily woman managed to wander the woods and spot hidden wildflowers but was unable to take her a short distance into the forest. But she didn't dare voice her complaint. She tucked her robe closer around her neck just as the door burst open and Dane filled the small doorway.

Again, her first thought when she saw him was that he was a handsome man in a rugged way. Her second was a stern self-reminder that he was not at all the academic sort she was usually attracted to. Men with more brains than brawn. Men like Colin. Nonetheless, she sat straighter in her chair and smoothed the hair from her face.

Dane scraped his boots on the mat, then took off his hat when he entered, nearly scraping the ceiling with the top of his head as well. When he saw her sitting at the table, his face darkened and she knew in an instant he was as happy about this arrangement as she was.

"Good morning and welcome," Maybelle called out, rushing to greet him.

"Morning, Maybelle," he said in a gritty baritone. His dark gaze darted to Laurel briefly and he grunted out what she barely translated as a "morning." She nodded in curt response.

Maybelle's eyes narrowed, witnessing the cool exchange. "It should be a lovely day," she said with extra warmth. "The sun's shining and will make the earth lovely for a picnic." She hurried to a large basket sitting on the counter. Opening it, her pale hands fluttered inside, rummaging through the biscuits and cheese, strawberries and cut vegetables. "And see what I've prepared? A picnic lunch! And I've even packed a nice bottle of peach wine, one of my better batches too. I want you to have a perfect outing."

"Don't go to trouble for us," he said to her, surprising Laurel with the gentleness in his eyes when he spoke to Maybelle. She didn't think he had it in him. "Just a few biscuits and a couple of apples would be fine enough for the short walk we'll be taking."

"Nonsense, it was my pleasure. And it won't seem such a short hike for a city girl like Laurel. She isn't accustomed to hiking all day as you are, and your long legs can go for miles without pause." She speared him with a no-nonsense look. "It's a leisurely walk we want today, Dane. Just an introduction to the forest, not an in-depth tour. She'll tell you when she wants to stop to sketch, and you will oblige her, won't you? Of course you will," she said, efficiently cutting off any argument. "Now take the basket, and Laurel, you hurry to take your sketch pad and be off before the sun rises any higher overhead."

"But . . ." Laurel felt the force of this petite general's quiet determination. "Wait a minute. What should I sketch? What am I looking for?"

Maybelle took a long breath, as one trying to swallow her frustration. "Try to relax, Laurel. Everything doesn't need to be so organized. Just go into the woods with Dane and look around you! Feel! And if while you walk you catch the fragrance of a tree or a flower, linger. This is often a signal that you are being greeted."

"Greeted?"

"By fairies," Dane said with a gleam in his eye. "What did you think she was talking about?"

Laurel glared at him and when their eyes locked she knew he dared her to contradict. Turning to Maybelle, she asked in a controlled tone, "So you want me to draw flowers?"

Maybelle smiled gently, drawing near to place a hand on Laurel's shoulder. "Draw flowers, if you will. It's a good start."

*   *   *

An hour later, Laurel thought it couldn't have been a worse start. Dane was being deliberately obtuse, walking several strides ahead without heed to her winded pace behind him. The only inspiration she was getting at the moment was to kill one stubborn mule of a man. At least he kept to the path, if you could call the narrowly trodden deer trail that meandered across the mountain a path. Every muscle in her body ached and her legs were burning with some kind of nasty rash that was driving her mad.

"Will you slow down?" she shouted out in frustration, huffing over a steep, rocky rise.

Dane stopped and turned to stare back at her. "If we don't keep up a good pace we'll never get there by the noon."

"Get where?" she shot back. "I thought we were supposed to be strolling at leisure. Looking, seeing," she said with exaggeration. "This is more like a forced march." Grabbing hold of a tree limb she hoisted herself up over the slippery face of rock. Once up, she slipped and fell right back on her rear.

"Stop fooling around," he said with annoyance. "I want to get to the pond. We'll eat our picnic there."

Laurel's boiling point had been reached and she'd had enough of his bullying. "We'll stop here," she ground out. Her jaw was clenched and if he knew her better he'd realize when she was in this mood, she would not be budged.

"It's not much further." His voice was gruff with impatience.

She ignored him. "God, look at my legs," she moaned to herself as she stretched her long limbs out in front of her. Clucking her tongue, she examined the mean, angry scratches that crisscrossed her from thigh to ankle.

He looked back at her legs. "You should wear long pants in the woods."

"Yeah, well, I thought this was supposed to be a leisurely stroll, not a hiker's grand prix." She looked at him and said accusingly, "You're doing this on purpose. Just to make me miserable and leave."

He didn't reply, but walked closer and glanced at her legs. Though his brow furrowed with concern, his voice carried indifference. "You've got a nasty rash of stinging nettle. Stay there, I'll get something to help."

"As if I'm going anywhere," she called after him. Then under her breath she muttered through gritted teeth, "I can barely move, you big clod." Moisture flashed in her eyes, as much from fury as pain, but she wouldn't give in to feminine tears. She didn't need him to tell her she had rash from stinging nettle. It was burning like hellfire but she'd die before she admitted it to him. She knew what game he was playing and he would not drive her from the mountain, she resolved. She just had to get through today and she'd never have to talk with him, look at him, or hike with him again. She grit her teeth, clenching her fingers into a fist so as not to scratch the rash and instead, mentally ran through a long list of curses on a certain mountain man.

She didn't hear him approach and he startled her when he crouched beside her. The soft flannel on his broad shoulder grazed her and she felt choked by his overpowering nearness. In his hands he held a cluster of green leaves.

"This is jewelweed," he said.

"I know what it is," she snapped.

"And I suppose you also know the juice from the stem will stop the itching."

She didn't and that fact burned as much as the nettle.

He moved with authority, breaking the leaves in his large hands. Then he reached for her legs. She jerked back when his fingers touched her skin. Dane turned to face her, his dark brown eyes glittering impatience. She nodded stiffly and without a word, he began rubbing the leaves one by one along her legs. His movements were brusque and impersonal, but she sensed a heightened awareness as his skin touched hers that both of them were trying to avoid. When one finger traced a particularly nasty scratch at the knee toward her inner thigh, her muscles stiffened in response.

"That's much better, thank you," she said abruptly,

shifting her body. It was the slightest movement but the meaning was understood. He dropped his hands and rose to his feet, stepping back and looking ahead at the path.

"We should get going then."

Laurel was loathe to start walking again. "This is a pretty spot. I'd like to take a moment to sketch it." It wasn't a lie exactly, she reasoned. It was self-defense. If she didn't rest she felt sure she'd collapse.

He grumbled something inaudible behind her which she took as a "yes." Pulling out her pencil and sketch pad from her backpack, along with a bar of chocolate, she settled more comfortably on the smooth ledge. Behind her she heard his heavy footfall and the scrape of denim against branches and swallowed her smile, smug that she'd won this round of tug-of-war between them.

Dane sat a few yards away on another boulder, carefully setting the picnic basket beside him. Despite the weight, he didn't seem the least bit winded, unlike her, who was wheezing and sweating like she'd crossed the Sahara.

The view was breathtaking, all vertical green mountains sloping sharply down to green pastures dotted with cows. As lovely as it was, however, she was arrested by the unguarded view of Dane. He appeared to be sculpted from the mountain himself. His nose was cragged, probably broken, and his finely chiseled cheekbones and his jaw of granite had a symmetry that was attractive in a man.

Intrigued, she pulled out her pencil and began to draw. As she drew her initial lines, she imagined that his heart was a bit of gray flint that would slice any finger that dared to touch it. But as she defined his eyes, she recalled that he had his gentle moments, too. Pausing, she studied her drawing and saw that she'd drawn a vulnerability in the eyes and knew instinctively that she'd gotten them right. He was a man of contrasts and as unpredictable as the woods they walked in.

Inspired, her hand began moving quickly over the paper and the image came to life. She was a trained observer and excelled at capturing telling details. She drew the deep creases that crossed his brow—worry lines, she'd always called them. Drawing them, she wondered what a man like him worried about. She didn't know anything about him, really. She couldn't imagine the woman who could abide in a dwelling with him. As she sketched he lowered his head, as though his mind was weighed down more by sorrow than fatigue, and her hand stilled, intrigued. When he raised his head abruptly again, she quickly turned her gaze to her work, lest he catch her staring at him. She didn't think he'd like the idea of her using him as a model.

"I see you're inspired," he called out to her. "Did you catch a glimpse of the little people?"

She snorted in reply, thinking to herself that she caught a glimpse of a giant. She flipped her sketchbook closed. "So you believe in them too?"

He shrugged. "I'm not saying one way or the other. I was just curious, is all. Many folk who come to visit Maybelle start seeing things they can't quite explain. They get all excited by the visions, and like the fools they are, hurry down the mountain to babble on and on to anyone who'll listen what magic or sprites they've seen, or music and whispering heard. They like to hear themselves talk, more likely. And to draw attention to themselves. To make themselves important somehow in the eyes of the world."

"What happens then?"

"Nothing. Who is going to believe that fairies are found in these woods? Other than a few fanatics who tend to show up from time to time. The same lost souls that chase UFOs." He shrugged. "But that's why I'm here. To keep fanatics and other unwanted visitors away." His gaze raked her from head to toe and she felt he included her in that group.

"Then you don't believe in fairies?" she asked, ignoring his rudeness.

His face hardened and he looked off in the distance again. "No," he replied.

She should have felt relieved that at least one other

person on this mountain was sane. "You say that as if you regret it."

He rubbed his jaw, taking his time to answer. "I've a lot of things I regret, Miss Carrington, but not seeing a fairy isn't one of them." He raised his eyes to hers and his expression was inflexible. "But Maybelle does believe in them. With all her heart. And I don't intend to see that heart broken. Not by you, not by anyone."

"What makes you so sure I'm here to hurt her?"

"You're here to paint fairies you don't believe in."

His words were simple and true. "Maybelle invited me to come as her apprentice. As an artist. Of course I knew that I wouldn't be painting landscapes. I'm here to paint fairies. That's a skill. But painting them and believing they are real are two different things entirely. For your information, first I'm a student of science, and as such I've been trained to observe, collect data, and then provide information. Reasonable, logical data, not fantasies or dreams."

He reached down to pick up a stone and throw it with force down the mountain. "And what does all your reasonable, logical data tell you about Maybelle Starr?"

"Don't you think I cringe every time Maybelle refers to fairies as though they were real?"

"Cringe? Or laugh?"

"I would never laugh at her. Or mock her, or never, ever, hurt her."

He stared at her, hard. "And the magic? The fairies?"

She sighed and lifted her palms. "I don't know. They're figments of her imagination. I recognize that. But I realize that imagination feeds her talent. It's her muse. Look, Dane, Maybelle possesses something I'm here to learn about. Something beyond mere talent. She has a gift of seeing what the rest of us can only imagine. Light, color, mood all come alive on the canvas when she paints and transports us somewhere." She paused, trying to recollect the feeling she had as a child treasuring the fairy pictures. "Otherworldly. That's magic enough in my book, and if I have to walk in the woods every day to discover that kind of magic and hopefully put it into my work—maybe even into my life—then that's what I'm going to do."

She stopped, bewildered by the rush of words and feelings she'd just expressed, and unwilling to discuss them further with this stranger. She began to stuff her sketchbook into her backpack. "I'm not here to hurt her, Dane. You'll just have to take my word on that."

When she looked up he was staring at her without his usual rancor. His face appeared puzzled, wary, as though he was warring with himself whether to believe her.

She didn't care if he believed her or not. She rose again, hoisting her backpack up onto her shoulders. "You said you wanted to get there by noon, so let's get hiking."

Dane didn't hurry to pick up the picnic basket and follow. He knew he'd catch up with her in but a few strides. Let her lead for a while, he thought to himself, since she seemed hellbent to do so. He chuckled, admiring that kind of pluck. It would be amusing to see just how far off track she'd go before she had to turn and ask for his help. Now that would be a fine moment, he thought, his first smile of the day breaking his frown. To hear Miss Know-It-All admit a mistake would be like music in his ears. She was so sure of herself. So haughty about that knowledge. He'd never met anyone else so contrary, not even Daphne. And he didn't trust her, didn't trust any of her type. They came to Fallingstar with their own agendas, unconcerned about who might get hurt in the process.

Though he had to admit to himself that he'd caught a glimpse of another side in her explosion a moment ago. He'd thought she was a cold one, but after that display of fireworks, he wasn't so sure. Not just her words, but in the passion behind them—and that flash of vulnerability he caught in her eyes.

Those fairy eyes. His hand came up to rub at his own eyes, as though to wipe the vision away. It pained him to see that unique color again, green the color of spring moss in the forest. Eyes that tilted upward with a saucy slant. Eyes that flashed with humor and just as quickly, with defiance. Eyes that brought back a tenderness of feeling he was loathe to fall victim to again. He knew those eyes and he'd sworn they were naught but a childhood dream.

No, no, no . . . The words ricocheted in his brain. He would not let his mind wander there again. He'd been but a boy when he thought he saw the fairies. A mere child when he played with them, befriended them—his only friends. He knew better now. It was only his loneliness and being in the mountains where a wistful mind could translate strange noises, lights, and other natural phenomena into something mystical and magical that had made him believe. He'd read of such cases in the books he studied. He accepted that this was the case with Maybelle, a recluse with an inner vision and a vivid imagination. For her it was a vision that served her well. Her paintings were world famous. But a visionary like her had to be protected because she believed in the magic. She could be hurt, as he had been hurt. He would watch over her as she had once watched over him and Daphne.

He heard something whispered in his mind, loud and insistent, *Could Laurel be hurt?* He stopped to listen more closely. The wind rustled in the leaves and he heard: *Laurel is hurt.*

Glancing sharply up, he didn't see her on the path ahead of him. A chill ran down his spine as he turned his gaze to the left and right, searching for her. But she was gone.

Daphne found Maybelle where she expected to—in the flower garden. She was kneeling, bent over the shoots already growing tall and strong in the late May sun. A trowel, spade, fork, and old wicker basket half filled with weeds clustered beside her feet, and hanging from a nearby rosebush was a sweater discarded in the midday sun. Beside her, a pair of rabbits nibbled lettuce and carrots laid out for them. When Daphne was a little girl,

Maybelle had told her that only well-behaved rabbits were welcome in her garden.

Daphne paused, resting her hand on the gate. This was the image of Maybelle Starr that she would always carry in her heart.

The more famous image of a lithe Maybelle Starr painting a canvas in the fields in her uniquely styled long dress, with her hem waving in the wind and her face obscured by a wide-brimmed straw hat, was the one the world had of the famous artist. This one photograph, printed on a full page in *Life* magazine almost twenty years earlier, was the only one ever allowed by Maybelle. It had stirred the imagination of generations of children and their parents. Like Tasha Tudor and Cecily Mary Barker before her, Maybelle Starr jealously guarded her privacy. Daphne never understood why she tolerated her success and fame with quiet resignation rather that triumph. When she was young Daphne used to dream she might paint like Maybelle someday, but her temperament was too hot and her talent lukewarm. And she didn't love it the way Maybelle did. She knew that was the key. So she told herself that someday she'd find her talent, and when and if she did . . .

She'd relish the fame and fortune it brought. She'd travel around the world as her brother once had. But she wouldn't lurk in rain forests like Dane did. She wanted to see the world, to travel its cities and be anonymous in the crowds, to walk down the streets and have people smile as she passed, not sneer and smirk the way they did in town. She wanted to see things, do things, experience adventures in her life. More than anything she wanted to get off this mountain and away from this nowhere town. And when the insurance money came in July, she was going to do just that.

So this final summer at home, she was pasting into her heart the images of things and people she loved best, like this one of Maybelle in the garden, in the same way ladies she knew pasted photographs into an album. Daphne never did like sewing dresses or flower arranging or picture albums or any of those other girlie things.

Maybelle was so good at all those homespun skills, but after years of trying, even she conceded Daphne couldn't, or wouldn't, be domesticated.

And why should she? She loved the wild things! The woods and all its secrets, the untamed animals, things hidden in the dark. It was these mysterious things that captured her imagination, and Maybelle understood this. Probably because there was a wild side inside Maybelle that Daphne saw, even if no one else did. They were kindred spirits, deep down. She knew this for certain when Maybelle gave up trying to teach her how to sew and introduced her to the bees.

And like a bee, she'd go from flower to flower, not sit around like a pretty bud waiting for one bee to pollinate her. She'd take the insurance money and go—and keep this image of Maybelle in her heart, which was the best place anyway, she figured.

Stepping from the shrubs onto the garden path, a pair of swallowtail butterflies took flight and fluttered about Maybelle's face. The squirrel scampered up a nearby tree and the rabbits perched on hind legs and sniffed the air with trembling noses. Alerted, Maybelle raised herself from the garden bed to face Daphne with a bright, welcoming smile, resting her soil-covered hands upon her apron.

"Isn't it the most beautiful day?" Maybelle called out.

"Gonna be a hot one," Daphne replied, removing her wide, slouch hat and wiping her brow with her elbow. "You shouldn't be in the sun at noon, you'll get scorched."

"Noon already? Goodness, where did the morning go? There just never seems to be enough daylight time in the spring. The garden's in such a state, there's a season's worth of work to do and then some. Just look at my poor lilies. Ravaged. The deer haven't been very neighborly, just helping themselves. And if they dare go near my herbs . . . Well, I'll have to talk to them about that."

"Where's Dane? He came up hours ago."

"Oh, he's on another errand right now. With Laurel.

Though I confess I miss his strong back to spread that pile of mulch. Make yourself useful and spread a bit of that hay in the lily bed, won't you? Mind you use the gloves lying by my basket. Rosie's making a fine contribution to the garden this year."

Daphne wrinkled her nose at the prospect of hoisting Elsie's composted cow manure and hay but readily bent to gather a shovelful and began spreading it in a thick layer. "What kind of errand could Dane be on?" she asked with between hefts. "I can't imagine he's any too happy about spending time with *her*."

"Why wouldn't he be? It's a wonderful day for a walk. He's taking Laurel through the woods, just to introduce her a bit to the lay of the land. A nice, peaceful hike to where the grass grows long and soft . . ." Her gaze drifted to the woods as her voice trailed off.

Daphne paused and leaned against the shovel. "Maybelle, are you matchmaking again?"

Maybelle dug a bit in the dirt. "Whatever do you mean? Matchmaking? Me?"

Daphne narrowed her eyes and nodded. "You *are!* Don't bother to deny it, it's written all over your face." Maybelle's hand shot to her cheek and Daphne laughed. Maybelle always took slang literally. "Believe me, it's a lost cause. Dane can't stand the snooty Miss Apprentice."

Maybelle sat back on her heels and asked rather haughtily, "Can't stand her? Laurel? There is nothing *not* to like about her! She's absolutely lovely, in every way. And talented. And as bright as the sun overhead." She returned to the soil and dug with spiteful strokes. "Not like her, indeed."

Daphne was caught off guard by the strident defense of a relative stranger. Maybelle rarely made friends or even acquaintances, so her seeming attachment to this apprentice was by all measures odd, and a bit too sudden. Dane's warning rang in her mind and her antennae rose.

"When do I get to meet the little goddess?"

Maybelle ignored the sarcasm. "I packed them a picnic lunch, so they might not be back until after three."

"A picnic lunch?" Her cheeks flushed as she felt the heat of jealousy rise. "Aren't you going overboard? I mean, she's supposed to be here to help you, not the other way around. You don't need to pack her a lunch."

"Perhaps not, but I wanted to. And I've made rhubarb tarts for tea. Close your mouth, Daphne, you'll catch flies. I know they're your favorite and I made them especially for you." Her eyes turned crafty. "My own special lure. Do say you'll come. Laurel won't know anyone else here and it would be nice for her to have a friend. Nice for you too. You're the same age, you know."

"I don't need any friends," she snapped. "I know all the people I care to." Then, seeing Maybelle's hurt expression, she said with a grunt, "But I'm a slave for your tarts so I guess I'll come by and be polite."

"How lovely. I've scones and cream cakes too. And if we're in the mood"—she raised her brows in a saucy manner—"I'll serve a bit of my special nectar juice."

Daphne's eyes widened. Maybelle's nectar was served only at the most rare of occasions.

"So she must be a pretty good painter to be getting the royal treatment."

Maybelle's hands paused in the soil, then she said hesitatingly, "Good enough."

"That's all?" she remarked, feeling another prick of jealousy. "Then why did you pick her to be your apprentice? I'd have thought she'd have to be the best darn fairy painter in the world for you to let her take over your painting career."

"She has the potential. I feel it, even if I can't see it quite yet. She'll learn."

"But that's crazy. Why teach her when you could find someone who already knows how to paint fairies?"

"It's not crazy. It's not even original. The Japanese masters always take on several apprentices who learn how to imitate the master's work. This is a great skill and it's an honor to be chosen to perpetuate a national treasure."

"So basically you're saying you want her to copy your work? Well, darn, Maybelle, if that's all you wanted you could have picked me!" She turned her face and lifted another shovelful of hay, ashamed lest Maybelle hear the hurt in her voice.

"No, Daphne. I don't want someone to paint exactly as I do. I want someone who can see the magic themselves and express it on canvas." Her face softened and she smiled sadly. "You do not love painting, Daphne, we both know that. You have to find your own magic."

"Yeah, right, if I ever—"

"Hush!" Maybelle interrupted, her hand held in an arresting gesture. She sat motionless, her ears cocked and her eyes wide, listening intently.

Daphne stilled instantly, but all she heard was a whistling between the trees.

Maybelle's face paled and she bolted to a stand, her eyes flashing with worry. Clutching her skirts in her fists, she took off like a colt in her bare feet through the garden, her straw hat blowing off without notice.

Daphne saw that she was headed straight for the woods. Tossing down the shovel, she ran off after her.

The deer path veered across a very steep, forbidding slope of the mountainside. Laurel frowned with annoyance, thinking Dane chose this treacherous terrain especially for her. She slowly passed around an enormous maple perched near the ledge, gripping its bark and trodding over several toadstools that grew between the thick roots at its base. Once past the dangerous spot, she took a deep breath and carefully placed one foot after another in single file, concentrating on each step. Suddenly, she felt a sharp pinprick between her shoulder blades.

"Ouch," she cried, jerking forward. Her ankle twisted on the soft earth and, arms flailing, she lost her balance. She hit the earth with a squelched yelp as pain exploded in her ankle. Before she could register it, she began rolling and rolling over and over like a rag doll down the mountain slope. She tried desperately to stop but the momentum worked against her as she plowed over stones, rocks, and sharp branches and sticks that cut, jabbed, and scraped. She came to a crash against a hard wall of rock, cracking her head and seeing stars.

When the world stopped spinning, she lay in the dirt, dazed and with a mouth full of grit. Seconds ago she heard a scream in her head that must've been her own. Now, the silence was deafening. Thorns and burrs poked through her clothing, stabbing her tender skin. With painstaking slowness she dragged herself to a sitting position, leaning heavily on her scratched arms and spitting out dirt. She raised her head, swallowing down the nausea, and saw that she rolled down to a small ledge on the mountain. With blinking slowness she realized that this massive pile of rocks had broken her slide. Thank God, or she'd still be rolling.

Her head drooped with wooziness and her hands trembled as she gingerly checked her arms then her legs. Nothing looked serious and she could move her fingers and toes. But if she thought she had scratches before! Angry cuts bled down her leg and on her head her fingers gingerly outlined the beginning of a goose egg. Her ankle looked ugly, however. It was swelling up and turning a nasty purple and blue. When she tried to move it, she cringed with pain. Feeling helpless, she craned her neck to look up the slope. Dane was nowhere in sight, nor was the path. She shivered, feeling the forest close in on her, as though thousands of eyes were watching her. She took a deep breath before panic set in.

"Hello! I'm here!" she called out. A few birds fluttered and rose in flight. "Help!"

This time she heard a low growl in reply, coming from deep within the cluster of boulders. Her hair stood on end as she slowly turned her head toward the sound. The massive wall of jutting granite appeared to have an opening, and it was from somewhere in that darkness that this growl emanated. Her breath came faster as she inched her way to a full sitting position, using the rocks as a crutch. She froze, however, when from the darkness of the cave crawled a large black bear with enormous padded feet and angry eyes—focused sharply on her.

*   *   *

Dane's feet ran sure and steady along the mountainside path. When he turned the curve he'd hoped he'd see her just ahead. What he saw instead brought him to a dead stop. The path narrowed dangerously along a steep slope around an enormous maple. But at its base, small toad-stools clustered in a neat circle. And inside the circle were a set of footprints. The blood drained from his face as he realized Laurel had walked right through the ring without notice.

A fairy ring.

It was a foolish thought, a reflex from years of living with Maybelle. He was as irritated as embarrassed to think of it. But it was there in his mind nonetheless, sharp and vivid as though written in neon. This was a fairy ring. *And woe to the one who stepped within its borders.* So Maybelle had always told him. She'd told tales of abductions. Of pranks and fairy mischief when they perceived a slight, as this certainly was. Maybelle had warned the fairies could be dangerous.

"Laurel!" he called out, leaping across the ring and studying the path ahead. "Laurel!"

From somewhere far below he heard the angry growl of a bear. Stepping to the steep ledge he saw a trail of broken branches and flattened grass that told him the full story. He took off down the hill, grinding his heels deep on the slant and grasping at branches to halt a fall. He had no time to lose. It was spring and bears were with their young. Black bears usually didn't attack, but a mother with her cubs could be dangerous. He took bounding leaps down with his long legs, not feeling the cuts in his hands, his heart pounding with worry that he wouldn't be in time.

After a sharp dip in the mountain he saw her. Laurel was sitting on the ground with her back pressed against the rock, staring straight ahead with panic etched on her face. Her face was pale against the scratches and mud that marred it and by her temple was a gash that might need stitches. But she was alive, his mind flashed with profound relief.

He followed her line of vision and what he saw next caused his muscles to tighten instinctively. He stopped short so as not to make a noise. A large black bear hovered near a cave making aggressive, guttural woofing sounds. At the mouth of the cave rambled her cub. He had to think fast and sure, for a female bear defending her cub was the most dangerous bear situation. She'd tear them apart with her claws in defense of even a perceived threat to her young.

He had to stay calm and approach slowly. Attacks were rare, but this mama bear had already been startled by Laurel. She didn't need more aggravation. He pulled a knife from the sheath on his belt and held it in the ready.

"Laurel," he called out from the brush in a low voice.

The bear raised herself to her hind legs and sniffed the air.

"Dane," Laurel replied with a whimper, afraid to so much as move her lips.

"Listen to me and do exactly as I say," he told her in a loud, firm voice. "Are you hurt?"

"My ankle. I think it's sprained." Her voice was enough to elicit a warning growl from the bear. Her cub replied with a mewling noise that seemed to make the mother more anxious. She began wagging her head in a threatening manner while emitting a series of low woofs.

Dane swallowed hard. An attack was imminent. He loved bears, had always considered them the guardians of the woods. But he knew their power and respected it.

"I want you to slowly rise when I tell you to. Don't do anything sudden. Just back away and keep on going."

"I'll try and run."

"No, do not run," he urged, trying to head off her panic. "A bear can outrun a horse and you'll only encourage its instinct to chase. You'll be prey."

"But what if it *does* chase me?"

"Then drop to the ground and play dead."

"Oh, God . . ."

The cub wandered from the cave and the mother instantly turned to it and growled out a warning, then swung her head back and bared her teeth at Laurel, charging a few feet closer before stopping. Laurel closed her eyes and ducked her head, cringing.

Dane couldn't delay a second longer. He leaped from the woods, placing himself directly between Laurel and the bear. "Go on, get out now," he ordered.

Laurel pulled herself to her feet and began limping away toward the woods, but her strange, wobbly movement only served to aggravate the mother, who reared again with an earsplitting roar. Laurel stopped, arms in midair, poised for flight.

Dane stepped aggressively forward, roaring back at the bear with equal ferocity. He picked up a rock and threw it, hard, hoping to discourage another charge. The bear dropped to all fours and retreated a few feet, but when she neared her cub she swung around again, snapping her jaws. Dane stood his ground, knife at the ready, eyes flashing in warning, looking every bit as dangerous and aggressive as the bear.

"Get going and if the bear charges, keep going. Fast," he said without taking his eyes from the snarling bear. "Don't look back, just get far from here. She won't chase you. I'll see to that."

Light from the sun glinted against the razor-sharp metal of the knife as time stood still. Laurel saw the man and animal as two equal opponents and knew if they clashed only one would be left alive. No one moved. No one so much as blinked. Death crackled in the air.

During the impasse, Laurel looked into the bear's eyes. Somehow she understood that this was not an act of aggression but a mother's defense.

"Laurel, get the hell out of here," Dane howled.

The bear's tolerance snapped and with a roar she charged Dane. In a flash, Dane's knife rose in his clenched fist.

Acting on instinct, Laurel leaped forward, thrusting herself between the bear and Dane. The bear roared forward like a tank to within a few feet of them. Laurel could feel the heat from the bear's breath and the spray of spittle from a growling jaw before the bear suddenly veered off.

The bear stood a short distance away with her ears flat back, waiting and watching. Then with a move surprisingly agile, the bear abruptly turned and lumbered to her cub and promptly chased it back into the cave.

For a second no one moved. Laurel, still standing rigid, closed her eyes and exhaled long and slow the breath she didn't realize she had been holding. The earth seemed enveloped in a profound silence and she felt somehow connected to it. Then, her shoulders slumped, her knees wobbled, and her ankle gave way. She might have slipped to the earth if Dane hadn't bent to scoop her in his arms. She felt safe and slipped her arms around his neck as though it were the most natural thing in the world. The bone of his shoulders was hard against her cheek and, closing her eyes, she caught the scent of his leather and skin.

"You're crazy to have done that, you know that?"

"Dane," she whispered against his neck but her throat was dry and it sounded muffled. She wanted to tell him that she wasn't crazy, that she knew, somehow, that the bear wouldn't hurt her.

"Rest now," he said in a voice that betrayed his emotion. "I'll carry you home."

Six

From high on the ledge, Maybelle held Daphne's hand as they watched Dane carry Laurel back home. Maybelle's eyes darted from the cave to the retreating figures while her fingertip tapped her lips excitedly in deep thought.

Daphne took off her hat and slapped it against her thigh. "How did she do that?" she asked in a husky voice. "That bear was out for blood and would've killed Dane sure, but Laurel stopped her cold. She just . . . stopped her. Was that brave or nuts? I've never seen the like."

Maybelle only shook her head and squeezed Daphne's hand, too moved to speak. She understood fully what had transpired on the ledge in the woods and rejoiced.

Dane carried Laurel the entire way home in his arms as though she weighed little more than a doll. Neither of them spoke but each was intensely aware that Laurel's nose touched the skin at his neck, and that her breath was warm, and that their blood raced in their veins. When they arrived at the house Maybelle hadn't yet returned, but he walked straight to the kitchen, where he gently set her down her on top of the counter. Her arms slipped away from his neck and she immediately wrapped them around herself to cover the awkward feeling of emptiness.

He cradled her foot in one hand, and with the other he carefully unlaced her hiking boot. "Gently now," he said in a reassuring tone as he tugged the shoe from her foot, taking it slow. Next he rolled her wool sock down from her ankle, exposing an already purple and yellow swollen ankle. His hands were tough and callused, crisscrossed with scratches, but he handled her ankle with the care and gentleness of a curator handling museum glass.

"That'll be tender," he said, eyes on her ankle. "You'll have to stay off it for a while."

She sighed her disappointment. "What a fiasco. I'm supposed to be hiking the woods, getting inspired. Not such a good start, is it?"

"I'd say it was a great start. You're alive."

He'd been avoiding looking at her, unwilling to attach a face to the feelings stirring within him. He'd decided she wasn't his type. She was from the city. Vermonters had names for people like that and none of them were flattering. Yet, his heart was pounding, and if he lived to be a hundred he'd never forget the sight of her, small and courageous, jumping in front of him to face down a charging bear.

He raised his eyes. She was sitting on the counter so her face was almost even with his when their eyes met. His heart stopped pounding and he thought he'd died. He'd thought he was prepared for the punch of those fairy eyes so near but he'd been wrong. Their color had changed from the moss in the woods to that of Emerald Lake in the summer sun, brilliant green on the surface, deep enough to drown in. He felt his breath still, then come back pounding as his blood hit a mad boil. It was not the mile he had carried her that brought his shortness of breath.

The air thickened between them as they stood a breath apart. *I could kiss her now,* he thought suddenly.

And just as suddenly, her gaze dropped.

The suddenness of his eyes staring deep into hers took her breath away. His eyes were the color of chocolate and as tempting. Lowering her gaze she saw the weathered, tanned quality of his skin, the fine stubble of beard that traced his jawline and patched his upper lip.

Ah yes, his lips, she thought to herself in what felt like a drugged silence. Thinner on the top, full on the bottom. A wide mouth on a wide jaw, one that devoured. She lingered there, liking what she saw, wondering, taking her time. Then, with a self-conscious, slow pace, she allowed her gaze to travel from his lips, past his proud, straight nose and, with another small sigh, she again met his eyes.

In that moment they both knew that something had changed between them, something deeper than mere attraction.

"This afternoon in the woods," he began in earnest, struggling for the right words. "What you did. For me. You risked your life, you realize that, don't you?"

"I did not," she replied with a self-effacing manner that he found attractive. "I only knew that I had to stop the bear or blood would be shed."

"My blood."

She paused. "Yes," she agreed slowly. "And hers."

He nodded. After a moment he said, "I thank you. And I'm beholden."

"No, no, you're not," she replied, unnerved by the fervency in his tone. Then, when she saw he meant to argue the point, she shook her head with resignation and said, "Okay, I see you're determined. I won't argue with you." She gave him a slanted look. "I'm not that strong at the moment. Let's just say that your carrying me all the way home in the woods more than compensates. I never would have made it out alive on my own. So now we're even. Fair enough?" She held out her hand.

With half a smile that cracked his stern composure, he took her hand.

"You've a small hand, with the bones of a barn swallow." They both looked at it lying still in his larger ones. "And like the swallow, you'll leave at the end of summer."

He was the serious type, one that didn't joke. She liked that, she decided, even as she withdrew her hand and tucked it neatly into her lap.

"Yes, I will."

His smile fled and once again his usual serious expression reclaimed his face and eyes.

The door swung open and Maybelle hurried through the rooms to her side, all pink faced and flustered. She rushed to Laurel's side and immediately began inspecting her wounds, muttering about what herbs and ointments she would need.

"I'm all right," Laurel assured her. "Just a few scratches and scrapes. I'm a bit shook up, though. There was this bear . . ."

"I know. I saw," Maybelle replied, holding Laurel's hands in her own. "I'm so proud of you."

Laurel's chest rose and color rosied her cheeks. "I didn't do anything."

"We'll talk about that later. For now, you just rest a moment and let me tend your wounds. Dane, you go on home now. We'll be fine."

"She hurt her ankle. Be sure and check on that," Dane said, turning to leave.

While Maybelle kissed his cheek, then shuffled him away, Laurel looked around Maybelle's shoulder, hoping to catch his eye. But he'd already turned his back. The moment between them was gone as quickly as it had come, and strangely, she already missed it. She leaned far to the right to watch him stride down the hall to the door, then leaned far back to catch sight of him through the greenhouse glass. Outside she was surprised to see a tall, lanky young woman with overalls and a flop hat leaning against a tree, waiting.

Dane hailed the woman who, on seeing him, arced her arm in an exuberant wave of welcome then threw herself into his arms in a fierce hug. The swift movement brought her thick, lustrous red hair tumbling down her shoulders and revealed a voluptuous chest that no overalls could hide. Laurel's eyes widened as hundreds of emotions flickered through her. She watched Dane wrap his long arm around her shoulders and together they matched long-legged strides down the mountain. Laurel leaned far over on the counter to watch their progress until they disappeared around the bend, feeling for the second time that day the sharp prick of pain—this time in her heart.

Later that night, after she'd soaked in a hot, lavender-scented tub and had her many abrasions treated with Maybelle's herbal remedies, Laurel sat at her window, wrapped in a thick terry-cloth robe and stared out at the moonlit mountains. *Such a mysterious landscape,* she thought, resting her chin in the fold of her arms. Fallingstar was a place that pulsated with an eerie magic. A place where the westerly winds whispered secrets in the woods.

The woods. Laurel shivered and gathered her robe closer around her neck. She was chilled to the bone but not from the bath or the cool night air. She was cold with fear. There was something supernatural and otherworldly about the woods of Fallingstar. They were teeming with energy, flowing and transmutable, as changeable as mood or thought. Not that she saw anything or anyone unusual, but there was no mistaking the keen sense she had all throughout her hike that she was being . . . watched.

And when she thought about her confrontation with the bear . . . That was beyond comprehension. Surely there was some logical explanation. She'd heard that sometimes bears bluff a charge then veer off. Could she have imagined that she had communicated somehow with the animal? She shivered again, cold despite the flickering fire Maybelle had laid for her in the cheery brick fireplace. She closed the window, locking it against the elements outside.

A soft rapping on the door diverted her attention and after acknowledging it, Maybelle entered the room carrying a cookie and a steaming cup of tea in a porcelain cup and saucer.

"I brought something to help you sleep. A sweet dream is the best tonic."

Laurel accepted the tea gratefully.

"I never dream," she said before taking a bite of the maple cookie. It melted in her mouth like butter.

"But of course you dream. Everyone does."

"Not me."

"You just don't recall them," Maybelle answered with authority.

Laurel's eyes crinkled. "I'm sure you have an herbal remedy for that, too."

"I do indeed. But I'm not sure it will help in your case," she said in utter seriousness. "I'll have to think on it awhile, but not to worry. We'll come up with a good and proper solution, you'll see."

"Maybelle," she began, gathering her courage, "something strange happened to me in the woods today. It's confusing and I'd like to talk to you about it, but I'm not sure how to begin."

"Begin at the beginning."

She set aside the tea and cupped her face in misery. When she looked up she dragged out the words. "This is crazy, I know, but if I don't talk to someone I'll be certifiable. Today in the woods, when I looked into the mother bear's eyes, I thought, that is, I *felt* that I could understand what she was telling me." She grabbed a fistful of blanket and squeezed as she moaned, "Isn't this unbelievable? I can't believe it's me saying this. Rational, logical me. But the truth is—I understood what the bear was saying, though they weren't her words exactly. It was as though I heard her words in my own head." She *tsked* and leaned her head back against the pillow. "It's so hard to explain."

"I understand you perfectly, Laurel," Maybelle said in her honest, open manner. "As would anyone who has had the experience. You shared a connection that transcended mere words."

"You've experienced this?" She felt relief knowing that Maybelle wasn't laughing at her, or worse, that she was losing her mind.

"Oh yes, dear, all the time. It's part of what I was explaining to you earlier, about how you should open your mind. You'll be surprised at what you hear and see."

"I just don't know . . ." she began sincerely.

"What don't you know?"

She laughed lightly. "If I'm losing my mind."

"Let's think back a moment, shall we? As a child, did you ever have an imaginary friend? Someone you talked to and played with, especially outdoors?"

Laurel felt a blush tinge her cheeks, too embarrassed to admit how she used to make believe she had a playmate who sat with her on the branches of the big weeping willow. She'd never admitted that to anyone.

"I remember I used to sing to the trees," she admitted.

"Did you?" Maybelle replied, brightening. "Good. That's a form of communication. And you didn't feel you were losing your mind then, did you? Of course you didn't. What about today? When you were in the woods, did you see strange flickers of light?" When Laurel shook her head no, she asked, "What about the feeling of being watched?"

Laurel's eyes widened and Maybelle nodded her head knowingly.

"Today?"

Laurel nodded.

"Hmmm . . ." Maybelle stroked the tassels of the quilt with such agitation she plucked several silk strands loose. "Dane told me that you stepped into a fairy ring today."

Laurel set her teacup on the bedside stand and looked at her with a puzzled expression. "I have no idea if I did or not. What is a fairy ring?"

"I should have told you about those. There's so much to teach you, Laurel, I don't know where to begin."

"Begin at the beginning," Laurel replied, eyes dancing.

Maybelle returned a commiserating smile. "Ah, that would be much too far back. Centuries, eons, time before time!" She picked up the teacup and handed it to Laurel to finish. "Fairies are everywhere. Yet they do have their favorite habitats. The woodlands, of course. Also intersections of any kind, such as caves, caverns, fissures in the earth, whirlpools, wells." She wriggled her fingers in the air. "The list goes on and on. Sometimes there are small portals that are marked by circular rings in the grass. Often these rings are bordered by toadstools. Fairies do love toadstools, you know. To walk around a fairy ring is a show of respect. To trounce upon them is viewed as an insult and," she leaned forward and said with urgency, "fairies take offense at even the smallest slight. They are capricious. You don't want to make them angry."

"I certainly didn't mean to! I . . ." She broke off and quickly lowered her head, surprised at her own words. Good Lord, she was talking as though she believed fairies actually existed.

"What made you fall, do you remember?"

"I twisted my ankle. The ground was soft and steep and I just tumbled down the slope."

"You weren't, say . . . pushed?"

Laurel raised her brows, shocked. "You don't think Dane—"

"My stars, no! Dane can be gruff but he would never hurt anyone unless it was in self-defense. But the fairies . . ." She pursed her lips then said in a low voice, "They have a dark side, you know. They can be spiteful."

She might have smiled in amusement except that Maybelle was so serious. Her strange, opaque eyes were wide and animated. "It wasn't a fairy, Maybelle. There's a perfectly rational explanation for what happened. I was stung by a bee and I jerked forward. I just lost my balance."

"A bee?" Maybelle latched on to this. "You mean you felt a quick stab? A sharp point?" Her voice was rising and her delicate chin jutted forward like a blade.

"Yes, but it was just a bee sting."

Maybelle rose to pace the room, her hands always busy picking up and folding Laurel's clothing as she muttered to herself, "How dare they? To one of their own? I won't have it. We shall see about that."

"I've been lucky not to have ever been stung so far," Laurel said in an attempt to douse the flame of Maybelle's fury. "I guess it was about time."

"Nonsense, of course you haven't been stung," she replied absently, opening the window a bit. The night breeze flowed in with the moonlight, carrying with it the sweet-scented elixir of the mountains that was so good for sleep. She reached into the pocket of her long skirt and pulled out a fossil sea urchin and placed it on the sill.

"You rest now," she said, returning to Laurel's bedside. She took the empty teacup from her hand, catching sight of the scratches on Laurel's arm that were already healing. "You'll find that my herbs will work wonders on those nasty scratches during your sleep. Not a single scar shall mar your fair skin, I promise." She bent to smooth the hair from Laurel's brow, pausing to look into her face with the warm tenderness that Laurel was beginning to expect from her.

Laurel looked into Maybelle's beautiful face and felt an odd choking-up inside, realizing she was already beginning to relish that tenderness. Maybelle was an earth mother. And though she was probably as warm and giving with every stranger that crossed her path, a touch such as hers, a mother's touch, was something that Laurel had craved as a little girl. Especially when the lights in her bedroom were turned off and she was left alone in the darkness with the odd, frightening creatures she imagined under the bed and in the dark, forbidden realm of the closet.

"Good night, Laurel dear," she said with a soft kiss on her forehead.

"Good night," Laurel said, stifling a yawn. "Thank you."

"May your sleep restore your body and your dreams replenish your soul," Maybelle replied, tucking the down blanket close beneath Laurel's chin. "I'll be going out for a little while. I often do at night, but I'll return soon. You're safe here. You've no need to worry. Not one little bit." Her eyes flashed. "No bees shall sting you again."

Laurel wondered why Maybelle seemed so upset over a little bee sting. It could have happened to anyone. Yawning, she turned to her side and tucked her hands under her cheek.

"Oh, Maybelle," she called out in dreamy afterthought.

The door, almost closed, swung back open and Maybelle's narrow face peeped in. Her silvery hair shone in the moonbeam. "Yes?"

"I was just wondering . . . I don't know anything about Dane. Is he married?"

Maybelle's opaque eyes crinkled in the corners and her mouth twitched. "No, he isn't. He is quite unattached."

Laurel knew Maybelle was amused by her question but she didn't mind. "Good night," she repeated and smiled again when Maybelle blew a kiss her way and closed the door softly behind her. The tea that Maybelle had served was making her sleepy; her eyelids were drooping low. Giving in to the urge, she yawned noisily one more time and drifted to sleep while the owl hooted its beckoning call outside her window.

Later that night, deep in a heavy sleep, Laurel didn't hear the thunder grumble in the mountains, or see the fiery show of lightening that streaked the sky over the woods of Fallingstar.

Seven

The following morning, Laurel awoke to the soaring crow of a rooster. She slowly opened her eyes and cursing the rooster, turned on her side and closed her eyes tight against the invading light. She might have drifted back to sleep except for the ringing clatter of metal against metal coming from down the hall.

Resigned, she stretched again and dragged herself to her feet, feeling every muscle in her body. The debacle of the day before came back to her with each movement she made and, pulling up her sleeves, she inspected the trail of scratches and bruises. *Whatever herbs Maybelle put into her ointment she ought to bottle and sell,* she thought to herself. She'd never had injuries heal so quickly. Only the ankle still had that ugly purple swelling. She rose slowly, adding weight to the ankle bit by bit. It was better, but a long way from well. If that was the worst of it, she decided she was lucky.

The early morning air was still nippy as she limped her early trek to the outhouse. The sun was low and had yet to burn off the fog that lay like a gray fluffy blanket over the mountains. Sparrows twittered in the trees overhead and the Robin was hunting his worm, but despite this, there was a peace at this early hour that settled deep into the bones. Laurel stopped to breathe in the sweetness of the early morning hours when the world was fresh and dewy, when everything felt new. Hope for a better day—a new start—sang in her heart.

She dressed quickly, easing her tender ankle into a

long length of denim and her arms into an old, blue cambric shirt, a thick cable sweater, and sensible brown shoes with thick socks to ease the swollen ankle. This late in the spring, the days started off chilly and one had to layer because as the sun climbed so did the temperature. Sweaters, outer shirts, and socks often hung on tree limbs, bushes, and chair backs by noon.

Limping only slightly, she followed the sounds of Maybelle's whistling and Amor's chirping into the kitchen with the ease of someone who had lived here for years. Maybelle already had a fire snapping in the woodburning stove that was taking the chill from the room.

"You're up with the birds this morning," Maybelle said brightly, wrist-deep in dough.

"The day starts early here."

"True enough." Maybelle hurried to measure teaspoons of herbs into a teapot and pour hot water. "And the nights are longer." She looked up searchingly. "Did you sleep well?"

"Yes, I did," she replied honestly. "That tea knocked me out."

"But you still do not remember your dreams?"

Laurel shook her head with a slight shrug. "Some people just don't."

Maybelle didn't reply as she poured the crimson-colored liquid that Laurel recognized as her own "morning blend" into a teacup.

"I'd like to do some chores for you today, Maybelle, though I don't know which I can get done with this ankle. It's much better, but I'm rather slow and clumsy."

"There's always so much to be done in the spring. Fences to be mended, seeds to plant, soil to till. Dane does most of the chores himself, but I'm sure we'll find something you can do. And I thank you for the offer. That's a good and willing heart you have, Laurel dear."

Laurel blushed at the compliment. "Dane works for you, then?" she asked while stirring her tea. She tried to sound as nonchalant as possible, but when she looked up at Maybelle's face. Laurel knew she wasn't fooling anyone.

"Yes, he's what you might call my caretaker." Her opaque eyes softened and she gazed out the window down the mountain. "But I rather think of him as the son I never had." She turned away from the window to gather a cup and saucer from the hutch. "I was great friends with his mother years back," she went on to explain. "Rosalind was her name. We were both young women struggling to survive, me with my painting and she with her son. We helped each other as women often do, and as the years passed, we were more like sisters than friends." She delivered the tea into Laurel's hands, her expression cloudy with memory. "When my paintings began to sell and I had a bit of money, I built the little house down the mountain for her and Dane to live in. It wasn't generosity. It was the height of selfishness. They were my friends, my family." She moved back to her dough and began kneading it with a vengeance.

"Till she married Joe Flannery, that is. Rosalind and I were still friends, but Joe was the jealous sort and mean-spirited. I never thought he treated my friend very well at all. Or her son. I don't like men like that and often told him so." A sorry smile crossed her face as she pounded the dough efficiently with her small fists. "I have always prided myself in speaking my mind, but I've learned it's not always wise to do so. Joe despised me." She sighed and turned back to her bread, kneading with a steady, firm hand. "Oh, he was a smooth-talking moocher, that Mr. Joe Flannery. The folks in town took to him readily. As did Rosalind. His quick smile and hearty laugh never fooled me. One only had to look into his eyes to see a man without morals who was only interested in himself. But he wasn't too proud to take any handout he could." She shrugged and wiped a bit of flour from her cheek in the manner of a pro.

"After they married, I allowed them to stay in my caretaker's cottage at the foot of the mountain, so he allowed our friendship to continue. Dane did all the work, of course, but he was a good son and we both knew he did it for love of Rosalind." A soft smile of remembrance erased the frown from her face. "She was a gentle-spirited woman, as fragile as a May flower. Men such as Joe Flannery trample such grace. And men like Dane Walden protect it."

Laurel felt stirred by the story, as well as by hearing Dane's full name for the first time. "Why did she stay with him if he was so awful?"

"Why do so many women stay with such men? But then of course, there was Daphne. He fathered her daughter and that made the leaving hard."

"Daphne is Dane's sister?"

"Half sister, yes."

Laurel felt a surprising relief at this fact. Maybelle must have misunderstood her raised brows for before she could speak Maybelle continued to explain.

"Joe Flannery is not Dane's father, a fact I'm quite sure Dane celebrates." She shook her head and her brows gathered in memory. "The man was brutal to the boy, uncommonly so. I still believe it's because he saw in young Dane a nobility that he knew he would never possess. And he tried to beat it out of the boy. Growing up, Rosalind sent him to me often, so he could be spared the switch."

Maybelle's face lit up again and she smiled brightly as her hands stilled in the dough. "Dane stole my heart the moment I saw his soulful eyes. I knew it was my duty to watch over him, to guide him as best I could. And I couldn't have found a more worthy, or I daresay more grateful, recipient of my love. He has a natural gift with plants and animals alike. Under his hand, plants thrive. He's always worked doubly hard for me, eager to please." She paused and Laurel was on the receiving end of a calculating gaze. "You see, Dane never expects anyone to be kind to him, and when someone is, he's slavishly loyal."

Laurel saw in her mind Dane's hard-set jaw and wary eyes the day she had met him. Then she recalled his fervent gratitude in the kitchen.

"What was he like as a child?"

"Oh he was a dickens, that one was! So full of joy and mischief. He knew the woods intimately, even then, and would sneak away for days on end. Joe would be furious and often rout him out. He has the cunning of a hunting dog, Joe does. But Rosalind and I never tried to stop Dane from hiding—we encouraged it—knowing as we did that in the woods was where he felt most safe."

"But he must've been so lonely."

Maybelle lifted her shoulders as if to say, *who knows?* "He chose his own friends. Foxes followed him home, rabbits nibbled from his hands, and even the birds flew nearby just to hear him play." She saw Laurel's inquisitive look. "He plays the violin, didn't you know? Just like his mother did. On warm nights with the windows open, you might hear his music soar up the mountain. It's a fine gift he has. On moonlit nights, I like to think she hears him playing." Her eyes took on a dreamy quality as she paused in her thoughts.

"What happened to her?"

Her expression grew solemn. "She got very ill. Cancer it was. And one day she . . ." she grasped for words. "Well, she left us. I was brokenhearted to lose my dear friend, but it was her two children who suffered the most."

"How old were they when she died?"

"Dane was thirteen and Daphne was only nine. Joe went from bad to worse afterward. Dane caught the worst of it when that miserable excuse for a father started in to drinking heavily. Dane came up the mountain here, to me, to escape Joe's brutality, but he never stayed away too long. He was worried about his sister. I would've booted the man out of my caretaker's house except he'd have taken the children with him. So, what could I do but put salve on the boy's wounds and try to soothe his wounded heart with love?"

Maybelle covered the smooth ball of dough with a flour-dusted cloth and put it into a warming box in the oven. "No boy should put up with what that boy had to put up with," she said through tight lips. "Something in him changed after his mother died. The little boy disappeared. Oh yes, he was becoming a man and those hormones were surging. But many men keep the joy alive inside them past puberty. While others, well, it's a sad sight to see a man without dreams.

"Anyway, a few years later Joe disappeared. I brought Daphne to my home and gave Dane money. I set him free, hoping he'd find his magic again. He traveled the world and when he was through, he returned home to me and Daphne, those who love him most."

Maybelle's love was a powerful thing, Laurel knew. She had undoubtedly saved the boy. But what about the man? She wanted to ask more questions about Dane— did he find the joy? Where did he go, and for how long?—but Maybelle had returned to her baking in earnest.

"Listen to us, talking the morning away. Have another cup of tea, dear," Maybelle said, handing her the steaming red concoction.

"Do you have anything for an itchy scalp?" she asked after a sip. "My whole head tingles."

Maybelle quickly turned back toward the stove and busied herself there. "I'll have to think about that. But I wouldn't worry if I were you. It's probably just a reaction to the water change. Well water can have so many minerals. I'll make your oatmeal. There'll be toast later, and maybe a sponge cake if I ever find the time to collect today's eggs. I just don't have the heart to ask Dane to take on one more chore."

"Let me collect the eggs for you," Laurel begged. "I'd appreciate a morning chore."

"But your ankle . . ."

"It's almost healed. Please."

"If you insist," she replied, but the relief was obvious in her expression. "I used to love to fetch them, but with my eyesight failing, I'm missing so many that I'm expecting many more chicks this year."

Laurel smiled, delighted at last to do something useful. Even if she hadn't a clue how to fetch an egg from anything but a refrigerated section of a grocery store.

"Perhaps you can ask Dane to bring you back in the cart along with my milk. He should be finishing the milking soon and I'd like to make butter today. And if I'm quick, I just might have time to make that sponge cake. We'll have such a nice afternoon tea!"

Maybelle's enthusiasm crackled in the air and Laurel could only wonder how such a diminutive woman could accomplish so much in a day, and still have time to paint world-class art. She felt Maybelle's enthusiasm tingle in her veins, even as she scratched at the curious tingling in her scalp.

After finishing her rib-sticking breakfast, Maybelle promptly shooed her away from the dishes, handing her a small wicker basket and giving directions to the hen-house. Laurel set off in good spirits, even if her pace was slowed by a tender ankle. The shortcut led to another plateau that overlooked a rolling hayfield dotted with cows. Above, the sky mirrored the landscape. White puffs of clouds sailed across the brilliant, azure skies. She paused to catch her breath and marvel at how the leaves on the trees had grown from pale to dark green just overnight.

The barns were everything a city girl like her expected a New England farm to look like. There were two tilting outbuildings filled with a selection of shovels and spades and other tools. Higher up the slope was another, newer, and much larger, weathered barn with its rear floor raised on stilts. To reach the barn she walked up a wide, stone-laid path that led to where the barn doors were flung open wide, welcoming. No one seemed to be about, but from within its shadowy portals she could hear the cacophony of moos, bleats, whinnies, and nays.

She made her way up the path into the coolness of the barn, sneezing as the multiple scents of animals, sweet hay, and earth assailed her. Sunlight filtered in through cracks between the wood planks and in the beams, dust motes floated. Her heart skipped double time when she spied a fuzzy white colt nuzzling its mother in one stall, and in another, a wobbly-legged calf nursing from a Jersey cow. The other horses and small goats were lazily chewing hay. Sparrows and swallows were flitting about from corner to corner, and a few doves cooed in the rafters. But no chickens.

Her ankle wasn't complaining, so she continued on her mission out from the barn, then down and around to the rear, where she heard a mad clucking. Hot on the trail, she rounded the bend calling out in a high, cheerful singsong, "Here chick chick chickee!" She stopped short when she saw Dane standing in the middle of a circle of plump, brown hens. He was scooping pellets from a bag and spreading handfuls to the ground. The dozen or so hens made a mad rush to wherever he tossed the pellets and greedily scooped every morsel, clucking noisily, and emerged hungry for more.

He looked up, and they stared at each other for a heartbeat. Then he surprised her by smiling, a pure, unguarded grin of welcome. Without his hat she could see the way his eyes came alive with it, shedding grace on his entire face. It was a handsome face, she thought, strong featured and square chinned. But it was his eyes that captured her, for today she spied a bit of the "dickens" Maybelle had described in them.

"I've come for eggs," she said, dragging her eyes away from his face to settle her gaze on the squawking hens around them.

"Well then, you've come to the right place."

Behind the slope the barn rested on pilings, leaving a lower barn open to an enclosed yard where the chickens seemed to have free range.

Dane casually tossed the remaining pellets to the ground, causing another flurry of wings around his high boots. His eyes, however, tracked her every movement. As she neared, he casually waved Laurel over. "Come on. I'll show you where they are. Mind your step." He was about to turn when he stopped, his eyes on her ankle. "You're up and about," he said with some surprise.

"Amazing, isn't it? Maybelle is a wizard with those concoctions of hers."

He nodded. "She is at that. I've had many a bruise or black eye mended by her wizardry. Do you need a hand?"

Even as he asked he was at her side, taking hold of her basket and her arm. She might have protested but enjoyed too much the feel of his strong arm beneath her own. There was a difference in his touch today, more solicitous, more concerned.

A large, brilliantly plumed rooster followed them into the henhouse, his scarlet wattle wagging. He was clucking loudly and eyeing them with his beady dark eyes.

Laurel looked over her shoulder and laughed. "He's suspicious . . . and he's right. I feel like a thief. And look, here come the reserves."

Dane rewarded her with another brief smile as a few more hens followed the rooster into the henhouse. "They're just begging for more food, greedy girls. And they're used to Maybelle coming for the eggs every day. It'll take awhile for them to accept you."

A series of wooden boxes were built high above the ground, which Dane explained pleased the hens and him both since it kept the nests cleaner. "Just wait while I finish the feeding and I'll come back to show you how it's done." He walked across the barn to scoop more pellets from a bin into the long wooden feeders.

A few hens fluttered back up to roost again on their nests. For a few minutes she bided her time, craning her neck as she studied the rafters, the bins, and the assorted tools hanging on iron hooks. She had no idea what they were used for. Eager to do something useful, she moved closer to the hens. They glared at her as she peered into the boxes. She was rewarded by finding a few eggs peeking out from the hay in several nests. Dane was still working with the feeder. How hard could it be to pick up a few eggs and put them into a basket? she wondered. She stepped closer to the nests. A few hens ruffled their feathers, uneasy.

"Easy now," she crooned as she began hunting for eggs from the nests without a hen. She captured one egg, then another, placing them gently into her basket, while the hens watched suspiciously. Emboldened with her success, she went to a nest with a hen hovering, and she said with respect, "Excuse me, Mother, but your job is to lay the eggs and mine is to collect them." She proceeded to competently collect the harvest of eggs without complaint. When she was done she heard Dane come up behind her in a hurry.

"I told you to wait," he said pointedly. "You could get hurt."

"Nonsense," she said with a jaunty smile. "Even a city girl like me can figure out how to pick up an egg and put it into a basket."

His face expressed suffering patience. "Some hens don't like to give up their eggs. Especially not these old girls. They'll peck at you and believe me, they'll draw blood. You have to learn to grab the hen's neck before retrieving the egg." He turned and stepped up to one hen and with a few quick, decisive movements, demonstrated the technique.

"Stop it, Dane," Laurel said, horrified. "That's no way to treat a lady. I can't imagine Maybelle doing that."

"She doesn't have to. She has this relationship with her hens that you don't."

"Oh no?" Laurel slowly but calmly walked up to the hen, clucking her tongue. Her movements were slow but sure as she gently, without complaint from Mother, collected an egg from her nest. Glancing up from under low lids, she caught Dane's drop-jawed expression.

"Don't feel bad," she said with a shake of her head. "It's a girl thing. We understand each other." With a smug smile she added another egg to her burgeoning basket. "It's not your fault God gave you testosterone."

He watched with amused amazement, which later changed to admiration, as she completed her task. She moved from nest to nest with an ease and grace not unlike Maybelle's. As he watched, he wondered again how wrong he'd been about her. He'd thought her chin was stubborn and her eyes sharp and critical. But he saw now that he was mistaken. As she cautiously plucked eggs from the nests with her delicate fingers, the pout eased into a smile that lit up eyes and could only be called gentle. And how did he miss the dimple in her left cheek?

"I have the makings for another sponge cake!" she announced with giddy triumph, lifting the basket laden with over a dozen eggs.

"And then some," he agreed, feeling her infectious delight.

"What will Maybelle do with them all?"

"I'll let you in on a little secret. Maybelle has an incurable sweet tooth. She loves cake, any kind of cake, and has been known to make three or four at a time." He laughed gently. "I always find something to do at her house around eleven in the morning. That's when she has her midmorning snack."

"And I'll just bet her cakes will be to die for. It's a date."

Their eyes met over the basket while she cursed her unfortunate choice of words. This new tension between them felt too much like flirting.

He found the pinking of her cheeks beguiling. "Would you like to meet the rest of the animals?"

There was no mistaking the friendly invitation in the tone so she hesitantly nodded her head, even though she'd never been close to farm animals before. "They're not mean, are they? They won't bite?"

"Haven't yet," he replied, and was rewarded with another smile.

Taking her basket once again in a courtly gesture, he guided her through the land mines of hen droppings to a far corner, where a ladder of wood was built onto the wall, leading to the floor above.

His hands seemed clumsy and large as he assisted her up the ladder. "Careful with your ankle now," he admonished as she tested her weight on the rung.

"I'm a big girl," she replied.

Seeing her slender form, he mentally disagreed. Her arms were no bigger than cattails. He felt certain he could snap them in two with a rough movement. As she climbed, he couldn't help but notice the gentle rounding of her hips, the waist he could span his fingers around, and the delicate bone of narrow ankle exposed between thick socks and the frayed hem of worn jeans. He dragged his gaze away to stare at the jaunty rooster, prancing with his brood.

"You'll need to fatten up if you intend to do farm chores," he said. "You're too thin."

She paused in her ascent and looked down over her shoulder. "Thank you," she said crisply.

"I didn't mean . . ." he said in a stumbling manner. "You're not unattractively thin."

"You're turning my head with compliments."

Dane felt tongue-tied with this woman. She made him think of a piece of delicate china and beside her, he felt like a big, clambering bull.

"I just meant, well, farm work can be tough and you're not used to it. You'll need to wear gloves," he muttered, looking away. "Your hands will get callused." He knew most ladies didn't like rough hands.

To his surprise she laughed lightly and it sounded to him like the gentle peal of bells.

"Oh, I shouldn't worry about that," she said, turning to finish her climb up the wooden slats.

He felt a profound relief that he hadn't insulted her, and he followed her quickly up the ladder to find her slapping dust from her hands and craning her neck to take in the lofty ceilings.

"It's a marvelous barn," she said, awe tingeing her voice. "So airy and well maintained." She looked over her shoulder and he felt the cool assessment in her intelligent eyes. "I assume you're responsible?"

He nodded and walked toward the cow at the far side of the barn, as much to tend to her as escape Laurel's study. "It's part of my job."

"I see," she said, following him slowly, taking in all the details of the place. He was leading the cow and her calf out from the barn when she said, "So you're a farmer, then."

"A good farmer," he replied.

She didn't doubt it. Keeping her distance from the animals, she watched Dane as he led the enormous brown cow to the center of the stable, parking her beside two stocky white horses at a feeding alley. Then he began laying hay, grain, and silage. A large watering bowl piped to the barn's water supply was beside this. When the cow's muzzle depressed a lever at the bottom of the bowl, a valve let in water and she laughed, thinking of bubblers in the school yard.

While the cow fed, Dane sat on a stool and milked, his hands moving in a smooth rhythm. It was a mesmerizing sight. The sound of milk hitting the pail brought two sleek barn cats running to beg for breakfast. The black one was larger and more aggressive; the smaller gray one's belly swung to and fro like an empty sack as she walked. They slunk in and around her legs like minks.

"Friendly, aren't they? What are their names?"

"Sticks and Twiggy. Sticks is a tomcat, very aloof. He only tolerates humans at mealtime. But Twiggy is a sweetheart. She's as hungry for affection as milk, though she's a lazy mama. She has a litter in the hayloft somewheres to tend to. It's her first and I don't think she knows quite what to make of it. I hear them mewling from time to time."

"More babies," she said on a sigh. "They're everywhere."

"It's spring," he replied matter-of-factly. "If you grab that metal bowl over there, I'll oblige them," he said, nodding his head in the direction of the bowl.

Happy to have a chore, she set the basket down to fetch the small dented bowl. Dane squirted with expert aim into the bowl and in no time it was filled with warm milk which the cats lapped up with relish. The scent of sweet milk filled her senses and she leaned against the stanchion to watch his hands confidently express the creamy liquid from the serene cow.

"Have you ever seen a cow milked before?" he asked.

"Oh, sure I have," she replied with a laugh. "They line the cows up at the local grocery store and we just stick our plastic gallon jugs right under a teat to fill 'er up."

He chuckled, not breaking his rhythm. "It's not difficult, just strenuous. Would you like to try it?"

She backed off, palms up. "No, no thank you. I'm not good with animals. Especially not big animals. I don't think they like me."

"The chickens seemed to like you well enough. Not to mention the bear."

"I haven't figured that out yet. It's strange, but up here I'm not so afraid of them. Maybe it's the farm environment. Truth be told, I never had much interaction with animals. We never had a dog or a cat because my father found them too dirty and too much a bother."

"Why don't you come and give this old girl a pat? Elsie's a lady and won't bite."

Laurel surveyed the cow as she lazily chewed her hay and frowned in doubt. She'd seen compact cars smaller than Elsie. "Are they anything like bulls? I've seen what they do when they're riled. With my ankle, I'm not in shape to run with the bulls."

He laughed loudly, causing a spray of milk to miss its mark and land on the floor. Sticks immediately came to investigate. "Trust me. A bull is nothing like a cow. And I promise you, he wouldn't tolerate me yanking his underbelly like this." After she laughed, he cajoled in a friendly banter, "Come on, don't be so timid."

Timid? She squared her shoulders then approached the cow with her arm out straight as a stick.

He laughed again and shook his head, muttering, "Hopeless."

"You said pet it, not hug it," she fired back. The hide felt like a scrub brush, not at all as soft as she'd expected. Elsie's large eyes rolled back to check out who touched her, then with a bored swish of her tail, went back to her cud.

"That should do it," Dane said, pushing back and patting Elsie's side with firm strokes. "Maybelle will be wanting her milk."

"I'm supposed to tell you that she wants to make butter."

"There'll be sponge cake for sure. Can I offer you a ride up? I'm taking the cart and you've probably gotten as much mileage from that ankle as you're going to get today."

"Thanks," she replied, grateful that she didn't have to ask.

He nodded, rose, and poured the milk into a tall steel container, the kind Laurel had seen in flea markets. He closed the lid and, carrying the container by the handle, came to her side to take her basket as well. Then, with a simple chivalry, he offered her his arm.

She didn't look at him—didn't dare. Instead, she rested her weight against his massive muscle and allowed Dane to guide her out from the barn to the little wooden cart. He was careful to take small steps for her sake, opening the door and lifting her into the cart as though she weighed no more that Twiggy.

As they rode off on their bumpy ride up to the house, neither of them spoke. But it occurred to Laurel that this self-described simple farmer was without question as fine and true a gentleman as she'd ever met.

Eight

A week passed while her ankle healed and still Laurel hadn't touched a paintbrush. She didn't say a word to Maybelle, deciding to wait instead for her to initiate the lessons. She sensed that Maybelle was biding her time, testing her out, although for what she couldn't imagine.

She wasn't suffering. The waiting was easier because she was also having a wonderful time going through *Fanny Farmer's Cookbook* for sponge cake recipes, using up dozens of the eggs that she gathered each morning from the henhouse. She'd never done much baking before. Sure, there were a few box mixes and chocolate chip cookies, but never a cake from scratch. Even the words *from scratch* were foreign on her modern tongue. There were almost as many varieties of sponge cakes as there were fairies: plain sponge cakes, cream sponges, daffodil, chocolate, angel food, and Laurel's favorite, Genoise.

By the end of the week there was a backlog of cakes. She carried cake to the garden at "elevenses," when Dane obliged her by testing samples of the day's baking adventure. She ate cake in the gazebo at four with Maybelle, scattering crumbs to the birds and leaving a hefty slice out for the fairies. "They absolutely adore cake and they're ever so grateful," she told Laurel in all earnestness. Laurel's inedible failures they fed to the hens, who were not so critical and cackled gratefully as they pecked at the unexpected treat.

Every morning she awoke to the rousing crow of the

rooster. After a filling breakfast of an omelet or pancakes or perhaps hot cereal and fruit, she gathered the eggs and fetched the milk from Dane. She looked forward to his casual smile of greeting as he fed the hens or milked the cow. Yet despite his seeming indifference, each morning he offered her his arm with a gallant formality and drove her back up the road to the house in the little horse-drawn cart. They didn't speak much on the short trip, but a glance or two between them conveyed a mutual pleasure in the ride. An easy peace was born between them in this early morning ritual, a natural joining as simple—and as rich—as the cream that rose to the top of the milk jars each day.

Laurel and Maybelle forged a bond as well. There was no shortage of chores and it seemed Maybelle was intent on teaching each and every one of them to her. One day Maybelle ladled thick cream into an old-fashioned butter churn and they took turns pumping the dasher, an exercise Laurel defied any gym to match. One day she helped make cheddar cheese in big, round molds sealed with wax. There were countless oil lamps to fill, candles to make, fires to set, floors to scrub, and clothes to mend. And this was just indoors.

Outdoors, the primary responsibility was the massive vegetable and flower gardens that required hours of weeding and hoeing. The month of May was ending and the seedlings were taking off. Soon they would be eating peas and spinach and before too long, tomatoes.

But it was the flower garden that drew most of their focus. Each morning after breakfast the two women gathered wicker baskets and gardening tools and headed for the flower beds. Like clockwork, by late morning, Laurel started to look for Dane to come to the garden in his worn tweed jacket and high boots. She always felt a flutter in her stomach when she recognized his steady gait as he climbed the mountain road, as strong as that of the powerful horse he led. Maybelle usually made some excuse soon after he arrived, leaving the two of them to work alone with the hummingbirds and bees busily feeding.

Laurel wasn't usually much of a talker, and Dane certainly wasn't either. Initially, he answered her questions, then asked some of his own. They didn't pry, but neither did they hold back. It was a slow start as they pushed past awkward moments. Yet, like the tender plants they tended in the garden, as the days passed their conversations gradually broke through and bloomed and ripened. When she heard him laugh the first time, her heart soared at the richness of the sound of it, like hearing a church bell unexpectedly pierce a quiet afternoon. After several days of working together, they fell into an easy comradeship.

"I can't believe I've been here a week already," she said as she pulled a weed from the lily bed. "Some days it feels like I just arrived. Other days I feel like I've been here forever. It's as though my whole body has slowed down. No, that's not right. It's more my whole pace has slowed."

He chuckled, nodding. "That's common enough around here. We're just not in so much of a hurry. Things work out in their own sweet time."

Dane was a few yards away replacing the rotted frame of one of Maybelle's raised beds. He was clad in his usual jeans, suspenders, and boots. But today the afternoon sun shone hot and he'd removed his outer flannel shirt. In his T-shirt she could see his muscles bunch as he sanded a new piece of rough-hewn wood. He had a farmer's body, she thought, hard, tanned and sinewy. Accustomed to hard labor and long hours. It seemed to her that he, like Maybelle, never stopped working. She remembered that the first time she saw him, he was working with wood. How wrong she'd been about him, how quick to make judgments.

"When I first saw you I thought you were a logger. I guess it's because you were carting all that wood."

"I am that, too," he replied, not looking up. "But I prefer to think of myself as a farmer."

"Maybelle tells me you do everything here—cut wood, manage the woodlot, care for the animals . . . Seems like a lot more than just a farmer."

He lifted his head at that and his eyes sparkled as he said with a confident smile, "All that *is* being a farmer," he replied. "It's what I am, and I'm good at what I do."

"But you're also a gardener, and there's a difference. Gardening is a skilled craft that requires years of study. Believe me, I know. I've studied horticulture for years. That's what my college degree is in." She meant it as a compliment, but the way he stiffened and tightened his lips revealed he took it as anything but.

After a moment's pause he lifted his head and said evenly, "I am a gardener. I know what I'm doing out here." His eyes met hers. "But school has nothing to do with what I know. I haven't finished high school."

She blanched, feeling the burn from his scorching gaze. So much of her self-esteem had come from her education. She'd led a secluded life surrounded by academics. But certainly she didn't feel superior to Dane in her knowledge of horticulture. They'd had so many discussions about horticulture during the past week, lengthy debates not only about the care of the plants but of breeding and genetics. And certainly he was a master in Maybelle's gardens, a rival of any master at Longfield.

"Dane, I'm sorry. I didn't mean that as anything but a compliment. I was so impressed with your knowledge, your expertise, I just assumed you had a degree."

"Learning doesn't only occur in universities, Laurel."

"No, of course not," she hurried to say, feeling that this conversation was going from bad to worse. How could she have been such a snob? "I shouldn't assume," she said humbly.

He appeared to be moved by her statement and struggling inside with a decision. Laurel waited with her hands on her thighs for what seemed a long time. Dane was a deliberate man in his thoughts, speech, and pace. She knew that a decision reached was irrevocable.

So when he reached out to pluck a primrose from the garden bed and reached out to hand it to her, she felt like melting with relief.

"Let's just say I had an apprenticeship of my own with Maybelle."

She smiled, liking that answer immensely. "That's an education I value highly."

"I know you studied horticulture," he said with a wry grin. "But what is it that you do, exactly?"

She shrugged and played with the leaves of the primrose. "Like you, I'm a jack of all trades. I guess I've always been a student." She laughed shortly. "It sure seems like I've been studying something all my life."

"I kinda figured that about you."

"Oh?" she asked with raised brows. "And how do you know that?"

"Everything with you has to be by the book, and I mean that literally. You rely on the printed word as fact rather than your own observation."

Her cheeks flamed. In science, this was a serious criticism. "I believe in a solid background of knowledge to support my observations," she replied in the manner of a textbook.

He cocked a brow. "Yeah, right."

She opened her mouth to defend herself against the sarcasm but he'd beat her to it by smiling and saying with utter charm, "Now that I know you better, I'm willing to overlook it."

She pursed her lips to hide her smile. "My goal is to become a biogeneticist," she continued. "That's someone who . . ."

"I know what it is," he interrupted as his knife sharply cut into the wood.

She blushed, realizing how condescending she had been again. "I'm sorry. I'm really not trying to be a snob. It's just that I'm always asked, so I just assume I should explain." He stopped sanding the wood to cast her a pointed look.

"I know," she said with a flip of her hands. "I'm assuming again." He certainly seemed very touchy about anything to do with academics. She could only believe that no matter what he might tell her, he wasn't comfortable with his limited education. "I work in a lab most of the time," she pushed on, hoping to restore normalcy between them. "In the past few years, I've done a lot of research for my father's projects. But for years before that, I also drew sketches of plants offered in the Longfield catalogues."

"Really?" he asked, pausing. His eyes measured her again and his voice revealed that he was more impressed by this revelation. "Then I've seen your work in the catalogues. You're good. Is that how Maybelle discovered you?"

The compliment was quick but flattered her enormously. "No. Years ago, when I was only sixteen, I was in a collective show of local young talent. Maybelle apparently saw my work and remembered it. Can you imagine my surprise when she wrote to invite me? It came from nowhere."

"Sounds like Maybelle," he said, and she was rewarded with the sound of his laughter again. "Your paintings must be very special."

Feeling the warm sunshine on her back and the glow of his flattery in her heart, Laurel tugged vigorously on a patch of clover. She liked the fact that they could lapse into a comfortable silence, unlike with her father and Colin, who would tune her out when they were busy, as though she were not even there.

Laurel leaned back on her heels and looked at her hands, coated with dirt like Dane's. She laughed out loud just seeing them.

Dane turned her way again, curious. "What's so funny?"

"My hands! I've spent how many years drawing, dissecting, and examining under a microscope countless varieties of flowers. I can name each and every one of them in both Latin and common names. But I've never had dirty hands before."

She raised her hands so he could see them. Her short nails were encrusted with dirt.

"Farmer's hands," he said with appreciation glowing in his eyes.

"Yep," she replied, heavy on the Vermont accent.

Their eyes met again and this time, held. The connection was very strong. Her mind stilled till all she could hear was the throbbing singing of the insects in the tall grass of the meadow.

Dane broke off, looking down again at his wood. With a mighty thrust, he began sanding again.

Laurel puffed out her cheeks.

"Working at Longfield Gardens," he said, "I'd have thought you would have had plenty of opportunity to work in the soil."

"Never," she said with a roll off the eyes. "I'd never be allowed to stick my hands in the precious Longfield soil. It's strictly maintained by a professional crew."

"What about at home? Not even a little patch of earth there?"

His tone wasn't critical and she answered honestly. "My father's gardens were always experimental, tended by his students. I wasn't encouraged to help. Quite the contrary, he'd rather I didn't. They were projects, you see. I guess that was the problem. I've always looked at flowers as scientific projects. Things to study, to measure and chart and to get results from." She looked at the long stem and pointed leaves of the lily in front of her and shrugged. "Other than a few window boxes, I've never bent my back over the plants like here. Having my hands in the soil, all bare like this, connects me to the earth in a way I've never experienced before."

"It's a shame to only see a flower through a microscope."

"Well," she said shyly, "there are the roses. I've always loved roses, all types, colors, shapes, sizes." Her eyes danced with excitement and she didn't notice him pause to rest his arm against his knees to study her. "I love the old roses that our grandparents cherished and the new cultivars too. They're such a delight. I even love their names, they roll off the tongue. *Pearl of Gold. Peace. Chapeau de Napoleon. Burglar Rose. Razzle Dazzle.* Aren't they lovely?"

He raised his brows in astonishment. "Does Maybelle know you love roses?"

"I don't know. I wouldn't think so. Why?"

"No particular reason, other than that she loves them too."

"Does she? But I don't see many here in the garden. I've looked for them and I have to admit I was disappointed to find her collection rather skimpy. She has rare varieties of everything else imaginable, but for roses, her selection is, well, standard. Lovely and well kept, mind you," she hurried to add, "but nothing thrilling."

Dane merely lifted his shoulder as though to say, *who knows?* "So, do you study roses too? Under the microscope?"

"Oh yes. My father is an expert in the field and spends months of every year tracking down old species. He's what's known fondly as a 'rose rustler.' "

Dane's face darkened with suspicion. "What does that mean?"

Now it was her turn to laugh. "He doesn't steal them, if that's what you're asking. Surely you know that roses are propagated through cuttings. And though *clone* is a modern word, the method is an ancient one dating back three thousand years. It involves nothing more scientific than a pair of cutting shears. But what he enjoys most is driving through the countryside and discovering some old, forgotten rose along a highway or behind a church in some graveyard garden in the middle of nowhere."

"And then he just goes up and helps himself?"

She didn't like the implication and scoffed at his question. "The bushes aren't hurt, and it's a darn sight better than digging up the whole rosebush. That *would* be stealing. Besides, garden roses don't reproduce true to form from seed. So thanks to my father, countless rose species have been preserved for posterity." Her pride in her father's work rang clear in her voice.

"You don't know the bushes aren't hurt," he said, sticking to his point.

"Well, of course we do."

He shook his head. "You're assuming again. Take my

word for it. There are some ancient species that must never be cut or they'll die."

Her hand stilled in the garden and she leaned forward, curious. She'd never heard of such a thing except in rumor. "Do you know of such a species? Does Maybelle?"

Dane shook his head and frowned. "I've heard of such a rose."

"Ah," she replied, taking a deep breath. "More fairy tales."

"Not fairy tales," he corrected. He set down his tool and slowly brushed the sawdust from his hands as he considered his words. "There are quests for old roses, rumors of old gardens that true rosarians pursue with a single-minded focus. Some spend entire lifetimes on the scent." He paused and offered a wry smile. "No pun intended."

"I've heard those rumors," she said, feeling an old excitement dance in her veins. Leaning forward, she spoke with a new fervency. "My father often spoke of a certain rose." She hesitated, uncertain of how much to tell Dane of something so personal.

"I'm intrigued. What's the story?"

She hedged, scraping a bit of soil from her nails. "My father isn't prone to reminiscing or storytelling, or even idle chatter. You should know he is a well respected specialist in roses, and a renowned collector whose accomplishments—"

"Yes, yes," Dane interrupted her. "I know who your father is. Anyone involved in horticulture would. Even me," he added in his self-deprecating manner.

Her eyes widened a bit at this admission from a man who seemed blatantly antiacademic. He was looking at her with his usual strength of focus. Despite his claims that he was not intellectual, a sharp intelligence shone in his eyes.

"Well then, you know that he's not the kind of man who is swayed by legend and rumor."

"I don't consider that a positive trait, but go ahead."

Laurel shifted her weight, nettled. "As I was saying . . ." She hesitated, bringing back to mind the memory of her father sitting on her bed, perhaps having finished reading her a book. At that quiet moment of tenderness, his eyes would mist as he looked out at the moon, and if she was very quiet and did not disturb him, he would sometimes lapse into the story of the rose.

"My father was born and raised in the English countryside, in Kent, 'the garden of England.' No one loves roses like the English—with the possible exception of Californians. At any rate, when he was a little boy, it was his job to care for the roses. Well, he much preferred hunting, archery, and cricket and though he grew up in the midst of gardens, he showed no interest in horticulture. Still, Father wasn't given much choice about the matter and at that time, he hated roses because they meant nothing to him but work. Until one day visitors complimented him on his excellent rose beds and encouraged him to enter a few blooms in a local contest. Well, he did, and he won. Nothing like success to spur one on.

"From that time on, he was hooked. He began raising many varieties and winning more contests. But when he became a young man, he longed for a bit more adventure. He began roaming the country for unusual roses. He spent days and days wandering about all sorts of places. He particularly loved old gravesites with the marble vaults, obelisks, urns, and among them, old roses. After finishing his college exams, he decided to reward himself with a hunt in the countryside. This trip was more of a lark. He was enjoying the view of the countryside as much as anything else when it happened."

She stopped to look at him, her eyebrow raised. Dane had stopped working and was leaning toward her, his head cocked in anticipation.

"He fell head over heels in love."

"With a rosebush?"

"Of course. He found the rose quite accidentally. A sudden summer storm rose up and he had to hurry to a rocky glen to wait it out. While pacing about smoking a cigar, he caught sight of a perfect blossom, the like of which he'd never seen before or since. He felt a tingling in his body as though he'd been struck by lightening. Such a rose! He's described it to me so many times I feel as if I've seen it myself."

She leaned back in the tall grass and, closing her eyes, she could see the rose in her mind's eye as clearly as if it were real.

"Bathed in the splendor of the setting sun," she said in recitation, quoting her father's words as verse, "was a single bush with a rose that held the tints of a maidenly blush against a whiteness so pure it was heavenly. This particular rose had every quality he sought in a rose: large flower, exquisite color, and a rich, fragrant perfume that was intoxicating.

"He was utterly mesmerized. Then on closer inspection, thrilled to the marrow. This was no ordinary rose. It was an important discovery. He knew it was an old rose, though not one he could identify. Despite being neglected, the bush flourished free of disease or fungus or insects. He tells me how he studied the plant, took copious notes in his book. He was about to take a cutting with his penknife when someone called out to him not to cut the bush. Looking up, he saw an exquisitely beautiful woman, every bit as enchanting as the rose blossom—and she captured his heart more so than the rose. He couldn't refuse her."

"What happened then?" A smile crept across his face. "Did he learn the names of either of them?"

Laurel nodded but kept her gaze averted. "The rose was a major discovery that formed the cornerstone of his career. He called it, *La Belle Rose*. The woman was my mother. He named the rose after her."

"La Belle Rose?" He rubbed his jaw in thought.

"Yes, have you heard of it?" she asked quickly, hope stirring in her breast.

Dane shook his head, dashing her hopes.

"I've never seen it either. It simply disappeared without a trace, just like my mother."

"Your mother disappeared? When?"

"At my birth. One morning my father woke up and she was gone. Left us both without an address, phone number, nothing. My father knew very little about her—except that he adored her. He was devastated and looked for her, but it was as though she'd fallen off the face of the earth. She never tried to reach us, not once in all these years. I think it changed him."

"How can you tell? You were only an infant."

"Naturally I didn't know him then, but I can't reconcile the free spirit who roamed the countryside in search of roses with the man I grew up with, someone so precise he plans every minute of his day. And there's something in his eyes . . . There's a faint glimmer, a wistfulness that slips into them on occasion and I know he's thinking of her."

"That's sad. He must have really loved her."

She nodded, plucking at the grass.

"Love like that is rare," he said in a distant voice. "He was fortunate to have experienced it, even for a brief moment in time."

"The odd thing is, over the years he's convinced himself that the whole affair was only so bright and beautiful in his memory." She suppressed a shudder of dismay and picked up her trowel and began attacking a patch of clover with a vengeance. "It probably was just his imagination," she added with a huffiness that came more from her heart than her effort. "Just a childish dream or some overblown memory. It's quite common you know, especially as one gets older. In my opinion, love is highly overrated. All those starry eyes and swoons are the stuff fairy tales are made of. It's certainly nothing I've ever experienced."

She didn't like the way his eyes were searching her, as though they were peering into dark and private corners of her heart. Quickly she turned her head away.

"It seems our conversation has come full circle," she said in summation, hoping to sidetrack the sentimental turn. "We're back to fairy tales."

"That's the natural course of things here at Fallingstar," he chided.

Laurel looked off into the dark woods in the distance and felt a shiver run down her spine. "It is indeed," she replied.

Later that day, as the sun set over the Danby mountains, Dane walked at a tired pace to the small farmhouse that he shared with his sister, Daphne. He loved spring and the resurgence of life he felt deep in his marrow. He had traveled around the world, but when the snow melted and the earth warmed enough for the tender green shoots to break the soil, there was nowhere else in the world he'd rather be than at Fallingstar. But spring was also a time for hard work and long hours. Everything needed doing in the spring, and he often felt like an ox in the harness, plowing through chore after chore with blinders on and a whip at his back.

It was a labor of love, however, and he never regretted a moment's effort. For this place—the land, the woodlands—was part of his own soul. This lifestyle, primitive as it may be, suited him. He wasn't one who expected an easy life. He craved the peace that came from privacy, a quiet mind, and an easy conscience.

Though he wasn't a spartan like Maybelle. His little house had modern amenities like running water and electricity, although it remained true to the simple lifestyle embraced at Fallingstar.

Simple sure isn't easy, God knows, he thought, bringing a hand to rub the perpetual ache in his lower back. On spring days like this, when the fence needed repair, the cistern cleaning, and the plowing done, the place needed two men, or even three. But he didn't often hire on extra men, preferring to keep a distance from the prying and curious. He was proud that he could work hard and long. To do less would have broken some covenant he shared not only with Maybelle but with the land. He had a kinship with the woods that stemmed from his childhood. He cleared the stream banks of trees and brush, leaving some for trout and beavers, and felled softwood. All in all, though, he'd achieved a fair balance that allowed for the tame and the wild to live peacefully side by side. Maybelle called him the caretaker. He had laughed and replied that was a mighty fine name for the hired hand.

He walked through the thick hedge of mountain laurel that his mother and Maybelle had planted when the house was built twenty years earlier. The sweet scent of the blossoms greeted him, slowing his step, stirring him as no other scent did. He'd never known the why or reason of it.

Tonight, however, as the scent enveloped him, he thought of Laurel. It was her scent, he realized with a dawning realization. He breathed in deeply, certainty flooding him as the sweet scent did. He accepted this realization as readily as he accepted the certain knowledge that they were meant to be together. He had felt it the moment she'd stepped in front of the bear. Carrying her home in his arms, that feeling grew to certitude.

As he pushed open the iron gate to his front walk, he wondered what it would be like to see Laurel sitting on the front porch waiting for him when he came home at night. He stopped again, a curious smile loping across his face. Why, he could visualize her sitting right there, neat as a pin, perhaps in the white wicker rocker, or perhaps leaning against a rounded pillar.

She'd like his house, he decided, looking at the two-story frame house with the gingerbread trim and the wraparound porch that was the only home he'd ever known. The house was still filled with charming notions, nooks and crannies that were hallmarks of Maybelle and Rosalind. And the house was his. The house and surrounding one hundred acres had already been deeded to him. Maybelle had wanted him to know that as a man, he had something of his own to work for.

"What are you out here daydreaming about?" Daphne called out through the screen door. A moment later it swung wide and she marched out, one steaming sauce-pan in her left hand and a mitt in her right. "This rice is as dry as dirt. And your chicken looks like a cinder. I thought you'd be back early tonight."

He looked at the rice and sighed, remembering the savory scent of Laurel's Brunswick stew on the stove and Maybelle's warm bread and freshly churned butter on the counter. They'd invited him for dinner but he'd refused. He didn't think he'd taste a thing with Laurel sitting across the table from him. He'd chew his tongue for sure. And he wasn't sure his table manners were up to snuff. The last thing he wanted to do was embarrass himself in front of a lady like her.

"It'll be fine, sis. Just leave it on the counter. I'm too tired to eat just yet."

Her eyes noted his hand on his back, the weary sag to his face and the staggered walk of a man who'd put in one hundred ten percent.

"You look worn out. It's too much for a single man, I keep telling you that. Maybelle tells you to hire on help. You should do it."

He took the beer she offered him gratefully and took a long swallow. "I don't trust anyone not to cause more trouble than they're worth. I'd rather do it myself."

"You just don't trust anyone, period. The list of chores keeps growing each year and soon it's going to be more than you can do even if you work round the clock. The frontier will get the best of a single man."

"Now don't start jumping down my back. You know I hire on for the big jobs and for all the haying."

"You need to hire on for other chores as well."

"You could help more."

"Nope," she said, shaking her head. "A thousand times no. You know I hate farming. The only thing I love is my bees, and I already put in twelve-hour days with them. You can't get water from a stone."

"Don't I know it," he replied with a lazy grin. "And you're one hard rock, no doubt about it."

"Very funny." She slanted her gaze. "At least I found my equal. Little Miss Apprentice. She's the tough one."

He cocked his head. "Now how would you know? You've never even met her."

"I know what you tell me," she said, following him into the kitchen.

He sat down at the kitchen table and stretched his long legs out before him. "Well, I was wrong about that. I find now that I don't know Miss Carrington at all."

Daphne studied his face and didn't like the dreamy expression she saw in his eyes, not one bit. She piled the clumped rice onto his plate in heaping spoonfuls. "Seems like you want to get to know her better."

"Maybe I do."

She tried making light of his serious tone. "Aw, you're just working too hard. You need to get out more. Meet some women. You're such a recluse, a hermit just like Maybelle. It ain't healthy."

"I suppose you think I should go out with you and the boys and go carousing."

"That's right," she said, dishing out the chicken. It hit the plate like a rock. "We have a good time. A little poker, a little beer, some laughs. We could even go to Rutland to some of them bars. There's lots of nice girls to meet there."

Dane eyed the dinner with dread, but his stomach was demanding. Taking up a fork he resigned himself to his fate. "Thanks, but no thanks. I'm not the type."

"We're back to that type thing again, huh? Well, Little Miss Apprentice sure as hell ain't your type."

He took a long draught of beer to wash the mouthful down. When he finished he wiped his mouth and said seriously, "Miss Carrington might just be exactly my type."

Daphne was silenced and her face reflected her worry. "How can you say that?" she asked in a rush. "She's a bookworm and you love the outdoors. When she thinks of plants she thinks of them in laboratories under a microscope. She doesn't *know* them like you. Did you know she told Maybelle she's just waiting on her chance to go to graduate school to be some kind of engineer?"

He frowned at his plate but didn't reply.

"On top of that, she's so pampered. Who does she

think she is? Maybelle waits on her hand and foot like she's some kind of princess."

"Pampered?" he snorted while sawing the chicken. "Hardly. Maybelle's put her through the paces. I've seen hired hands put in fewer hours. You're the only other person I know who can work a day like her. And she doesn't stick her nose in a book all the time," he said defensively. "She's out in the garden side by side with Maybelle with her hands in the soil. There aren't many women like that, least not that I've met."

"And what's that all about? Her and Maybelle are getting all chummy all of a sudden. No one does that without expecting something in return. What does she think? That Maybelle's going to leave everything to her?" Her dander was up and she was wagging her finger. "I've heard about cases like that, where young folks move in with older ones just to collect when they die."

He barked out a laugh and shook his head. "Maybelle's hardly dying."

"No, but her eyesight is going. She'll be dependent someday soon."

He sobered and captured Daphne's gaze. "True enough. We talked about that very issue. I seem to recall you saying that you didn't want to live with her. You wanted your freedom." He silenced her retort with a stern look. "You had the chance and turned it down. It's not fair to be riled now just because Laurel's taken it."

"It's not just that," she argued back. "You have to be blind not to see how Maybelle's gone overboard for Laurel. I didn't believe you at the time, but now I'm thinking maybe you were right when you said Maybelle was vulnerable now, with her sight going and all. I went up to visit the other day while Laurel was out and do you know what I found out?" She narrowed her eyes with meaning. "Guess who's sleeping in the special bedroom? Just guess." When she saw Dane's stunned face she nodded smugly. "Yep. Laurel."

His hands rested on the table. "No one has ever slept in that room."

"See what I mean?" she said, glad to see the first sign of worry in his expression.

Dane saw in his mind's eye the image of Laurel and Maybelle baking cakes together, in the garden together, making candles, churning butter—and soon, standing at an easel with canvas and paints. Side by side. He'd watched an affection blossom between the two women that was a thing of beauty to observe. They'd both been lonely in their lives and it seemed only good and natural that the two women would form a bond. He imagined it was like this with his mother and Maybelle, and that notion pleased him, assuaging any doubts.

He went back to finish his meal. "It's Maybelle's room, Maybelle's house, and Maybelle's decision. And she made a good one, as far as I can tell."

Daphne was white with fury. "Since when did you get all moon-eyed over her?"

He looked at his sister's rigid stance and hard expression and asked calmly, "Since when did you get so hostile?"

"I'm not. Why should I be? I don't even know her. I'm just worried about you."

"That's rot. You're upset because you're so jealous of the affection between Laurel and Maybelle that you can't spit straight. Don't you know yet that Maybelle has plenty of love to go around? You don't need to be jealous. And you sure as hell don't need to be so damn stubborn. Go on up and meet Laurel. Give her a chance. I know Maybelle's invited you for tea every day, and every day you stand her up."

"Not her, exactly. It's just that I hate those things. Tea and cakes. That's a little too girlie for me."

"Well, little sister, you can't have it both ways. If you want someone to be thoughtful to you, you have to be thoughtful back. You run off to the mountains for days on end without a word to anyone. Does it ever occur to you that I might worry?"

"Hell, I come by it honestly! Maybelle's forever taking off into the woods. And you used to go for days.

And our parents damn well disappeared for good in them!"

He rubbed his jaw in consternation, knowing it was the truth. "Well, as far as coming to tea or stopping by to say hello, it wouldn't kill you to make an effort, if only for Maybelle's sake. God knows she's done a lot for you."

"You too," she fired back.

"And I know it."

She shut up, knowing no one on earth could criticize his devotion to Maybelle.

He mopped his face with his palm, leaning back from the table. He was weary beyond words. "Face it, Daphne. You've never really been there for Maybelle."

"I can't help it if I don't like doing the stuff she does," she replied, collecting his empty plate and silverware with an angry swipe. "I find it so boring! Is that a crime?"

"No," he said more gently and without accusation. "It's just who you are. Our own wild one. We love you and don't want you to change. But you have to accept that Laurel enjoys working with Maybelle . . . and that Maybelle is having a nice time teaching her. I'm happy for her. Happy for them both." He speared her with a look. "As you should be."

Daphne stuck out her chin combatively. It was clear she wasn't giving in.

"If you don't mind, I'm going to excuse myself, take a hot shower, and go to bed. I'm too tired to talk about this anymore tonight."

"Well, sweet dreams, brother," she said in a voice loaded with sarcasm. "I don't need to guess who you'll be dreaming about."

He frowned and dragged his exhausted body up the stairs. He knew that it wasn't only the hard work that was exhausting him. If tonight was like the last five nights, he would indeed be dreaming of a certain blond woman with fairy eyes. And he wouldn't get a moment's rest.

Nine

After two weeks of waiting, Maybelle surprised Laurel when she greeted her return from the henhouse with a tray of paints and a canvas.

"I've been watching and waiting for a signal that you felt at home," Maybelle said as she handed her a long, paint splattered cotton duck apron. While she talked, her hands busily tied another similar one around herself. The ruffles that traveled from the neck of the sky blue dress to the floor-length hem were flattened by the wide shoulders of the blanket-sized covering. "Yesterday, when you left a slice of cake out for the fairies after tea, I knew your heart was in the right place."

Laurel opened her mouth to deny that she'd left the cake for the fairies, but she couldn't voice the objection—for she had. She honestly didn't know for sure whether she left the hefty slice because she'd seen Maybelle do this every day after tea, or because she was falling under the spell of Fallingstar. So she closed her mouth and kept her peace.

"I've gathered together a few supplies for you," Maybelle continued. "I know you've been very patient. And isn't it a marvelous day? So grab the easel resting by the door, will you?"

Laurel watched the fireball of action hurry down the hall, arms laden with a large basket of supplies and her long skirt flowing behind her. Maybelle was as flighty as one of the fairies she loved to draw.

And as enchanting. Maybelle's cheery enthusiasm

was infectious. Feeling a surge of joy, Laurel carefully placed her basket of eggs on the wood table, then took after Maybelle at a trot. She followed Maybelle to the meadow that separated the gardens from the forest, a bit of land that Laurel had always thought of as the natural, graceful transition piece between the civilized and the wild. A perfect spot to begin her apprenticeship, she thought as she approached, lugging the easel.

"Here's a hat for you to wear," Maybelle said in a motherly tone, offering her a wide-brimmed straw one that tied under the chin with a long scarf. "We can't have you burning your tender skin in the hot summer sun." Maybelle was always concerned with such things as skin, hair, nails, and other such issues of beauty. Having grown up alone with her father, Laurel wasn't accustomed to thinking of such things. If she wore a hat and sunscreen, it was because common sense told her to. The sun's rays could prove cancerous. Maybelle, however, was more alarmed that her lovely white skin might turn leathery. Still, Laurel admitted to herself as she took the offered hat and dutifully tied the trailing scarf under her chin, she enjoyed the mothering.

Once the easel was in place, the paints organized, and Laurel was settled in front of the canvas with brush in hand, Maybelle clasped her hands nervously and surveyed the scene. Laurel waited anxiously for the sage advice she was sure was coming.

"All set then?" Maybelle asked. When Laurel nodded eagerly, Maybelle nodded and said with forced cheer, "Good! Well, I'm off then. Have fun!" She clutched her skirt in her hands and spun on her heel to make a hasty retreat.

"Maybelle, wait!" Laurel called out, her arm outstretched as though to catch the fleeing woman. Maybelle stopped and, with a long sigh, turned to look at her over her shoulder. "Where are you off to?" Laurel called out. "I thought . . . well, I mean . . ." She swallowed then said almost sternly, "Aren't you going to work with me?"

Maybelle seemed flustered, pinned like a butterfly eager to fly off. "Whatever for, dear? It's your painting, not mine."

Laurel had come to expect such a reply from Maybelle, but she dug in, determined to get direction. "Yes, I know it is," she said with determined patience. "And I will paint something. But you agreed to teach me. You promised," she urged, her voice insistent.

Maybelle's face fell, like a child's caught at her own game. "I did, yes, I recall." She frowned petulantly then started back toward the canvas with slow, dragging steps. "I'll try, Laurel, but as I said, I don't know the first thing about teaching."

Laurel felt like some bully on the playground and it felt all wrong. She was the student here, not the other way around. She resented having to beg or bully for the teaching she'd come for. When Maybelle returned to the canvas, Laurel saw with a start that Maybelle was truly anxious about teaching.

"Perhaps if we don't think of it as teaching," Laurel suggested gently. "What if I just watched you awhile? I'm sure I could learn a lot if you just talked aloud about why you do what you do and how. It doesn't have to be formal teaching."

Maybelle's eyes sparked to life as this concept took root. "Well, since you put it like that, I suppose I could. Yes, perhaps I even should." Her face brightened. "We'll pretend we're just having a chat, shall we? A little of this and a little of that, nothing too serious, right? Well then . . ."

She rolled her trailing sleeves back and went to the canvas. First, her hands fluttered at the small jars of paints, opening them and considering the palette of colors. Laurel could almost see her mind at work, so focused was her attention. It seemed as though she wanted to hurry and start right off or lose her nerve.

"I . . . I haven't painted in a very long time," Maybelle confessed as her hands trembled among the brushes. "My eyes you know . . ."

"Neither have I," she volunteered. "I think that's why I am so afraid."

Maybelle's eyes met hers and their gaze met in a silent understanding. "Afraid?" Maybelle said, tossing her shoulders back. "Nonsense. What's there to be afraid of?"

Laurel laughed and nodded in agreement.

Maybelle reached up to pluck the jeweled pins from her hair and to slowly unwind the long braids from around her head. Laurel watched in fascination as the thick plaits tumbled down and flowed free from their strict bindings. The wind caught the hair, playing with it, waving it free in the wind like a shimmering silver-capped wave. She stood as still as one of the nearby trees, head cocked slightly and her eyes closed, listening. Laurel listened too, hearing the whistle of the wind that sang high in the trees. For a long time Maybelle stood quietly in this position as a faint smile slowly spread across her face. Laurel watched as one transfixed. Maybelle's face seemed to lose years as she stood and listened. The worry lines around her mouth and eyes eased, as did the deeper crevices across her forehead. Her whole body seemed to loosen and she swayed in the wind like the lithe branches of a tree.

After a long, peaceful stretch of time, her eyes snapped open—so fast it brought Laurel's back up with a start.

Maybelle stared hard at the canvas, her strange eyes glazed as one hypnotized. Then she picked up her brush and twirled it before the canvas like an expert swordsman. Laurel licked her lips, waiting. In a quick, fluid motion, Maybelle dabbed her brush in blue, poised it in the air, then in a rush, dove at the canvas. Laurel took a step closer, her mouth open and her curiosity bubbling in her veins. She'd never seen an artist work in such a fevered burst of inspiration, and she could only watch in awe before a master.

Maybelle's brush seemed to fly with a will of its own across the canvas, sometimes diving into the jars of color, then darting back to the canvas in a burst of speed. Before her eyes, the blank canvas was coming to life. But not with a depiction of a delicate fairy perched on a flower, or dipping daintily in a woodland pond. There were no wings or flowers of any kind.

Instead, over the course of the afternoon, what Laurel saw was light in motion—a flowing radiance of astral blues, greens, reds, and silvers that illuminated the canvas as well the spirit. As she watched, Laurel thought of Maybelle's definition of a fairy as forms of energy. Seeing the shimmering, luminous aspects before her, she had a first glimmering of understanding of what she'd meant, as well as a deep awe. Laurel could only stand before the canvas and watch with her arms hanging at her sides and her heart trembling in her chest till Maybelle finished with a final, flourishing jab.

As she did, hours later. Maybelle's head drooped as her hand lowered from the canvas. She seemed physically exhausted, as though all her energy had flowed directly from her, through her brush to the canvas.

"It's wonderful," was all Laurel could say in way of praise. No words could describe the magic found in Maybelle's colors. "There is no possible way you could teach me to paint like this," she said in a soft voice.

Maybelle looked for a long while at the painting she'd just completed, then shook her head sadly, as though in remorse. "My eyes are so bad now, I can't paint the fairies as I once did. As my public wishes me to paint them. I simply cannot make out the lines." She reached up to gently rub her eyes. "Now I paint more what I feel than what I actually see." She faced Laurel, her eyes troubled. "I'm sorry, Laurel. It's not you who is the failure, but me. It's not that I'm unwilling to teach you, it's more that I am unable. I should have been more honest with you, told you plainly that I would not be able to see well enough to instruct you stroke by stroke. But I was worried that you would be disappointed and leave, and I so much wanted you to stay and try. I have such faith in you."

"Maybelle, don't speak of failure! This painting is a wonder, a masterpiece. Nothing I've ever painted can come close. Look at your colors, your mastery. It's abstract, yet it's not. Quite simply, this *is* a fairy. I know it," she said in a whisper.

A faint smile replaced the worry on Maybelle's face. "Do you think so? Why, if you think so, then that is all I need know. You see the fairy?"

"In a manner of speaking, yes. Maybelle, you know I don't see them in real life, but if I were to imagine energy come to life, then this would be it."

"Fairies *are* energy! They are transmutable. Oh, don't be discouraged, you must have faith and wait for them to present themselves to you in whatever form they will. They will, I just know it. For me, I see them in this pure form now. I have seen them take many other shapes over the years. For fairies are seen not with the eyes but with the heart."

She sighed and cupped Laurel's chin in her hand. "I cannot teach you this."

For the first time, Laurel felt she was beginning to understand. Her thoughts were swirling like the colors of the paint before her. "I don't know how to get the feelings from inside of me to out there on the canvas. But I'll try."

"And you will succeed, with faith," Maybelle said with a tender smile. "And a little help from the fairies."

An hour later, Laurel stood alone in the meadow with the canvas. Before her, countless flowers sat patiently waiting for her to fill the blank whiteness of the canvas with their colors: scarlet poppies, late-blooming daffodils, and sweet-scented lilacs from the shrub border. Any one of them would do as a model.

So what was she waiting for? She rolled the wooden paintbrush in her hand, feeling its weight, uncertain of making that first brushstroke. *I'm waiting for a little magic,* she thought to herself.

"Let me guess," came a deep voice from behind her. "This is the painting of a polar bear in a blizzard."

Laurel yelped and jumped back, straight into Dane's chest. She heard his chuckle over the pounding in her ears as his strong hands calmly and gently held her steady.

"Easy now," he said in the low tone she heard when he gentled his horses. "I didn't mean to startle you. You just looked a bit lost so I thought I'd come by and see how your work is coming along."

She adjusted the tilting brim of her straw hat and brushed wayward gold tendrils from her face. "You can see for yourself."

"How long have you been at it?"

She scratched her head, then checked her watch. "Let's see, including the time I've been staring out trying to choose a flower, about an hour."

"Thoughtful, aren't you?"

His eyes crinkled in the corners and she knew he wasn't mocking her, just gently teasing.

"There are just so many flowers out there, and they're all so beautiful." She twirled the brush in her hand, frowning. "And I feel as though anything I paint won't do them justice."

With his hands on his hips he looked out over the field of flowers as a father would his children. "Which one do you like best?"

"The lilacs, definitely. I've always loved them."

"Then start with what you love."

It made such simple sense. She nodded her head, agreeing, then smoothly changed the motion to shaked her head in the negative. "I can't," she confessed. "I feel absolutely frozen. I just know anything I do won't measure up."

"You're setting yourself up for failure. Just paint the one you love best, the very best that you can. Worrying about anything else is futile. What medium are you using?"

"Acrylics. Maybelle wants me to paint what comes to me without going over and over it. I'll have to paint quickly because acrylics dry so fast." She tapped the brush against her cheek as she stared at the blank canvas. "I know what she's up to. She doesn't want me to ponder. She wants impulsive strokes."

"Instinctive."

"No doubt," she said with frustration. "I've already sketched dozens of plants down to the last stamen. I can do that well enough," she said with emphasis. "But Maybelle wants me to capture the essence of the flower, whatever the heck that is. I mean, what technique, what medium do I use to achieve that?"

"Hold on a minute," he said, holding up his palm. "I have an idea." He walked quickly across the meadow on a direct path to the lilacs. Pulling a Swiss Army knife from his rear pocket, he flipped it open and, with a quick flick of the wrist, cut a sprig from the shrub.

She watched him as he returned, closing the distance at a steadfast pace. Even with his wild, tawny hair and sun-weathered skin, he looked like an old-fashioned gentleman caller carrying posies to his girl. She felt a flutter inside thinking that he was bringing them to her. She watched his powerful gait across the meadow. His shoulders were broad under his blue flannel shirt, his hips slim in rugged, worn jeans, and the knife looked as natural in his roughened hands as the tender lilacs did.

He averted his gaze as he handed the flowers to her. She took the lilacs, feeling almost as shy in kind, and she immediately bent her head to sniff their sweet, heady scent. With her eyes closed, she didn't see the softening of his expression as he watched her, face in the flowers. When she lifted her eyes, he was studying her.

"Why are you looking at me like that?" she asked, blushing.

"If you could see your face right now," he said, "you'd see the essence of flowers."

Her blush deepened and she lowered her gaze. "The scent of lilac is pure ecstasy," she murmured. "What technique do I use to paint a scent?"

"I don't know about painting, but I know Maybelle. She doesn't care one whit what technique you use or what medium. That isn't her way. I'll bet she's more concerned that you should know what's possible."

"I know, I know," she replied, seeing again in her

mind the burst of energy on Maybelle's canvas. "But that's Maybelle. As far as she is concerned, anything is possible."

He stepped closer to take her hand from her hair and hold it. "Is that so hard to believe?"

She winced. How could she explain to him a lifetime of fighting off just such a belief? "Yes, it is," she replied softly. She stepped back.

He heard her. He stepped forward. "Trust me for a moment. I want you to do what I say. It's an exercise that Maybelle once taught me. No, don't argue. Just do it." He grasped her shoulders to keep her from walking away. "Come on. What have you got to lose?" he said cajolingly.

"My sanity," she quipped.

"Just relax." He took the lilac branch from her clenched fist and held it out in front of her, near her frowning face.

"First just take a deep, cleansing breath. Go on . . . good. Now another." He could see her frustration in the tension of her cheeks as she blew the air out. "One more."

Her eyes flashed with impatience.

"Now look at the lilac. Take your time. Examine it, just as you would under a microscope." He could see the suggestion take hold as she tilted her head. "Do you see the bark?" he continued, stepping closer. "The petals? How would you describe that shade of purple?"

Her beautiful lips moved from pout to ponder. He brought the lilac up and gently stroked her cheek with the petals. Her face was porcelain-perfect and her eyes glazed a bit as her lids lowered to half mast. His stomach tightened as though he'd been punched.

"How does it feel?" he asked in a low voice.

She replied with a soft sound in her throat.

He had to concentrate to keep his hands from trembling. Very slowly he dragged the soft petals along the long line of her delicate cheekbone to rest beside her nose. "Now this time, close your eyes and smell the sweetness again."

He watched as her lids dropped and she inhaled the heady scent. Her long, spiky lashes fanned her sun-kissed cheeks. When her lips parted in a breathless smile, he stared at lips that looked to him as delicate and pink as flower petals. He had an almost over-whelming urge to move a fraction closer to taste their velvety sweetness.

It took all his willpower to hold back and to focus on the exercise. For her sake. "With your eyes closed," he said in a steady voice, "bring the image of the flower to your mind. Do you see it?"

He spoke softly now, near her ear, and he, too, was enveloped in the scent of lilacs intermingled with her own scent of mountain laurel. It was intoxicating and made the blood swirl in his head.

"See the blossoms unfold now," he said in a husky whisper. "Petal by petal. Take your time. . . . Look deeper in the center of the blossom. What do you see now?"

Laurel saw the lilac in her mind, the purple petals, so soft and fragrant. She felt her shoulders lower as the vision clarified and she felt both peaceful and stirred. She focused her concentration on that center, sensing that what she was looking for was just within those blos-soms. But try as she might, she could not open the buds. Eager to touch it, her hand reached out for it, but the blossom remained elusive, just beyond her reach.

Then she felt something feathery soft on her out-stretched hand.

Her eyes flashed open. Poised on the curve of her hand, its gossamer wings basking in the sunlight, was a yellow and brown swallowtail butterfly!

Her heart beat rapidly but she didn't jerk her hand back or cry out. She remained still, fascinated by the delicate fanning of wings and the way the sunlight fil-tered through them, as though through watered silk. For the space of a breath the butterfly stayed, exposed and vulnerable. Then, with the blink of an eye, it flew off.

Laurel's held breath eased out with a wide grin of delight.

"Dane, did you see it? Wasn't it the loveliest thing you ever saw?"

Staring into her eyes, he thought she was the loveliest thing he ever saw. But he said nothing, only nodding in agreement, matching her smile.

Laurel spun around to catch sight of the butterfly's flight. "There it is!" she cried to Dane, pointing. "And look. Another! And another . . ." She saw two more, then three, four. . . . A dozen butterflies, yellow, blue and orange, fluttered among the blossoms.

With a laugh of animated delight, Laurel ran among the flowers to join them. Amazingly, the butterflies did not fly off as she approached, but rather, drew nearer. They circled her arms, her head, alighting from time to time as though to kiss her before they took off again. Laurel couldn't believe this was happening to her, that she could feel such joy in the attention of these delicate beings. She heard a sweet, joyful music in her head that filled her heart and head with light. It filled her to bursting and hearing the music, she began to dance. Laughing, she raised her arms and began to twirl as the butterflies fluttered around her.

Dane had never seen the like. She was like some ephemeral creature, some enchantress, dancing hip-deep in flowers wreathed by a score of butterflies of myriad colors. He couldn't believe his eyes, but there was no doubt that the butterflies were dancing with her! What kind of woman was this, he wondered, watching her as one watched a movie, feeling apart from the vision. He felt a stab of loneliness that comes from a longing for the innocence that he saw on her face.

Laurel's laughter pealed through the air and her small-boned hands swayed in the air like the branches of a willow in a summer's breeze. He was drawn to her—to her voice, to her beauty. Drawn to be her partner in this summer's dance.

She didn't turn away or stop dancing in embarrassment, as he thought she might. Instead she reached out to take his hands in her own and welcome him. They held hands as children do, arms outstretched and raised high. She smiled and tilted her head back to laugh freely. Together they waltzed in the flowers as the butterflies circled them. It felt natural for them to dance together, to hold each other in their arms and whirl, as though they'd done it hundreds of time before.

He slowed his steps to a stop, still holding her, still looking into her eyes. Her eyes never left him, but her smile dissipated and her eyes took on a curious, innocent look. Dane felt the scorch of doubt. He'd been burned before by believing that the love and splendor he saw in a gaze like this was real—only to learn later that that what he thought was love was only design.

But what if the look in Laurel's eyes was sincere? Or if her trembling was not coquettishness but gentle modesty? What if all that he'd dreamed these past nights could come true?

One by one, the butterflies flew off, leaving them alone in the garden, hands held, gazes locked. Dane lowered their arms. With a gentle tug, he drew her nearer.

She did not resist, gliding easily forward as though spellbound. He drew her in, closer, until her chest was against his and he could catch the sweet scent of mountain laurel. Her scent. He guided her hand to rest on his shoulder then his hand glided down her arm, her shoulder, tracing her spine to meet his other hand in a cinch around her slender form. She fluttered like a butterfly caught in a net but his arms encircled her, holding her captive. He moved again, one sure step, just enough to pivot his hips against hers and angle her head up toward him.

She thought she might slip back, swoon, fly away, but his eyes, dark and full of intent, pinned her. As his head lowered she felt her body stiffen and shake. A final whimper caught in her throat.

Then his lips were on hers, alighting as delicately as a butterfly. As before, she dared not move, keeping still as she experienced the light sensation of his lips grazing against hers. She dared not even breathe. His lips gently kissed the corners of her mouth. His tongue traced the lines of her parched lips, ah, so sweetly. She melted against his chest and as her lips parted, the whimper escaped from her throat as a sigh. Closing her eyes, she knew she was captured.

He heard her sigh as a song of welcome, and his grip tightened around her triumphantly. Possessively. His lips pressed harder, eager now, even hungry, to taste the nectar of her lips. Emboldened by her response, his kiss deepened as his hands grasped her tighter to clasp her against him. Once again he felt as though he was destined to hold her, to make her his own. It was a senseless notion born of his senses. The touch of her, the scent, the taste—all wordless testaments that she was his.

She felt his desire as domination. There was a strength to his kisses that she expected, a finesse that she did not. She'd been kissed many times before, but never like this. He literally took her breath away. When he pulled back, releasing her slowly, she was dizzy, as though they'd waltzed in circles and she'd lost her balance.

The kiss left her confused. She needed decision, direction. Not this dazed blankness that had her searching for her own name. The butterflies, the dancing, the kiss . . . it was all too much.

"Dane," she said after releasing his hands. She smoothed her hair with her trembling fingers. "This cannot happen again."

"Yes it can, if we want it to."

"But I don't want it to."

His composure slipped, releasing a moment of hurt before he marshaled it back. "Why not?" he asked with his characteristic bluntness. "Don't tell me you didn't enjoy the kiss. I wouldn't believe you."

She shook her head. "No, it would be a lie to tell you that. But I shouldn't be kissing you, or anyone else." She paused, then pushed forward. "I'm not free. I'm with someone else. We're . . . engaged."

His face stilled, then his gaze darted to her left hand. "I don't see any ring."

She massaged the bare ring finger on her left hand. "It's more of an understanding. We're to finalize our decision when I return in the fall."

He relaxed his posture and rested his hands on his hips, nodding as though making a private decision. "The way I see it, there's no ring on your finger, so there's no commitment made." His eyes grew smoky again with intent. "And I'm interested. And more to the point, I'm here." He took a step closer to her.

Laurel put up her palms to stop him. "Dane, don't pursue this, please."

"I will pursue this, Laurel Carrington," he said in his deliberate manner. "I will pursue you. With every ounce of my being. The sun won't rise or set on a single day that I won't make my intentions known." Then, as though mentally reining himself in, he paused to run his hand through his hair and offer a one-sided smile. "Don't look at me with fear in those big eyes of yours."

"I'm not afraid of you," she replied. "I simply don't want to have to deal with this right now."

"I won't do anything that you don't want me to do."

"I know you won't," she retorted, her back rigid. "I won't allow it."

His smile turned crafty. "But you do want me to kiss you."

Her toes curled. "You're mistaken. It was . . . fun," she said, holding her hands tight before her. "But I'm not here for a casual roll in the hay."

His eyes flashed. "And you're mistaken if you believe I'm only interested in you for some quick sex. I told you before, there is a connection between us I've never experienced before. And you felt it too. I see it in your eyes."

"You see far too much in my eyes," she replied, looking away.

"That's true enough." He paused, then took her hand in his and played with her fingers. "I'd be lying if I didn't admit that I'm very interested in the sex as well. It will be fine between us, Laurel."

She felt as though all the butterflies had just returned to flutter in her stomach.

"But that's not all I'm interested in. If you'd rather I didn't kiss you just now, then I'll hold off until you do." He stepped back to give her more space. "But make no mistake, Laurel Carrington. I am pursuing you."

Her head was still swirling, and it took all her focus and determination to break away from the hypnotic intensity of his eyes. "I can't stop you from wasting your time," she replied crisply. "As long as your pursuit doesn't become a problem for me." She turned and headed back toward her paint supplies. As she made her way across the field she could feel the heat of his stare on her back as hot as the sun.

During the next week, he pursued her in her thoughts as she picked up her brush and painted short, spontaneous strokes of purple and green on the canvas. He pursued her in her mind as the shadows lengthened and she moved from room to room of the quaint berm house, lighting oil lamps. He pursued her as she soaked in the small, claw-footed porcelain tub before the fire and poured hot, scented water over her head, shoulders, and breasts. He pursued her as she lay in her narrow, down quilted bed, eyes on the ceiling, while the wind flapped the Irish lace curtains at the window. Every minute of the day, his face loomed before her in her mind's eye.

The cool mountain breeze wafted in carrying haunting music. She closed her eyes and listened to the high, mournful song. It was the sound of a violin—Dane's violin. Lord, he was pursuing her with his music as well. For she had no doubt he was playing this song for her. It was rich with sensuous emotion and the plaintive notes of longing. The music filled her with a strange, heated desire that was new to her, and again she felt the same heady confusion she'd experienced after his kiss.

Laurel sat upright and furiously rubbed her eyes, waking up from the sensuous dream that there was any hope for a relationship between herself and Dane Walden.

They had nothing in common. They came from different worlds, had different backgrounds, education, goals. What kind of a life could they expect to share together?

When she made a mental list of all the ways in which the two of them were wrong for each other, the list was long and weighty. On the other side of the column she tried to list the reasons why they might be well matched. On that side she could think of only one item: the kiss. It was a weighty item. Her hand traced the tender skin of her lips and her eyes drifted close. She could feel again the tremors caused by the feel of his lips on hers. She'd been lost in his kiss, clinging, aware only of him in the world. She couldn't ever remember feeling that way with Colin.

Colin. Her eyes snapped open. *I'm an awful woman,* she moaned. Untrue, unfaithful, un . . . well, she'd come up with another word, but the point was she had no right to betray Colin's love for her. He was waiting for her, patiently, as he'd waited for the past three years. Good, true, honest, loving Colin.

She quickly rose from her bed, intent to rummage in her drawers. Under a pile of socks she found what she was looking for. A small black jeweler's box, the one that Colin had slipped into her hands with a fervent squeeze as she was leaving for Vermont. He'd asked her to accept this ring as a symbol of his eternal love and devotion. He'd also asked that she wear it on her return to Delaware, so that he would know that she'd accepted his proposal of marriage.

Opening the box, she pulled out the round diamond ring set in platinum. The Tiffany setting was the epitome of classic elegance, like Colin. She picked up the ring between two fingers and held it up to the moonlight. The many facets of the well-cut stone sparkled eerily in the blue light, cold and hard, like a chunk of ice.

If she put the ring on her finger tonight, she would have her answer for Dane. According to his primitive code, he would see the ring as a signal that she was not free. Her common sense told her to do it, to end this nonsense about pursuing and kissing and heaven knew what else. It would be a relief not to have him *pursue* her. She was here to paint, after all, not to fool around.

She held the ring over her finger, but still she hesitated. It was as though part of her wanted to slip the ring on her finger and another was tugging in the opposite direction. She thought of Colin with his white-blond hair and mustache, his slim body handsome in well-cut suits and his tapered, elegant fingers. Then she thought of Dane with his hair as wild as a lion's mane, his broad shoulders in stained flannel, his roughened hands and his face as chiseled as the mountains he adored. They were opposites on the spectrum, as different as purple and yellow, city and country, perhaps even civilized and wild.

The sweet string music of the violin floated through the window once again, wooing her with its gentle, seductive song. She held the ring poised over her finger, then with a fateful sigh, she lowered it in defeat. She couldn't put it on. Not yet.

As if on cue, Omni hooted in the distant woods, calling her to sleep.

She would wait to make this decision. Tonight she was too tired, too confused, too filled with the music of Dane Walden. She reached over to place the diamond ring on the small wooden table beside her bed. Tomorrow she would rise with the sun and put Colin's ring on her finger.

But tonight, she thought, with an indulgent smile spreading across her face, she would listen to Dane's music—and hopefully dream.

Ten

She awoke smiling. Filled with a lassitude that spread from the tip of her head to the tip of her toes, she yawned noisily and stretched, relishing the feel of linen sheets on her naked body.

Naked body?

Her eyes popped open and she ran her hand brusquely down the familiar terrain of skin. Where was her nightgown? She didn't remember removing it. Pulling back the sheets she sat up, feeling lightheaded as though she'd waltzed the night through. And she had the damnable tingling in her head again. Reaching up to scratch her scalp, she wondered for the hundredth time what she might be allergic to. She didn't have lice or ticks or any other such thing because she'd scoured every millimeter of her head. While she gave her scalp a thorough scratching she searched the room and found her nightgown neatly folded on the chair beside the window. Her hand dropped into her lap as she stared dumbly at it. When had she bothered to neatly fold her nightgown after tossing it off in her sleep?

Shaking her head, all she could think was that it must have been some dream. And quite a dream at that. Too bad she couldn't remember any of it.

With slow movements, she began her morning ritual: a visit outdoors, a washing of her face with fresh water from the pitcher, and a quick brush of her hair. The boar bristles against her itchy scalp elicited a groan of pleasure and her ritual slowed down to relish the downright luxury. While she stroked, her mind drifted to her dream, for she felt strongly this morning that she'd had one. She recognized the telltale signs. Her arms and legs felt heavy, her skin dewy, and deep within she was filled with sexual longing for . . . someone. Who was he?

Her hand stilled and she closed her eyes, trying to see past the gray mist to the face just beyond. He was standing there, with his hand outstretched toward her. Closing her eyes, she tried to capture the man's image, she could swear she knew him, but the harder she tried, the faster it vanished.

"Oh, this is too frustrating," she murmured. She'd never recall her dreams. Bringing the brush to her head, her hand stilled as she caught her reflection in the mirror. She blinked, then blinked again. It couldn't be possible. Her hair was touching her shoulders!

Setting down the brush she played with the long strands of golden hair, letting it slide through her fingers like silk. She couldn't remember ever having hair this long before—nor having her hair grow so quickly. There must be something healthy in the mountain water, she mused, admiring her reflection.

Laurel never gave much thought to her looks. Her father eschewed feminine vanity and had only praised her intelligence. But today, with her cheeks fuller, pinker, and her golden hair longer, why, she thought modestly, she might even look pretty. She liked the way her hair swirled when she turned her head from left to right and the way she could pile it all up on the top of her head, or let if fall down in a veil around her neck.

Perhaps she wouldn't cut it, she decided. Maybelle seemed to believe letting her hair grow long would help with her inspiration, sort of like Samson she supposed, her lips twitching with mirth at the thought. Maybelle did have her notions . . .

And she was nothing if not persistent. She noticed two barrettes lying beside the water pitcher that were not there the night before. They were of the same unique style that Maybelle always wore in her hair. How sweet of her, she thought with fondness for Maybelle's seemingly endless generosity.

The jewels in her hair reminded her of another jewel, and another decision she would have to make. She supposed she should do the responsible thing. It was cruel of her to lead Dane on, to flirt and dance, no matter how much she might enjoy it. Her commitment had to be to Colin.

She walked to the bedside stand with a heavy tread. Her gaze flickered over the small oil lamp, the half empty glass of water, a paperback novel.

But the ring wasn't there.

Feeling a fluttering of panic, she searched under the novel, on top of the bureau, then fell to her knees and scoured the floor and under the bed and between the hooks of the rug. Oddly enough, she found her missing watch, but Colin's diamond ring was gone.

"My ring is gone!"

Maybelle stopped pumping water in the sink to take in Laurel's stricken face. "Which ring is that, dear?"

"My diamond. My engagement ring from Colin."

Maybelle's face pinched. "Oh," she replied, then returned to her pumping. "I hadn't realized you were engaged to that young man. Well, not to worry."

"But of course I'm worried! It's a very important ring to me, and it's just disappeared."

"I've told you, missing things have a way of turning back up," Maybelle replied, her task finished. Drying her hands on her crisp white apron, she offered Laurel a commiserating smile. "You'll find it, rest assured."

"How can things just vanish then turn up again?"

"The fairies, of course, my dear. They are terrible borrowers and they especially love sparkly things. If your ring has disappeared, I'm sure they are just admiring it."

"Wait," Laurel said, holding up her hand. "Don't tell me any more. All I want to know is that you're sure it will come back."

"As sure as I can be."

Laurel found that reply far too ambiguous for her taste. "Fairies, indeed. It's got to be here somewhere. I'll just look around again." A tantalizing scent caught her attention and started her mouth watering. "What kind of tarts are you making today?"

"Rhubarb cream," Maybelle replied, pinching the edges. "We've a fine crop this year and I'm still hoping Daphne will deign to join us for tea. She's not one for sitting about and having a good chat, but she does love rhubarb cream tarts." She looked up and mischief sparkled in her eyes. "One of these days you just know she'll have to succumb to the temptation."

"I hope so. I'm eager to meet her. Dane says she isn't very social, but neither am I. So perhaps we'll get along. Do you know where she might be today? I could walk down and personally invite her."

Maybelle was hesitant. "You could, as long as you don't get your hopes up. Daphne can be hard to find, and be blunt spoken when she is."

"Oh, I don't mind. I'm used to it. My father can be quite direct."

Maybelle's hands stilled on the dough for a moment. When she began laying tops to the crust, she said in a distracted manner, "Your father—he's turned hard then?"

"Hard? No, I wouldn't say that," she replied, quick to banish that impression. "He's just matter-of-fact. He has no time or patience for nonsense."

"Hard," Maybelle confirmed to herself. To Laurel she asked, "Is your father well?"

"Yes, very. At least he was when I left him. My dad isn't much for correspondence, and of course, there's no phone here. I've written him several times."

"And he hasn't written back . . ." Maybelle pinched the remaining tart crusts in pensive silence. "Do you expect he'll come for a visit? To see how you are?"

Laurel shook her head and leaned against the counter, crossing her arms tight around herself. "No, and I wouldn't expect it. He's going on a monthlong tour of rare roses in Europe next week. He's something of an expert in that field, you know."

"So he's going back to England?" Her tone was wistful.

"Why, yes, he goes almost every year. Have you heard of him? Arthur Carrington?"

"Vaguely. He's become something of a celebrity, hasn't he?"

Her tone implied disdain rather than awe. Laurel chafed, knowing that though her father's reputation was built on scholarly research, he did enjoy the limelight.

"How long will he be in Europe?"

"It varies. For most of the summer, I should imagine."

"That long? Do you know how to reach him? In case of an emergency, I mean."

There was something troubled in her manner that made Laurel wonder at the source. "He always gives me his itinerary. You aren't worried something will happen to me, are you?" She laughed lightly. "Maybelle, I'm a grown woman, after all. It's been years since my father sat up at night after curfew."

"Not at all," Maybelle replied quickly. "I was just curious if you knew how to reach him—just in case. Now," she said, slapping the flour from her hands and deftly changing the subject. "Those tarts are finished. I'll pop them into the oven and then what do you say to some breakfast?"

"I'll serve the cereal," Laurel volunteered, feeling ravenous. Waking up to a rumbling stomach was a new experience for her. "I want to hurry and go straight out to paint today." As she poured out the hot oatmeal into two ceramic bowls, she asked as nonchalantly as possible, "Is Dane coming to work in the garden today?"

"I suspect so," Maybelle replied, pouring out a cup of Laurel's red tea. "There's still so much to do."

Suddenly, Laurel felt her appetite wither. "Do you know what time he's expected?"

She looked up coyly. "You might know that better

than I. It seems to me he makes a habit of being there when you are."

"Strictly coincidence," Laurel replied, quick to douse any further speculation. "I can assure you it isn't because I plan it that way. I go out strictly to work. In fact, I was hoping to avoid him completely today." She sat down and picked up her spoon in a manner that emphasized her point.

"But why?" Maybelle's face fell. "I thought you two were getting along so well."

"We were." She swallowed down her oatmeal. "Until he ruined it with his ridiculous notion that we belong together."

Maybelle's eyes widened as her spoon hovered in midair. Then, lowering her hand, her eyes narrowed in speculation. "Dane said that you belonged together? Do you mean to say he is interested in you? As a woman?"

"Well," she said with a light laugh, "when you put it that way, I'm not sure how to reply. Yes, I'm a woman and he's interested. In a nutshell, he says we're connected somehow. He says he can feel it. Have you ever heard of anything so ridiculous? Wait," she interrupted, "don't answer that. I don't think I want to hear your answer."

Maybelle's flush deepened and she brought her hands to her cheeks, the very picture of surprise. "He feels you're connected? Does he really? Why, I never would have thought . . ." She dropped her hands and looked searchingly at Laurel. "And you? Do you feel this connection?"

Laurel set her spoon down, aghast. "No, of course not," she lied, not willing to encourage Maybelle. It was obvious that Maybelle was fascinated with the possibility of a little romance at Fallingstar. "I don't know why the two of you are so enchanted with the notion of some"—she wriggled her fingers in the air like a spell—"connection. Why must everything be so mysterious here? There's a very natural explanation for what's going on. It's called sexual attraction. He's attracted to me and yes, I'll admit I'm attracted to him. But there will be no romance. I'm engaged to be married—practically—which is why I don't want to see Dane today. We need a little distance between us until he gets past this fantasy that he's pursuing me. I'm here to paint, Maybelle. Not play."

Maybelle's face grew winsome and she turned toward the birdcage to make high trilling noises deep in her throat. Amor hopped to a perch closer to Laurel and chirped sweetly, cocking his head till Laurel was convinced he was speaking directly to her.

"He's such a flighty creature," Maybelle said, pretending to be cross at the goldfinch. "Do you hear him making up to you like that? It seems Dane's not your only conquest."

"I've suddenly lost my appetite," Laurel said, standing in a huff. She took two quick gulps of her tea, cleared her bowl, then grabbed her easel and supplies. "I'm headed out to the orchard, if it's all right with you. You said the apple trees were in bloom and I'd like to try and paint them. I believe Dane said something about working with the roses today so I'll avoid him entirely." She stopped and tilted her head. "Where might the roses be? I've not seen roses anywhere except for the polyanthus at the gate. I absolutely adore roses," she said with a hint of longing in her voice. "Don't you?"

Maybelle stood very still and her face shifted into a pensive expression. "Yes," she said in a distant voice, as though she were afraid to breathe. "I do."

"I hope someday you'll show me where they are," she replied, bending at the waist to pick up her backpack of supplies. "As for today, I think I'll be safe in the orchard. If you see him," she said, pausing at the door, "remember. Mum's the word."

Maybelle waved, then watched her walk off down the road burdened by her bulging backpack and lugging her easel. She had to stop to rest every few steps.

"What a determined girl she is," she said to Amor. "So much like her father." Then, with a sparkle in her eye she said on a sigh, "And she loves roses . . ."

*   *   *

It had rained during the night, leaving the earth steaming in the steadily rising morning sun. It would be another unseasonably warm day. The combination of hot weather and rain brought forth a bountiful crop of dandelions that brought a golden glow against all the vibrant green of the rolling hills and pastures below.

Laurel found the sight of so much gold against green breathtaking and her hands itched to paint. Her father would view the vista with a scowl. Dandelions were nothing to him but troublesome weeds that had to be routed out of his gardens. Maybelle had seen them and immediately exclaimed she'd have to harvest the tender leaves for dandelion wine and salad. It was, Laurel realized, a matter of point of view.

As she made her way back down the path, Twiggy kept her company. "Go on home now," she told the cat when they passed the barn. "You mustn't be a derelict. Your kittens will be hungry now, too. Go on with you, home now."

Twiggy paused in seeming indecision, eager to continue on the journey, needing to get back to her babies. With a switch of her tail, she turned and made her way back to the barn at a dainty trot. Laurel smiled, already inordinately fond of the young cat. She'd never had a pet and, like it or not, Twiggy seemed to have adopted her. While she rested her easel on her foot, she listened for the sound of mooing from the barn.

All seemed quiet in the big gray structure, which meant Dane had brought Elsie and his horses to the pasture for the day. She was sorry she had to avoid him. She'd miss their new friendship, but what choice did he leave her? With a sigh of resignation and telling herself it was for the best, she hoisted the easel and veered off the main path across the meadow on a beeline for the orchard.

She was breathless when she arrived, as much from the beauty of the sight of an apple orchard at its peak in springtime as from the long, laborious walk. The rows of trees stood as glorious and resplendent in pink and white as a line of spring brides in full gown. Walking among them, Laurel was enveloped in a profusion of sweet-scented blossoms, more glorious than she'd imagined, every bit as fanciful as a fairyland. With each gust of balmy wind, the heavy branches creaked and waved, releasing a flurry of delicate petals into the air to float about her like confetti. The air was thick with the heady scent of the blossoms and she was enveloped in the low murmurous humming of hundreds of bees feasting on nectar.

She chose to set up at a far corner of the orchard where several ancient and proud maples clustered. They would provide shade as she painted. She lugged her supplies further, but as she drew nearer the maples, the buzzing grew louder. The air throbbed with it. She entered the cool shade carefully, resting her easel and backpack on the ground in a choice spot. Then, curious, she followed the sound of bees to the further edge of the woods, where the land was higher and the maples gave way to pines. The humming seemed to come from the center, obscured by a thick curtain of boughs. She felt a thrill of excitement as she followed the buzzing, walking over a soil rich with pine needles and fern.

As quiet as a hare she pushed back a pine bough and peered into the cluster. Her heart gave a wild beat when she saw a neat row of white boxes, some stacked three to four high. Working among them, lifting the lids and pulling out thin drawers full of buzzing bees, was Daphne.

Daphne's bees was all she could think, both amazed and fearful at the sight of what felt like a treasure trove. There were thousands of them, and from a distance they looked to her like vibrating, flying stingers. Daphne didn't seem the least afraid. She moved among them wearing nothing but a long-sleeved shirt, overalls and gloves, humming a peculiar song, as though she hadn't a care in the world. Her movements were like those of her brother, spare and smooth. There were no wasted steps, nothing was jerky or sudden.

Laurel didn't want to startle Daphne or the bees, so

she carefully and slowly pushed aside the pine bough and made her way closer, humming a tune of her own. When she'd traveled twenty feet, Daphne looked up and spotted her. Her face reflected surprise at first, followed by tight-faced annoyance. She went back to her work without so much as a hello.

Remembering Maybelle's warning, Laurel waved her hand and smiled. "Good morning," she called out cheerfully. "Am I disturbing you?"

Daphne remained bent over a hive. "What do you think?" she called back.

Laurel took a step closer, every bit as stubborn as Daphne. "I've come to invite you to tea. Maybelle would be so pleased. She's made rhubarb cream tarts especially for you."

Daphne paused in her work, then said in an offhand manner, "I might come. For Maybelle's sake."

That stung but Laurel accepted the reply as a yes. Daphne concentrated on her task of efficiently opening the boxes with a tool, humming her strange tune that seemed to communicate with her bees. Surrounded by her bees with her red hair shining in the sunlight like flame, she looked to Laurel like some woodland goddess. The hives were as busy as hub airports as the bees, their hind legs laden with pollen, flew back and forth from the bountiful orchard to the hive.

"There are so many," she said in a low voice so as not to disturb the bees.

"Yep," Daphne replied, not looking up. "I keep sixty thousand bees here, and more at other locations. I don't like folks to know where I keep my bees." Her voice implied that Laurel was spying.

"Who am I going to tell?" She stepped still closer, losing her fear as she watched the bees circle Daphne in their busy manner and go about their business without notice of the two humans. The humming of the bees was hypnotic, luring her forward. "They seem friendly enough."

"My bees are well behaved," Daphne replied, and

Laurel didn't miss the pride in her voice. "I only have sweet-tempered queens."

"And yet they seem to tolerate you."

Daphne delivered a measuring look at Laurel over her shoulder. She seemed mildly amused. "They trust me," she replied in an easier tone. "I'm gentle with them, that's important. Bees don't like to be rough-handled and they let you know it, believe me. Once the bottom of a hive fell off while I was carrying it and I got the worst of it. Dane took pictures of my face to remind me to wear my veil."

Laurel noted that Daphne was not wearing a veil. She watched a bee circle around her own head warily. "They stung you? And you still do this?"

"They didn't mean nothing by it. Bees aren't aggressive, but they are wild. People forget that. And I don't like to wear gear. It's cocky, I know, but as I said, I have this thing about trust. Once given and received, it's a bond."

Another bee joined the scout to circle closer around her head. Laurel stood still but kept her eyes on the pair. "So you think they know you?"

"Sure. Bees have a keen sense of smell. See them bees hovering at the entrance of this hive? Those are guards. They smell the bees trying to get in and only allow the ones with the queen's scent to enter. The thing to remember with bees is to be alert."

Laurel was on full alert. A small regiment of bees had collected about her and were humming over her head. "So," she said, speaking in a low, slow voice as she took measured steps back. "They only like people who smell like the queen?"

"Yep. I'm just another worker bee, like all the rest. There's a saying that's true enough: When the queen is in place, all is well."

Laurel couldn't move. All didn't seem so well with these bees. In a matter of seconds the sunshine filled with a thrumming, consistent buzzing as a steady stream of bees poured out from a hive to hover around her in their crazy, zigzag dance. Laurel, breathless with fear, took another few, mincing steps further back from the hives. She couldn't recall if she was supposed to run or lie still like with a bear.

Her mouth was as dry as a desert and she croaked out, "Daphne? I can't recall. If they get too close, am I supposed to swat bees away or stand still?"

"Don't swat them!" Daphne called back, her eyes still on the honeycombs. "That's a sure way to rile them, and when you do, they'll come after you. If that happens, just get the hell out and cover your face."

"I can't!" she cried out.

Daphne turned around, alerted to the fear in Laurel's voice. What she saw left her frozen. Hundreds of bees were circling Laurel in a dance pattern, swirling jubilantly, round and round her like a maypole. Sentries, guards, workers young and old were swept into the humming music of this extraordinary midair dance. Within seconds more, a swarm formed around Laurel.

"Stay calm," Daphne called out, fear clutching her throat. It was too late for her to run and the bees didn't seem angry. They seemed curious, even joyous. "They're not interested in stinging you. Just don't do anything to threaten them, okay? Laurel?"

A muffled reply was all she heard. Laurel was standing with her arms ramrod-straight to her sides, not daring to move a hair as the swarm of bees grew larger and larger around her.

Daphne turned heel and ran to her truck to collect a face veil, blanket, and her smoker. She had to hurry. Time was of the essence. Being in a swarm was terrifying, and if Laurel started swatting, the bees would start stinging. With that many stings she'd be dead for sure.

At the truck, she spotted Dane walking at a leisurely pace across the meadow in their direction. Relief surged through her veins. "Dane!" she cried out, waving her arms over her head. He must have heard the panic in her voice because he took off toward her on a run.

She grabbed for her gear, her heart pounding and ran back to the hives. What she saw stopped her short. She stood unsure of what to do next. Behind her, she heard

Dane's steps. Raising her hand, she stopped him as he approached, shushing him so as not to disturb the bees.

For her bees had landed. They clustered in the thousands on Laurel's outstretched arms, hanging in tight bundles like brown sacks. Their humming took on a more contented note, loving, like the lulling of a summer sea.

"Laurel." Dane's voice was a choked whisper. He felt powerless to do anything to help her. Laurel stood quietly with her eyes closed as though deep in meditation. "Daphne, what should we do?"

Daphne's hand raked her hair, clutching at the ends. "I'm not sure. I don't understand this."

"We've got to do something!"

"Easy now. We don't want to rile them. Okay . . . the bees are swarming, but it's a small swarm. The weather's right for it." She began moving closer to Laurel in smooth, easy steps, firing up her smoker as she moved. "We want to stay calm, Dane, or she'll get stung. They've parked on Laurel, God knows why."

"They parked on Ed Willis last summer."

"But that was on purpose," she exclaimed, her patience stretched. "Ed captured the queen from a hive and set it under his chin." She kept her voice calm, almost singsong as she moved closer. She never took her eyes off Laurel as she studied the pattern of the bees. They were clearly nonaggressive. If she didn't know better, she'd swear they were waltzing for their queen. "Then a second person shook the bees from a frame right down on him. Bees don't just park on humans on their own. Bees settle when they catch the scent of the queen." She stopped and turned to look at Dane with eyes wide.

"Wait a minute. Didn't you say some butterflies were dancing with her the other day?"

He nodded.

"Damn, I've heard stories about this, but I always figured they were old wives' tales. But now I'm not so sure." She looked again at Laurel, standing still with her eyes closed and a queer smile on her face. "Goddamn if she's not charming the bees."

Dane's worry was not lessened in the least. "Get them off her," he said, his voice tense and graveled.

"Dane?" Laurel's voice sounded distant against the thrumming of bees.

Dane and Daphne looked up sharply.

"I'm glad you're here."

"You're doing great," Daphne said, licking her lips.

"I think . . . I think there's something about a queen. Do they need one?"

"That could be why they swarmed. I'll have to check the hive," she called back. To Dane she said, "They'll rest for a while while the scouts search out a new hive."

"How the hell long will they rest?"

"It could be hours. Even overnight."

Now Dane swore and slammed his hands on his hips with impatience.

"Look, we'll just proceed as though she were Ed Willis and start taking the bees off of her, nice and easy, okay?" She slipped the veil over her face, muttering, "I just hope this works." She'd taken a swarm of bees off from lightposts, garages, tree trunks, bushes, empty tubes . . . but never from a woman's arms. She hoisted her smoker and began releasing a plume of gray smoke over the bees on Laurel's arms.

"Grab that hive over in the far corner, the last one," she ordered Dane. "That's right, now bring it on over closer." After he'd done so, Daphne moved close to Laurel, who still stood with her eyes closed and a faint smile on her lips. *That's right, kiddo,* she thought. *Be a good ol' Buddha.* She swung her arms in a wide arc, back and forth in a kind of rhythmic dance as she spread a cloud of smoke around Laurel.

"Laurel? Now listen carefully. It's time for the bees to go home. This may sound crazy, but somehow I think you'll understand. Can you tell them that? Tell them to go home."

She waited a moment as Laurel's brows furrowed in concentration. Meanwhile, Daphne said in a low voice to Dane, "We'll have to act fast. Get that white tablecloth and bring it over here. And some of that tape. Laurel?" she said as she and Dane approached. "We're gonna surround your arm with a sheet. When I say so, I want you to give yourself a firm shake, like a dog with fleas. That'll knock most of the bees off. Not too rough, now. I'll keep smoking while you shake. Ready?" Under her breath she whispered to Dane, "If they go after you, run like hell."

"I'll be damned if I'll run away leaving two women to fend for themselves."

"Stop being a hero. They're enamored with Laurel, any fool can see that."

"What about you?"

"They know my smell. If they get mad, it's gonna be you they go after." She swallowed. "I think." In a louder voice she called out, "Okay, Laurel, easy now. We don't want the little darlings to take off again."

At the cue, Laurel firmly but gently shook her arms while Daphne brushed her arms with utmost care. Little by little the docile bees were encouraged into the sheet, first one arm, then the next. With nimble fingers, Daphne taped the two sides of the cloth together with masking tape, tearing off strips quickly with her teeth.

Laurel remained motionless as she and Dane carried the bulging sheet to the ready hive. "Go on home now," Laurel crooned to the bees.

Once the bees were dumped back into the hive, Dane released the empty cloth and strode straight to Laurel, who had not yet moved a muscle. She stood so still, as though in a kind of trance. He was wary of touching her. She must be terrified, he thought. She didn't know a thing about bees. He gingerly took her hands in his, bringing them forward to hold them between them.

"It's all right now," he said in a soft voice. "You can open your eyes. There's nothing to be afraid of."

Laurel's long, sooty lashes blinked several times before she fully opened them and focused her eyes. When her gaze met his she smiled drowsily, like someone who had just awakened from a deep sleep.

"I'm not afraid," she replied, still with that drowsy

voice. "I knew they wouldn't hurt me. They came looking for a queen, is all. They thought I might be able to help them." A strange smile flitted across her face. "Isn't it strange that they'd think that? I, who know nothing?"

Daphne, who had overheard, closed the lid of the hive and drew closer to Laurel, her attention riveted.

"What do you mean? You heard them? Like how? They talk or what?" Her tone was belligerent. Disbelieving. Tinged with jealousy.

"I don't know," she replied, exhausted, turning away. "I want to go now."

"Leave her be," Dane said sharply, taking Laurel's arm possessively. He'd wanted his hands on her, his arms around her. It was torture standing by with his big hands useless, watching while the bees lingered.

Daphne watched them go, her brother's arm protectively wrapped around Laurel as he guided her back across the meadow. Daphne was forgotten as well and she felt suddenly cold and abandoned. A thing left carelessly behind in the fields like the art supplies. Forgotten not only by her brother, but by her bees.

Her bees, not Laurel's, she thought jealously. Who was this woman that everywhere she went she charmed the bears and butterflies and bees? The only other person she knew who could do that was Maybelle. And Dane, when he was young.

Not her, never her. All her life she'd envied the way the critters would come up to Dane and sit while he played the violin, or the way chipmunks nestled in Maybelle's pockets while she painted. No matter how still she sat or for how long, they never came to her. Except the bees. They welcomed her as one of their own. She'd never taken the gift for granted. She'd worked as hard as any other worker bee for them and because of them, she'd always believed she had some magic in her, too, that charmed them. She was serious when she told Laurel about that trust.

And today she felt as though that trust had been broken. She'd been betrayed—as any queen bee that had been supplanted by the young virgin princess. *Damn that*

Laurel Carrington! Why'd she have to come here in the first place? she thought as she begrudgingly began to pick up her smoker, the bee brush, and sheet. Everything was fine before she got here. She and Dane and Maybelle, they got along all right. Now it was all changed.

It was just as well she was leaving, she decided in a huff. Dane was bewitched and Maybelle didn't know that Daphne was alive. And her bees, well, they wouldn't miss her. She'd been a fool to think they would, she thought as she dumped her gear in the back of her truck.

"Hey there, Bizzy Bee."

Daphne's heart stopped for the second time that day. She stood silent as the grave, unmoving while her mind whirled back in time to place that raspy voice. Only one person in the world had that voice and it chilled her to the marrow. Only one person in the world called her by that nickname.

But he was dead.

Eleven

"**D**on't you have nothin' to say to your own father?"

Daphne loosened her grip on the truck and turned in degrees to face the voice.

It was him. Joe Flannery.

Her shoulders slumped and she could have wept, not tears of joy that her father, long thought dead, was in fact alive—but tears of regret. Dane's words flashed through her mind—*he'll be back*—and even then, some part of her knew it was true. But she couldn't bring herself to believe it. The hell this man had put her through had ended the day he disappeared. Now here he stood in the shadows and he was all too human to be a ghost.

"I've nothing to say to the likes of you," she said in a voice as brittle as the pine needles she stood upon.

Anger flashed across his face as quick as lightning, replaced just as quickly by the familiar grimace he always tried to mask it with.

"Still got your gumption, I see. Just like your old man. I always liked that best about you. And look at you! You've grown up. You were but a girl in pigtails when I left, but now . . . You're almost as tall as I am. Ain't no doubt who your father is. You never were no small, gentle thing like your mother was." His face shifted and he scratched behind his ear with a faraway look into the woods. "God rest her soul."

Daphne closed her eyes tight against the shame of being compared to her father. When she opened them again, they'd turned as hard as coal and held as little warmth. She took her time studying him. The past seven years hadn't been kind to Joe Flannery. He looked more than ten years older with the lean, mangy wariness of a wolf. His hair was sparse and graying, and he was so thin his faded jeans hung loose on bony hips. But his eyes were sharp over thick cheekbones.

"I thought you were dead," she said.

Joe Flannery laughed, a strange sound in the back of his throat. "Why sure I am! And now I've come back to life. And do you know why?" He squinted and pointed his finger her way. "I'll just bet you do. I lived a lifetime of hell and now I'm ready to collect a little bit of heaven. One hundred thousand dollars' worth of heaven." He broke into a spiel of laughter that set her teeth on edge.

"Just how do you figure you can collect that insurance money if you're not dead?"

"Well, that's a problem, that's certain."

He rubbed his jaw, but his eyes danced. It was clear he was already set on his plan, and Daphne knew in that moment that his scheme involved her. She stood ramrod-straight, as she had as a child when he stood her in the corner with a bowl of water on her head for some perceived infraction of a rule. One drop spilled meant a harsh slap or a privilege taken away, a missed meal, or, worst of all, a strike against Dane. Her father sought out ways to divide them, and it was Joe's private torture that he never could.

When it was clear Daphne wasn't going to respond, he stuck his hands in his pockets and walked around in the manner of a scholar expounding on a theory.

"Seven years I waited, real patient like, to collect my just reward. And it's due me. Life never gave me any breaks, so the way I figure it, a man has to create his own. When your mother walked away into them woods and never came back, folks blamed a bear or such, and looked the other way." He squinted his eyes and looked as though he were splitting a hair with his teeth. "But I searched them woods from hill to dale and I'm telling you I never found no bones or torn clothing or nothin' to tell me my Rosalind got herself ate up by no bear."

Daphne turned her head toward the woods, remembering the way her mother had insisted on going alone every day at twilight into the embrace of the forest. When she didn't return one evening, only she and Maybelle were not surprised. They were not grief stricken, like Dane had been. And Joe. Not because those two men loved her more than the women, but because the women understood Rosalind better.

"She weren't the type to run off," he continued, "so I guess I'll never know what became of her, specially not dyin' the way she was." He rubbed his jaw again and his manner was sorrowful. "I like to think she went off to the woods to die like an old dog when it's time is come."

Daphne felt no pity for the man. All she could think was how he'd treated Rosalind like a dog when she was alive.

"Yep, she always loved them woods," he rambled on. "Anyway, I figured if the folks could believe she died in there without no proof, then why wouldn't they believe I did too? So I staged my disappearance, bein' clever enough to drink a lot and make the boys at Tuttle's think I couldn't get over the loss. Left a few things in the woods, to make it seem I was hurt and all." He laughed again, a hiccuping sound. "Afterwards, I hid around for a while till I heard folks tell that I was grief stricken and went off to die. See? I knew then that my idea had worked. I just had to stay away till the money came in. Didn't dare to come back till now."

"Great. Just don't expect us to welcome you back. You abandoned Dane and me, don't forget. And now you to plan to gyp us out of the only thing you left us—money."

He waved his hand as though to brush away her argument. "I knew that Maybelle Starr would look after you. She always did want to take hold of my children and I figured I might as well take advantage of her damn nosiness."

"How convenient. I don't suppose it occurred to you to leave word to your own children that you'd run off? At least once in seven years."

He shook his head. "Couldn't do it. Seven years is a long time to lay silent and those insurance guys, they're just waiting for me to slip up. And besides . . ." His face turned stony. "I didn't trust Dane not to turn me in. Or Maybelle, if they knew the truth. The money wouldn't matter none to them."

"But you think it matters to me?"

He grinned broadly. "Like I said, you're my kid."

The fact that what he said was true made her insides twist. "Not anymore. As far as I'm concerned you're still dead." She turned away in an angry rush, walking over to her hives to check that the bees had resettled. He stood quietly in the shadows, biding his time. She worked slowly, hoping he'd just go away and never come back, but of course he didn't. He was still waiting for her by the truck when she returned.

He drew closer, leaning against the fender, chewing a bit of grass. "I saw what happened here with that Laurel girl. She's new around here, isn't she?" He chuckled again, a rasping sound that inflamed Daphne to hear again. "That girl's got herself some of those special powers like Maybelle Starr, don't she?"

Daphne stopped loading the truck and swung her head to peer at him sharply.

"I never saw bees act like that," he said. "And I've seen plenty. All this time everyone thought the bees were charmed by you. Well, girl, you got yourself some competition."

He was like a bee under a shirt, buzzing around, stinging left, right, and sideways in the most tender spots. She fought the urge to slap him.

"Just what do you want from me?" she spat out in a fury, slamming the truck door shut. "Let's not pretend you came home because you care."

"You wound me."

"That's it," she said. "I haven't got time for this. You can talk to Dane."

"Wait." His smirk fled from his face to be replaced by the hardness she was more familiar with. He moved closer and she could smell alcohol on his breath. He stood in her face and she saw he was as surprised as she that now she was as tall as him. Feeling strong, she stared him in the eye.

"Here's the deal," he said in a low, conspiratorial voice. "I need you to collect that money for me. We both know I can't walk in there and get it for myself. And I sure as hell can't ask Dane. He'd turn me in faster than he could spit. You're my kid. My blood. You've got to do it. I'm counting on you."

She narrowed her eyes and hated herself for considering his offer. She'd waited for that money for too long to lose it now. "Why should I do this for you?"

"Because I'm your father."

She released a short, angry laugh. "Yeah, right."

Joe pursed his lips, taking her measure as a gambler would before placing his bet. "I've been watching you the past few days since I got back. Things aren't going so good for you here, are they? I'd like to give my kid a little money to get out of here. Go see the world. Dane did. Maybelle gave him the money. I don't see her givin' you no money. So I'm planning on splitting the money with you, seventy-five–twenty-five."

"I want fifty-fifty."

His ears flushed as his face turned mean. "You'll get nothin' if I turn up alive."

She shrugged. "Neither will you, except maybe a jail term for fraud."

His face mottled and she knew she had him. He wouldn't collect a dime without her. Nor would she collect without him. They needed each other and the thought stuck in her craw.

"It's a deal," he said, and though his voice was begrudging she saw a spark of admiration warm the ice in his eyes. He stuck out his hand.

She stared at it, seeing in the configuration of bone and flesh her own doom. It was a Faustian deal. But what choice did anyone leave her? No one needed her here, or wanted her here. She might have stayed for the bees, but now it appeared they'd turned on her too. She didn't matter to anyone or anything. The thought stung and the venom spread.

Joe was right, she decided, her mouth tightening. Hadn't Maybelle given Dane money to go? Maybelle hadn't offered her any to make her world brighter. Now she only cared about some stranger. What had Joe said? Something about creating one's own breaks in life? That sounded true to her. She needed to get away and she needed money to do so. This was the first break she'd ever had. And even if the devil offered it to her in exchange for her soul, well, by damn she would take it.

Daphne pushed back her hair from her face with her palms, taking a deep breath. Behind her, the bees thrummed their constant song. Tuning them out, she reached out and took her father's hand. "It's a deal."

Dane stood in Maybelle's front room clutching yellow roses in his large hands and gazing longingly down the hall at Laurel's closed bedroom door.

Maybelle took the roses from his hands, clucking her tongue and gently pushing him back. "You're wringing the life from these beauties. I'll put them in water. Come follow me, Dane. I won't have you go in there and disturb her rest."

"She's been in there for three days," he said, worry tingeing his voice. "Are you sure she's all right? She should see a doctor to be sure the bees didn't sting her."

Maybelle glided quickly to the kitchen, calling over her shoulder, "Pump the water for me, would you please?" While Dane obliged, she went to the hutch to select a porcelain vase. "Of course the bees didn't sting her. They wouldn't, you know. Not her."

"Why not her? Even Daphne gets stung from time to time."

Maybelle plucked a few dry leaves from the roses and asked quietly, "Have you ever been stung, Dane?"

Dane's hand rested on the pump, perplexed. He'd never really thought about it before, but now that he had, he wasn't sure. "I don't remember ever being stung, but then again, I don't tend bees."

"But you tend the garden. You toil in the fields day after day. You've spent a lifetime studying plants."

"Dumb luck," he replied, turning to pump the handle hard. Water began pouring out into the sink and Maybelle hurried to fill the vase of flowers.

"There's nothing dumb about you," she replied with a stern eye.

Dane scowled as he always did whenever the slightest nuance referred back to his school-age nickname, Dumb Dane.

"Is there something in the herbs you give us?" he asked, going back to the original subject. "Something that keeps the bugs at bay?"

Maybelle arranged the roses with a deft hand, pausing only to bring her face near and breathe in the scent. She closed her eyes in delight. When she raised her eyes again, she looked at Dane with a loving eye that held sadness.

"Yes, the herbs," she replied, bringing the roses from the sink to the table. "I'll bring these roses in to her when I bring in her tray."

"May I bring them to her? I won't stay long."

Maybelle shook her head. "No, my boy, you can't. Don't scowl at me, she doesn't want to see anyone. And I think you in particular. You can be forceful when you've got your mind set, as immovable as rock. And I believe, so can she." A wry smile flitted across her face. "You've met your match."

He ran his hand through his hair and his eyes gleamed. "I believe I have indeed. Come on, Maybelle, let me see her. Just a glance."

"Out with you. I'll deliver your roses and let them speak for you—a sight more eloquently, I'll daresay." Then, her expression softening, she patted his shoulder and said as she guided him out the door, "She'll be up and about in a day or two and out in the garden once again. You know you must trust the course of fate, dear boy. One cannot rush things to suit himself."

Maybelle was as good as her word. A short while later she carried a tray of soup and bread and Dane's roses into Laurel's room as twilight settled in the mountains. Laurel was still sleeping when she entered the room, so she set the tray down on the table beside the bed, then opened the windows wide. The fairies of the twilight realm were agents of self-growth and transformation, and she invited them in with the cool night's breeze.

She moved to sit on the mattress and to enjoy a stolen moment looking upon her daughter's face. Did every mother think her child's face was most tender when sleeping? she wondered. She wouldn't know, having never enjoyed this simple joy in the past twenty-one years. Every morning since Laurel's arrival she'd tiptoed into her room to fill the pitcher with fresh scented water and to pause and gaze at her daughter's face.

She marveled at how she saw bits of herself in Laurel's fine bone structure, the tilt of her large eyes and the color of her hair. She saw more of Arthur. Hungrily she took in details that reminded her of the face she had loved more than any other. Loved even still. The dimple that carved deep in her cheeks when she smiled, the fine, straight nose, and most of all, her pouting lips—all just like Arthur's. Such a tempting mouth Arthur had. She'd often thought she'd been drawn to it like a bee seeking nectar from the rosiest blossom. Or perhaps more apt, like the moth to the flame.

How pleased she was that their daughter had his mouth.

How sad that she also had his wariness. This troubled her most of all, for she saw signs of the fey in her daughter. Surely the wildlife saw it—they always recognized the fairies and adored them, unlike the humans, who were blind to them. Except the children, she amended. The young ones still could see the Other floating about them when they opened their eyes to them. It was a shame Laurel had missed opportunities to recognize her gifts growing up. Her childhood had been robbed from her with Arthur's focus on her cognitive skills while ignoring her imagination. Nature had not been able to reveal her secrets and the Good Folk could not reach her.

Nor was she allowed to even try.

Maybelle scoffed, her fury against Arthur flaring. No pet indeed. How cruel to keep a child so isolated, offering her only test tubes and logic for amusement. Arthur could be the worst kind of human.

And the best, she thought on a sigh, remembering. When he loosened his guard, she had seen an innocence in him that was utterly beguiling. More pure and heartfelt than most. He had an aura that shone like gold. Perhaps more precious because he held it back, like a secret treasure he shared with only a few. And wasn't Laurel his daughter in this way? Afraid to reveal the child inside? Afraid to believe?

Laurel stirred in her sleep. Maybelle waited and watched as she blinked heavily and slowly focused. "Yes, it is time to awaken," she said softly, stroking the hair from her face. "You've been asleep for twenty-one years. Knock three times," she said aloud, recalling an ancient chant. Her heart danced in her chest. "My child, you must awaken. You are on the threshold of what is and what is to be."

Laurel's lids fluttered, then slowly lifted. Her first sight was the loving vision of Maybelle's smiling face. She felt suffused with peace.

"How long have I slept?" she asked in a groggy manner, rubbing her eyes.

"This time? About six hours. You've hibernated for days, you know."

Laurel's brow creased in a frown. "I'm sorry. I didn't mean to worry you. I've been so tired and . . . It's hard to explain. I feel like I've been turned inside out and my heart and mind, even my soul, is exposed. It hurts," she said, a plaintive note slipping into her voice.

"Growing pains," Maybelle murmured, patting her hand.

She shook her head. "I'm not doing very well here, Maybelle. It's not your fault. You've been wonderful. But this apprenticeship just isn't working out. To be totally honest with you, I don't think I have the talent. I never knew what you saw in me in the first place. I try."

"You mustn't try. No one can ever measure up to another's expectations."

"I've given this a lot of thought the past few days and I think . . ." She paused while her fingers ran up and down the beribboned trim of her quilt. "I think I should go back home."

"No." Maybelle paled as a fissure of fear run down her spine. "Please don't go," she said. "It's too soon to quit now, you've only just begun. No dear, it's much too soon."

She spoke with an urgency uncharacteristic of her, causing Laurel to sit up a bit against her pillows. "It's not about quitting. I don't want to waste your time. You could still find someone else."

"I don't want anyone else. I've waited for you for long enough. You're the right one, the only one. You must trust me. Laurel, you think you haven't learned anything here. Think again. In the past few weeks you've learned a million skills that you mustn't take for granted. Here at Fallingstar you've eliminated much of the outer noise and now, close to nature, you're beginning to hear and feel its presence. It frightens you, I know. It's different and you don't understand it. I know you want to go back home, where everything is understood. But believe me, the only way you will open up your painting is to open up your spirit."

Laurel shivered again, not able to bring herself to deny it this time. "I know you're right, Maybelle, and that's what frightens me. I'm experiencing something new that I can't pretend to understand. It's a kind of communication. I experienced it with the bear, then the butterflies, then again, very strongly, with Daphne's bees. It's not that I have some supernatural power, or even that I'm particularly unique or special. It's just that when I hear the bees or dance with the butterflies, I simply understand, as a child might understand when he hears words spoken to him. Does that make any sense at all? I'm not hiding indoors because I'm afraid of the bees, as Dane thinks I am. I'm afraid of what's happening to me." She rubbed her eyes with her fingers and groaned. "I don't understand."

"Oh, not to worry. Fairies are notoriously hard to understand. They communicate in the most curious ways, through riddles, music, dance, tricks. In your case, my dear, they've tried three times to knock on your consciousness. Hello in there!" she said, tapping Laurel's forehead with her fingertip. "Answer!"

Laurel rubbed her eyes, forlorn. "I don't know how, and I'm not sure I want to try. I came here not only to learn about painting, but to learn about myself. But I'm more confused than ever. I haven't a clue who I am."

Maybelle reached into her apron pocket and pulled out a strip of braided leather attached to a smooth white stone with a hole in the center. "I want you to have this, Laurel," she said, handing the stone to her with reverence. "I've saved it for you, waiting for the right moment to give it to you."

Laurel took the stone in her hand. It was smooth against the pads of her fingers, more like glass than stone. But it was just a stone. "Is there some significance to this?"

"This isn't any ordinary stone. This is a stone with a hole bored through it after countless years of water dripping on it. Not ocean water, oh no. Only the water of a brook or pond will provide the magical powers of a bored stone. When one looks through it, one can see the fairies."

Laurel sighed, thinking that this was but one more of Maybelle's riddles. She stared at the bored stone in her palm, feeling the weight of it. Maybelle spoke of such things with such sincerity, and on nights such as this, after experiences such as hers, she was less sure of what was real and what was not. She lifted the stone and with some hesitancy peered through the hole, moving her arm and hand in tandem as she searched the room.

"I only see you," she said matter-of-factly. She hadn't really expected to see small beings with wings.

Maybelle only smiled.

"Why do you give the stone to me now?"

"You seem to be in quest of answers. And . . ." She paused to close Laurel's fingers around the stone. "I thought tomorrow we might move from flowers and begin to paint fairies."

"Maybelle," she said with a warning tone, dropping her hand back to the bed. "I didn't see any fairies with the stone."

Maybelle laughed lightly, her strange, opaque eyes sparkling with mirth. "You're always so serious. I've hired a few young girls from the town to come as our models. I often use them for inspiration. I've a box full of lovely costumes I've sewn up just for them to wear and the girls have a wonderful time playing dress-up. We always end the session with tea in the garden and I promise them plenty of cream buns and cinnamon rolls if they sit still."

"Then we'll paint pretend fairies," Laurel said, greatly relieved. "With models. How wonderful!" She refrained from saying, how normal. "I'll try my best."

"Then you'll stay?"

"I'll stay," Laurel replied, leaning back against the pillows, feeling the weight of her decision.

"Well then," Maybelle said brightly, her eyes sparkling. "You must eat your dinner and gain your strength. Tomorrow will be a busy—"

The night was rent by a cracking explosion in the woods, followed by another, in rapid succession. It was very near.

"What was that?" Laurel asked, sitting rigid. "It sounded like a firecracker."

Maybelle sprang to her feet and hurried to the bedroom window to peer out. She stood motionless, her small hands clutching the frame. Back in her bed, Laurel sat rigid, clutching her sheets, listening. There was a rustling in the night wind. Omni hooted with an uncommon urgency.

"Hunters?" Laurel asked in a hushed voice.

"No, I don't think so. It's not the hunting season. Not that it matters. I never allow hunting on my property. But there's no question that was a rifle's report." Maybelle's eyes were alert and she tilted her head and closed her eyes, her ears tuned to the outdoors in concentration. "There's a disturbance in the woods."

Laurel shivered and rose from her bed to join Maybelle at the window. Standing shoulder to shoulder as they gazed out into the darkness, she felt the eerie tension creep up her spine. She thought of calling only one person for help.

"We have to get Dane," she said.

Twelve

Further down the mountain, Dane was already sitting on the edge of his bed, pulling on his boots. His mouth was set in a firm line and his eyes burned with fury behind his shock of sleepworn hair.

"Are you going to check it out?" Daphne asked when she came to his bedroom door. Her brown eyes were black with worry while her hands busily tied the sash of her frayed chenille robe. They both knew the answer to the question, but she had to ask it anyway.

"Yep," he replied, stomping his heel, then rising to a stand. "No rifle has a business in my woods."

"But you don't know who's out there. Most folks around here are afraid of these woods, so you know whoever's out there is either not from these parts or just plain crazy. You might get shot."

He looked over his shoulder and replied with a cocky grin. "Whoever's out there will have to see me first."

"Don't," she exclaimed, grabbing his arm as he passed through the door. Her voice was unusually high and urgent.

"What's the matter, Daphne? It's my job. Besides, there's no man alive who knows these woods better than I do." He patted her hand on his arm, then said with a noisy yawn, "Be a pal and make me some coffee while I get my gear. I want to leave right away."

She released him with reluctance and watched him walk off in his determined manner to the basement where she knew he stored his rifle and ammunition in a locked safe. He rarely used the weapons, and then only to put a critter out of its misery when it was sick or dying. But everyone in town knew Dane was a crack marksman.

As she made her way to the kitchen, she was wide awake as fear percolated in her veins. Worry weighed heavily on her shoulders, drooping them. Dane was so headstrong, too stubborn for his own good, she thought, spilling coffee as she measured it into the pot.

"Don't go," she cried, muffling her voice with her palm. There was one man—still alive—who knew the woods as well as he did. A man who wouldn't think twice to use a gun.

The woods at night were like a remote island, far from civilization and human contact, an entity unto itself. Dane followed the narrow path carved into the soft grass, fern and wild undergrowth by his own heels. He passed scores of maples, oaks, birches, and pines in the gray darkness of a long summer's night. As he walked, he listened. All sounded normal enough. Whippoorwills sang accompanied by the twittering of creatures unseen in the brush. Overhead there was a rustle of the leaves in a breeze and from yards away, the sharp snap of a branch broken, probably by a deer.

All the drowsiness he'd felt was gone as his instincts sharpened and he sensed his prey. He crouched, held his rifle close, and took on the mantle of night. He moved swift and silent. His eyes gleamed in the paling moonlight with the thrill of the hunt.

When he passed the base of the enormous hawthorn, he crouched and searched in the darkness for sign of the fairy ring, but it had disappeared. A few yards beyond, he peered over the ledge, but the night obscured all trace of Laurel's fall. He was about to move on when a high whimper of an animal caught his attention. His hackles rose as he moved closer to the ledge to listen. Again he heard the piteous cry. It came from below, near the cave of the bears.

Dane moved slowly down the slope, not wishing to disturb that mother bear who could run as fast uphill as down. His boots slipped in the damp dew and he could barely see through the heavy foliage and a blur of branches. In the pale moonlight the enormous mounds of granite shone like the white monoliths of a temple.

And on the ground, lying before the jutting stone as some great sacrifice, lay a large animal. He placed his feet cautiously on the earth as he drew nearer. From the shadows, he saw that it was the mother bear that he'd tangled with before. Another, smaller shadow moved in erratic circles around the mound, mewling piteously. Dane lowered his rifle, feeling a heavy sadness overtake him.

The mother who had so furiously defended her cub lay dead, shot by a rifle's bullet, leaving an orphan behind. Dane took a final sweep of the area. No one else was near; whoever it was who shot the bear was long gone. He'd have to wait until daylight to search for clues. He clicked the safety latch on his gun and stepped out from the brush to the open ground.

"Poor little fellow," he said, holding out his hand to the cub. "Lost your mother. I know what it's like and I feel for you." He felt a familiar heaviness in his chest as he brought the image of his own mother's face to mind. "You'll never be the same, boy," he said to the cub.

The cub ignored him, cried more loudly than before, then scampered closer to his mother, not understanding why she wouldn't stir.

Dane felt his anger stoke against the brute who would shoot to kill. A fired shot in the air would likely have frightened her off. It was a senseless kill that left a stranded cub in the wild to die as well. He crouched to stroke the cub's head and this time, the bear cub didn't scamper away.

"So what are we going to do with you?" He couldn't leave the cub; it would never survive. He was a healthy cub, round and clear-eyed. And hungry. Reaching into his back pocket, he pulled out a granola bar that Daphne had given to him to ward off hunger. Unwrapping it, he waved it in the air close to the cub. The cub sniffed, and like most children, was enamored with the scent of sugar.

"Come on, little fella. Let's play follow the leader. Come on," he cajoled, tossing the cub a bit of cookie when he wandered back to his mother. "I know you'll miss her. But now you need a new mama. Come on." He smiled for the first time that morning. "I think I know just the one."

By the time he broke from the woods into the clearing, the sun was afire in the pink sky and the quiet twitterings of the night were now heartfelt songs of newly awakened birds. In the distance he saw smoke rising from the crooked chimney of the quaint berm house and he knew Maybelle was stoking the old potbellied stove for her morning ritual of bread baking. His stomach growled in anticipation as he tossed the last crumb of cookie to the cub.

"Come get it, and don't be such a baby," he said in a cajoling tone. "I'm starving, too. You've got to be a big boy now and not so afraid. And you like the cookie, don't you? That's right. Come along now."

He chuckled as the roly-poly cub ambled from the edge of the forest in search of a crumb of cookie. Poor thing was probably hungry for his breakfast and it had been a long walk for the cub. He'd shown plenty of signs of fatigue mingled with playful curiosity along the way, stopping often to check out a strange scent, to chase a rodent, or just plop down and rest. Dane had worried he'd have to carry the cub all the way home. After they'd left his mother's scent, however, the cub followed Dane—and the cookie—more closely. This touched him, for it had been a long time since an animal had followed him. When he was young, he'd befriended all sorts of animals. They'd come to him and . . .

Dane closed his eyes and shook his head, chasing off

the memory. He didn't want to recall those early years. The doctors had told him he'd been a sad and lonely child with a vivid imagination. He accepted that explanation for his memories—memories that everyone had told him were crazy.

The cub had stopped following and was sniffing a patch of Maybelle's mint. He gave a sharp whistle that brought the cub's head up, then took off again toward the gardens and house with the bear cub not far behind. Dane hoped Laurel would connect with the young cub as strongly as she had with his mother. If not, Maybelle would certainly tend to the orphan until he was old enough to return to the wild. But it was Laurel he really hoped would adopt the cub, partly to help her overcome her fear of the wilderness and, if he was lucky, partly to bind her closer to life at Fallingstar.

As though hearing his thoughts, she stepped out from the house, one hand shielding her eyes as she looked their way out over the gardens. She waved her hand in a long, arc of welcome over her head. His heart skipped a beat at the sight of her, thinking how different this greeting was from the first time he walked her way across this same meadow. Was it only a few weeks ago? It felt like a lifetime. He'd been a brute that afternoon, deliberately goading her with his quipped replies. He didn't like strangers and city strangers least of all.

His heart swelled seeing her now, wearing one of Maybelle's long, flowing skirts, the long strands of her golden hair catching the wind. She seemed so changed . . . or was it simply he who had changed?

He lifted his arm to respond with a wide wave of his own, even as he swallowed down the hope that rose in his chest. A wave of welcome was a far cry from the kind of response he wanted from her. He wanted to feel again her softness in his arms, the trembling of her lips under his. He was tortured by the memory of that one kiss as no other. There had been no reservation in her kiss, he recalled, his blood racing as he walked toward her at a clipped pace, his eyes riveted like an animal's.

Slow down, boy, he reminded himself, slowing his step. Despite the "yes" of her body, her mouth still said no. He was honor-bound to hear that and obey. Even though the feelings she aroused in him were primal, he was a man, not an animal.

He turned his head and whistled. "Come on, slow poke," he called out, combing his hair with his hands then grimacing as he rubbed the stubble on his cheek. "Look at us," he said to the cub as it ambled to his side. "We're a sorry sight this morning. No offense, but we both can use a bath." He laughed as the cub stumbled over a rock, then picked himself up to trot closer to his outstretched hand. "I guess we'll have to rely on our charm."

Laurel paced before the greenhouse window with worry since the moment Daphne had galloped up the mountain, riding bareback on one of Dane's horses. Sliding off its back she reported that Dane had gone out into the woods to investigate the gunfire. The three women remained in a tense silence as the minutes ticked by endlessly. Maybelle had prepared a special calming tea and declared with certainty that no danger would come to Dane in the woods. He was a skilled tracker, she said, and he knew the woods as well as the gardens. Laurel was comforted—until Maybelle had added that Dane was also loved by the wood fairies who would watch over him. At that, Laurel had silently rocked her forehead in her palm.

It was Daphne, however, that unnerved her the most. Cool, detached Daphne was pacing and clasping and unclasping her hands as she chewed her lip. Maybelle and Laurel cast worried glances at each other several times as the night dragged on to dawn.

Time and again Laurel's gaze was drawn to the window that overlooked the meadow to scour the horizon.

She couldn't tolerate the thought that something could happen to him, that what they shared between them— this new friendship—could end. Inconceivable. She'd never had such a relationship with a man before, and to think that she had sent him away for the past several days, had refused to see him, made her bunch her fists and pound her thigh as she stared out at the empty horizon.

When she saw him emerge at last from the darkness into the soft morning light of the clearing, her heart rose like a bird taking flight at first light. "He's here!" she cried out.

With his rifle swinging in his arm and his long, tired strides, she thought he looked like a soldier returning from war. She hurried outdoors, telling herself as her heart quickened with each step he drew nearer that she felt this way simply because she'd never worried about a man before. Her brain whispered back that was because he was *the right man.*

But he isn't the right man, he can't be, she argued to herself, even as she waved her arm over her head in welcome. They were from different worlds, with different dreams. Yet her body contradicted her by shivering as he drew near enough for their gazes to meet and lock across the field. She felt the forcefulness of his presence—and his intentions. What was it about him that conveyed such power? Who was this man? she wondered. Despite his incredible strength, he had a gentle manner. Despite his gentle manner, he was not deferential. He did not proclaim his presence nor was he self-effacing. He had a confidence so rooted he did not question it.

Noble, she thought, as the word sprang to mind. Dane Walden may have been simply born and raised, but he was as noble as the wilderness he was so at home in.

"Dane!" she called out, running to meet him. She stopped just short of throwing herself into his arms. For a heartbeat she teetered on the brink of balance, her hand hovering in the air between them, her lip caught between her small white teeth. Laurel struggled with her instinct to touch him, to physically feel the connection she felt in his gaze. Memories of the kiss they shared before, in this very meadow, rushed through her, eliciting desire for another. Yet the few inches between them felt like miles, too far to overcome.

He hesitated too, his eyes lined with fatigue. He recalled the kiss as well and he held his body tense and his arms at his sides lest he follow his instinct to reach out and grab her in his arms.

One moment passed as they waited, holding back. Then, in the next, they both stepped forward. Just one step and she felt his strong arms wrap around her, the chafe of denim and flannel against her cheek, smelled the dewy green of the woods in his clothes and the soap of his hair. She reached up to run her fingers through the softness of that dark brown hair, then tilted her head back to stare into his eyes. They were filled with wonder at her show of emotion mingled with a determination not to let go of her.

Their heads drew together slowly. Tilting her lips to his, she felt a rush in her head, dizzy as though they'd waltzed again. Again she felt that she'd danced with him many times and that she was a breath away from something magical, elusive. If she just leaned forward, just the slightest bit . . .

They both heard the joyous shouts of Maybelle and Daphne as they sang out their hellos. They both went still with frustration. Smiling at each other, they both drew back. Dane curled his arm around her shoulder, holding fast as she tried to scoot away. She felt the blood rush to her cheeks as they turned to greet the women.

Maybelle's step slowed and her eyes sparked with maternal pleasure at seeing Dane's arm possessively wrapped around Laurel's shoulder. But Daphne burst forward, leaping without restraint to wrap her arms around her brother in a bear hug, effectively nudging Laurel out of Dane's grasp. Laurel stepped back, self-conscious and embarrassed at the public show of affection between herself and Dane. As she watched the mutual affection between brother and sister, she moved further away, almost tripping over something large and fuzzy—*and alive*—at her feet.

With a yelp she leaped forward, spinning on her heel to glance quickly back over her shoulder to see what it was that she'd bumped into. In her haste, everything was in a blur, and to her horror, all she could make out as she began running away was some small, grunting brown animal—and it was chasing her!

In a rush of adrenaline, she took off across the meadow, vaguely hearing the sound of hooting laughter in the background and Dane's voice rising above it, calling out, "Laurel! Laurel, stop!" She glanced again over her shoulder but that animal was still chasing her, lopping along clumsily like some rabid beast. While looking over her shoulder she ran smack into Dane, who had run to intercept her. Hitting his shoulder was like hitting a brick wall. She slammed against his chest then bounced back, hitting the hard-packed ground with a graceless thud. In a flash, the animal was beside her, licking her face, nudging her with its paws.

"Go away," she called out, flipping to her belly and covering her face. "Call it off," she cried. "Dane, hurry!"

To her mortification, Dane was hovering over her, laughing and pulling back the creature, but he certainly wasn't in any hurry.

"Make it stop!" she yelled from under her palms.

Daphne had run up beside them, hooting out loud while she and Dane tried to keep the animal from lunging back at her with more licks. It grunted and mewled piteously in restraint. Only when she heard Maybelle's gentle, belllike laughter join in, did Laurel know she was safe. She pried open her fingers to peer through. Over the grass, she looked up to see Dane and Daphne on their knees, still chortling, rubbing the large, furry head of her attacker.

"A bear cub," she said with wonder and surprise in her voice. Lifting up her head and leaning on her elbows, she watched the playfulness of the cub with Dane. It was like some large, roly-poly puppy. *She was afraid of a bear cub*? Then in answer to her own question, she shook her head and laughed out loud.

"Where did it come from?" she asked Dane, drawing herself up to a sitting position.

The cub saw her movement and lunged forward toward her again, but Dane's large hands and arms held the cub at bay. "He's smitten," he said between laughs. "I don't know what's gotten into this guy."

"Probably the same thing that got into those bees," muttered Daphne.

"Most likely," agreed Maybelle, watching the scene unfold from a distance.

"But what does he want?" Laurel asked, eyeing warily the cub as it struggled to break free of Dane's grip to run to her.

"You," Dane replied, holding tight.

"No, that's silly," she replied, but her heart melted seeing what looked to her like a living, breathing, stuffed animal. And it was staring at her with big brown eyes filled with what she could only think was adoration and longing. She'd never had a pet before . . . As her fingers touched the soft fur and the cub scrambled to press against her, making short woofing noises, she told herself that he was just hungry for affection as all babies were. But when he flopped down on the grass beside her and rested his head contentedly in her lap, she could no longer deny that the cub had chosen her.

"Really, Dane, what does he want? Is he hungry? I don't have any food on me."

"He wants a mother," Dane replied soberly.

She looked up and met his gaze. In an instant, she understood from his dark look who the little bear's mother had been. She heard in her mind again the clear message of the mother bear's concern for her cub. Regret filled her as she shook her head and looked with a new tenderness at the orphan cub. "Is she dead?" she asked.

Dane nodded, grim-faced. "That was the rifle shot we all heard."

"Did you see the guy?" Daphne asked. She was white-faced with worry.

Dane shook his head and Daphne visibly relaxed.

"Son of a bitch was a coward," Dane said with disgust. "Killed the mother cold and left the cub to die. And it would've if I'd left it there."

"He probably thought the bear was going to kill him, same as she almost killed you," said Daphne.

Dane sent an angry look her way. "He had a gun in his hand, he was well protected. He didn't have to kill her. He had no right to be in these woods anyway, much less with a gun. Whoever it is, he'd better not show up on this property again or he'll have to deal with me." He spoke with a low, controlled fury that was very much like a warning growl.

"So the bear cub followed you here?" Laurel asked.

Dane rubbed his jaw and hid a smile. "In a fashion. You could say I encouraged him to follow me, figuring we could find some way to care for it. Just until it's big enough to fend for itself out in the woods. Then I'll take him back and set him free."

"You can't bring him down to the barn," Daphne said. "He's wild and the other animals won't like it. Little bears become big bears. There'll be trouble."

"I know it," he replied. He looked up at Maybelle with an innocent smile. "We'll have to find another spot for him."

She followed right up. "Couldn't you build a little shed for him up here by the house? Surely we could take care of him for the summer. And besides, I don't think he wants to be separated from Laurel."

Dane turned her way and offered a wink that was more devil than angel. "I think he's adopted you."

"Me?" She stared at him in disbelief. "Oh no, no. He's just exhausted, the poor thing." Even as she denied it, her hand lovingly stroked the cub as it slept, head in her lap.

Dane watched the movement with a tug of envy. "He is that. But he's also smitten. And an orphan. His real mother's not coming back and so he's picked you."

"But," she stammered, "why not Daphne? Or Maybelle? Now there's the perfect mother for this little guy."

Amid the protests, the cub squirmed, climbing further

onto her lap. She looked down at him and couldn't help feeling a wave of pity. "He thinks I'm his mother?" Her brow puckered with worry. "You poor, misled creature that you'd think someone like me is your mother. I don't know the first thing about how to take care of a bear cub."

"I'll help you," Dane offered, moving closer to lean over her and stroke the cub behind its ears.

While Maybelle sighed with delight, Daphne exploded with frustration.

"Well, that's just great," she exclaimed, throwing up her hands. "The two of you can pretend you're the bear's mother and father. What a nice, rosy little family you'll make. Well, it makes me sick. I'm out of here."

That said, she turned and walked off across the meadow in a huff, but her sentence floated in the air afterward. Laurel ducked her head and fervently stroked the cub's head.

Dane cleared his throat and rose to a stand. "Wind's changing," he said, looking up at the sky. "There'll be rain by nightfall. I'd better get going if I plan to build a lean-to for this little guy to sleep in. I was thinking of putting it along the west wall. There's a nice patch of level land I can base the structure on. Needn't be too big."

"You know best," Maybelle said. She smiled. "But you must be starved after all night in the woods. Come inside and join Laurel and me for breakfast."

Dane shook his head. "I can't. I know a cow that's waiting to be milked. I'd best take that fellow down to the tractor barn with me. I can put together a little pen while I build his house."

"You work much too hard," Maybelle said in a scolding tone that was more loving than not. "Be sure to quit early today and get some sleep."

Dane stretched his shoulders wearily, then mopped his hand with his face. "We'll see. I've got a lot on my plate and it's just dawn." He walked over to Laurel to fetch the sleeping cub. She relinquished the bear reluctantly.

It made mewling noises when Dane lifted it in his massive arms as he would any large pup.

"So what are you going to call him?"

"I don't know. He's been through so much, somehow I don't think Teddy will cut it. We need to think of something that suits him."

"How about Trouble?"

"Let's not encourage that." She stroked the cub's head as he slept on. "We could call him Sleepyhead."

Dane frowned his disapproval. "What kind of name is that for a guy?"

"Have you considered Vincit?" said Maybell. "It's Latin for 'conquer.' I should think that suits our little champion, wouldn't you?"

"Vincit," Laurel repeated, testing the name on her lips. It was short and easy to call. "Yes, I like it. So little fellow, how does Vincit sound?"

The cub slept on, oblivious.

After they all laughed, Dane hoisted the bear into a better position in his arms. "Will we see you at the barn later?" he asked as he turned to leave.

"As soon as I finish up here."

"Good." His eyes gleamed over the cub's head. "I'll be looking for you."

He nodded his farewell, his hands being full with bear cub, but his eyes lingered on Laurel before walking from the garden. Laurel hurried to climb up to her favorite perch overlooking the road. It was a large, flat boulder as large as a small car that dipped in the center, making it perfect for sitting and reading a book. On the ledge, she brought her knees close, wrapping her arms around them and waited, watching for Dane to clear the garden and shrub border and become visible again on the road.

Maybelle noted all this, as well as the lingering glances of the young folk with a mother's affection and apprehension. Though her eyes were dimming, she could still see the luminous auras around them that attested to their true feelings. Did they realize yet that they were in love? she wondered. Humans could be so very dense about such things. Some were more intuitive than others, but overall, she didn't find the lot to be very high on the cosmic ladder. Dane was an exception, she thought, watching the tall, handsome man walk down the mountain carrying the cub as though it were a sack of potatoes.

Her line of vision moved to Laurel. She watched Laurel's delicate fingers, so much like her own, come to her cheek in a self-conscious gesture as she gazed at Dane walking down the mountain road. The look on her face was definitely more than friendly. No matter how she might deny it, there was love in that gaze.

Oh, how she'd hoped they might spark an interest—they were her two most beloved people on the earth. Her daughter and the son of her best friend. Wouldn't Rosalind be pleased?

"Oh hush now, I'm not meddling," she replied to the voices in the trees. Then with a jaunty shrug of her shoulder she said, "And what if I were? I'm her mother, after all. If I don't have the right to see to my own daughter's happiness, then who else does?"

Even as she set her course, however, she worried. Was the real reason she was so eager to see Dane and Laurel matched merely in order to relive her own history? Her own and Arthur Carrington's.

"Fiddleheads," she said aloud, convincing herself that a little intervention was necessary to see her daughter happy. She hoped their love would blossom and grow, as hers and Arthur's had not been able to. She wanted for her daughter to know a love as beautiful and treasured as La Belle Rose.

"I'm going in," Laurel called out as she climbed from her perch. "Coming?"

"No," Maybelle replied wistfully. "I think I'll stay here a bit and enjoy the sunrise. You go on."

Laurel nodded, loosening a tendril of hair from its pin.

As she watched her daughter tuck the lock of hair behind her ear and saunter back into the house, Maybelle smiled with pride. Laurel's hair was coming along quite nicely, if she did say so herself. Why, the potion she mixed each morning for her tea was working wonders!

Already her hair was touching her shoulders. And such hair it was, so lustrous a gold it made the sun look away with shame. Her hand absently traveled to her own hair to tuck in a lock as she puffed her chest with pride. Hair like *that* could only come from the fairy in her.

She felt a familiar pang, thinking as she had countless times the past twenty-one years how much she had missed in her daughter's life. If only Laurel could have grown up to recognize the fairy in herself. . . . If only she could have been there to teach Laurel the tradition of the fey . . . If only . . .

Maybelle brought her fingertips to her forehead, forcibly stopping herself from this dangerous game of *if only* before she spiraled into a darkness that was hard to lift herself out from. After Laurel's birth, she'd fallen into this pit of despair many times. Only a tincture of time, her friendship with Rosalind, and the belief that she'd see her daughter again pulled her through the darkness and helped her to understand that she had to be patient.

Faith in true love had been her only salvation. True love withstood all obstacles; it could not be diminished by time. She believed this—had to believe it. It was the bedrock upon which she'd built her new life here at Fallingstar. It was what kept her going, day after day, despite the harshness of a simple lifestyle and utter loneliness.

She turned her head to look up the slope toward the house she'd built on this remote mountain ledge twenty-one years earlier. Puffs of gray smoke spiraled from the stovepipe chimney into the morning sky. Laurel had started breakfast. What a thoughtful child she was, Maybelle thought with pride. Arthur hadn't done all bad.

And now it was her turn to be a parent. She wanted to do something special to help bring those two young ones together. To give true love a chance, and just maybe help Laurel discover the magic inside her. What . . . what . . . she wondered?

Her head came up and a grin widened across her face. Of course! The summer solstice!

Thirteen

If those were fairies, she'd never met such a spoiled, complaining, whining bunch of babies in all her life!

Laurel dumped her paintbrush into the pot and wiped the paint splatters from her hands with swipes of frustration. They could all go home for all the inspiration they were providing.

"We're bored," one of the little darlings whined petulantly.

Laurel rolled her eyes at the hundredth complaint she'd heard in the past two hours. Maybelle had hired the three eight-year-old girls from the local town to pose as fairies for her benefit, explaining that she'd used the local children frequently over the years whenever she wanted to paint childlike fairies. She kept a box of dressing-up things in the studio for just this purpose. The little girls loved wearing the costumes, especially when they pinned on wings and applied rouge to their cheeks. Laurel had a devil of a time trying to keep them posing instead of jumping around the studio pretending to be flying.

For the past three days, Laurel had spent more time fetching juice, helping them out of their costumes to go to the bathroom, and imploring the girls to stand still than in actual painting. Today was the last day, thank heavens, and a now familiar headache was hammering at her temples.

"Time's up, my little fairies!" Maybelle exclaimed as she entered the studio carrying a tray full of pink-frosted cake she'd baked just for the occasion, adorned with the wildflowers she adored. "Come see what I've prepared for you! You know fairies simply adore cake, don't you?"

The little girls, well versed in the world of the fae, squealed in glee, clapped their hands and gathered around the sweets with their silken wings flopping like colorful butterflies. The girls simply adored Maybelle. She was the maven of the fairies—no one knew more about their legend and lore. And what was best of all, she painted the fairies as no one else, convincing the children, and the world of believers and fans outside the confines of Fallingstar, that she was somehow magically connected to the world of fae.

Mostly, however, Maybelle was fun. Whenever she stepped into the room the world seemed a bit brighter. Laurel understood this, feeling the same incomprehensible charm that seemingly flowed like light from the diminutive woman. With her, the children were on their best behavior, behaving like good little fairies. Not like the harpies they were when alone with her. In contrast, they delighted in disobeying her all afternoon. Even now, Dorothy, the leader of the group, looked over her shoulder and stuck her tongue out at Laurel.

It took all Laurel's self-control not to stick her own tongue back out at her. Standing alone by her easel, watching the girls flutter around Maybelle and drape their thin arms around her adoringly, Laurel felt a bit left out, not an unusual sentiment for her. She had always been shy and tongue-tied with aggressive, chatty girls such as these. Ignored, she remained at the other end of the studio and continued cleaning her brushes.

What did it matter if they liked her? she asked herself. When she was little, the other girls made fun of her then, too. They'd mocked her large, tilting eyes and her quiet manner. And when she'd tried very hard to be their friend, to open up enough to tell them her greatest secret—about her imaginary friends—they'd doubled over with laughter and teased mercilessly.

Which was why, early on in her life, she'd shifted her

attention away from parties and jokes and the usual childhood games to gardening and drawing and accompanying her father on his horticultural hunts. Her father was wonderful in the way he always included her and never talked down to her because she was a child. She adored him for that, for giving her some purpose, and worked very hard to please him. In her mind, the mother she'd never known was like the frivolous girls at school, concerned only with beauty and popularity, and she'd resolved never to be like them. Like her mother.

In time, Laurel gave up her imaginary friends in the garden, gave up her beloved painting and fairy books by Maybelle Starr, gave up believing in such things as Santa Claus, the tooth fairy, wishes on a star. It was then, too, that she stopped remembering her dreams.

Instead, Laurel became an excellent student. It no longer tortured her that she didn't have much of a social life with kids her age. She knew lots of people at Longfield who were friendly and interesting and thought she was someone of value. So she filled her hours after school working at her second home: Longfield Gardens. While other teenagers went to movies and played sports, she sketched plants for the catalogues and went on expeditions with her father.

Laurel let her father direct her life. She didn't question whether the lifestyle suited her; she accepted it for what it was and made the best of it. When he had decided she'd sketch plants rather than paint landscapes, she had said yes. When he had chosen Cornell for graduate school, she had said yes. And she had said yes when her father introduced her to Colin Whitmore.

She swished her brush in the turpentine with quick strokes while realizing with a start that saying no to Colin's proposal was the first time she'd ever refused her father's will and stood up for herself. Coming to Fallingstar to live with Maybelle was another no. And in saying no to him, she was saying yes to herself.

Her stirring slowed as a smile of wonder crossed her face.

So what if these little children didn't like her? She

shouldn't be so self-conscious about it, she realized. Maybelle liked her, the bees and butterflies liked her. She gave the brush a quick, jaunty swish. And most of all, Dane liked her.

A flush of satisfaction rushed through her just thinking of the past few days they'd spent building the small house for the bear cub. She'd never known hammering wood and pitching hay could be such fun.

"It's not very good."

Laurel swung her head around to find Dorothy's head, so close the freckles across her nose loomed large. The girl was chewing a piece of cake and looking through squinted eyes at the painting of the three "fairies" she'd worked on all morning. In it, Laurel had tried to capture the mischief that she'd seen so wonderfully rendered in Maybelle's paintings of fairy children. Looking at her painting, however, she thought her own fairies looked more devious than sweet.

"You know what? You're absolutely right," she replied with a short laugh. "It stinks." Picking up her paintbrush, she dipped it in blue and made quick slashes across the painting, destroying it.

"Why'd you do that?" The little girl was horrified.

The other two girls clustered around them, each exclaiming their distress that Laurel ruined "their" painting.

"Because I don't like it either," she replied, making a smiley face with her strokes. Behind her, the girls giggled. She turned to look at them. Their faces were smudged with pink frosting and their fairy wings askew and suddenly she saw them for the children that they were. Delightfully carefree, even if a bit naughty, and certainly not responsible for whether or not she had the ability to paint a proper fairy.

"Maybe we can try again sometime," she said, wrapping her arm around two of the girls' waists. "I have to get the hang of it first, but when I do, maybe you'll come back? We'll have more fun and when I'm done, I'll give each of you a painting. How about that?"

The three girls' mouths dropped open in astonishment

and their eyes widened. Then in unison they clapped their hands and danced on the balls of their feet with delight, in the same manner they did with Maybelle.

Maybelle stood back, tapping her chin as she watched. "Come, children," she called, waving her fingers in the air. "Finish your cake, spit spot. I promised your mothers that you would leave promptly at three."

"Aw, do we have to?"

As they finished their cake, Maybelle came to Laurel's side and tucked a long tendril back from her face. "How are you?" she asked, her opaque eyes peering deep into Laurel's.

"I have a lot to learn. Like how you ever managed to get any painting done with fidgety children?" She brought her hands to her forehead. "They wouldn't do anything I told them to do!"

"And did you order them to pose for you?"

She looked up to see Maybelle's lips pursed and one brow arched.

"Yes, I did," she confessed with a light laugh. "I was a regular field marshal. *Do this—do that.* I treated them as I would any hired models I've used in the past, only these models didn't give a darn about working for scale or getting hired back, and they sure weren't about to play by my rules. They showed me, all right. All they did was bounce around and laugh and play."

"Just like children. And," she said with a smile, "like fairies."

"But how do you paint them if they won't sit still? There were so many times I caught an expression of joy or mischief on the children's faces and I wanted to capture it for the canvas. But just as quickly as it came, it disappeared. So I got frustrated and angry, which of course was self-defeating."

"Learn to capture a special moment and keep it in your heart. I promise you if you are ever fortunate enough to see a fairy, remember her, for she won't linger. Just like a child's smile." Then she turned toward the young girls, clapped her hands, and announced,

"Time for fairies to fly away home. Come along, dainty dears!"

By half past two, Maybelle and Laurel had changed the children out of their costumes, wiped their little hands and mouths, and hustled them homeward. Laurel remained in the studio to clean the mess and to dump the series of paintings she'd completed in the past few days into the trash, where, she decided, they belonged. Her mind was a million miles away and she didn't hear the door creak open.

"I take it you didn't have such a great day."

She immediately recognized the deep voice and didn't jump or shriek. She only wished she'd been quicker about tossing away the paintings. She knew Dane well enough that he'd want to see them and think nothing of going about helping himself. She turned her head to look at him and saw his brown arms under the rolled sleeves of his cambric shirt already reaching out to pick up one of the canvases from the table. His dark hair fell over his broad forehead as he looked down.

"Don't look at them," she rushed to say, cringing with embarrassment that he see her obvious lack of talent. "They're awful."

"They aren't that bad," he said.

Her cheeks flamed and she reached out to take the canvas from his hand. "Yes they are. They're worse than bad. They're terrible. We both know it." She ripped up one particularly bad picture of a fairy-costumed Dorothy trying to point her toe, supposedly on a leaf. To her eye, the painting looked like the fairy was trying to kick it.

"I don't think you've captured quite the right mood," he said, trying hard to keep a straight face.

His humor only served to fan her frustration.

He took advantage of her distraction to grab another canvas from the bottom of the pile. Seeing what he was up to, she reached out to snatch it back but he raised it high over his head.

"Dane, give it back!" she cried out, but her laughing gave her away. In the manner of a game, she jumped up, trying to take it back, and neither one of them could resist laughing as he dangled it high from her reach.

Between jumps and laughs, she was enjoying this flirtatious game immensely, feeling childish but then again, not caring if she was. After a few fruitless lunges, she swatted at him in feigned pique and quit. They both knew she had as much chance reaching the painting as she had grabbing hold of the highest leaf of a tree.

"I'm doing you a favor," he said. "You'll go tearing everything up before anyone gets a chance to see what you've done."

"That's the point, you bully," she fired back. Then, stepping back and wrapping her arms tight around her chest, she shrugged and said, "Go ahead. I'm sure your opinion doesn't matter to me in the least."

It was a terrible lie. She knew it and cringed as he lowered his arms and stood quietly looking at the painting. One of Dane's qualities was his brutal honesty. He wouldn't assure her the painting was good just to humor her, as he wouldn't tell her a dress was flattering or a dessert delicious if it were not true. She prepared herself for the onslaught. He studied the canvas in his usual brooding silence while she writhed inside. For in that moment she realized that next to Maybelle, she'd rather he liked her paintings more than anyone else.

This one wasn't one of the series of fairy paintings she'd worked on with the girls. The canvas in his hand she'd painted just for herself, a bit of pleasure between the tortuous hours in the studio. It was a depiction of Vincit, the bear cub, inside the warm and secure outbuilding that Dane had constructed just for him. She'd come upon him sleeping when she brought him his dinner.

"You've caught his sweetness," Dane said.

Laurel's shoulders lowered and she neared to study the painting in his hands. The backgrounds were not developed yet but the sleeping cub wasn't too bad, she'd decided.

"Do you think so?" she asked, hesitant to accept the compliment.

He half turned, so close now that she could see the

texture of his tanned and weathered face. "I do. You can tell he's dreaming of romping in Maybelle's lily bed again. I told you that you should have called him Trouble."

They both laughed, recalling how the cub's first day's outing had ended with his disastrous foray into Maybelle's lilies. Maybelle had come running from the kitchen, her arms flailing, her gauzy gown flapping behind her in the wind, to shoo the cub away. Afterwards, she'd scolded him for being so naughty. "You won't be invited back unless you learn to behave," she'd told the bear. Whether it was her imagination or not, Laurel would never know, but she'd have sworn the bear cub lowered its head in a sorry sulk.

"This painting is very good," he said in all seriousness. "It has more emotion than the fairy ones. You see? It's a good thing I intervened. You've made your first sale. I'd like to buy this one, if you'll sell it."

Her brows shot up. "Buy it? Don't be ridiculous. It's yours. Take it, please. It's the least I can do for bringing the cub to us in the first place, then building such a nice little house for it."

Dane accepted the gift readily and her chest swelled to watch him study it again with obvious appreciation etched on his handsome face.

"Thank you," he said. "I know just where I'll put it."

"You know, Dane, I've never seen your house. I've only passed it on the road." Her tone hinted at an invitation. She was curious to learn more about him, his style, how he lived, what he did at night when she wasn't with him.

Dane lowered the painting, his interest shifted to focus solely on her. "Will you come tonight?"

It was such a sudden invitation. Direct and demanding, like Dane. "It doesn't have to be tonight," she said, stalling.

"Why not? I can't offer you a meal," he hedged with a shrug. "Trust me, you'll fare better with Maybelle. But I can make some coffee."

Laurel's eyes widened with desire. "Did you say coffee? Do you mean you've had coffee down there all this time and didn't tell me?"

He laughed and nodded. "If I'd have known coffee was such a lure, I'd have tried it much sooner."

She closed her eyes with longing. "I'd have been at your mercy."

His eyes flashed and his smile turned crafty. "Really? So you're at my mercy, are you?"

She took a step back. "That's just a figure of speech. Don't let it go to your head."

He took a step forward. "So, how do you like your coffee? Black? With cream? Sugar?"

"With cream and sugar." She swallowed thickly. "Please."

His voice lowered a notch. "Ah, sweet," he murmured.

She licked her lips, then caught his gaze dart immediately to her mouth.

"Hot? Iced?"

She couldn't comprehend how such an innocent conversation about coffee could be so titillating. "Hot . . ."

"Very . . ." he agreed in a murmur, lowering his head.

She opened her mouth to say something, anything. The minute his lips touched hers the sentence melted away.

As did her bones. His kiss sent a scorching blast of heat straight down her spine, sizzling away any resistance she might have mustered. She felt her knees weaken and her back soften as all the light, magic, and cosmic forces that she'd tried to capture in her painting swirled within her now.

His grip around her tightened and she knew as the kiss deepened that he was not going to let her slip away. His kiss was more hungry and demanding than Colin's, and she certainly never felt like this when Colin's lips met hers. For Dane made her every bit as hungry for him as well. She felt starved for his kisses, knew one would never be enough. Her fingers trembled as they climbed his back to his neck, were she tightened her arms around and drew him lower, closer. Her fingers fisted in his soft hair while she feasted.

He responded to tighten his grip, leaning forward over her while his tongue expertly explored her mouth. The hunger in her grew and grew until it was a gnawing, ravenous need that only he could fill. So when she felt him pull away, she felt a sudden mindless despair and clung tighter, pressing herself against his chest.

Dane opened his eyes and saw hers inches from his own. They appeared as limpid green pools that he could drown in. Her eyes always had the power to enchant him, but dreamy with longing like they were now, they were bewitching. He had to pull back or not be responsible for what came next. He didn't want their lovemaking to be quick and explosive, not the first time. Laurel was special. He wanted it to be slow with enough time to savor the emotion and the sighs.

He reached up to loosen her arms from around his neck, kissing her hands softly when she whimpered in her throat.

As the air cooled around her, she took a moment to slow her pounding heartbeat and catch her wits. She'd never lost control like that before. Colin's kisses never made her throw all caution to the wind. She looked up and saw Dane dragging his hand through his hair and exhaling a plume of air. *So,* she thought with wonder mixed with conceit, *he felt it too.*

Her hands were trembling when she reached back to lift her long hair from her moist neck. The cool air was calming and she took a long, steadying breath.

"Will you come tonight?" he asked. "At seven?"

Her impulse was to say yes, but she felt the need for caution. Walking to the easel, she began placing lids on all the jars of paint, screwing them on tightly. "I don't know if I dare."

His lips twitched and he said with a teasing drawl, "I'm just inviting you down for a cup of coffee."

Such an innocent invitation, but looking into each other's eyes, they both knew that neither of them were fooled. Would he press for more if she said no, or would he wait for her signal that she was ready for more than just the offered coffee? Would she be made to feel so hungry again that it would be she who demanded more?

He caught her worried expression. "I mean this, Laurel. I'd be pleased if you just came down for coffee. Your company tonight would be enough."

A wave of relief flowed through her and she had her answer. Of course Dane would respect whatever pace she chose. "I'm not sure it's enough for me. I can't pretend that I don't desire your kisses," she said shyly, feeling another blush burn her cheeks. "It's too late for that. But it's not just about the two of us. There is Colin . . ."

"Not him again," Dane almost growled. "He's not even here."

"But he is." She tapped her forehead with her fingertip. "In my mind."

Dane leaned over to place a gentle kiss on the very spot her finger touched. She closed her eyes, feeling drawn to him again, feeling again the same rush.

"Do you think of him when I kiss you, Laurel? Is he there then?"

There was a conceit in his voice but she couldn't deny the truth. "No," she replied, shaking her head. "And you know it."

He nodded his head smartly in confirmation. "Nor do I think of any other woman. I tell you, Laurel, we're meant to be together."

"Dane, please." She put her small hand between them as he stepped closer again. "It's too soon, too fast. I've only been here less than a month. We hardly know each other."

"I know all I need to know about you."

"Well, I know almost nothing about you," she countered, stepping back. She had to think fast and hard because his hands were smoothing her hair from her face and he had that look in his eyes that promised another kiss.

"Then come tonight. For coffee." He paused and his

smile sparkled in his eyes. "And for whatever else you might want."

"All right, I will. Come for coffee, that is."

"Whatever you wish."

His eyes had too much of the devil in them to believe his angelic smile. She raised her brow and pointed a finger at him. "And none of that instant stuff for me."

He surprised her by tossing his head back and roaring a laugh. "I was thinking the same thing."

She wasn't nervous until Maybelle began to hover over her like a mother hen. Laurel was shooed out of the kitchen at dish time with the suggestion to change into something pretty and feminine for her evening with Dane. Perhaps a dress? she'd hinted. Or perhaps a flowing skirt?

Laurel had thought about changing into something a tad nicer than the gabardine slacks and cotton blouse she was wearing, but to do so would only encourage Maybelle further. And, she thought, perhaps Dane as well.

She was standing in front of her mirror, at her wits' end with what to do with shoulder-length hair, when Maybelle strolled in with her arms laden with assorted brushes and elaborately decorated pins and combs of every sort imaginable. It was on her lips to tell Maybelle to take them away and leave her be, but she quickly recalled how twilight was the saddest time of the day for Maybelle. Laurel often caught her standing alone, gazing longingly out at the woods. She'd sigh, not moving until the sun disappeared into the darkness. One night Laurel had asked what was the matter. Maybelle had simply smiled sadly and said she was visited by the twilight fairy, the one who travels between darkness and light to remind one of past joys and sorrows.

"She and I are old friends," she'd said.

Laurel suspected that Maybelle hid some deep inner sorrow that she shared with no one. So on this night, rather than disappoint Maybelle as twilight approached,

Laurel said yes to whatever joy she could offer Maybelle in return for all the joy she'd given.

They didn't spend a long time together before the mirror, but Laurel would never forget those precious minutes. She'd never known the gentle touch of a mother's hand combing her hair, and she thought to herself as Maybelle lovingly guided a brush through her long tresses that this was as close as she'd ever come to that experience.

Maybelle was in a particularly chatty mood. She talked on and on, peppering her monologue with compliments on Laurel's beauty, but Laurel's eyes were closed and all she was aware of was the gentle tugging of her hair as Maybelle's tiny fingers expertly wound the sides of her hair in braids, then pinned them at the back of her head with an amethyst clasp. When she finished, she cupped her hands over Laurel's shoulders and looked into the mirror.

Laurel opened her eyes and the two of them stared at the reflection in silence. She saw Maybelle standing behind her, her silvery hair wound around her head in multiple braids and pinned with large combs on either side of her head. Her own head was directly beneath Maybelle's, her golden hair pinned back as well, accentuating her large, tilting green eyes.

"I never noticed it before," she said with wonder in her voice, "and I don't know if it's just because my hair is longer now or that our eyes both seem to tilt up a bit, or what. But we look a little alike, don't you think?"

Maybelle's face softened to a bittersweet smile. "I think there might be some resemblance," she said softly. "Though the light is poor," she added, stepping back and turning quickly away from the mirror. "But if you think so, my dear, I am highly complimented."

"It's me that is complimented. You're so beautiful, Maybelle. I can't imagine ever being half so lovely."

"Oh, dear girl, surely you have a better imagination that that!" But Laurel could see she was clearly pleased with the compliment. "Now off with you before you turn an old woman's head. I hope you and Dane have a lovely time together. Here, I've made berry tarts for you to share with him and Daphne. He loves berries, you know. Now hurry off, and don't be alarmed if I'm not here when you return."

She was about to beg Maybelle to be careful, but shut her mouth in a tight line and took the basket filled with tarts instead. During her first few weeks, Laurel had worried for her safety and often said as much to Maybelle. In time, however, she came to understand, as Dane and Daphne did, that Maybelle had her own way of living her life and she wouldn't tolerate any change or meddling.

The sun was still shining when Laurel began her walk down the mountain toward Dane's house. Her heart felt light and she swung her arms as she paced around the first bend of road. Yet it wasn't long before she entered the shadowy darkness of the foliage that formed a thick, green tunnel over the narrow gravel road. Her arms stayed close to her side while her eyes scanned the blackness just beyond the little stretch of road. It would be night by the time she returned, and, craning her neck to view the impenetrable wall of foliage overhead, she doubted any moonlight would filter through to light her way.

As twilight descended, she could see the guttering of the small white courtship lights of fireflies. There were so many out tonight. Suddenly, from the corner of her eye she caught a sudden, quick movement and a flash of light. She jerked back, turning her head sharply. There was nothing was there.

Her heart raced like a rabbit's as she caught her breath. *It must have been a firefly,* she told herself, rubbing her suddenly cool arms. Yet, she'd never known a firefly to be so bright or so fast. What was that Maybelle was always saying? Something about twilight being a time of betwixt and between, a favorite romping time for fairies. The thought gave her pause. She stilled her body and wondered, could it have been a . . .

No, no, no, don't even go there, she scolded herself. Taking a step forward, she began her trek again with determination, picking up her pace to get through the woods as quickly as possible. She shivered and scoured her surroundings. Again it felt as though dozens of pairs of eyes were staring out from behind leaves, within the knots in trees, and hidden in the brush, watching her every move. It was a creepy feeling, as unwelcome as it was frightening. She told herself it was just the animals and birds. Maybe a deer too. *Bambi,* she thought with a smile of relief. There was nothing to be afraid of. She began to whistle, hoping her noise would scare off any unwelcome visitor.

She passed a quaint, twisting little brook with rushing white water skipping downhill. It was an idyllic place, mystical, bordered with a slope of bright green moss that crept right up to the borders of the brook and contrasted sharply with the whiteness of the stones. The gurgling water made its own kind of sweet music. Drawn to it, she wandered from the road to pause before the brook and listen. The water was so clear and sparkling it seemed transparent, but strangely, as she stared into it, she did not see her reflection.

It must be the lighting, she reasoned, though she could see the mirrored images of the leaves over her head. Bending lower, she crouched closer to the brook. The water looked so inviting, so refreshing and cool. It seemed to shimmer in the blue light like icy silk. She couldn't resist reaching out to run her fingers through the water. It was so cold her fingers tingled. Suddenly, that mild tingle zinged and shot straight up her fingers throughout her body. She jolted back, whipping back her hand and holding it protectively. Her heart pounded wildly and from somewhere in the trees came the faint sound of twittering. Laurel's gaze scouted the surrounding area, her shoulders hunched and her damp hands clasped tight.

"Is anyone there?" she called out.

The wind whispered in the trees, but the high twittering ceased. She was enveloped in a deep mountain silence.

I must be getting skittish, she told herself, rubbing her still tingling fingers. *My nerves are a wreck to jump at a bird call.* And the tingling in her fingers was simply from the icy water. *It's only your overactive imagination*, she reassured herself. Nothing at all. Drying her hand on her shirt, she rose again and made her way back to the road. This time, however, she kept to the road at a steady pace.

"I live here too. I don't have to go anywhere." Daphne was holding her ground.

Dane mopped his face with his palm, counting to ten. It was 6:45 and he'd have to hurry to shower and dress before Laurel arrived. He'd wanted everything to look its best. "You don't have to. But I'd appreciate it if you did."

Dane and Daphne stared at each other, at an impasse. She'd hit the ceiling when Dane asked her to leave the house for a few hours so he and Laurel could have a little time alone.

"Besides," he said, feeling the rumblings of temper stoking in his gut at her obstinant silence, "you had plans to play poker in town tonight. So what's the big deal?"

"I changed my mind," she said with a thrusting out of her chin. "It's a woman's prerogative."

"Damn it, Daph, what's the problem? You've never pulled that one before. You're just being a brat because you've got it in your mind not to like Laurel. It's your own fault the two of you aren't friends. She's made every overture, not to mention Maybelle's invitations, but you won't have any of her friendship."

"I'd say the two of you are friendly enough for the both of us."

"And that's another thing," he said, holding his temper in check. "What the hell difference does it make to you if I decide to spend time with Laurel Carrington? It's my life and I've never welcomed your sticking your nose in where it doesn't belong. I like her. A great deal.

So you might just as well get used to the idea because I plan to see her. A lot. Got it?"

"Fine," she snapped, flopping down on the sofa and locking her arms around herself. "See her all you like. Bring her around. I'm sure I won't mind. As long as she stays out of my way."

"It's always about you, isn't it, Daphne? What bothers you, what suits you. It's no wonder you're in such a foul mood so much of the time. Why don't you try looking beyond your own needs to see to the needs of others once in awhile?" He flipped the towel over his shoulder, then said in a lower voice, "You might find you're a happier person if you do."

He walked out toward his room, closing his bedroom door behind him.

Daphne curled her knees close and rested her chin upon them, scowling. She'd rather he'd have ranted and shouted at her, called her names, and kicked her out of the house. That kind of anger, like her father's, she could shut out or even laugh at with disdain. Dane never did that, however. He never shot out with malevolence. He was a powerful man. He'd been a strong boy too, capable of settling disputes with his fists if he'd chosen to. It just wasn't in him to deliberately hurt someone, not even when they mocked his size and strength, egging him on. He'd taken it all in, never complaining or acting out against them or his mother. Not even against Joe, though he deserved it most. Until the day a boy hurt her.

She was twelve at the time, tall for her age and over-developed. A boy known to be a bully had spread lies about things she did with him behind the schoolhouse. Daphne had squared off with him in the playground during lunch. The teasing escalated to anger, which culminated in his shoving Daphne, knocking her to the ground and bloodying her lip.

She could still feel the rush of love and pride she'd felt that afternoon when she saw her brother, walking straight-shouldered and ham-fisted toward them on the playground. His gaze was deadly. She hadn't seen that look before or since. The other kids saw it too, for they parted before him like a wave as he made his way to her side. With a tenderness she expected from him, he helped her to her feet, dusted off her legs, and looked into her face. She saw the mottled rage in his eyes when he saw the blood on her lip. It frightened her. He turned by degrees. When the bully caught sight of Dane's face his cynical smile slipped. Dane walked toward him. The boy raised his fists and swung, hitting Dane squarely in the pit of his stomach. Dane didn't even slow down. In one smooth move he delivered a single right hook that knocked the bully to the ground. Dane didn't stand over him to gloat, nor did he acknowledge the slaps on the back of other boys. He ignored everyone but his sister, helping her home with the gentleness that was at his core.

After that, no one ever bothered her or Dane again.

It made his criticism all the more a burn right dab in the middle of her stomach. She had a bad feeling about her deal with her father. Guilt, more likely. It was wrong, she knew it, just as she knew it was Joe who shot that poor bear cub's mama. She'd waited for him to come by every night, looked for him in the apple grove when she tended her bees, to tell him . . .

Tell him what? She wrung her hands. Tell him she wanted out? That no money was worth this torture? But she wasn't sure. This was her one chance out of here. People like her weren't given more than one shot. But for sure she'd tell him to lay low and stay away from Fallingstar.

Except he didn't come around. And there was no way she could tell Dane about it, even though some nights she lay awake trying to come up with the right words. For one thing, he'd go after Joe and get himself hurt or worse. And the other was he'd see her for the cheat she was.

She shook her head and squeezed her legs tighter against the twisting in her stomach. She could stand a lot of pain, but not the loss of Dane's love. He was all she had in the world, she couldn't risk that. Sure, she was being a crab lately, snapping at anyone who drew near. But she felt cornered, trapped, locked into a losing situation with no way out.

Dane came from his room in his terry robe, barefoot, with his long hair dripping water from his shower. His eyes scanned the room with a worried expression.

"Daph, have you seen the iron?"

"The what?" she asked, her eyes as round as her open mouth. "I haven't seen one of those around here since Mom died. Hell, Dane, I'm not even sure we own one."

He frowned and headed toward the kitchen. She heard him opening and slamming the cabinets, banging around pots and pans. He emerged with a victorious smile and an old iron with a frayed cord in his hand. He looked just as she remembered he had when he was about twelve coming home with a line of fish for dinner.

"Oh hell," she said, dragging herself up on her feet. "Give me that ol' thing. I'll iron your shirt. Though I can't believe you're going through all this trouble just to see Laurel Carrington. You see her every day. Oh, never mind," she muttered, seeing his lost expression. "Go on. You go make yourself beautiful for your date."

His dark eyes gleamed with gratitude, making her feel small for not helping him clean up the house earlier when he'd asked. She was just being obstinate and he hadn't asked twice. He closed the door behind him and she felt the twist in her gut again when she heard him whistling. This was no good. She didn't like the way things were heading.

She plugged in the iron, and while it was heating up, took the time to pick up her papers and trash from the living room and fluff up a few pillows. She ironed his shirt with care, remembering all the hints her mother and Maybelle taught her. When she was finished, she hung it on a hanger, put the iron neatly away, turned on some soft music, then grabbed her purse and car keys and without a word, quietly left the house.

Fourteen

The sky was a rich turquoise color by the time Laurel finally spied the slanted slate of a rooftop in a clearing of the dense green. A little further down the road and she could spy gabled windows overflowing with soft yellow light. *At last,* she thought, as her heart lifted and her gait loosened. A few minutes later she broke through the foliage tunnel into acres of open, rolling hay meadows. The mountain breeze was cool on her cheeks. As she passed through the tall hedge of shrubs surrounding the house, she caught the heady scent of flowers in the night air.

She paused at the entrance, drinking in the sight of Dane's house. Even in the darkening light, she found it beguiling. She didn't know why, but she'd expected something ordinary, perhaps a straight-walled, unadorned farmhouse or some slipping-down shack. Neither Dane nor Daphne seemed to be homebodies.

The Victorian-style house, however, radiated warmth and charm. Gabled windows arched over an enormous wraparound porch adorned with clever, curling bric-a-brac and gracefully rounding spindles, all painted a bright white against the dove-gray wood. The porch led her gaze out to the long perennial bed that bordered the house. She couldn't see much more than the rounding curves of the bed's design and the shadows of prolific flowers in the moonlight.

She sighed in appreciation.

"So, you like the house?"

Dane's deep voice piercing the silence caught her by surprise, but his presence never startled her, as though he was always but a step away. She turned toward him, smiling, her head tilting as she considered his transformation. Gone were the stained jeans and flannel shirt. He'd changed into tan gabardine slacks and a plain white cotton shirt, worn open collared, its sleeves rolled up. The whiteness of the cotton was almost iridescent in the moonlight against his dark tan. *How wonderful he looks*, she thought.

"It's a wonderful house," she replied.

"Maybelle built it for my mother."

"That would explain the charming touches," she said, noting his freshly shaven cheeks and the damp ends of his hair along his neck.

"It was a labor of love," he said, looking over the house with obvious pride.

She noted the fresh paint on the trim, the straight edges to the garden and the freshly mowed lawn. "It's obviously a labor of love for you as well. I wasn't expecting anything quite so elaborate. Or so big."

"Maybelle and my mother worked together on it and, knowing them, they were indulgent and just didn't know where to stop." He took her hand in a casual move and led her to the front porch. "It's cozy, but it seems real big when I have to heat it in the winter. There are four bedrooms and as many fireplaces to tend. But believe me, living with Daphne, especially when we're snowbound, there are days when I think we could use more room."

She laughed as he opened the front door to a small foyer of more Vermont slate covered with bright hooked rugs, probably made by Maybelle. It was the living space of hardworking people with an eye more to well-utilized space than charm. The walls were the color of faded linen and the upholstery was worn and covered with afghans, an old trick to hide tears and holes. Magazines were stacked along the wall, hooks by the door were filled with coats for all kinds of weather, and below them stood a line of boots.

Dane seemed eager that she feel at ease in his house, and she did her best to keep her voice light and cheery, despite the nervous twisting of her stomach. She was very aware that she was alone in his house and that his dark brown eyes never left her face. She kept her own gaze averted.

"I'll get the coffee," Dane said after a long silence.

She blew out a stream of air and followed him into the kitchen. The ceilings were higher than Maybelle's berm house, and she noticed that Dane could walk through the rooms without scraping the top of his head. It was a small kitchen compared to Maybelle's enormous one, but unlike Maybelle's there was a refrigerator, a gas stove, and even a kitchen sink with running water.

She moved toward the counter where Dane was spooning tablespoons of coffee into a filter. Laurel's mouth began watering just catching a whiff of the coffee. "It's been such a long time . . ."

He turned to look at her face, close at his shoulder. Her hair was pinned back from her face, drawing his attention to her eyes, which were closed in a kind of ecstatic smile as she inhaled the scent. He paused for a heartbeat, the tablespoon still in the air, to absorb the punch of it. His gaze traveled to her pink, full lips and he felt a craving all his own. *Yes indeed*, he thought, *it has been such a long time.*

She opened her eyes and he was stunned by the sudden sight of enormous green eyes, so close and focused on him. They widened at seeing him staring down at her and she quickly lowered her head. But her telltale blush gave her away, and he thought to himself he'd never tire of that heightening of color on her cheeks.

He served the coffee in his mother's best china cups. They rattled in his big hands as he served them, and he cursed himself for being a fool. Why was he trying to impress her? Dainty things like teacups painted with lilac sprigs, plates of sugar cookies, and curved women like Laurel Carrington rattled his insides as well. He'd spent most of his life living with Joe and Daphne, or with a bunch of men roughing it in the rain forests. What did he know about such things? He felt much more at home with big mugs and sandwiches and . . .

She took the cup from his hands and smiled at him gratefully. His insides tumbled and he decided he could eat off prissy china for the rest of his life if she ate across the same table.

"Maybelle's all excited about the Summer Solstice party," she said, pouring milk into her coffee. "She's been out gathering wildflowers and supplies from the woods for days. And we're sewing new dresses to wear too. They're so lovely! Maybelle's is white and mine is a soft rose and we're making a soft gold one for Daphne, which should be perfect with her red hair. They'll have long, flowing sleeves and hems that will trail behind us." She added a teaspoon of sugar, then pointed the spoon at him with a squinting eye.

"You'll have to wear something terribly romantic to fit in with us lovely ladies."

"Maybelle's already delivered my shirt." He rolled his eyes and grabbed a tart. "Only for Maybelle."

"I can hardly wait for tomorrow night."

"The weather should be fine. No clouds or rain."

"I don't think Maybelle would allow it," she said, stirring her coffee.

Their eyes met and they smiled, each knowing the words were spoken in jest, but each also silently acknowledging that Maybelle had some uncanny power over nature.

"Will Daphne deign to come?"

Dane lifted a shoulder. "Who knows? But she knows how much the summer solstice means to Maybelle, so I think she might make the supreme effort."

Laurel set down her cup and fingered the rim. Hesitantly, she said, "Why doesn't she like me? I've tried to speak to her, but every time I approach her she walks away."

A sigh rumbled in his chest as he stretched out his long legs. "It's not you," he replied, deciding to answer honestly. "Not directly. It's your relationship with Maybelle. I think she's jealous."

"Jealous of me? But why?"

"You may have noticed Daphne has her own kind of femininity."

"More like an Amazon, I'd say."

He laughed and nodded. "True enough. It's hard to believe she used to be a shy thing, quiet as a mouse. Growing up, our house was a war zone with Joe Flannery constantly firing out missiles with no warning. But after that I went away to travel, and Maybelle brought Daphne to live with her. Maybelle never had the same expectations for a girl that most folks around here do, and she certainly doesn't tolerate any of the local gossip or opinions. With that as her role model, Daphne grew up to explore her own tastes and inclinations. And she wasn't the type to dress up or flirt with the boys. She likes boys well enough, mind you, but to hunt and fish with. She thinks of them as pals. Though," he added with a snort, "I can't say they feel the same about her. Many a heart's been broken 'cause Daphne won't have those boys making love to her."

"I'm not surprised the boys are agog. She's knock-down gorgeous." She said this matter-of-factly, without a hint of jealousy.

Dane rubbed his jaw, the same one that had been punched many a time in defense of his beautiful sister. "She's always considered her looks a problem rather than an asset. She'd rather be plain, I do believe, so no one would look at her twice. Not that she's shy anymore. Not at all. Maybelle turned a shy, sad kid into a strong and confident woman."

"But I don't understand why she doesn't like me."

"Well," he said, allowing his gaze to travel down from Laurel's waves of golden hair pinned back with an amethyst clasp to her lavender, crisply ironed blouse to her delicate fingers resting around the rim of her cup. He was pleased as always to see no ring on her finger. "Maybelle is very feminine, in a dainty kind of way. Like our mother was." He averted his gaze. "Like you."

In the awkward aftermath of that comment, he reached out to offer her a tart. When she shook her head, he took one for himself. "None for you? You're still so thin a good gust of wind could blow you away."

"I don't know why. I've been eating nonstop since I've arrived. Maybelle and I cook and bake up a storm."

He dispatched the tart in a single bite. "That's what I mean. You two are having a great time together. It was never like that between Daphne and Maybelle. They enjoy each other's company, but Maybelle never could interest Daphne in household arts. Or painting, though she tried."

"Ah, now I'm beginning to see. Then I come along and she sees Maybelle and I doing both together."

"Right. And to boot, you have the same eerie connection with wildlife that Maybelle has. And that Daphne covets. It's killing her that the animals love you, wild and tame both. But mostly, it was her bees."

"I didn't do anything," she said, her eyes appealing. "It just happened."

He nodded. "Of course. It's natural. She knows that just as she knows there's not a damn thing she can do to change it. You've a rare gift." He reached out to place his hand over hers on the table. "And anyone can see how you're beginning to appreciate that part of yourself. It's a beautiful thing to watch. Like watching a flower unfold in the sun."

Laurel lowered her head again and slowly extricated her hand from his. "I think you're seeing far too much in me."

"I don't think you're seeing near enough."

"Tell me about yourself," she said, sitting straighter in her chair. She knew he was very good at asking questions and listening, revealing very little about himself. "What's all this about going to the rain forests? I think that sounds terribly exciting."

"It was a lot of work." His voice was expressionless. The chair scraped as he rose to collect the coffee pot.

"What kind of work did you do there? Maybelle said something about how you studied plants?"

He put his hands on his hips and pursed his lips. Then, with decision, he put out his hand toward her. "If you want, I'll show you. It isn't much, but with your background, you might find it somewhat interesting." He spoke in a self-deprecating manner.

She took his hand and rose, eager to see his work. He led her to a room just off the kitchen. The small room was cluttered with industry. One wall was lined with bookshelves so full they tilted precariously. Dusty stacks of agricultural magazines and tilting piles of papers with curled edges littered the floor, along with a stray shoe, an old camera on a tripod, and a rusted file cabinet. There was an old roll-top desk against another wall from which paper, pens, photographs of plants and Lord knew what else overflowed from every drawer, nook, and cranny. Even the walls were plastered with a *Farmers Almanac* calendar pinned over the desk and a bulletin board covered with bits of papers. On another wall, however, were sketches of plants that were tacked carelessly onto the wall with pushpins. Her breath caught in her throat and she was drawn directly to them.

Where did these come from? she wondered, as she stood quietly before them, studying. A few were species of plants she recognized, but a few stunned her because she'd never seen them before.

"These are masterful," she said at last, awe in her voice. "The detail is remarkable. And the skill . . . Who drew them?" She turned toward him. Dane's face was still with apprehension. "You drew these?" she asked, though she already knew the answer.

"They're not much," he said modestly. "I'm no artist. I've always sketched what I found on my walks in the woods, just for my own collection. When I was in the rain forest, however, I had no choice but to draw what I discovered and collect specimens when I could. The destruction of the forests is going on way too fast and I didn't know if I'd ever get another chance. It's a damn shame. Thousands of acres are being slashed and burned every day."

"These two," she said, indicating the two genera she didn't recognize. "Are they known or did you discover them?"

"I'm no expert," he said without pretense, "But I've not seen them recorded anywhere. That's why I've got them pinned up there. I'm still trying to find out. So you don't recognize them either?" When she shook her head no, he seemed pleased, even excited. With a spark of enthusiasm, he bent to rifle through his desk in a desperate hunt through an enormous mess of papers, drawings, empty cups, and ashtrays. He found what he was looking for and with a sigh of relief, pulled out a large painter's file and laid it out on the desk before her. Momentarily silenced, she leaned over, eager to see.

"Here are some of the others I've drawn," he said, pulling one painting out, then another while he talked. "I've painted them to catch the magnificent color. Most of them are species you'll recognize, but there are a few I'm still studying." He reached up to scratch behind his ear in a self-conscious gesture. "I don't have much time now, what with all the work to be done at Fallingstar."

She had to sit in the creaky old desk chair or slip into it. One look at the collection of drawings in vibrant color had her weak at the knees. As he silently turned one sheet after another, she marveled how one was even more beautiful than the next. When that file was finished, he tugged another out from under a mountain of paperwork. Opening it, she gasped with surprise. Genus after genus was described with detailed descriptions and information on the flowers included in the color drawings. The information was expert, including exhaustive records, maps, charts, and seasonal weather variations. Even a cursory study revealed that the observations were recorded in the nonemotional, thorough manner typical of a professional field researcher. Yet at the end of each entry was a remarkable summary that was filled with personal observations and conjectures that could only have been written by a very knowledgeable—even brilliant—mind.

Her mind blurred as she tried to connect this concept of Dane Walden with that of the simple and honest but uneducated field hand he presented himself as. She stared down at what she could only describe as masterpieces. Why, hers were amateur compared to this level of work.

She looked up to see him leaning back in the chair beside her, idly leafing through the records, totally unaware that the floor was dropping out from under her. She looked at those long fingers she'd seen hundreds of times before, a few scratched by bramble, his nails short but clean. A farmer's hands, he'd called them. True enough. But also the hands of a scholar. And an artist. *And who knew what else?* she wondered wildly.

He must have sensed her sharp perusal because he looked up to catch her gaze. His brows furrowed and he lowered the papers slowly to his table.

"What's the matter?" he asked.

"I don't know what to say," she replied in a soft voice. "The drawings, your records . . . they're unbelievable."

The tip of his ears turned scarlet and he said brusquely, "I told you they weren't very good. Just my notes is all. I thought you might want to take a look. I didn't think . . . well, never mind." He reached out to scoop the papers back into the file.

Laurel put her hand on his, stopping him. He had misunderstood. "Dane, don't you know how good this is?"

His hand stilled beneath her own as he registered her question. He turned his head toward her so slowly it was as though he had a new thought with each degree. His eyes were filled with wonder. "Are they?" he asked.

"Of course they are," she replied. "But you have to know that. Wait a minute." She jerked her hand back. "Are you playing games with me?"

He appeared puzzled. "What do you mean? What games?"

"This," she said, indicating with her free hand the files on the desk. "You told me you didn't even finish high school. Why would you tell me something like that?"

"Because it's the truth."

She skipped a beat. "Do you mean you graduated early and moved right on to college or what?"

"College? I just said I didn't finish high school. Why

are you asking me about college?" Now he seemed on the defensive as well.

"Because you had to have studied somewhere! These entries and sketches are scholarly. There's too much knowledge and expertise here to pretend otherwise." Her temper sizzled with feelings of betrayal. "What do you take me for? I may not be up to your caliber but I'm not a fool. Either you're lying or these aren't your notes. Did you even draw the sketches?"

His face grew thunderous but he spoke in a low, deliberate voice that had her sitting straighter in her chair. "One thing you should know about me. I never lie."

"But this doesn't make any sense," she said in a hurry to douse the flame in his eyes. "This work, my God," she swiped a lock from her forehead. "Surely you know what you've got here."

He quirked a dark eyebrow. "A bunch of notes from my travels. So what?"

"A bunch of notes . . ." she murmured, rubbing her forehead, beginning to understand. Could he really not have a clue how important his discoveries were? Much less the level of research. "There's one thing I don't understand," she said, leaning forward to peer into his eyes. "What about your colleagues? The other researchers in the field. Surely they must've talked to you about your work. I mean, didn't you all compare notes periodically?"

His grin was more a smirk and he leaned back in his chair again, resting a booted ankle on his knee. "I never said I was a field researcher. You're jumping to conclusions again. Who would hire me at that level? I had no credentials, no degrees." His smile slipped. "I have no illusions where such things are concerned. I signed on as a grip. They needed a strong back and paid me minimal wage for it. Believe me, there are lines drawn between their type and mine that aren't crossed. I didn't care. I went to the rain forests because I wanted an adventure and I was curious. For myself. Is that so hard to accept?"

"No. Well, maybe yes," she replied, thinking of most

of the researchers she knew. Publish or perish was a fact of life in academics. "So, am I to understand that no one has seen all this?" She looked down at the papers on the table while experiencing small explosions of glee in her chest.

"Well, Maybelle has, of course. We've gone over them many times. She sometimes recognizes a few genera that I don't. I wasn't joking when I told you I apprenticed with her. She knows more about plants than any book I've read, and I've read plenty. I doubt any of those scholars you revere so highly can hold a candle to what that lady has tucked away in her crafty little mind."

A hardness entered his eyes and spread across his features. Even his voice sounded hard when he spoke again. "I don't pretend to be some brainy guy out of college with a fancy degree and a cushy job. I read what I like, study what I'm interested in, and go about my own business. I never claimed to be smart or an expert or anything else but a farmer." He speared her with a look that sliced right through the chaff. "What you see is what you get."

She stared back at him, not the least unnerved, blinking as though seeing him fully for the first time. *So he was self-educated*, she realized, as all the pieces of the puzzle fit together. She'd heard of such people, geniuses who did not do well in school and were often teased or mocked by teachers and students alike. Often, they dropped out. From time to time they popped up again as adults to become the darlings of the world of academia.

"You realize what this means," she said.

He narrowed his eyes in suspicion. "No."

"You could compile all your notes and drawings and write a professional paper. What journal wouldn't publish it? Wait, that's wrong. What am I thinking? You could write a whole book! Don't you see, Dane? No one will care if you've got a degree or not. Your work will stand on its own." Her voice was rising in its enthusiasm. "Why, I could help you! I'm very good at organizing and editing. It's what I do for my father all the time. But he's never done anything as impressive as this. Your drawings alone are spectacular, but you've done it all. And who knows what excitement will occur if some of these plants are now extinct." She brought her palm to her mouth in silent exclamation. "My God, Dane, I just realized. These might be the only evidence that these plants ever existed. You'll zoom right to the top of the field! You could go anywhere."

He leaned back in his chair and studied her excitement with that intense power of observation she was now familiar with, except that this time she felt as though she were another specimen he was about to dissect.

She lifted her shoulders helplessly and said in a weaker voice, "You might even become famous."

Rather than respond with the enthusiasm she expected, he looked as though he'd just eaten a bad piece of fish.

"Thanks, but no thanks," he said.

Laurel's smile collapsed with her enthusiasm. "What do you mean, no thanks? No, you don't want my help?" A new thought entered her mind and she felt a scorch of embarrassment. "If . . . if you don't think I'm good enough, I'd understand. I was only offering to help."

"You said earlier tonight that you didn't know anything about me. I thought you were wrong. Now I know it's true."

She was taken aback by the coldness in his tone. She felt a shiver of apprehension, for the first time worrying that his interest in her, one that she'd tried to discourage, might actually have died after all. She tightened her lips and held herself straight. "Go on," she said.

His eyes narrowed. "What makes you think I even want to achieve this academic fame you seem so enamored with?"

She opened her mouth to reply, "But I just assumed," but she shut her mouth before the horrid words escaped again. She'd learned to assume nothing at Fallingstar.

"I have nothing but contempt for those people who pursue knowledge for the sole purpose of achieving fame or money or the esteem of others," he continued, pounding her with the anger of his words. "What do I need with that kind of fawning? That simpering, self-serving pandering? This work is mine. Mine!" he said, bringing his fist to his chest, his voice rising to as close to a shout as she'd ever heard from him. "Don't tell me what to do with it or what I should feel."

Her own breathing came heavier as her fury sparked. "I thought you might feel excitement about your work. Some passion."

His dark eyes flashed. "You talk of excitement? Of passion?" He leaned closer till his face was inches from hers and his breath came as fevered pants upon her cheek. His gaze fell to her lips before slowly rising back to her eyes. "What do you know of excitement? Or passion, Miss Laurel Carrington?" he said in a low, suggestive voice.

Her mind flashed back to her scene with Colin Whitmore, when she'd asked him if he felt passion. The truth, she saw now, was that *she* had not felt it. She opened her lips to reply, but no words came out.

"I thought so," he said and pulled back to stand. "Well, let me enlighten you. The excitement comes from the hunt, Miss Carrington. The passion comes from the doing. And the satisfaction comes from knowing that it's mine."

She reached up to rub her cheeks with her palms, giving herself time to catch her wits. She thought of her father, whose whole career was based upon his success at discovering rare species for the sole purpose of sharing that discovery with the world. She'd spent a lifetime supporting his endeavors. Dane's argument, his heated beliefs, mocked her father and her.

"You don't care that you're hoarding all this information like some hermit miser?" she fired back with a heat she'd never experienced before. "Or that you're secreting away this precious knowledge, not even bothering to share it with mankind?"

"Share it?" he exploded. "They'll exploit it! In the name of progress, science, and industry, it's a feeding frenzy out there that's destroying not just the rain forest but the whole planet. I'll not have a hand in it. I won't be a part of it and I sure as hell won't play that game."

"Don't you feel any sense of responsibility? How can you be so selfish?"

"Careful now," he ground out, placing his pipe between clenched teeth.

Her temper was too hot for caution now. She rose to a stand before him, her chin up and her eyes like bright green flames. "So it's enough for you to hide away on this mountain? Ha! I say it's nothing but a retreat from the real world that exists outside the boundaries of Fallingstar. You and Daphne and even Maybelle. You're all hiding out here. From what? That's what I want to know. What are you so afraid of?"

The fire in his eye banked as she spoke, and in the resulting silence, turned cold.

"What do you know about me, or Daphne or Maybelle?" he asked in a deadly voice. "You say we're hiding? Not true. We're defending ourselves, and our lifestyle, from those who would seek to mock us, to ridicule us, to tear down what we've built simply because they do not understand. You don't know what we've been through!" he roared.

"You talk about sharing this precious knowledge?" He waved his hand with disgust over his papers on the desk. "This is nothing. Oh yes, I've tried to explain the things I've witnessed. Do you know what happened? I was persecuted. Laughed at. Called dumb, retarded, a dreamer. And worse, God, so much worse. I left school. Left town. I've been to doctors who've explained away my core beliefs as dissociation, delusion, or the retreat of an abused child into fantasy."

He paced the room, trailing a faint gray smoke from his pipe and filling the room with the scent of apples. When he spoke again, his voice was calmer. "And you ask me why I don't share my knowledge with the world?" He set down his pipe and walked to the window, raking his hands through his hair as he gazed out.

She felt a million miles away from him. Separated by a deep gulf that she worried could never be crossed again. When he turned to face her the anguish and anger had dissipated, replaced by a despair she'd never seen in him before.

"I don't want to talk about this anymore," he said in a tired voice. He flipped the file closed over his drawings. "I should drive you home."

She clasped her hands again and straightened her shoulders, disguising a deep hurt she felt inside. "Yes, I suppose so," she said in a strained voice. "It's getting late. Thank you for inviting me."

He led her to the front door, then opened it for her. As she passed by him, she wished he would take hold of her arm again, as he so often did at the barn. If she just felt his touch she might find the courage to say she was sorry, to say something that would splinter the wall of ice building between them. But he didn't, and neither did she. The icy barrier was already too thick. She passed from his charming house out to be swallowed by the dark.

"Wait here," he said, going down the porch steps and walking away toward the truck.

She did, staring up at the moon with anguish. *The evening was a fiasco*, she thought, digging her hands into her sweater pockets. Her fingers met with something hard and smooth. She pulled out the small object and held it up to the moonlight. It was the bored stone. In the light of the nearly full moon, it seemed to take on a shimmering luminescence. How did the stone get into her pocket? she wondered.

She was distracted by the firing up of the truck's engine. She tucked the stone back into her pocket as the battered pickup truck rolled before the house. Dane didn't jump out to come around and open the door for her. He merely stretched over the front seat to flick open the door for her.

She climbed in and sat as far away from him on the seat as possible. With a spinning of tires and spitting gravel, they lurched forward and began their drive up the mountain in a heavy silence. The engine whined as it climbed. Laurel saw Dane's large hands cupped around the gear shift and wondered again how such hands could paint such magnificently intricate detail. She turned her head to look out the window before she allowed her gaze to wander to his face.

Outside the darkness was pierced with the relentless flashing of countless fireflies. They seemed to follow the truck as it made its poky way up the winding, soft road. *Hurry, hurry,* she whispered in her mind. She couldn't wait until they arrived at the tidy berm house where Maybelle lived—and that she now felt was her home. The wedge between her and Dane was like a physical stake in her heart and each moment she sat next to him in this horrid silence it dug deeper. She had to hold her breath and blink rapidly so she wouldn't embarrass herself and cry.

She thought they'd never reach the top, but at last they did, rounding the curve to see the warm light of welcome flowing out from the small, mullioned windows. Laurel's hand fumbled at the car door for the handle.

Dane's hand shot out to grasp her arm. "Laurel, wait," he said, his voice husky with emotion.

She wouldn't turn around to face him. Couldn't. But neither did she struggle away.

"I'm sorry," he said. "I shouldn't have reacted that strongly. There's a lot of history you don't know yet."

The apology kept her from stepping out from the truck. The pained tone in his voice forced her to turn to look at him. His head was bent and a lock of hair fell across his forehead, half veiling his eyes. Yet even in the shadows, she saw that his fury was spent. All she saw now was sorrow.

"I seem to remember you pointing that out," she replied softly.

A short silence stretched long. His hand traveled down her arm and hesitatingly took her hand. She held her breath as he fumbled with her fingers, considering his words.

"I . . ." He stopped, then lifted his gaze to capture hers. "I'd like to change that. I know I can be a bear. It's hard for me to open up. It's not my way. But I'd like to try, with you. Try to talk to you more, to let you know more about me. And I'd like to learn more about you as well, Laurel Carrington."

She swallowed hard, feeling the air thin between them.

"Would you like to do that?" He looked down at her hand again and rubbed the narrow span of skin between the knuckles on her ring finger. "Or would you rather not? I'm asking you to make the decision. I'll abide by whatever you decide."

She knew he was referring to Colin. Common sense told her that she should carefully, kindly extricate herself from her relationship with Dane. After tonight, especially, common sense told her that there was no future for them. They wanted different lifestyles, cherished different goals. He despised all that she held dear. All that she shared with Colin.

But looking into his eyes, so vibrant with a passion she'd never seen in a man's eyes before, she couldn't think of Colin. He simply didn't exist.

This time, her heart guided her, not her mind. She reached up to brush away the lock of hair from his forehead. "I don't suppose it could hurt to get to know each other better," she answered in a soft voice.

His hand darted up to take hold of her hand again and bring it to his lips.

Her hand trembled in his, like her lungs as they expelled a breath of air.

"Do you have many secrets, Miss Laurel Carrington?" He kissed each of her fingers.

She licked her lips and gave her head an erratic shake. "No. Do you?"

His eyes sparkled over her fingertips. "Many."

Her heart skipped a beat. She sighed and leaned forward. "I thought you might."

He slipped his arms around her. "I thought you might not."

"I guess you'll be doing most of the talking," she said, attempting to smile.

But Dane cut off the smile, stopped all the talking,

with his lips. Once again she felt a sudden surge of heat whip through her. The heat burned away her resistance, softening her bones till she seemed to melt into his arms. She knew that if she let it go, she would lose all control and that could be dangerous. She would be consumed.

Her head slipped back and she trembled as his lips trailed from her lips down her neck, sending plumes of heat throughout her body. Pulling back with a murmur of surprise, she took deep swallows of air to cool the fire.

"We weren't talking." Laurel reached up to find the pin that was dragging from her mussed hair, but with trembling hands she was getting the amethyst caught in tendrils.

"No." Dane reached out to deftly pluck the jewel from the hair. Handing it to her, he said, "But we were definitely communicating."

She was grateful that the darkness hid her smile. "This is happening so fast. We shouldn't rush things."

"Laurel, we aren't rushing things. Believe me."

"I should go in."

He leaned forward and the look in his eyes was decidedly wolfish. "Yes, you should."

She felt the pull of his desire as though he had her tied to an invisible string that he could tug and she would just slide forward. She jerked back with a final push of will.

"Good night, Dane," she said, lifting the latch, opening the door, and slipping out of the truck.

He was smiling and his eyes were like banked fires. "I'll see you tomorrow night. I plan to play the fiddle, so wear your dancing shoes."

"The summer's solstice!" Suddenly the joy of patching up with Dane, of having a party to look forward to, of simply being young and having a date with a handsome man on a glorious summer's night made her feel giddy with anticipation. She waved good-bye, then spun on her heel and hurried to the small house, turning just in time to catch sight of the red brake lights of Dane's truck bumping down the road and disappearing into the darkness.

What was this feeling expanding in her chest making her feel free and wild, like one of the fairies she was drawing? She didn't want to go inside. She wanted to run in the meadow and dance under the stars! Oh, to-morrow night couldn't come fast enough. Who knew what the fairies might have planned for the night of the magical summer solstice? She laughed aloud, just for the joy of it.

Before the door closed, she heard the echo of her laugh ringing in the woods.

Fifteen

Laurel awoke shivering to finding her comforter kicked off, sheets wrapped around her legs and her nightgown tossed onto the floor. Once again, she was nude. Her woozy mind awakened as she disentangled herself and slowly sat up. Something heavy lay against her breast and, looking down, she was surprised to find the bored stone looped around her neck on the leather string. She wrapped her fingers around it, yawning and blinking, trying to recall when she'd put the necklace on, trying to bring to mind her dream that lingered till dawn.

The same dream that she had most nights of her life. It seemed very real last night, and this morning she felt the memory of it was so close—just there within reach. As though she could reach out to pull back the veil and see it.

He was there. She knew him, the look of him, his scent, the sound of his voice, the touch of his hands on her body. She knew him with every sense of her body. So why couldn't she remember him at dawn? Not remember his beloved face, or even his name. Since arriving at Fallingstar, she'd begun to see through the fog of her dreams a bit more, though the shapes remained blurred and the details shrouded by the mist of memory.

He was more insistent, more demanding since her arrival. But of what? Of some awakening? Of a long-cherished dream coming true?

She squeezed her eyes tight, but as always, the answer was obscured by the haziness of her memory. It was like looking into the pond and not being able to see her own reflection in the rippling water. Groaning with frustration, she lifted the heavy length of hair from her shoulders to the top of her head. A strange lassitude soaked her limbs, leaving her sighing with anticipation for something elusive.

Amor was chirping loudly in his cage in the kitchen, signaling Maybelle's presence. She dropped her hands, sending her hair cascading down her shoulders as a smile chased away her worries. Mornings at Fallingstar were far too busy for lazy ruminations. And such a day it would be, she thought, excitement coursing through her veins. No more thoughts of night dreams. It was the morning of June 21—the summer solstice! She rose and dressed quickly, buttoning her cotton blouse as she hurried down the hall, stopping only to right the tilted picture frames en route.

The kitchen was bustling. Amor and Maybelle were both hopping about with animation, making high trilling noises in their throats as though they were having a heated discussion. The black wood stove was already ablaze and steam billowed from the teapot.

Soon her very own scarlet-colored blend of herbal tea would be brewing. She could almost taste its sweetness. Setting the table for breakfast, she thought how happy she was here, living this simple, idyllic lifestyle. True, the routine of each day was rigorous without the comforts of electricity and plumbing, but it was also peaceful. She could hear the birds and insects call out their morning songs through the open window. She could hear herself think. Funny how the old stresses and pressures of her life in Delaware seemed so far away. In only a short time, Fallingstar had become home.

They were finishing the morning breakfast dishes when they heard Dane's whistle outside the door. Laurel sat straighter in her chair. A moment later he appeared at the door wearing jeans, rolled-up shirtsleeves, and high leather boots, carrying a polished aluminum urn of milk. He entered, ducking his head as always under the low ceilings. His dark hair was wild on his head and his eyes lined with fatigue, but his gaze was sharp as he searched her out immediately, settling on her with a sure and knowing grin teasing the edges of his generous mouth. A blush as bright as her tea stained her cheek as she saw instantly that he was recalling the night before, the kiss, the argument that brought them a step closer rather than further apart. In that flash of communication she felt the punch of it anew. Her hands fumbled at her teacup as she bent her head for a hasty sip.

Amor chirped loudly and Maybelle nodded, seemingly amused.

"You look as though you didn't sleep well last night," she said, stepping forward to collect the urn of milk from his arms.

Dane wouldn't allow Maybelle to carry it and walked past her directly to the pantry. "Wild dreams is all," he replied, setting the milk pail down.

Laurel swung her head around, eyes wide.

"Why, what a coincidence," Maybelle exclaimed with a bit too much lilt in her voice. "Laurel was just telling me about her dreams as well. Seems she's been having them all summer, haven't you, dear?"

Laurel choked on her tea and began coughing, unable to reply. But she didn't miss the eaglelike probe from Dane when she glanced up.

When she caught her breath she sat back in her chair to find three pairs of eyes fixed on her, Maybelle's, Dane's, and even Amor's. "Why are you looking at me like that? I've just had some crazy dreams. I'm in a new environment, in the mountain air, it's to be expected. And besides, I don't recall them anyway."

"Yes dear, I'm sure that's it," Maybelle cooed. "It's just amusing that both of you dream of dancing, is all."

Dane shot Maybelle a suspicious glance. "I never mentioned dancing."

Laurel folded her arms across her chest. "Nor I."

Maybelle's large, opaque eyes blinked several times from under her finely arched brows. "Didn't you? But you must have, at one point or another, or how else might I have known? But it's true, isn't it? You both dreamed of dancing?"

Laurel held her breath as the misty veil opened and she saw herself in her dream, in a place filled with trembling green leaves and dewy blades of grass and bright stars twinkling near a white moon. She was swirling with his arms tight around her, cheek to cheek, hip to hip. She felt again the joy of it, the magic of being with him. Her breath came hard with this first gleaning of her dream and her gaze darted to Dane, searching his face. She found him standing stiffly, studying her as well with questions etched across his features.

"I . . . I don't remember," she stammered out.

Dane simply leaned back against the counter and shrugged noncommittally.

"Well, Elsie was certainly cooperative this morning!" Maybelle said, clearing the air. "She provided a generous portion of milk today for our party. We'll have enough for puddings and a rich trifle." She licked her lips. "But only if we stop chatting and begin our preparations. Come, children, no more dawdling."

"Dawdling?" Dane said, turning a smug face toward Maybelle. "While you two ladies were sipping tea, I've not only milked the cow and fed the animals, including that rascal bear cub of yours, I fetched your eggs to boot. And Elsie wasn't the only one obliging. I've a full two dozen in the cart for you."

"How delightful!" Maybelle exclaimed, clapping her hands. "I'll have to bring the girls some cake."

"Thank you," Laurel said, her eyes shining. It was very like him to think of doing her chores today, when she'd be so busy with the party preparations.

"Well, Laurel," Maybelle said, "we've cakes to bake, puddings to prepare, and flowers to gather. We've not a moment to waste."

"I'll be off then." Dane's gaze searched out Laurel. "I'll be bringing the fiddle, don't forget. I don't know about dreams, but I intend to dance with you tonight." He flashed a grin that sent Laurel's toes curling in her shoes.

Maybelle caught Dane's sleeve as he turned to leave, tugging him back. "Dane," she said with her eyes entreating, "do tell Daphne to come. I'll not accept any of her excuses today. I expect her here at twilight without fail. Tell her it's a command performance!"

Maybelle paused as her face softened. "Tell her," Maybelle said softly, "that I said *please*."

Maybelle and Laurel spent the entire day in preparations. Puffs of gray smoke spiraled in the clear blue sky all morning while Laurel baked sponge cakes and dozens of lady fingers for the trifle in the woodburning stove. While she baked, Maybelle scoured the woods for wildflowers. Laurel was just setting the last cake on the windowsill to cool when she caught sight of Maybelle crossing the meadow, her hair wrapped in a colorful scarf and her large basket spilling over with countless flowers. Vincit whined in his pen when he spied her, eager to be released to race across the gardens to meet her.

As the afternoon wound down and the party lay in readiness, Laurel and Maybelle each took a luxurious scented bath, well worth the several trips back and forth from the stove as they hauled warm water to their tubs. Laurel sunk low into her claw-footed tub, relishing the scent of mountain laurel as the hot water enveloped her.

She'd never had such day, never known such excitement in preparing a party. She'd read about such things, heard talk of the heady thrill of dressing up for a special occasion, but had told herself it was just another fairy tale. Now she knew it was not. The magic was in knowing how to make the fairy tale a reality. Maybelle had shown her how one person's determination for joy could change an ordinary day into something extraordinary.

Stepping from the bath, she stood before the open window and allowed the warm air of the first night of summer to dry her skin while she breathed deeply. Her skin tingled with anticipation and she couldn't explain why each nerve felt so alive, or why she bubbled inside with joy, or why she had the strange urge to run outside as naked and wild as a creature of the forest to dance in the meadow. It took all her willpower to step away from the window and not clamber out.

Maybelle had told her that Midsummer's Eve, when the earth had reached the midpoint on her journey around the sun, was a night of magic. It was a time of betwixt and between, a favorite time of revelry for the fairy kingdom.

She felt it had to be true. The magic felt so close tonight.

She went to the bureau to pick up her brush and stand before the mirror. Her skin was pink from her bath and the cool white of the bored stone appeared lustrous between her breasts. She reached up to touch it, marveling at the transformation she'd undergone in a month's time. Her body had rounded out to curve at the right places, and hard physical labor had defined her muscles to erase the image of a scrawny young girl and replace it with that of a lovely woman.

Nothing had changed as much as her hair, however. What was once a short mass of thick, unruly curls had grown out into a long mane that cascaded past her shoulders in golden waves. It was as if Maybelle was right, that her hair was an outward symbol of all the changes that were going on inside her head as well. For she *was* changing, growing in so many ways.

A knock at the front door drew her out of her reverie. She set down the brush and slipped into her robe before hurrying through the hall to answer the door before Maybelle was disturbed from her afternoon nap. She was surprised to find Daphne at the threshold, her face drawn and guarded.

Laurel tightened the robe at her neck against the chill of the gaze and felt her own shoulders, soft as butter a moment ago, begin to stiffen. They stared at each other a moment, each waiting for the other to speak. Laurel's stubbornness won out.

"I got word to show up at twilight or else," Daphne said begrudgingly. "So here I am."

"Maybelle will be glad to see you," she replied in a tone that implied only the older woman was pleased.

Daphne's brown eyes narrowed. "Aren't you going to let me in?"

Laurel stepped aside, holding the door open while Daphne passed by without comment into the front room. She tossed her hat onto the chair with the familiarity of someone who had lived here. When she passed the sofa, however, she stopped and placed her hands on her hips.

"Well, well, well, what have we got here?" she said. "Looks like Maybelle's magic fingers have been busy." Her words may have been sarcastic but the tone of her voice and her expression reflected her awe.

Laurel crossed the room to stand beside Daphne. There on the sofa were three neatly folded dresses, one white, one rose, one gold. Each was made of the softest gauzy fabric, and lying on top of each gown was a beguiling wreath of fresh flowers entwined with ribbons to match the color of the dress.

Laurel reached out to finger the flimsy rose gown trimmed with lace as fine as a spider's web. "She spent hours every night for weeks bent over these. She practically had her nose to the fabric to see clearly enough."

Daphne bent to finger the fabric of the gold dress between her fingers. The fabric was so fine it caught on the rough calluses of her hand. "It's so soft," she murmured.

"She's amazing, isn't she? Her love of beauty shows in everything she does, not just her painting."

"Did she make those cute little butter molds? The ones with the fairy and toadstools? I used to love those as a child. It killed me to cut into them."

Laurel nodded and smiled. "And you should see the picnic. She's packed up her best china, the ones with the hand-painted flowers, and a snowy white linen tablecloth and napkins. She makes everything so special. I wish I could be more like her."

Daphne let the fabric slip away. "Not me. I'm not like her at all. And I can't wear anything frilly like that."

"Why not? I think you'll look lovely in it. The color suits you."

Daphne snorted and wiped her nose more for show than need. "In case you haven't noticed, I'm not exactly the frilly type. I wouldn't be caught dead in something like this."

"You don't have to be any type to wear the dress," Laurel replied with a chilly smile. "Just kindhearted. Maybelle went to a lot of trouble to make this for you and the least you could do is wear it in the woods. At night. In the dark, where no one else will see you."

With an equally chilly smile, Daphne replied, "So now *you're* protecting Maybelle as well? You and Dane make quite a pair. He chewed me out to come, and now you're chewing me out to wear this frilly dress. I suppose if I wait a moment, Maybelle will come out and chew me out till I agree to do something else."

"Nothing much, dear," came Maybelle's voice from behind them. The girls started and turned their heads to find Maybelle standing there, rosy from her bath and her hair still damp at the edges. "But a bath would be lovely for you, don't you think? Laurel and I have already finished ours, and I've already poured hot water in the bath in your old room. I added lilac scent. That's still your favorite, isn't it?"

Daphne's shoulders slumped in defeat and she closed her eyes as tight as her lips. "I should've known," she said on a sigh. Then, opening them again, she fixed Maybelle with a wicked grin on her face that reflected love, not anger. "And next I suppose you'll be wanting to stick all sorts of pins and clasps in my hair too?"

"Only if you insist, my dear," she replied guilelessly. "After all, there are the flower wreaths."

An hour later they each emerged from their rooms dressed in long, diaphanous gowns worn in airy layers. The fabric gathered tightly under their breasts to accentuate their fullness, then tapered down the arms to drape at the wrists and flow in the wind. Maybelle was resplendent in the white gown trimmed with seed pearls. Her silvery hair was wound in multiple braids gathered

around her head and crowned with a wreath of spectacular white roses and more seed pearls.

Laurel's alabaster skin was complimented by the rosy
gown trimmed with feathery lace through which the out-
line of her slender form was discernible. She wore her
hair long and loose with tiny plaits gathered around her
head and adorned with a wreath of tender blush roses.
In contrast, Daphne was striking in shimmering gold
with a bold tapestry trim. Her red hair was a riot of curls
and waves temporarily tamed by a ring of brilliant yellow roses.

"We are the three Graces," Maybelle said, putting out
her hands. "Come, join hands."

Laurel and Daphne glanced at each other with reproach, neither of them willing to make the first move.

"Come, children, we must be united tonight for the
magic to work. Come." She dangled her fingers impatiently.

Laurel stepped forward to take Maybelle's hand. Encouraged by the gratitude in Maybelle's eyes, she stuck
out her left hand in invitation to Daphne. After a reluctant pause, Daphne lifted her chin and with elegant carriage, stepped forward to take both their hands in hers,
uniting them in a circle.

Maybelle glowed with happiness. "Tonight is a night
for enchantment," she announced. "There can be no
room in our hearts for anger or hatred or distrust. Only
love." She squeezed their hands and looked at one, then
the other. "I love you both, so very much. I want so
much for you both to be happy."

Laurel felt moisture threaten her eyes and, looking at
Daphne, was stunned to see her brown eyes tear up as
well.

"Now it is time to begin our journey to the site of the
celebration. Dane will have everything at the ready. We
shall feast and drink and dance. It will be a night we'll
never forget!"

Maybelle led them like a high priestess in a solemn
procession through the profusion of violets and blues of
the iris, bachelor's buttons and speedwell. Vincit tagged

along, following Laurel closely in his leather leash wreathed with flowers. Laurel felt a quickening in her heart as she approached the barrier of the deep woods. Tentatively, she placed a foot in the threshold where scrubby grass changed to mulched earth and the light changed to dark. Another step and she was inside what felt like the fairy bowers. The air was tense, as though countless eyes watched her every move. She took a deep breath to steady her nerves when she heard a soft voice whisper her name. Her breath sucked in while she listened, turning her head to see the branches move above. Vincit tugged at the leash, eager to follow the other women into the trees.

"Don't stand there!" Maybelle called back. "That's a portal, an intersection where two worlds intersect. Powerful forces are at play today and there's mischief afoot! Come quickly forward! And mind your hem, the branches are apt to snag!"

Laurel took hold of a fistful of fabric, lifted her skirt and hastened forward, soon enveloped in the dense forest. Instantly, the air felt different, smelled different, *was* different. Her senses tingled with vibrations of energy as though she'd been plugged into some power source. And, as always, she had the feeling that she was being watched.

"Come, Vincit," she called to the cub, and quickened her pace to catch up to the other two women, staying close.

Deeper and deeper into the woods they journeyed, far beyond the point Dane had taken her. Yet she wasn't the least bit tired and she realized with a ripple of satisfaction how much more fit she must be now in comparison to when she'd arrived. They wound in and around trees, across steep slopes, and past countless burrows and dens of woodland animals. After a long trek, Maybelle turned and informed them that they were almost there.

Laurel felt her excitement build with her curiosity. Just ahead she could see a clearing and she breathed, "At last!"—not because she was weary, but because she was anxious to begin the festivities, and most of all, to see Dane. He had been in her thoughts all day—while she baked the cakes and stirred custard, as she soaked in the scented tub, and while she languorously stroked her hair.

They passed through a green veil of shimmering leaves into a secluded meadow dominated by a pond and surrounded by ancient trees that stood tall and dignified, like pillars around an amphitheater. The shimmering waters of the pond were a mirror to the sky, reflecting the varying hues of blue. Wisps of mist swirled over the expanse of water and in the fertile green surrounding it, Laurel saw touches of gold and pink and white. Her heart fluttered in wonder as she walked out from the dark woods into the sylvan tranquillity, imagining how she might paint it.

The high, sweet song of a violin sang out across the valley. Laurel turned toward the music and saw Dane standing on a level bit of ground not far from the pond. A violin was clamped between his shoulder and chin, and his long arm moved in a rhythmic motion, back and forth, across the instrument. He was playing Debussy's Nocturnes, a haunting theme. How did he know it was a favorite? Dane's eyes were fixed on her and she smiled, feeling their connection across the field of grass.

A firm tug on the leash jerked her attention and in a flash, Vincit burst from her hold and ambled off toward the table and the baskets of food. Laughing, she went to join Maybelle and Daphne at the long table that Dane had already set up for them beside the pond. A number of baskets clustered nearby, and beyond the white horse nibbled the soft grass in the shade. It was short work for the women to drape the table in Maybelle's crisp white linen, set the four place settings of china, arrange candles in small, polished silver lanterns, and begin to unload the bountiful feast.

Laurel brought Dane a glass of the ale that had been cooling in the pond. He set aside his violin and took it gratefully.

"You look beautiful," he said. He took a long swallow, finishing it in short order and handing her back the glass. Then, after a quick wipe of his upper lip, he bent low to her ear, so close she could feel his lips move against the fine hairs of her head. "I could feast my eyes on you and that would be enough."

She felt a shiver of pleasure, but replied with a light laugh, "That won't be necessary, I'm sure. We've more food than we can possibly eat for dinner and we're counting on you to prevent us from carting it all back. You look quite handsome yourself," she added, looking over his flowing, cream satin shirt. It gathered at the neck and cuffs with a modest flair of ruffles, revealing a glimpse of his broad, tanned chest.

"Thanks to you, I'm revived. What shall I play?" he asked, lifting the violin to his shoulder once again. "Something a bit more lively, perhaps?" With a wink, he broke into a reel. His fingers flew up and down his instrument and she couldn't keep her feet from tapping.

Maybelle came over to link arms and dance with Laurel in the soft grass. They twirled their skirts around them in a carefree manner. As before, butterflies fluttered near, making the dance all the more joyous. Laurel spotted Daphne standing in the shadow of an elder tree watching them with a pained expression on her face. Laurel knew that kind of pain and hurried over to grab Daphne's hands and pull her into the dance.

"I can't dance," she complained, tugging back. "I don't know how."

"Neither can I! Come on, no one could be more left-footed than me. We'll just pretend we know how," Laurel replied, holding fast to Daphne's hands.

Maybelle came to take Daphne's other hand and urge her. Daphne feigned reluctance but she wasn't fooling anyone. Secretly she was delighted to be forced into the fun. While Dane played on, the three women joined hands in a circle again. Slowly at first, then faster, they swirled round and round while the butterflies fluttered overhead. There was a freedom in their movements and in the way they lifted their faces to laugh into the sun.

Laurel felt something shift between herself and Daphne, and looking at her, she knew that Daphne felt it too. Her eyes, so much like Dane's, lost their wariness and sparkled.

The reel ended, making them all laughingly catch their breath in dizzy gasps. Maybelle wandered off to stand by the pond and stare out in solitude. Laurel turned to catch the gazes of Dane and Daphne. Dane came up behind Laurel and silently slipped his arm around her waist.

"She'll be all right," he said. "It's twilight."

Laurel nodded and leaned against his chest.

"Dance with me," he said.

She turned her head, surprised. "But there's no music."

"No matter," he said, turning her around and drawing her closer.

"I don't know how. I . . . can't," she stammered.

"You can't break a promise," Daphne exclaimed. "Now go on out there and dance with him."

Dane's face registered his disbelief at hearing his sister encourage him to pay court to Laurel.

"I'm not very good," Laurel said, her hands grasping her skirt and lifting it from the grass. "I really don't know how to dance."

"I do," he replied, stepping closer.

"I seem to remember someone telling me to pretend," Daphne called out in a gentle tease.

She felt his arm slip around her waist and with his other, he lifted her palm up to his shoulder. His eyes held hers as securely. "Now follow my lead . . . and breathe."

He moved to the left, and she to the right, tripping over her long hem. "I can't," she hedged. "I'm too clumsy."

"Again," he said in his calm, resolute voice.

He repositioned his hand at her waist and took another step to the left. This time she followed him. He stepped again, and she followed, tripping on his toe. Then again, counting out, "One, two, three. One, two, three," in a steady beat. She felt awkward, as stiff as a board in his arms, but he wouldn't slow down or release her or give her the chance to back off with a quick, "Thank you, that was lovely."

Then, in the background, a piercingly clear voice began to sing in a high soprano. Laurel turned her head in surprise to see Daphne standing still and straight, legs together and her face lifted to the sky, opening her heart in song in a voice as pure and stirring as a canary at full throat. The sight of her singing solo, dressed in her filmy golden gown with her wild red hair flowing in the breeze was mesmerizing. She was exquisite.

Dane's hold tightened and he held her closer to him as he matched the pace of their dance to Daphne's song. Around and around they waltzed across the soft grass of the valley as the sky darkened around them. If she looked into his eyes and stopped thinking of the timing or the steps and just let go, she fell into a natural rhythm with Dane. It was impossible, she knew, but she felt as though she'd danced with him a thousand times before.

Dane's eyes bore into hers, searching, wondering, and she knew he was experiencing the same sense of déjà-vu. The song ended too soon, just as they were beginning to click and dance in sync. They stood for a moment looking into each others eyes, each silently asking, *did you feel it too*?

"The summer solstice feast awaits us!" Maybelle called out, drawing the three of them to the table.

Dane led Laurel to the table and pulled out her chair, then the chairs of the other two women, taking the seat opposite hers. Maybelle served the plates full and they laughed and chatted while they ate, without any hesitation or reserve. Even Daphne dropped her mask of indifference and for the first time Laurel saw the humor and kindness that endeared her to Dane and Maybelle.

When the meal was ended, darkness deepened around them like a misty veil. The violin music was replaced by a thrumming chorus of peepers and insects. Overhead the full moon had emerged brilliant and victorious while nearby, Venus pulsed. The pond altered in the moonlight, too, changing to a silvery expanse that seemed boundless to the eye.

"Come, children," Maybelle said, rising to a stand. "The summer solstice is a magical time for having wishes granted, especially for affairs of the heart. Tonight, lovers around the world are sending their hopes and dreams to the stars. Let's join them."

Laurel cast a furtive glance at Dane.

He arched a brow suggestively.

"You all go on and have a good time," Daphne said with a hint of sarcasm. "I'll hang around here. I don't have any wishes for affairs of the heart."

Maybelle offered her a knowing look and said, "The solstice is a night for purification as well. If there is something that bothers you, you can seek resolution."

Daphne paled in the moonlight.

Maybelle bent to retrieve four torches from the basket by her seat. She lit them one by one in a ceremonious manner and handed one to each of them.

Laurel held hers before her with her eyes wide.

"It is time to make known our wishes. Dane, please bring out the little rafts you constructed," Maybelle went on. "Laurel, could you bring the extra cake and some candles? And Daphne, you'll need the jar of honey and a piece of paper and a pen. Hurry, children, follow me to the pond. The fairies are expecting us. I can feel it!"

Oddly enough, as she scrambled to collect the small sponge-cream cake they'd lovingly decorated with wildflowers, Laurel felt it too. She'd felt the presence of the Others since she entered the forest, but now, in this place, in the moonlight, their presence was tangible.

Maybelle led them in a torchlight procession to where the pond emptied out to a smallish brook. Laurel realized that this was the beginning of the same brook she had knelt at the other night. A ribbon of moonlight seemed to flow without break from the sky right into the pond to ramble down the mountain in the water. At the pond's edge, they each received a small boatlike raft made of twigs and were told to put a small candle in each one.

Maybelle went to Laurel, then Daphne, and plucked roses from the wreaths around their head.

"It's a very simple procedure," Maybelle told them all. "First, you must make a wish. Then, transport your wish from your mind to the rose with a kiss." She closed her eyes and after a brief pause, bent her head to kiss a rose. "That is all there is to it. But remember, the wish must come from the heart." She handed them each a rose.

Laurel noticed that she gave Dane one of her own blush roses with a secret smile. It was a sweet enough game, Laurel thought, as she fingered the delicate rose in her hand. Love and kisses and roses—harmless enough. Then why did she feel it was of such import? She chewed her lip, unsure of what to wish for. Affairs of the heart? What if her heart was confused? What did she dare wish for? She sneaked another glance at Dane in time to see him bring the rose to his lips.

He was quick enough with his decision. How like him. She wished it was as simple for her. Glancing over at Daphne, she saw her tossing the rose in her hand like a baseball. It was pretty clear there was no war raging in that particular heart. When she looked over at Maybelle, however, she saw with a start that her strange eyes were focused on her.

The wish must come from the heart, she had said. But what if she didn't know her heart?

She released a sigh and decided that instead of a name of a lover, she would wish for insight. She closed her eyes. "If there is magic out there," she said silently, moving her lips, "then I wish for some magic that would enlighten me. Please, I wish to know my own heart."

While Laurel made her wish, Maybelle went to Daphne's side and deftly caught the careless toss of the rose in midair. Taking her arm, Maybelle walked her a few feet away to offer her the privacy of distance.

"Daphne," she said gently, "I know something troubles you very deeply and I'm pained for you. Don't toss away this opportunity. Write whatever it is that bothers you on this piece of paper. Quickly, while it's fresh in your mind. Do it, and you'll feel better. I promise."

Daphne frowned, unsure of whether she wanted to play one of Maybelle's mystic games. This was all very well for fun and feasting, but when it came to serious belief, she wasn't eager to be part of it.

And yet, the pain of her dreadful secret was digging deeper each day. She could hardly breathe for the pain it caused her. Perhaps if she wrote it down, just put the words on paper, then some of the pressure would be released and she could think clearly and find a solution out of this trap she found herself in.

"What the hell," she muttered. "It can't hurt." She took the pen and paper from Maybelle and scribbled on the piece of paper her secret: that she had sold her soul for the insurance money.

"Ready?" Maybelle asked, her head turned away so as not to pry.

"Yes," Daphne replied, subdued.

"Good." Maybelle faced her again, her face sympathetic. "Now give me your hand. Hold your breath." Quick as a wink, Maybelle stuck Daphne's finger tip with a pin.

"Damn!" Daphne cried out, and tried to tug her hand back.

"No, mustn't touch it. Squeeze out a drop of blood onto the note. One drop should do it."

Daphne grumbled to herself that if she'd known blood would be drawn she wouldn't have done it. But in for a penny, in for a pound, she figured, so she squeezed the drop of blood onto the paper.

"You certainly have your dramatic moments," she said to Maybelle.

"Do you think so?" she replied guilelessly, handing Daphne a jar of her honey. "Now if you'll smear the note with honey, you'll be finished. No, don't ask why, it's far too complicated to explain now. Just do it, then fold the paper and place it in your raft beside your rose."

"What are they doing over there?" Laurel asked Dane. They were watching Daphne and Maybelle huddled together a few yards beyond them.

"I don't know. My guess is that it's unlikely my little sister has any love affair she needs help with. Maybelle is probably offering her some other spell so she can join in the fun."

"So that's what you think this is? Just some fun?" she asked. Laurel wanted him to say yes, that he was just humoring the older woman. Yet she knew in her heart she'd be disappointed if he did.

"I think that there are many unexplained mysteries in the universe," he said seriously. "All ceremonies serve a purpose. If only to cement a commitment or a belief in the mind and heart of those who participate." He leaned closer and, pinning her with a look laden with promise, he added, "I have no need of these ceremonies, if that's what you're asking. I know my wish." He raised the single blush rose in his palm to her eye level. It seemed so small and fragile in his large hand. "I know the affair of my heart."

"Dane . . ."

"All ready now?" Maybelle called out as she walked to the table. "Now there's one more step of our ritual, but an important one. Gather near, and bring your roses." She lifted a crystal decanter of her homemade wine from the table.

"Nectar!" Daphne breathed.

Dane said nothing, but Laurel sensed that he was caught unawares. He turned his head and she saw that he was impressed. She'd heard that Maybelle's nectar wine, as painstakingly derived from the blossoms of wildflowers as the essence of any perfume, was reserved for only the most special of occasions.

"Hold the roses in your hands and don't spill," she said. With a gracious solemnity, Maybelle poured a small amount of the amber colored wine into each rose blossom. "Now drink!"

Daphne and Dane drank theirs readily. Laurel looked at the liquid that cupped in her rose like dew with speculation.

"It is like a fine cognac," Maybelle said with a gentle laugh. "Quite delicious."

Laurel sniffed and caught the intoxicating scent of flowers, as fine as the rarest perfume. She brought the rose to her lips, tilted her head and with a fateful sigh, sipped. The nectar was indeed like cognac. It was perfumy and sweet and slid down her throat with a dry, tingling heat. It was wonderful.

"Well, then, let's proceed, shall we?" Maybelle said with a clap of her hands. "You may place your roses into your rafts and light the candles. Dane, could you please bring me the cake?"

"Which one?" he asked with a teasing grin.

"Don't be impertinent," she replied with a sentimental slap. "You know very well which one. The small white one with lattice decoration and all the wildflowers on it. Laurel spent hours decorating it."

He chuckled and did so, placing the cake onto the large raft. This cake was to be sent along with their wishes as their gift to the fairies. Reaching up, Maybelle plucked a white rose from her own wreath, then bent to place it in the center of a ring of white candles. They then took turns lighting the small candles in each boat.

Maybelle straightened and moved to stand at the highest edge of the pond. In the silver moonlight she appeared wraithlike. The whiteness of her gown and roses around her head shimmered with a luminescence. Maybelle stood quiet and still with her eyes closed for some time, as one in prayer. When she opened them again, her strange eyes appeared even more opaque, shining like twin moons. Maybelle then picked up a strip of birch and held it ceremoniously out over the small flotilla of rafts.

"We gather tonight to celebrate the summer solstice!" her voice rang out. "On this, the shortest night of the year, we stand at the threshold of illumination. We welcome all those who will help us on our journey to understanding."

She lifted the wand high into the air. Laurel didn't know if it was her imagination or the wine, but the fireflies seemed to be gathering closer from the pond and circling around Maybelle's outstretched hands.

"We gather together in the garden of shimmering delights," she continued in her melodic voice, "knowing that you are listening. We gather together in the hope that you will grant our wishes tonight."

She lowered her hands and smiled at each of them sweetly. "Now send your wish home."

Laurel joined the others in bending low to the edge of the pond. It was a surprisingly emotional moment. She told herself it was the moonlight and talk of magic, but she felt a surge of hope as she gave her little raft of twigs a shove and sent it on its way. They stood together on the bank and watched the pretty sight of the candlelit rafts reflected in the pond with their honor guard of fireflies. They slowly bobbed in the gentle current, bumbling over the smooth pebbles on their way down the brook. The current picked up as the mountain dipped and in a short while, the soft glow of lights disappeared into the darkness.

Dane came to stand beside Laurel, placing his hand on her shoulder. Daphne wrapped her arms around herself and stood apart while tears flowed down her cheeks. In the distance, Maybelle stood by the pond surrounded by dozens of glowing lights.

With a secret smile, she watched the gentle unfolding of the wishes of her beloved young ones.

Sixteen

Omni hooted outside her window.

"Yes, I'm coming," Laurel replied with a yawn as she pulled back her down blanket. Her head swirled and her body felt strangely light. She wasn't quite awake as she rose from her bed. She felt as though she were somewhere betwixt and between, as Maybelle would say.

From the kitchen, she heard Amor chirping excitedly. Laurel blinked in a sleepy stupor and turned to look outside her window. The moon shone bright and full in the inky black sky. It was still night, she realized. She remembered the long journey home from the pond, slipping out of her gown and crawling into the warmth of her bed. Why would Amor be chirping as though it were dawn?

Suddenly, a light flashed by her head. Her eyes snapped open and, swinging her head sharply, she caught sight of a bright light flying out her window. She rushed to the window to follow it, grasping the sill to lean far out. In the garden, she saw several more glowing lights, larger and more bright than fireflies, all heading toward the meadow in an erratic, even joyous, pattern. Omni hooted again, three insistent cries, and in the kitchen, Amor's chirping escalated in excitement. Her heart began to beat wildly in her chest. Something strange was happening tonight.

"Maybelle?" she called out, hurrying out from her room up the short flight of stairs to Maybelle's room. "Maybelle?" She rapped at her bedroom door. There was no answer. Very quietly, Laurel pushed open the door to peer inside. Moonlight poured in from the large circular window, bathing Maybelle's room in a silvery light.

"Maybelle?" she called again as she tiptoed into the room. She'd never been in Maybelle's bedroom before, and she held her breath lest she disturb her. An elegantly curved wooden desk sat before the enormous window. On it were several pieces of paper, a few small boxes of assorted sizes, and a feather pen in a silver stand. The whimsical bed was made of cut tree limbs with its branches bent and twined to form a curved canopy. And it was empty.

A glow of lights outside the window drew her attention. Curious, she walked closer to look out at the marvelous view of the meadow and the woods further beyond that this higher vantage point provided. Her eyes widened and her breath caught in her throat.

"I must be dreaming," she thought, blinking hard and bringing her hands to her cheeks.

For out in the meadow she saw a sight that defied logical description. The meadow itself was like a stage, engulfed in a condensed cloud and illuminated in a silvery light so bright it could have been midafternoon. The moon cast a magical tint to the shimmering leaves and grass, reflecting the dew like thousands of tiny diamonds.

In the center of the meadow, dancing in the moonlight, was a young woman, a woman more lovely than any she had ever seen before. Her limbs were bare; her hair was long down her back and swirled around her as she gracefully danced, as silver and as flowing as the moonlight itself. She seemed otherworldly, a sylph, so free and uninhibited was her joy and complete absence of self-consciousness as she danced with the dozens of white lights that surrounded her like pulsating stars.

Laurel placed her hand on the window glass and pressed closer. She felt drawn to the woman, drawn to the meadow. While she watched, the woman slowly stopped dancing and faced the window to stare up at her, motionless. Laurel's breath hitched and she drew back sharply, suddenly aware that the woman knew that she was up there, spying. In a graceful movement, the woman reached out her hand and beckoned.

Suddenly the room was filled with the lights of dozens of small opalescent beings, one more beautiful than the next, shining in every color. They sparkled and shimmered with an almost transparent shine, and Laurel knew with a rush of joy what she was seeing.

"Fairies," she exclaimed, and she was filled with a radiance that lit up heart and mind. She was surrounded by the musical sound of silvery bells as they swirled around her, gently urging, guiding her out from the room, down the stairs, and toward the open door. Laurel felt light and giddy, slipping off her nightgown as she glided across the grass, still wet with dew.

This may be a dream, she thought, but it seemed more a shimmering reality than anything she'd ever experienced.

The woman in the meadow awaited her, smiling with a tenderness and sweetness that was dazzling. As she drew near Laurel could not take her eyes from the woman's smooth, unlined face and her large, slanted green eyes, illuminated in the moonlight. She was compelled to go closer.

"Laurel," the woman said in a musical voice, holding out her hand.

Laurel reached out to touch the hand and felt a flow of energy surge through her like the one she'd felt in the brook. It sparked a memory deep in the farthest regions of her mind. She felt the heat of tears flow down her cheeks as she smiled into the woman's face.

"Mother," she replied.

Dane was roused from a deep sleep by several sharp pin pricks, like the poking of pins, in his back. Grumbling, he swiped the offenders away and turned on his side.

"Damn," he cursed as he felt another quick stab on his shoulder. He sat bolt upright to scour the area, scowling. He was stunned to find that he was sleeping in the woods. Blinking heavily, he scratched his head in a stupor as he registered the shadowy trees and shrubs that surrounded him. What was he doing here? He didn't remember coming to the woods. The last thing he recalled he was climbing into his bed, thinking of how beautiful Laurel looked in her filmy gown. He mopped his face to waken. *I must've had a bit more to drink than I thought,* he told himself. It had been a long time since he slept on the ground in the woods. He rubbed the sore spots on his back, mumbling, "Damn insects."

He dragged himself up, slapping the dirt from his jeans, when a sudden flash of light crossed his line of vision. He turned his head, eyes squinting, and leaped to follow it as it bobbed wildly through the trees. That was *no* firefly.

He chased it through the dark woods into a fog that suddenly grew so dense he could not see his hand before him. He pushed forward, arms out, hoping to climb out from the valley into clear air. Suddenly he burst through into a mysterious silver-lit meadow where delight reigned. He paused and stood still, his eyes growing wider with a sense of wonder, shaking his head and telling himself that he must be dreaming.

There were many wondrous sights to be seen, but all Dane focused on was the sight of one young woman who danced with a fairy gracefulness to a haunting, deeply sensual music. Her golden hair cascaded like waves down her lovely body as she danced, oblivious to him or anyone else save the small bursts of light that encircled her head like constellations. She was wraithlike, moving her gently rounded hips and slender arms with an unworldly seductiveness.

The other woman dancing with her saw him standing there, transfixed, and beckoned him to join them.

He stepped forward into the magical light with a confident stride. He knew where he was now, was sure of it. He recognized this mist, this music, these wisps of color. He was in his dream, the same one that he'd had for many nights. All this was a dream and he rejoiced in the knowledge, because very soon, he would have Laurel in his arms again.

The woman gently tapped Laurel's shoulder as she stepped aside. Laurel turned and saw him coming toward her. The misty veil that had obscured her dream from her for so many years parted at last and she recognized the man with whom she'd danced each night in this magical meadow. Her heart leaped and she smiled, opening her arms in happy welcome.

"Dane," she said as he approached and took her in his arms. "I should have known all along that it was you."

There were no faulty steps or clumsy movements this time as he led her in a swirling waltz around the meadow. They glided and swirled in circle after dizzying circle with finesse and grace. The glowing lights surrounded them, trailing wisps of color that bound them closer and closer like transparent ribbons. Staring into each other's eyes, they were alone, dancing in the sensual music, two beings locked in a dream.

Not close enough, he knew, as he felt the familiar hunger gnaw at him. Not damn close enough. Each night he tossed in his sweaty bedsheets, aching for the touch of her, the feel of her in his hands. Each morning he awoke with the savage unrequited desire for her, knowing that he'd spent the entire, restless night dreaming of her in his arms. He could smell her, almost taste her on his lips when the light of dawn passed his eyes. And each morning he felt the nagging longing and loneliness that he knew only Laurel could ease.

The love of Laurel.

This was his wish. To have Laurel's love, in body and soul. He wanted her for his own, true, but he wanted her to love him as he loved her—purely, with devotion and without reserve. Surely a union as perfect as that could only be granted by the fairy realm.

The music around them ceased and the shimmering lights around them fluttered about for a moment. She felt a feathery whirring about her head, then the fairies flew off into the distance to appear as twinkling stars in the evening sky. Dane took her hand from his shoulder and brought it to her lips.

Laurel saw in his eyes what was to be and shivered, not in fear but in a delicious anticipation. What was to come was simply the fulfillment of her dreams.

His hand moved to her hair, long and luxurious now, a heavy weight upon her back. He lifted the skein with his hand, then bent to lower his lips to the base of her neck, warm and throbbing where the pulse beat faster.

"I've wanted to kiss you there, from the moment I first saw you. There was so much neck then, and so little hair," he murmured, his lips still along her neck. He inhaled deeply. "And the scent of you is always with me. Mountain laurel."

He let the hair slide between his fingers to fall again down her back. Then, taking her hand again, he led her to a spot under an elder tree, where the grass was as thick and soft and the dense foliage of a lowered bough served as a canopy.

He stretched out on the ground and raised his gaze to her. She stood before him, naked in the moonlight, as pale and still as alabaster. She was so lovely with her slender limbs poised and draped with hair as fine as silk, so perfect with her gently rounded breasts tipped in a rosy pink that rivaled her lips, that he wondered how he dared to think that she would deign to lie with him. But this was a dream, was it not? In a dream, couldn't he claim what he wouldn't dare in reality?

He reached out his hand and smiled in invitation. "Come, Laurel. We've waited too long already."

Slowly, shivering, she lowered to lie beside him. He turned to blanket her nakedness with his body.

"Are you afraid?" he asked, searching her face.

She shook her head. "No."

He didn't quite believe her. Cupping her heart-shaped face in his hands, he lowered his lips to kiss her once, chastely, on the forehead. Then he stretched over her to pick a clover from the grass. With a gentle question in his eyes, he twirled the pink clover by its long stem and asked, "Do you see the petals?"

Her eyes sparkled and her lips twitched, revealing she remembered that day in the garden when he'd helped her with her painting.

"Now close your eyes," he said. Her lids fluttered and closed. As he had once before, he ran the soft petals of the clover from the place on her forehead that he had kissed, around her temple and down her cheeks to her lips. Her full, pink lips curved, revealing a bit of moist tongue that darted out to touch the clover.

He felt the punch of it and took a long steadying breath. With extreme restraint, he dragged the delicate head of clover from her lips down her throat, trailing afterward with gentle kisses. He slowly circled her breasts with the petals, then the delicate bud of her nipple, and heard her suck in her breath when his lips followed the same path. His own hand was trembling, eager to toss away the flower and feel with his own skin the silkiness of her. He held back by force of will, remembering that he wanted it to be slow and gentle with her. For her.

"How does it feel?" he asked, his voice rough with desire.

"Like I'm still dancing," she replied with a soft sigh.

Dane held himself back, satisfying himself with the sight of Laurel, soft and pliant in his arms. He dragged the clover further down her body, over the curve of her hip, down the valley of her abdomen. When the flower teased the gentle hair of her mound, Laurel's long lashes quivered again and she moaned softly, arching her back to wrap her arms around his neck.

He tossed the clover into the dark with a frustrated flick of his wrists. Worthless weed. How could he compare it to the sweet flower that lay before him? He saw her as an opening blossom, more sweet and tender than any he'd ever beheld. He longed to caress her, petal by petal. With a sudden impatience he pulled back to drag the clothes from his body.

She opened her eyes when he pulled away, feeling the cool evening air rush between them. In the dim light she watched him slip the satin shirt off from his head, tousling his hair even more than she had with her hands just moments before. In the darkness his silhouette rose above her as powerful as the mountain that loomed in the distance. His chest was hard and defined, he shoulders broad and straight. When his hands went to his belt she sucked in her breath. She felt bold in this dreamworld, and reached up to touch him. Her fingertips grazed his skin as lightly as a feather. She marveled at how hard he was where she was soft. How firm where she was pliant.

She slowly circled his chest with her fingertip in the same manner that he did with the petals and marveled at how the muscles of his stomach hardened in ridges as she passed over them. Lower her finger traveled to trace again the length of him, as hard and probing as granite, and she smiled wickedly to see him close his eyes with desire.

Dane removed her hand, gently lowered it to the soft grass, holding to it tight. With his free hand he brought her pleasure till she felt dreamy-eyed and floating once again, lost in a swirling mist of a dream.

"Close your eyes and see the blossoms unfold now," he said in a husky whisper. "Petal by petal. Take your time. . . . Look deeper in the center of the blossom. What do you see?"

As once before, Laurel closed her eyes and saw a delicate blossom in her mind. Soft, velvety petals of rosy pink, deepening in the center to a deep magenta. The petals quivered and trembled under the gardener's care, glistening in dew, unfolding petal by petal.

While her eyes were closed she felt him plunge suddenly within her. A deep, piercing, soul-reaching filling that brought a gasp to her lips and sent her arching against him. The outer petals were fluttering wildly now, but the core remained elusive, hidden deeper still.

And deeper still he plunged, again and again, sending her teetering on the edge. Her mind whirled in turmoil but she couldn't rush the delicate petals, despite her pleas. "Hurry, hurry, please, hurry . . ."

He did not, taking his time. "Open, Laurel," he demanded, relentlessly stirring her to the core.

She focused her concentration on that center as the petals eased open with agonizing pleasure. She grew desperate, grasping for them, clawing. But try as she might, she could not open the buds. It was there—just beyond her grasp. She arched high, reaching. He plunged hard and deep. The petals vibrated, convulsed then flung wide, opening fully to him to reveal the exquisite bliss at its core.

She was engulfed in a sweet fragrance that intoxicated her, filling her senses and sending her soaring into the dream lights. She shuddered, fulfilled, then floated effortlessly through a vivid blue-black, coming to rest in the security of Dane's strong arms.

She was awake. She was asleep. She was nestled and secure in that nebulous mist between the two worlds. All her unremembered dreams, all her vague glimpses into the shadowy realm of her unconsciousness led her to one, true awakening.

She loved Dane. Simply. Completely.

She opened her eyes to see several fairies sitting on the canopy of branches, watching and smiling with delight as they showered her with flower petals. Beside her, Dane was asleep, his one leg lying heavily over hers, his arms wrapped possessively around her.

This was her wish, she realized with wonder. To know her own heart.

"Thank you," she whispered to the fairies, her eyelids fluttering. She heard a twittering in the leaves. Nestling closer to Dane, she fell into a deep sleep. The last thing she heard was the sweet song of a violin.

Seventeen

Laurel pried open an eye, then shut it again quickly. She must have overslept, she thought, rising slowly. She made it a few inches before she groaned and reached for her head. It felt like it would spin right off her shoulders. In fact, her stomach was spinning, too. Opening her eyes, she found the room did likewise.

"How much did I drink last night?" she groaned, squeezing her eyes tight. She had some wine with dinner, but not that much. "Oh lord, let me live and I swear I'll never touch the stuff again."

Three brisk and unbearably loud knocks sounded on the door. A second later, it swung wide and Maybelle strode in, as gratingly cheery as the sun.

"Good morning!" she chimed out. "I thought I heard some sign of life in here. Look what I've brought you. Some breakfast in bed. You slept in this morning and I thought you deserved a special treat after such a busy day." She set the tray down on the bureau. "And night," she added briskly.

"Take it away," Laurel groaned, flopping back on her pillow. "Even the smell of those pancakes makes me sick."

"Nonsense. You just need a little tonic. Nectar has this effect on some folks, I'm sorry to say."

"The nectar!" Laurel groaned. "That's what did this to me? Vile potion. I hate it. I never want to even smell it again."

"Don't make such a fuss. You'll find it's quite delicious once you get used to it and well worth the mild headache you might get the following morning."

"I don't have a mild headache. I think I'm dying."

Maybelle was unsympathetic. She bustled about in her usual animated way, picking up the rose gauzy gown from the floor, wrinkled and stained with grass, and her rose wreath, withered and tired. "Come drink your tea," she said, offering her a steamy cup.

Laurel dragged herself to a sitting position and pried open one eye to stare at it. "That's not mine. It's brown."

"I've made you a special remedy. Drink this and you'll soon feel right as rain."

"An antidote, you mean." Laurel took the cup and drank the brew down. It wasn't as sweet as her red concoction, but it had a richer note.

"Did you have a good sleep last night?" Maybelle asked. She had her back to Laurel and was busy folding her clothes into tidy piles.

"I guess," Laurel replied absently, setting the cup down on the tray.

Her hand froze in midair. In a sudden rush, all the memories of the night before burst through the mist and flooded her mind. Music and mists. Dancing and . . . Her hand trembled, shaking the teacup and spilling the final drops of her tea. Could it be possible? Was she remembering her dream? Was it a dream?

She looked down at her nightgown, at her bed. Her hand rose to clasp the bored stone around her neck. All was as it should be. She remembered being nude in her dream, and sleeping in the forest. It had seemed so real . . .

She rose from her bed and walked to stand in front of her window. She didn't see the red-winged blackbird perched by the rain barrel, or the spruces at the crest of the hill. She saw only visions in her mind that were so vivid she blushed just to think of them. Dreams! She had no idea dreams could be so true to life.

"I can't believe it," she said, shaking her head. "I remember my dream! I really do. There was music and . . . fairies. Yes," she said, bringing her hand to her cheek in wonder. "I saw them, in my dream, anyway. How lovely they were, just as I'd imagined they'd be."

"This is such good news," Maybelle replied. "I just knew it would happen. What else do you remember?"

Laurel put her hands to her forehead and closed her eyes. Once again, the mist parted and she saw herself, dancing in a cloud with *him*. Making love with . . .

"Oh, my God," she muttered, her jaw dropping. "I dreamed of Dane." *I always dream of Dane.*

"Our Dane? Really?" Maybelle cocked a brow. "How amusing."

Laurel wrapped her arms around herself, remembering *his* arms. Remembering . . .

She walked to the mirror and stared at her own reflection. She saw a face but it was as blank and empty as the rippling water of the brook. The woman in the mirror with the drab cotton nightgown and sullen face was not her. She raised the bored stone to her eye and squinting, peered through the small hole at her reflection. In her mind's eye she saw herself as she was in her dream. The woman who was spontaneous, joyous, who was so unencumbered by rules and restrictions that she could dance nude under the stars without inhibition. Someone who could love freely and without doubt. *That* was the woman Laurel wanted to be.

Dropping her hand, she turned and said softly, "Tell me about dreams, Maybelle. I don't understand them. Are they merely the mind's playground where curious things happen? Or do they speak to us?"

Maybelle came closer. "Dreams are the bridge between our world and the fairy world, a place where all things are possible. If you journey to the fairy realm, you embark on a journey within yourself."

Laurel listened, sensing that she was on some threshold. Her mind was spinning, no longer from the effects of nectar but with new thoughts and ideas. She was close, so close she felt if she could just reach inside her mind and rummage about she'd find the answer she was looking for at last. How could she bring the answer out of herself?

"Maybelle!" she exclaimed, knowing suddenly what it was she had to do. She began to pace the floor, absently rubbing the bored stone between her fingers as she talked. "I need paint, lots of paint. And a canvas. Not a small one. Not even a four footer. I need a big canvas, the biggest one you've got."

Maybelle's eyes lit up and she tapped her fingers against each other. "Of course. I have all that, in the studio. It's all at your disposal, my dear. You know that."

"I've got to paint. It's the only way I know how to get these feelings out of me. But I must hurry, Maybelle, hurry fast before I lose them."

"Then run, girl, straight to the studio. I'll see that Vincit is fed and the eggs collected. Don't let your inspiration fly away. Run!"

Laurel ran to the studio, her feet flying across the gravel. She was driven by a single-minded focus again, such as she hadn't felt in many months. The kind that enabled her to work for hours without a break on a research project, or write all night long to finish a paper, or stay in the fields searching for a specimen until the last ray of sunshine disappeared on the horizon.

She entered the studio and locked the door behind her. Next she opened the windows wide to the mountain morning air. Then she went straight to the corner where a few weeks ago she'd seen a five-by-four stretched canvas and wondered how Maybelle could ever paint anything to fill it. Dragging the canvas across the studio floor, she wondered to herself if it would be big enough to hold her thoughts.

Laurel painted for hours and hours, past breakfast and lunch, and at the dinner hour she still couldn't stop. She painted with a fury of passion and deliberation that she'd never experienced before—with an inspiration that she didn't understand. What she felt now couldn't be explained or analyzed. Her feelings were tumbling out as fast as shooting stars. She could only paint fast and furious to try to catch them all on canvas before they evaporated into sparkling dust. Her brush dipped into many colors, but mostly blue, of every hue and tone. And silver too. Oh, that silver light! She was having a hard time capturing that strange moonlight. When she struggled too hard, she found the work suffered. Only when she let go did the colors come alive.

The sun outdoors burned as feverishly. The first day of summer was an unusually hot day in the Northeast, with temperatures near 90 degrees. A pall of heat seeped into the studio. Twiggy climbed through the window at midday to curl up in the cane chair to sleep. Apparently it was too hot in the barn or she was fatigued from the demands of her kittens. From time to time she'd lazily raise her head to look at Laurel as if to say, *how can you work on a day like this?*

She continued to paint, barefoot, her hair pulled back in an elastic, still dressed in the nightgown she'd awakened in, splattered now with paint. Beads of sweat formed on her brow and above her lips but she pressed on, oblivious to the world as she dug inside herself. She was driven to work until it was done, however long it took.

Dane walked into the kitchen and promptly banged his head on the wood-beamed ceiling. The stars he saw were not in the least like the ones he'd dreamed of the night before. Those were beautiful and twinkling while these . . . He winced, thinking these were black stars imploding on themselves and would kill him—or did he only wish they would.

"Mind your head," Maybelle said, hurrying to fetch the milk and eggs from his hands. "Ever since you sprouted up in your teens you've have trouble with those beams. Either you have to shrink or I'll have to raise the roof."

"Most likely I'll just have to be more careful," he replied with a pained voice. "Does that bird have to chirp so loud? Can't you put a muzzle on him?"

"He doesn't mean it," she said to Amor, feeding him a bit of lettuce. Then looking askance, she added, "You seem to be a bit worse for the wear this morning."

Dane only grumbled something under his breath and went to pump some water from the well. When the water gushed out he stuck his head under it, sighing mightily when the cold water hit.

"I made a batch of tonic for Laurel. I don't suppose you'd like some too?"

"Does a bear ... Never mind," he said, raising his dripping head and giving it a shake. He reached out to take the towel offered by Maybelle. "I'm just grouchy. Yes, please." The cold water helped, though his head was still pounding like a kettle drum. He rubbed his hair, feeling his head was made of glass, when it registered. "You said Laurel was ailing?" His voice revealed his worry.

"Mmm-hmmm," she replied. "The nectar."

"Ah," he replied, nodding, well aware of the possible side effects for a novice of Maybelle's brew. It had quite a kick. He sometimes got a headache, like this morning's. "I suppose she's still in bed, then. Will she be all right?"

"Oh my, yes. The tonic works wonders. She's up already and at work in the studio. She's all fired up." Maybelle paused to neatly fold the towel Dane handed back to her. "Apparently she had quite a dream last night."

He swung his head around too fast and winced from resulting pain. "A dream?" he croaked. "Laurel remembered her dream?"

"She did. And quite a dream it was, too. Something about fairies, and dancing, and ... Why, I believe she said you were in her dream."

The pounding in Dane's head ceased as he stared, slack-jawed. Laurel dreamed of him? Of dancing with him? But he had had the same dream. How could such a thing be possible? Suddenly the pounding began again in an even more fevered tempo. He brought his palm to his forehead. He couldn't think. God, he could barely breathe.

"Drink up, young man. You'll feel better in minutes."

Dane took the potion gratefully, downing it in a single

gulp. He stood with his hands on hips and stared out the greenhouse window in silence. He was grateful Maybelle knew when to keep silent. After a few minutes, the pounding receded, like the retreat of the marching feet of a thousand soldiers. He sighed with relief and accepted Maybelle's offered glass of water gratefully.

"I dreamed of Laurel last night, too," he said in the air of a confession. "But then again, I always dream of her."

He refrained from telling Maybelle just how vivid last night's dream was. He could have sworn he held her in his arms, made love to her as he'd dreamed of doing for so many nights. Last night he had told her he loved her. And she had loved him in return. It was a simple love story, one told over and over again throughout the millennia. But for him, it was new and fresh and pure. It was because of Laurel. He'd never known he was capable of such love.

And it was all a dream. It made the waking up this morning alone in his bed again all the more painful. His face fell and he rubbed his eyes against the fresh prick of regret. Last night's powerful dream was undoubtedly the effect of the nectar. He raked his hair from his face, relieved that at least the headache was gone.

"I must go," he said, walking over to place a kiss on Maybelle's head. "You looked beautiful last night." He was gratified to see Maybelle's face suffused with pleasure at the compliment. "All my ladies did."

He took a last look around the kitchen, hoping to catch a glimpse of Laurel. The house was quiet and empty. When he stepped outside, he felt as though the only sunshine he craved was housed in the little studio perched on the mountainside.

It wasn't until the sun began to set again and she began to lose the last remnants of her precious light that Laurel's arm dropped to her side.

The heat abated as the evening sky took on hues of pink clouds in a blue sky. A tender summer breeze blew in over the north mountain ridge. Laurel's shoulders slumped as she walked to the chair that Twiggy had vacated. She slid bonelessly into it and propped her feet on another, utterly drained, incapable of thought. If she could have walked, she might have made it as far as her bedroom to clean the paint from her skin and collapse into bed. The possibility of another dream was almost enough to make it worth the supreme effort of rising from the chair.

Knocks sounded on the door again. "May I come in?"

Laurel smiled, and called for Maybelle to come in. She had knocked several times during the day asking if she was hungry, or thirsty, or in need of anything at all. She imagined Maybelle standing at the door, ear pressed.

Sure enough, Maybelle entered carrying a tray laden with cheese and biscuits and fresh salad from the garden. "You simply must have an evening snack," she said with the lilt of hope in her voice. "You haven't eaten a thing all day."

"I'm too exhausted for hunger," she replied, but because Maybelle brought the tray, she added, "but this looks perfect. You were very kind to bring it to me. I'm a big girl, you know. You needn't worry."

"It brings me pleasure to prepare things for you." Maybelle tucked her hands in her apron and walked about the studio, not the least bit discreet about letting her gaze roam the room.

"I suppose you want to see what I've been working on."

"Well, I admit I am a bit curious. You had this wild look in your eyes this morning and you've been locked away all day. Do you mind if I look?"

Laurel took a bite of cheese and shook her head. "Of course not. You're my teacher."

"I'm not," she replied quickly, but walked eagerly toward the large covered canvas. With a quick flip, she tossed the cover over the top then stood back to study the painting.

In the fading light of twilight, the silvers and blues of Laurel's painting took on a mystical glow. Laurel couldn't help but rise to a stand to admire her own work, not due to vanity but because it didn't feel like her own. Despite it being so fresh, she couldn't remember painting those tilting green eyes quite so bright, or the silvery hair to look as though it were a river of starshine. Most of all, she had no idea how she was able to make the woman's eyes so real that she could see the love and tenderness pulsating in them. The work was truly inspired.

Inspired by Maybelle. How could she have known when she began painting the fairy that the image she would create would be her mother's? Or at least as she dreamed of her mother last night. But it made sense, now that she could step back and critique the completed painting. The fairy she'd painted dancing with her in the moonlight had the face of Maybelle Starr. After all, she was the only mother figure she'd ever known.

Maybelle's hands were fluttering at her lips and her chest was heaving with excitement. "I knew it . . . I knew it. . . . I am so fortunate that my sight has lasted long enough to see this. Oh Laurel, I can't begin to tell you how I feel. It's magnificent. Wondrous. It's all I'd hoped for—and more."

Laurel's head swirled with the compliments. Modesty prohibited her from believing it. "Really? You aren't just being kind?"

"Fiddleheads! You know how good this is, you must. The detail in the fairy is exquisite, but most importantly you caught her expression. Why, I'll call my agent and have the contracts drawn up immediately."

"Hold on a minute," Laurel said, putting her hands in an arresting gesture. "I've just painted one painting. I'm not quite ready for all that."

"But whyever not? This proves you have the talent to paint fairies. This is superb, every bit as good, or better than anything I've ever painted myself. The dealers are already pressing for more paintings."

Laurel hesitated, looking from the emotional painting to the emotion on Maybelle's face. "Don't get me wrong. I'm grateful for the offer, I really am. It's just that I'm not quite sure I'm ready to give up my other work, my other life outside of Fallingstar, for a career as an artist. That's too big of a commitment."

"Isn't that why you came?"

The time for the whole truth came, without secret motivations or hidden agendas. She could do nothing now but be totally honest, with Maybelle and with herself. Maybelle gestured for her to sit beside her at the open window. "Let's chat, shall we?"

With a sigh, she came to sit beside her.

"The truth is," Laurel began, "I didn't know what I came for when I first arrived. Of course I wanted to be your apprentice, to learn from you and consider the choices at the end of summer. I was sincere about that." She picked at the paint on her nail. "But you see, I really didn't have a lot of choices, at least none that I was keen for. I was feeling trapped and desperate. I'd set my cap to go to Cornell for graduate school. I was conceited enough to believe I'd get in." She puffed out air. "It was a blow when I didn't."

"There are reasons for such things," Maybelle hastened to interject. "Sometimes fate has other plans."

Laurel shook her head. "No, I have to face the facts. I wasn't good enough." She didn't want to talk about Colin and his proposal. It was too personal, and she realized now, he didn't really have anything to do with the life decision she was making now. "I know it sounds trite, but the main reason I came was not to learn about paint, but about myself."

"Trite? Never, my child. To know thyself is to have magic and power."

"I believe that," she replied, scooting to the edge of her seat. "That's why I had to paint this picture. Last night I had the most wonderful, vivid dream. It is more real to me, more meaningful in so many ways than anything else I've ever experienced. I caught glimpses of myself as I've always wanted to be. Of how I know I can be, if I just try. I knew what real love meant.

"And when I awoke this morning, I was ill, not from the nectar, but from the realization that that experience was just a dream. I was bereft. Adrift. I didn't want to lose touch with the magic I'd experienced, and yet, I don't know how to hold on to it. So I had to paint, to thrash out my confusion in the best way I knew how." She turned to look at the wondrous painting of herself and the younger, more radiant version of Maybelle dancing together with the fairies.

"I think I understand my dream now," she said quietly. "In order for me to know myself, I have to reconcile my relationship with my mother. I never told you this, but I never knew my mother. She abandoned me when I was born." She shrugged lightly, but the hurt still lingered, very deep. "I never heard from her again. Growing up, I tried to pretend it didn't matter. After all, it was she who left without knowing me. I did nothing wrong. But in my bed at night, I'd cry, wondering why I was so lacking that my mother could not love me."

Maybelle's hand reached out to clutch Laurel's tightly. "I'm sure that's not true. Sometimes there are circumstances—"

"No, it's all right," Laurel interrupted. "I'm no longer a child. I need to deal with the truth. I know, really I do, that there was nothing lacking in me. And I'm not looking to blame my mother or hold her up as some evil being responsible for everything that goes wrong in my life. You're probably right. Something may have happened that forced her to make the choice she did. I can accept that now and forgive her. And more importantly for me, I had to accept that in many ways, I am like her." She shook her head.

"You don't know how big that is for me to say. All my life, my father made me believe that to be like my mother was the worst possible defect. She was the embodiment of everything I should strive not to be. With this goal, he rooted out any hint of spontaneity, instinct, or irrational thought. He didn't want me to paint." She saw the horror on Maybelle's face and laughed sadly. "He wasn't some villain. He loved me very much and took the best care of me he knew how. But he was very deeply hurt when my mother left. She didn't just abandon me, don't forget. She abandoned him as well."

Maybelle rose from her chair and went to stand in front of the open window. The breeze lifted the gauzy fabric of her dress at her sleeves, but other than that, she was as still as a statue.

"When I came to Fallingstar . . ." she paused. "When I met you, everything began to change. It's like this person inside of me, this spirit that was dormant for so long, clamored to escape and be heard. Even though I didn't want to let her out because I was afraid of her, terrified of all she represented, because she was so like my mother. I saw this as a fault, remember. Then I heard the bear, and the bees. Things happened here that I can't explain logically, but I see now as gleanings and small gifts. Maybe it's because I'm closer to nature, or that I'm simply paying attention. Maybe it's because we all harbor the spirit of a fairy, somewhere in our soul. But suddenly I see my love of surprises and fancy, my ability to hear nature and the sweet sound of laughter in my head, my lifelong fascination with fairies and elves and all things magical and mystical not as faults or weaknesses, but strengths. Qualities that I should release and celebrate rather than tamp down under the chains of logic and propriety."

She rose and went to stand before the painting. "Don't you see, Maybelle? All those qualities are symbolic of my mother. I had to see my mother before I could see myself. To love her so I could love myself. Look . . ." She gestured toward the painting. "Our hands our joined." A smile flickered across her face as she looked at the face she drew of her mother.

"It's no wonder that she appeared to me in my dream as some form of you, Maybelle. You've shown me more love and maternal tenderness than anyone else I've ever known. You are the mother I never had."

She turned toward Maybelle, who was being uncharacteristically quiet. She was surprised to find her standing with her hands on her cheeks, weeping. She couldn't remember ever seeing Maybelle cry.

"Whatever is the matter?" she asked, hurrying to her side. "Are you all right?"

Maybelle's fingertips stroked her cheeks and she looked at them with amazement, even while nodding her head. "I'm crying!" she exclaimed, shocked. "Look, tears! But I never cry. I don't shed tears. We can't. It's such a human thing to cry." She sniffed and wiped her cheeks, her fingers still trembling. "Something has shifted, I feel it," she said, turning to Laurel, her face shining. "It must be the magic of this painting, the magic that I see so resplendent in you."

She walked to stand before the painting. Clasping her hands before her, she studied it for a while, occasionally tilting her head to catch a detail. Somewhere in the room a bee droned, and from the outdoors she could hear in the silence the distant rumbling of Dane's tractor gathering hay.

"I'd like to tell you a story," she said, her eyes still on the painting. "But first let's pour some tea and sit by the window. Stories are always so much better told and listened to when one is comfortable, don't you think?"

So they sat together on the cane chairs pulled before a small wrought-iron table. They ate cheddar cheese on biscuits and drank sweet mint tea. Twiggy came to join them, jumping through the open window and announcing her arrival with a meow. She settled in Laurel's lap and nibbled a bit of cheese while Maybelle began her story.

"There is a tale among the fairies of an exceptionally beautiful and exceedingly vain fairy whose favorite pastime was to tempt poor mortal men with visions of herself, to make them fall madly in love then leave them without thought or concern. One fateful day, however, this fairy met a handsome mortal who loved her so dearly he named a rare rose after her.

"Flattered, the fairy visited the rose and the gentleman every year when the rose bloomed in midsummer. For several years." She sighed and her eyes sparkled. "Then the unimaginable happened. They fell in love." A smile spread across her face as she grew more animated. "Their love was as passionate and fiery as a falling star. And as doomed."

Laurel couldn't help but be drawn into the story. She leaned forward in her seat, her attention riveted.

"Once their love affair was discovered by the fairy queen, Mab, the fairy was punished for her disobedience in the severest method possible in the fairy world—exile from the fairy troop. The fairy was condemned to give up all that she held dear: her lover, her child, and the world of fae. When the fairy cried out in anguish that this was true love, the fairy queen took pity on the brokenhearted subject. Mab offered her the small consolation of dancing with the fairies each year at Midsummer's Eve. And one chance to break the curse.

"When her child reached adulthood, she would be allowed to reconcile with her child, and meet her lover once again—as she was, older and without her youthful fairy beauty. She would be able to test whether their love was indeed true or glamour. If her mortal lover declared his love for her once again under a blue moon, the curse would be broken."

"Did her lover recognize her?"

"In fairy tales, only a true lover can see past the disfigurement to the real beauty beneath."

"So what happened? How does the story end?"

"I have no ending to the story. How do you wish to see it end?"

Laurel leaned back in her chair and stroked Twiggy's soft fur. She could feel the thrumming purr under her fingers while she thought. She understood why Maybelle told her this fairy tale. It was possible that her mother had no choice but to abandon her. Possible, too, that her mother truly had loved her father.

"I'd like to see it end with the whole family being together again. Happy."

Maybelle's eyes saddened. "That is human thinking, the belief that the family is paramount. In the fairy world, the most important aspect of life is to be one with the troop."

Laurel was appalled. "So if the curse could be broken, the fairy would leave them again? Just go flying back off with the troop? That's horrible. What kind of an ending is that?"

Maybelle's face grew drawn and pensive. "Would the child forgive the mother if she understood?"

Laurel's face clouded and she shook her head. "No. How could she?"

Maybelle reached out to lift the bored stone from Laurel's chest. Raising it to her eye, she peered through it, straight at Laurel, then let it drop again to hang around Laurel's neck.

"Laurel, you are a woman now. Try to see the story from an adult's perspective, not one-dimensionally. Nothing in life is all good, or all bad. Fairies know the course of fate is not always smooth. If you've studied your fairy tales, you would know that all the endings are not happy. But they are moral and just. Isn't that enough?"

"No!" exclaimed Laurel, taking the story to heart. Twiggy jumped from her lap to seek out a more peaceful resting place under the table. "This may just be a fairy tale to you, but it rings too close to my own story for me to accept the pain of my mother leaving me again. That's too sad, too cruel." She rose to walk to the painting and stare at it, strangely comforted by the vision of herself and her mother, holding hands. "I'm sorry, Maybelle, but you're not a mother. You wouldn't understand how a mother feels to hold hands with her daughter again, how important that bond is. I can't believe my mother would leave me a second time." Wrapping her arms tightly around herself, she said, "Besides, it's my dream. It can end any way I want it to."

Laurel never wanted her dreams to end. For the next three weeks, when Laurel awoke in the gray mist of a country dawn, she didn't move in her bed, didn't open her eyes so that she could hang on to the trailing remnants of the dream that still floated in her subconscious. Even as her mind began to focus she put aside her ego and asked the fairies to come to her, to help her visualize a scene or an image that she could paint that day. Oh, and the fairies came to her! In this place between sleep and awakening, this place of betwixt and between, the fairies showed themselves, pulsing into focus in all their glory. They danced in her head, fluttering diaphanous visions as translucent as their wings, spinning origins of ideas as wispy as cobwebs, and illuminating her heart with inspiration.

Laurel painted her dreams. Every day after chores she went directly to the studio to release the fairies in her mind. They arrived on the blank white canvas as bits of color, gradually emerging into shapes and forms with personality and messages. She didn't thank the fairies; Maybelle had told her they disliked maudlin expressions of gratitude. She told Laurel to thank them by spreading the light with joyful living and kindness to others.

So Laurel tried to open her mind and her heart. She took long walks in the woods, listening to the whispers in the trees and the music of the gurgling brook. She learned to look for the fairy world around her, shimmering in a drop of dew, slithering away in the form of a crimson newt, hidden in the twisted convolutions of a rotting tree trunk, shining in a loved one's smile.

Often, Dane would walk with her, holding her hand, taking her down winding paths bordered by wildflowers and along mountain ridges that afforded spectacular views that she might never have discovered on her own. They talked little, preferring to walk in a companionable silence and just listen to the woods, sharing an occasional amused glance or a look of awe. And in the walking, they took steps closer to each other.

It was a quiet time, a period of growth and transformation. As the moon journeyed soundlessly through its phases, Laurel discovered that the world of fae was not something she could find in books or through deliberate searching. She found fairies in the air, water, and earth. In all forms of nature. But nowhere did she see them more illuminated than in her own heart.

Eighteen

Dane was awakened from his sleep by a persistent knocking at his front door. He rose to open it, surprised to find Maybelle standing at the threshold. His senses sharpened. She hadn't stepped foot into this house since his mother had died. The night was deeply dark; it was hours before dawn. Maybelle's hem was soaked with dew, her face was pinched with worry and she wrung her small hands. Mopping his face, he swung open the door and ushered her in.

"Is everything all right?" he asked, his voice scratchy with sleep.

Her small hands fluttered at her lips and she appeared distraught. "Dane, I've been thinking and thinking, going round and round with this. A blue moon is coming. Sooner than I'd expected. The signs were there and I missed them—how could I have been so careless! Time is of the essence. I know what must be done, and it must be done quickly."

"Anything, Maybelle. You know that."

She looked into his eyes and smiled tremulously. He could see the relief soften her face and lower her shoulders.

"I want you to take Laurel to see the roses."

Dane's eyes widened and he was momentarily silenced. "The roses? Are you sure?"

"Yes, quite sure. There's no time for delay. I want you to take her there. Today."

He could not believe his ears. Maybelle had never

allowed anyone to visit the roses, not even the most welcome of visitors. They were her greatest secret. She held them sacred, and in caring for the rare species, he had learned to feel the same about them. Not even Daphne had ever heard of the roses, or the fissure.

But this wasn't just anyone, he realized. This was Laurel. Even he could see the bond between them that was sacred as well.

"All right," he agreed with a solemn expression. "I'll take her there at first light."

Laurel came to breakfast to find Maybelle busily preparing a special picnic lunch.

"No chores today!" she exclaimed while Amor chirped loudly beside her on his highest perch. "Dane is taking you on a special expedition." Maybelle bumped into a chair as she hurried across the kitchen to greet her. "Clumsy me . . ."

Laurel stepped up to kiss Maybelle's cheek. "I love surprises."

Maybelle's face brightened and she cupped Laurel's cheek in her hand. "Do you? Dear child, that is music to my ears."

Laurel was shocked to see tears well up in Maybelle's eyes and it nearly brought some to her own. Recently, Maybelle's eyes moistened at the slightest thing.

"Let me help you squeeze all that into my backpack," she said, turning away, sniffing.

Dane came for her as she finished her hearty breakfast. As always, he filled the door with his presence, and on seeing him, her heart as well. Dane was very much a part of her day, her every waking hour—and her sleeping hours too. She dreamed of him every night, and while not as vivid as that first, unforgettable dream, it was comforting to be in his arms, if only in her mind.

They left together in a festive mood, walking side by side across the meadow at a steady gait. They hiked across familiar terrain while the sun rose high in the sky, but as the morning wore on, all traces of the trail disappeared. They entered a deeper part of the woods she'd never traveled to before. She was dressed for the journey in tough jeans and a long cotton shirt. Her hair was wound like Maybelle's in several plaits close to the head and wrapped with a scarf. Yet the brush scraped and clawed at her clothes and burrs clung to her shirt.

They pushed over a high ridge, then headed down past a bog where the ground grew soggy. They had to step on rocks and fallen timber to escape the mud. Not far beyond they came across a small forest pond, not much more than an oasis surrounded by shadows and spruce. A deer leapt from sight as they approached.

They lunched here on sandwiches and oranges, enjoying the peacefulness of the place and each other's company. It was a short break, just a brief time to rest their legs. Then they were back on their feet, zigzagging across the steep terrain. Up, up, they hiked as they painstakingly made their ascent up the mountain. The woods altered, becoming less scrubby and more open as enormous trees arched above them, creating a canopy of intertwining branches through which the sun dappled. These ancient hardwoods never saw a chainsaw. As she passed through the tall, noble trees she felt the same reverence she would in a cathedral.

They climbed the last yards out of the forest to a grassy knoll high on a cliff. Twenty feet away, the ground seemed to drop away suddenly into a deep ravine. Across it, they faced another steep incline, far fiercer and nobler than the others. A flow of white water tumbled down the cliff in a series of small waterfalls into the ravine. Dane took her hand to steady her.

It was exhilarating to stand perched high at the top of the world. Laurel felt the wind at her back and tugging at her scarf. She had to reach up and hold it while she turned to gawk back at how far they'd journeyed so far. She could see the steep slope of the mountain they'd just climbed and far beyond, the rolling valley dotted with neighboring cows. To the left she could catch half of the barn peeking from behind the foliage. She squeezed Dane's hand, then looked forward again at the sheer face of rock.

"Up?" she asked, disbelieving.

His eyes crinkled and he shook his head and pointed. "Down," he replied.

Holding his hand tight against vertigo, she crept to the edge and peered over the cliff down into the fissure in the earth. It appeared fathomless. The rock wall was covered in patches with green stain and black earth and here and there, bits of purple groundcover. It seemed too deep and menacing for any man, woman, or beast to dare to approach.

"Down in there?" she asked, incredulous.

He locked his arms around her, pulling her close. His dark brown eyes danced with mischief. "I could tell you I was kidnapping you. Tell you I was Hades and you were Persephone, and I was whisking you down into the underworld."

The wind caught her laughter and it echoed around them as she replied, "I would remind you that Persephone's kidnapping plunged the world into winter. Surely a farmer such as yourself wouldn't wish for that."

He warmed to the game, pursing his lips as he conjured his next challenge. "Then I am a fairy king and I've captured you. I intend to lure you through this portal into my magical kingdom. You will live there with me forever, never to return." He tightened his grip and leaned far over her, bringing his face close to hers. "What would you say to that?"

She looked at him with uncertainty. High on this precipice with the sun warm on their faces, the wind swirling around them, and the sound of waterfalls in her ears, she felt again the sense of timelessness and otherworldliness she always felt in his arms. She didn't know what to call this feeling that left her confused and breathless. But if it was magic, then she wanted to believe in it and keep it alive between them forever. She would go anywhere on the earth, or beyond in the realm of dreams or fairies, as long as she was with him.

"I would say I am your captive," she replied with a lilting voice. "Take me where you will."

Though spoken in jest, it was the answer he was hoping for. He took her face in his hands. He looked into the fairy eyes that had enchanted him from the first and he saw the golden treasure he had sought, that long ago he'd stopped believing existed: love. His chest constricted and he lowered his lips to hers in kiss that was all the magic he wanted in his life.

When he pulled back her sigh was as sweet to his ears as the wind whistling high in the treetops. "It is me who is the captive," he said, his voice hoarse with desire. He longed to say more. To blurt out the truth—to tell her that he loved her. He opened his mouth, but she leaned back in his arms and laughed lightly, taking his words as a continuation of the jest. He clamped his mouth shut, cursing himself for a sentimental fool.

"We'd best be on our way," he said, releasing her from his arms and taking hold of her hand. "It's a long, long way down."

He wasn't kidding, she thought to herself several times during the descent. They were climbing down into a narrow fissure of the earth on a path that twisted and turned through a rocky maze. Several times she thought they'd lost their way when they'd come to a wall of granite. Each time he'd squeeze her hand and guide her though a narrow aperture that was invisible to the naked eye. They had to climb over boulders and under slabs of granite that jutted straight out like monoliths.

The light grew faint and gray as they descended into a dark, cavernous area where toadstools thrived and glacial erratics formed bigger than bulldozers. The deeper they climbed, the more the light narrowed as it squeezed through rock, looking more like beams from multiple flashlights than daylight. Her teeth chattered, but she wasn't sure if it was due to the sharp temperature drop, the dank mustiness, or to the excitement as they journeyed into deeper darkness.

Dane kept a tight grip on her hand. She told herself over and over again as they traveled to the bowels of the earth that she might not know what to expect at the end of the trip, but she trusted Dane completely. He moved at the steady, confident pace of a man who knew where he was headed.

"Not too much further," Dane assured her when her knees began to wobble from fatigue. "It's just around the next bend."

They rounded a corner and the decline flattened. With a sigh of relief she saw a circle of light at the end of the long, narrow path. Light! It lightened the heaviness of her fear and she felt a resurgence of energy. A little further and the dank tunnellike feel and musty smell dissipated. Dane's hand clasped around hers as he picked up the pace, eager to reach their destination. She couldn't help but feel the excitement too.

He paused where a veil of ivy fell across the portal, obscuring the view. His were bright with anticipation, like a boy's about ready to show off his prize. "Are you ready?"

Laurel could only nod, not having the slightest idea what it was she'd find beyond the wall of rock. He pushed back the green curtain, tugged her hand, and led her in.

She stepped through the vines, out of the shadows into a large, sun-filled circular arena. Blinking in the brilliant sunlight, she craned her neck, gazing with slack-jawed amazement at how the rock walls narrowed toward the open sky like a hollow volcano. Except instead of poisonous gases and molten lava, what was funneled in through the cone was sparkling sunlight and swirling gusts of air redolent with the overpowering scent of musk roses. Small rivulets of water tumbled cheerily over cragged walls to splash in a green pool with the tinkling sound of bells.

She looked round and round and round in a breathless silence. When her gaze caught sight of the bed of roses, however, her breath sucked in and her knees once again felt watery. Such roses! The bushes clustered in a small, raised garden in the center of the arena. They appeared as the royalty they were, princesses of every color.

She dropped her backpack to the ground and slowly approached them, her hand outstretched, eager to touch.

There was an air of unreality here. This lush garden of roses didn't belong down here in the bowels of the earth. She raised her nose and sniffed the air. It was warm and moist here, as humid as the tropics.

She stopped just feet away from the roses and drew back her hand. "What . . . where are we?" she stammered.

"Maybelle's rose garden."

Her eyes quickly scanned the small enclosure. More roses, ramblers and climbers, creating splashes of pink, yellow, red and white spilled out of cragged rock that served as urns. Some stood as straight and tall as little trees while others crept along the rocky wall with their thorny tendrils, creating the loveliest trellis of blossoms.

Her hands opened and closed at her sides. She didn't know what to think, what to do. Roses? People didn't grow roses in underground fissures! But there they were. A great repository of old roses basking in the warm air and sunlight. But this particular grower was Maybelle Starr. Suddenly, the idea didn't seem so far fetched.

"Why would she go to so much trouble to grow them here? She has marvelous gardens already."

"These are not just any roses. Come, take a look. I think it will all become perfectly clear."

She passed through a patch of lush lavender, releasing the heady scent as her leg brushed the leaves. Ordinarily she might have stopped to appreciate the scent, but her attention was only on the roses. There was a natural, unrepressed, even sensual disorder in them, so unlike the clipped, trained, highly pruned roses of Longfield. She walked among them in awe, reaching out to touch the velvety blossoms in full bloom. On one bush there were smallish pink blossoms of an authentic cupped pattern, and others with larger petals, plump and ruffled of delicate pastels. But there were also blossoms of the darkest, blood-red crimson she'd ever seen and next to it thrived a small shrub with dainty yellow roses with a knot of gold.

"They're all old roses," she said, her voice unsteady. "But . . . I can't place them. Those few with the large blossoms might be remontants, but I don't see evidence of pruning so I can't be sure." She rushed to another, bending low in study. "And this rambler . . . It might be a descendent of Île de France. But I've never seen such gigantic blossoms." She went from plant to plant, making comments and exclamations feeling a heady rush of excited confusion.

Then she saw it. Separated from the others, growing in a small, sheltered raised bed near the pond, surrounded by evenly matched quartz rocks that sparkled in the ray of sunlight like diamonds. It was a dramatic shrine, as natural and mystic as any Druid altar. A spectacular bush that stood proud and regal, unparalleled in beauty, a queen among the roses.

Laurel's hands dropped to her side. "La Belle Rose," she breathed.

"Yes," Dane replied somberly behind her.

This can't be happening, she thought, her head swirling. This had to be another dream. She even pinched herself to make certain.

Walking slowly, dragging her feet, she approached the rose that up till now had lived only in her imagination. She crouched before the rose, reaching out to touch with trembling fingers the flawless, saucer-sized petals of a brilliant, pure white that tinted to blushing pink at the pouting edges. Bringing her nose to the blossom she was engulfed in a fragrant cloud of delicious, heady perfume.

"I never believed she really existed," she said, drawing back to rest on her heels, her eyes still on the rose-bush. "My father spoke of her so often, described the flower so lovingly that I could picture it in my mind. And yet, it was always some dreamy vision, some girlish apparition that I eventually outgrew. I never thought I'd really see it. To be honest, as I grew older, I thought the whole story was nothing more than a lonely man's fantasy." She paused to touch one velvety petal with one fingertip. "And here it is."

"I'm sorry I couldn't tell you about it before. Maybelle is extremely secretive about these roses. They are not merely old, they're ancient. Maybelle is a connoisseur, not an academician. She has a profound knowledge of the field and infallible intuition. I don't know how she came by it, but it doesn't matter. What you see here is undeniably the most prized and rare collection of old, unknown roses ever accumulated."

"But how do they survive the Vermont winters? This is hardly rose country. I'd have thought she'd be in England. Or California."

He lifted his hands. "The fissure. The pools are in actuality hot-water springs. The warm air collects here, mingles with the warm sun to create a greenhouse, perfect for roses."

"A Shangri-La. I've heard of fissures, but in Tibet. Not here in Vermont!"

"Who's to say what secrets lurk in the world?" he asked, his eyes daring her to question him. "This fissure is here. The roses are here."

"They are!" she exclaimed in excitement, her eyes becoming two green flames. "I can't begin to understand the whys or wherefores—but La Belle Rose is here. I must contact my father immediately," she said in a gush. "He'll be so thrilled! It's the miracle he's been waiting for!"

"Tell your father?" Dane was appalled. "No! You can't tell anyone. No one is to know about this garden. Especially not a rose rustler like your father."

"How dare you talk like that about my father?" she said fiercely, taken aback by his vehemence. "He's worked hard and long to preserve roses that would have been lost. Who are you to criticize him—much less to me?"

"I'm the one who preserves these particular roses from men such as your father," he fired back. "I knew you shouldn't have come here. But Maybelle insisted."

"You make it sound as though we are out to destroy the roses."

"Some will, whether they intend to or not. Men like your father have no respect for the past and care only about the future, their own futures. Think, Laurel, what would happen if they saw these roses? Would they enjoy them, marvel at them, perhaps describe them in their books? Would that be enough? Or would they consider them just another resource and come at them with their red-handled clippers shining? I've seen it happen, again and again. As far as they are concerned, resources were put on this earth to exploit." His eyes flared with indignation while he thumbed at his chest. "Well, not on my watch."

She couldn't speak, her angry retort sputtered on her useless tongue. She began to rise to her feet, but with a speed she didn't expect he reached up to catch her wrist in his large hand and pulled her back to the earth.

"Do you remember our conversation weeks ago about rose rustling?"

"I do." She looked down at his hand on her arm, pointedly. "You were upset about it, then, too."

His eyes were like burning dark coals. "I was. I told you then that there were some roses that could not be cut or grafted. Rare species that would wither and die if they were."

Laurel's brow furrowed and she turned her head to glance at La Belle Rose, then back at him with a worried question in her eyes.

"Yes," he replied. "One cut into her cane and that would be the end of her." His fingers loosened on her arm and said in a calmer tone, "Laurel, you must understand. Maybelle has hidden this magnificent rose, all these rare, fragile species, from the world lest the inevitable happen."

"The inevitable? Dane, you have this morbid fear that the world will discover your secrets and destroy them," she argued back. "First your own discoveries in the rain forest and now these roses. Don't you have any faith in mankind? Are they all such heinous devils in your eyes?"

He took a long, drawn-out breath but did not answer. He simply released her arm and turned his head away toward La Belle Rose.

"My father isn't at all like the men you've described," she said, gently making her point. "He discovered this rose, years ago. He loves it. And he has a right to know it's here. To see it again. My father would never do anything to hurt La Belle Rose."

"As you would never do anything to hurt Maybelle?"

She gulped back a breath of air and rose quickly to her feet, this time unhindered by Dane. "I'll ask her permission first. Of course."

Dane rose with a grace unexpected in a man his size. "Then you're decided? After all I've told you. After all you've seen and done here at Fallingstar, you will still tell him?"

"I must."

His eyes narrowed as he studied her, his teeth tightly clenched like he was splitting a hair. "I see your stay hasn't changed you, after all."

She stiffened, but her eyes flashed fire. "I see I was right about you from the first."

There, she thought. The hurtful things were said. They couldn't be taken back. She winced inside even as she stared angrily back at him, her chin thrust and her mouth pinched tight lest they tremble.

"I'll take you back to the house," he said, turning, not offering his hand. "I can't see why Maybelle asked me to take you here in the first place."

"She knows I had to see La Belle Rose," she cried at his back. "Don't you understand, Dane? Maybelle knows what I must do."

He didn't reply. He bent to pick up her backpack and flung it over his shoulder in a rash move that revealed his scarcely contained rage. Then, in characteristic silence, he began to walk away, leaving her to follow.

"Hello, Dad? It's me, Laurel."

"Are you all right? You're not ill, are you? Was there some kind of accident?"

She held the telephone receiver so tightly in her hands her knuckles were white. If she didn't, they'd tremble so hard she'd drop it. Her decision weighed heavily on her shoulders, not because of Maybelle, but because of an unwarranted sense of betrayal to Dane. It wasn't fair that he should make her feel this way. Maybelle had not only given her permission to call her father, she had insisted that she do so, as soon as possible. Dane had stared at her with his eyes round but soon his face clouded with disappointment, confusion, and finally fury before clamping his jaw set and leaving without a word.

"I'm fine, just fine," she replied, twisting the cord and scanning the small restaurant in town that she had to drive to to reach a telephone. A mother and her two young children were sitting at a small square wooden table covered with paper placemats, scooping up spoonfuls of dripping ice cream. "Are you sitting down? No, really, are you?"

There was the sound of a chair scraping and a huff of breath. "All right, I'm sitting. Now what is it you have to tell me that is so important you felt compelled to call me halfway around the world and drag me out of a lecture? I thought it was an emergency."

"No, it's a miracle. Father, listen. I found it. La Belle Rose. I've actually seen it."

There was a long silence on the other end, save for the sound of his heavy breathing. She imagined him reaching for the ironed handkerchief he always kept in his breast pocket and mopping his forehead with it.

"You did hear me?"

"Yes, yes." The answer came breathless. "How can you be sure?"

"I'm sure. And it's everything you ever said it was. There are a number of rare species of roses here, all of them virtually unknown."

"Here? Where's here?" he wanted to know.

"It's the most amazing thing. They're here in Vermont, kept in a secluded fissure."

"A what?" He sounded impatient, eager to rout out the facts.

"Oh, Dad, I can't begin to explain it to you. You'll just have to come see for yourself."

"Where are you? Still with that artist?"

"Yes. Maybelle Starr's place. It's called Fallingstar. When can you get here?"

"As soon as possible!" The excitement in his voice was ringing across the wire. "I'll cut short my lecture tour, rearrange my ticket. I'll . . . I don't know what I can manage, but I'll be there as quickly as I can. In the meantime, I'll ring Colin. He'll want to be there too."

"No, Dad. Not Colin," she rushed. "He may not be invited."

"Nonsense. I'll send him in my stead until I get there. This is too important. I need him. La Belle Rose—found! I can scarcely believe it. My God, if you could see me. I'm crying like a baby."

Tears welled in Laurel's eyes as well. Tears in her father? They were as rare as tears in Maybelle. She said a hasty good-bye and hung up the phone, leaning against the wall feeling as winded as though she'd run a marathon. Looking up, she saw the children at the next table looking up at her with wide-eyed curiosity, ice cream mustaches on their lips. Beside them, their mother cocked her head while lazily stirring the cream in her bowl, no doubt listening to every word.

Dane's warning about gossip and idle curiosity about anything concerning Maybelle Starr and Fallingstar rang in her memory. She hastily straightened and left the restaurant, feeling the heat of their stares on her back.

Down in the valley, Daphne wiped her brow with her elbow and looked out at her day's work. Four lines of hives, white boxes neatly piled one on top of another in groups of three, were lined up in the north meadow. *It's going to be a good year*, she thought, sighing with exhaustion. She needed it, seeing as there wasn't going to be any other source of income for her. *Yep*, she thought with a ripple of pride. It might just be her best year yet. There was a profusion of daisies this year, not to mention black-eyed Susans, dogbane with its pink bells, pink and white steeplebush, pale yellow cinquefoil, and creamy Queen Anne's lace spreading wide and as delicate as the lace it was named for. Her bees would be happy here, she thought, listening to the contented thrumming in the hives.

Happy bees were productive bees. She tugged off her work gloves and slapped the dirt from them against her thighs. Every bone in her body ached. Moving bees was a tremendous amount of work that went on for days and days. Had she ever before been so tired? She still hadn't caught up on enough sleep since the summer solstice.

Her slapping ceased as a wide grin creased the soil on her cheeks. But man, oh man, it sure was worth it. She hadn't had such a grand time in she couldn't remember how long. And the kicker was, she didn't touch a drop of drink. Other than the nectar, that is. But that didn't count. She never got woozy or drunk from the nectar, and unlike Dane and Laurel, never got sick neither. Ever since the party she'd only felt great. Soaring, like she'd lost the weight of the world.

It was that crazy wish that did it, she was convinced. Maybelle was right. Sometimes you just had to give a name to your troubles to face them. Once she saw her shame written down on the slip of paper, all slicked over with her honey, she knew she could deal with it. What was she so afraid of? She'd made a mistake. She was angry and hurt and that made her greedy. But no more. Laurel wasn't a bad sort. She even liked her. And it was clear her brother was crazy for her. She might not be rich, but she'd be at peace. Yes, it would all work out.

Once she found her father, that was. She'd looked everywhere for him, in every dirty hole she passed, both in the woods—and in the town. Not that she expected him to show his face and be recognized, but his thirst for drink was powerful and she wouldn't put it past him to be stupid enough to do anything for a bottle. She tossed her gloves into the back of her pickup and went to gather her supplies. He'd show up one of these days, and when he did, she'd tell him.

She was distracted by a rustling in the verbena bushes, then saw a glimpse of a yellow T-shirt.

"Whoever's there, come on out!" she shouted.

A slim, wiry man with stubby hair on his chin and head stepped out from the foliage. "Hey there, Bizzy Bee."

She felt the usual knee-jerk reaction on seeing her father: to spin on her heel and run far away. But another urge, more powerful, forced her to stay.

"I've been waiting for you to show up," she said in an easy drawl that masked her nervousness. "Where've you been?"

He wriggled his brows as though he knew a private joke. "Here and there and everywhere."

"I'll just bet. Like in the woods. That was you that killed that bear, wasn't it?"

"What if I did? She weren't no use to no one. She came growling at me and got what she deserved. For all you know, she'd be the one that ate your mother."

Daphne's eyes snapped up to glare at him. "No bear killed my mother. Cancer did."

"Don't matter none, does it?" he fired back, a morose tone entering his voice. "She's dead and gone." Then, the scowl lifted and he chuckled as he added, "Just like me."

Daphne swallowed hard and raked her hair from her face. "I want to talk to you about that."

"Good, 'cause that's what I came here to do." He came closer, walking from side to side in a weaving line. The wind carried the scent of sour whiskey before him. "It's seven years next Wednesday and we've got to come up with our plan for collecting the money."

She wrinkled her nose and rocked on her heels. "There won't be any plan. I'm not doing it."

His smile wobbled but remained fixed by force of will. "What are you talking about? We agreed. You'll go claim the money and then we split it. Fifty-fifty. Seems cut and dried to me. There's nothin' to worry about. Nobody's the least bit suspicious." His smile hardened. "We had a deal."

"You don't get it, do you? I'm out of the deal. It's fraud! That's a capital offense. Not to mention it's morally wrong. My mother wouldn't want me to do it." She shook her head. "Don't worry. I won't tell anyone I saw you." She saw his dark eyes glitter with menace, a look she knew too well. She turned on her heel and started walking toward her truck as fast as she could.

She didn't get more than a few steps when she heard him come running up behind her. It all happened so quickly. She didn't have time to do anything but raise her hands to her face as he grabbed her elbow and spun her around.

"Don't you be saying anything you'll be sorry for," he ground out.

She lowered her arms, keeping her hands in a fist before her. "You stay away from me, hear? I'm not going to do it. I'll only be sorry if I go through with it."

His arm swooped up, balled in a fist and came down hard, straight to her face. She wasn't expecting it so fast, and caught a blow to the side of her face. She hit the earth shoulder first, cringing with pain. Pain ricocheted in her head and she could taste the salty taste of blood from her lip. She rose slowly up on her elbow to see two worn and dirty boots standing near her nose.

"You'll do what I say, or there'll be more coming. You hear me?"

She remembered him saying the same thing to her mother and no matter what Rosalind did, the beatings continued. And Dane . . . Was Joe such a fool that he'd think a beating could change her mind once it was made up? If he did, he never knew her.

She shook her head. "I won't."

She saw the boot rise and cringed. But the kick she expected never came. Instead he stomped the ground, spraying dirt in her face.

"You'll be sorry you crossed me, Daphne Flannery," he ground out. "Damn sorry."

Nineteen

"**H**ow quaint. The place positively screams Hans Christian Andersen." Colin sniffed and gave Maybelle's house another quick, assessing sweep of his eyes. "Or should I say, it's Grimm."

"Don't be that way," Laurel admonished him, laughing.

It felt so good to laugh. For the past twenty-four hours since her phone call to Arthur, she'd been on tenterhooks at Fallingstar. Maybelle had been unusually tense, dropping things, being more clumsy than usual and staying close to the house. At twilight the older woman sat at the greenhouse windows alone with Amor in a pensive silence that stretched for hours. Dane was a bear and had snarled at Laurel when Maybelle tripped over a watering can in the yard, blaming Maybelle's condition on the fact that strangers were arriving at Fallingstar. Blaming it all on her.

Dane . . . Why had he come to mind again? she asked herself, chewing her lip as she watched Colin remove his suitcase from the trunk. Each time she thought of him, it pained her. He had grown cold and withdrawn since their return from the fissure, more like the recalcitrant man she had met on her first day. When he heard the news that Colin was due to arrive as well as her father, his eyes iced over but he said nothing. He only walked away.

Laurel walked along the stone path toward Colin and leaned over to deliver a sweet kiss on his cheek.

"What? You've been gone for a month and that's all the welcome I get?" Colin asked.

It was unfair to pass her sadness of heart on to Colin, she thought, as she brightened her smile and hurried to wrap her arms around his neck and welcome him with a fierce hug. He surprised her by turning his head and capturing her mouth for a long, lingering kiss. His lips felt thin and dry and she didn't feel the rush she'd come to expect whenever she kissed Dane. Trying to ignore the disappointment, she told herself that this kiss was lackluster because, after all, Colin had just arrived after a long drive, he was tired and she was nervous, and he'd caught her unawares When he released her, seemingly pleased with the effort, she smiled with as much enthusiasm as she could muster, but all she could think was how strange it was to look at a man face to face without leaning back or going on tiptoe.

It was a handsome face, she told herself, with sensitive pale gray eyes, fine bones, full lips, and an attitude that spoke of breeding, education at the finest schools, and wealth. Odd, but she'd never noticed before how *soft* Colin was. Elegant, certainly, in his tan summerweight suit worn with appropriate brown wing-tips and a sporting yellow tie. He was charming and witty, no doubt. How different was Dane's tanned, muscled body, his jaw of granite, his dark, foreboding eyes, and his utter contempt of suits and ties. It was disturbing to realize, but to her mind, Colin appeared, well, doughy.

"However did you manage up here for so long?" he was saying to her. "It's in the middle of nowhere. I took my life in my hands just getting up that road. I never saw so many ruts and hairpin turns, and I swear to God I narrowly missed hitting a deer. It just came out of nowhere, almost sent me crashing into the ravine."

"Fallingstar's isolation is part of its charm. It's a bit foreboding at first, I know. It took a little getting used to." She linked arms. "Come on, let me show you around. You'll see for yourself how special this place is."

They passed through the seemingly impenetrable

hedge of Rosa Rugosa Alba that bordered the berm house to stand at what she knew was a particularly good vantage point of Maybelle's rollicking, rolling gardens. "Now see what you think." She peeked up at his face.

Colin stood straight-shouldered and still, expressionless save for the faint color that stained his cheek. She smiled with satisfaction. The sight had hit her like this, too, the first time she saw it. She sighed and faced the wind, allowing her gaze to glide around the mountains, the valleys, the way the clouds traveled from the north over the ridge. Showing a stranger the sights for the first time, she suddenly realized how much Fallingstar had become her home, how much it had come to mean to her.

A sweetly fragranced breeze lured them to stop staring and come into the garden. He turned to smile and for the first time in months she saw the old spark of the friendship and the mutual love of gardens that they'd shared for years flare in his gray eyes again.

"Shall we take the tour?" she asked.

She led him past an old maple with a blooming climbing rose rambling up its trunk into the main garden. They spent a lovely hour strolling and commenting on the many rare species of plants in Maybelle's collection. He stopped several times to study a plant at length, pulling a notebook out of his vest pocket to furiously scribble notes in it. He was bent over the bladelike leaves of a rare species of lily when Dane entered the garden. Laurel stiffened and felt a flush creep over her body when she saw him stop suddenly to glower at them. They faced each other across the long sweep of garden. His arms were filled with shovels, a fork and a hoe. She clasped her hands before her and steeled herself for the blast that was sure to come. He'd be rude. He'd challenge Colin in some way, she saw it in his stance and in the narrowing of his eyes.

Dane swaggered forward with the long handles of his tools pointed outward, looking like a Druid warrior on the charge. He didn't spare her a glance but kept his eyes fixed on Colin.

The clanging tools heralded his arrival. Colin, still bent over the lily, lazily turned his head, barely acknowledged Dane's approach, then returned to the lilies, ignoring Dane, who came to an abrupt stop before them. Laurel's toes curled, knowing Colin assumed Dane was the hired help and thus summarily dismissed him, in the same manner that she'd seen him dismiss the army of gardeners hired to tend the acres of Longfield. Shame tinged her cheeks as she realized, wasn't that just how she'd treated Dane when she'd arrived?

"Colin," she said, taking hold of his arm to distract him. She knew that, like her father, once absorbed he tuned out completely to the outside world. "I'd like you to meet Dane Walden. He's the master who tends these gardens. And a dear friend."

She emphasized the word friend as a compliment, hoping to impress upon Dane her desire to end the silent feud between them. Instead, it had the effect of oil upon a flame. Dane's eyes glittered dangerously and he paled slightly under his tan.

Beside her, Colin drew up sharply at her words. He raised a brow and looked at Dane shrewdly.

Laurel saw Dane as Colin would. He was shabbily dressed in muddy boots, jeans stained with iodine, and an old, well-worn blue shirt with its sleeves rolled to the elbow. His tawny hair was windblown and wild and his hands were as strong and broad as the shovels he carried. Yet no one could miss the power and masculinity that oozed from the towering man who glowered at Colin from under scowling brows.

Colin slipped his arm around her waist in a possessive manner. Although his expression was implacable and his smile polite, his attitude was deliberately condescending. "Any *friend* of Laurel's is a friend of mine."

Colin didn't know Dane as she did, didn't see the fury behind his narrowing eyes.

"She exaggerates," Dane replied coolly.

Laurel bit her lip, dismayed that he would not even call her friend.

"Oh?" Colin replied, still smiling. "Then you're not friends?"

Dane lifted the corner of his mouth in a sardonic grin and glanced at Laurel in a seductive manner that spoke clearly of the passion that had passed between them. She felt Colin's arm tighten around her waist but his smile remained fixed.

"You misunderstand. I'm not a master gardener," Dane replied. "I'm a farmer."

"Really?" Colin said with a slight laugh that was terribly insulting. "Well, no matter what your title, I assure you the garden is absolutely marvelous," he said. "I've never seen the like. Tell me, are the roses here?"

Dane's eyes flashed.

"No, they're far off," Laurel quickly interjected, waving her hand toward the woods. "In there somewhere."

"I'm very eager to see them. Can we manage it today?"

"No," Dane growled.

Colin seemed taken aback by Dane's vehemence. "Very well then. Tomorrow?"

"I'm afraid . . ." Laurel began, hoping to douse the flame in Dane's eyes.

"You can't see them at all. They're private."

Laurel closed her eyes, furious. "This isn't your decision, Dane. It's Maybelle's. Colin . . ." she hedged, placing a hand on his sleeve. "There is a possibility you won't be allowed to go. I know," she said, holding up her hand to ward off the torrent of complaints that were coming, "you've come a long way. I told Father not to send you. We'll just have to wait until he arrives and can talk to Maybelle Starr."

"This is ridiculous!"

"So go home," Dane retorted.

Before they could get into an argument, she hurried to ask Colin, "By the way, where are you staying? At the Wallingford Inn?"

Colin looked at her with surprise. "The inn? No. I thought I was staying here. With you."

She saw Dane physically react to that statement and

felt a rising panic. "You misunderstood," Laurel exclaimed. "There is only one spare room here, and that is reserved for my father. It's a small house," she added, the implication clear.

Colin's manner grew more frigid, even as his smile grew wider. "Then perhaps I can stay just until your father arrives? You're quite right, it's such a charming place." His tone changed, became more smoky. "And I've missed you."

"I'm sorry, Colin, but it's really not my decision. This is Maybelle's house and she is a recluse. It was a great concession for her to allow my father to stay. I really couldn't ask, it wouldn't be right. Especially as she isn't feeling very well."

"You can stay at my place. I live right down the road."

Laurel swung her head around to stare at Dane in disbelief. His face was inscrutable and he looked only at Colin. What was he up to?

Colin was obviously wondering the same thing as he considered the proposal. "Why, thank you, Dan," he replied at length. "That's very accommodating. I accept your offer with thanks."

"The name is Dane," he replied gruffly, not bothering to return Colin's smile or his handshake. "Laurel can show you the way." He hoisted his armful of tools, then, with a brief but piercing glance directed at Laurel, he walked away into the garden.

"Well," Colin huffed, withdrawing his hand that had been left hanging in midair. "These mountain men certainly do have their local color. It should be quite an adventure bunking up with one."

Laurel rolled her eyes and said a quick prayer. Colin had no idea.

Early that evening, they received a telegram from Arthur announcing his arrival at four o'clock the following afternoon. Maybelle excused herself in a flutter to retire to her room, claiming she wasn't well. Laurel worried that Maybelle's retreat was because of Colin's presence, but when she saw her pale skin and agitation, she agreed that it would be better for Maybelle to rest. While Colin freshened up, she prepared a fresh salad from the garden and served it with a hearty soup and slices of Maybelle's homemade bread and butter. She brought a tray into Maybelle's room, then shared an intimate, candlelit dinner with Colin.

He talked incessantly. She listened politely, wondering how she was ever interested in all the idle gossip from Longfield. More interesting was the success of his most recent publication, but the story was marred by the backbiting involved in the fierce "publish or perish" competition. As the meal ended and the red sun began to lower in the western sky, Colin's voice grew lower, more intimate. He changed his course of interest, moving on from the topic of biogenetics to her. He went on and on about how much he'd missed her, how awful it was of her to leave him for such a long time, punctuating his comments with hand holding, brief kisses across the table, and meaningful glances.

Laurel stifled a yawn and glanced over at Amor's cage from time to time, worried that the little goldfinch, too, was ill. He'd puffed up his feathers and tucked in his head without a peep. It wasn't usual for him to nest until well after sunset, and never when people were in the kitchen. Colin laughed at her when she expressed this to him.

"Your imagination is getting the best of you," he warned her.

Laurel said nothing, but wondered if what he said wasn't exactly true—and rejoiced in it.

After dinner, they sat outside on the bench that faced the garden. Colin's arm was wrapped around her shoulder. After the tumultuousness of the past several weeks, there was a quiet comfort in the familiar. Her relationship with Dane was an emotional roller coaster. She knew Colin. He was safe and secure. She leaned toward him, resting her head on his shoulder. But as she stared out at the stars, she found her thoughts wandering down the mountain to a certain man of few words. It occurred to her that she'd shared more in the silences with Dane than she did in all the talking with Colin.

"Darling, you're a million miles away."

"What?" She blinked heavily and turned her attention to Colin. "Oh, no, I'm sorry. I was just thinking how much I love it here. And I know you will love it too, if you just give it a chance."

"I could say the same thing about me." He reached down to lift her hand and hold it up to view in the dim light of the crescent moon. "I was hoping I'd see you wearing my ring when I arrived."

Laurel tucked her hand back, cringing. She'd have to tell Colin about the missing diamond ring. She raised her head and collected the words. "Colin," she began, then cleared her throat. A sweet-smelling breeze swirled around them, playing with her hair. She reached up to tuck it behind her ear, but Colin's hand reached out to do it for her. He rested his hand along her chin line.

"You look different," he said, running his fingers down the long length of hair, playing with it. "More feminine." His eyes grew smoky. "More sexy. You've filled out some, your skin is glowing. And your hair—it's amazing. I can't believe how much it's grown."

"Must be the mountain air."

"Whatever, it suits you. Everything does. You look so beautiful." His hand tightened on her shoulder and he leaned in, closing the gap. "God, I've missed you."

His mouth crushed hers in a kiss that was as devouring as it was possessive. His lips trembled with desire and she felt crushed against the wood bench as he pressed down upon her. She was confused by this rousing passion from him. Sex had always been pleasant but rather perfunctory between them. She closed her eyes tighter, trying to will her body to respond, to feel the same shivers of desire. But it simply would not. She felt nothing, except a pressure against her lips that was unpleasant and an urgent, grasping at her breast that was annoying.

Colin wanted to make love and would press his intentions, she was sure of it. And she was just as sure she did not want to make love with him. It felt wrong.

She pulled back, extricating herself from his tight grasp. Looking up at him, his lips a magenta color from the kiss, his eyes half closed and still dreamy with desire, she knew without question that it was more than just not wanting to kiss him. She could not pretend any longer that what they shared was some form of love. Or that they could create a comfortable life together, work together, have children together. Or that as they lay in their shared bed, she would be satisfied that she was well loved, cared for, and not alone. She knew better now. She knew what love was. She knew she loved Dane.

But love wasn't enough to base a marriage on. What was it her father had told her? *Shared goals, beliefs, dreams—these are the building blocks of a solid marriage.* These she shared with Colin, not Dane. Her head spun with contradictions. She felt the hammering of a headache beginning at the base of her skull.

"It's getting late," she said, smoothing her hair back from her face and creating more of a distance. "It's been a long day for both of us."

"Laurel, let me stay here, with you. It's been such a long time."

"You can't. I can't. Maybelle's upstairs."

"I'll be quiet." He reached for her again, more insistently.

"Colin, no," she said unequivocally, disentangling herself and pushing him firmly away from her.

He groaned and leaned back, rubbing his eyes. "I simply don't know what's going on between us, Laurel," he exploded. "But it can't continue for much longer. You said you wanted passion from me."

"Physical passion and emotional passion are not the same thing and you know it."

He shook his head, then shrugged with impatience. "I've been a very patient man. No one can deny that. You say wait, and I wait. You say show passion, and I show passion. But there's an end to my patience." He stood up and straightened his pants. "I thought I could wait until the end of summer for you to respond to my proposal, but I find I can't. I'm only human, a man with natural needs." He took her hands and with a finality that reminded her more of a father than a lover, he said, "I'll expect my answer before I leave. One way or the other, Laurel, you must decide."

Dane twiddled the pencil between his fingers to the tempo of the tall clock in the hall, wondering why that Colin guy wasn't at the house yet and whether he was still with Laurel, which of course he knew that he was. The night passed by with agonizing slowness while he wondered what were they doing up there. He feared he knew the answer to that, too. He threw the pencil across the table and reached for a bottle of scotch, pouring himself a couple of fingers, neat.

Damn, but he didn't want to fall in love. He didn't believe in it, having seen what love did to his mother. Her marriage to Joe crushed the joy from her life and changed her.

He'd known many women, all over the world, but not a one made him wish to linger in her arms. After a few months, maybe a year, he couldn't wait to escape their clutches and move on. Long ago he'd decided he wanted to live alone, like Maybelle.

And then he'd met Laurel. Just the thought of her rocked his self-made world. When he woke up in the morning and when he went to sleep at night, she was always there, floating around his mind. He'd known right away that she was the one. He didn't know how or why—it wasn't his style to analyze the hell out of something. And when he saw her in his dreams, he'd been fool enough to believe in the dreams once again. To believe that dreams could come true.

He didn't count on her not wanting him. He tilted his head and downed the scotch in one gulp, squeezing his eyes against the burn of it. It felt good, a counterbalance to the burn he felt in his heart.

Out in the hall he heard the front door click and the creak of the floors. He glanced at his watch, frowned. Nine o'clock. It was about time that Colin Whitless came back from the house. He walked to the hall and was surprised to see not Colin, but Daphne creeping to the first step of the stairs. Dane stepped out of his office and called her name.

"I'm going to bed," she called back, scurrying up the stairs.

"Hold on," he ordered, flicking on the light. Daphne ducked her head, sending a shock of fiery hair over her face. She looked like she'd slept in the woods all night. Bits of grass clung to her jeans jacket and hair and the clothes looked dirty and crumpled. She looked a mess.

"Where were you last night?" he asked, storming closer, his voice rough with worry. "I thought we'd agreed that you'd call when you'd be out all night. I worried like hell, wondering where—" He broke off catching a glimpse of purpling skin on her face beneath the shock of hair. The hair on his neck bristled. "Let me see your face."

"It's nothing," she said with a backward wave of his hand. She took a step up the stairs but he was quicker, taking the stairs two at a time to catch her arm. Daphne twisted away, turned her head, but his hands were already on her shoulders and he was much too strong for her to even attempt to escape.

Slowly, gently, he took her chin and turned her face toward him. When he saw her beautiful face marred by a swollen and bruised left eye, the blood drained from his face and he felt a violence well up in him like a hurricane.

"Who did this to you?" he hissed. His fingers were digging into her shoulders.

She shook him off angrily. "Nobody. I fell."

"Like hell. Tell me, Daph. Was it Tom Higgins? He's been sour since you brushed him off." His breath came hard, making his voice raspy. "Just tell me who it was."

"I told you, it was nobody. Now leave me alone." She stomped down the stairs and into the kitchen, fetching a beer from the fridge. He followed right behind her. She flipped off the cap, leaned against the counter and took a swallow, watching him warily. He bided his time, helping himself to a glass of water, then leaning against the counter to drink it. He thought she looked hunted, and he couldn't bear to think of anyone hurting her. Not his baby sister.

"Daphne," he said, setting his glass down on the counter. "You don't fall down and get a black eye."

She groaned with frustration and swiped back her hair. "God, Dane," she cried. "You're such a pest. You never give up, do you? I said it's no big deal but you just won't let it go. I've been moving the bees over to the north meadow, okay? You know what grueling work that is. I missed my step and fell. Like a damn fool, I hit my head on a branch going down. It happened, it hurt like hell, and I'm not proud of it." She shrugged indignantly, turning away from him. "I went to sleep in the woods like I always do after I move my bees. I'm sorry if I didn't tell you, but you've been pretty damn touchy lately. Maybe I was trying to get away from you, too. End of story. So I'd appreciate it if you'd just let it drop."

There was a long silence that stretched uncomfortably. Dane studied his water glass.

"Look, Dane, I'm not some little girl that needs her big brother to solve her problems for her anymore. I have my own business, I support myself, and I like to think at twenty-one I can come and go as I please."

He nodded his head, lips tight. "You'd tell me if you needed my help, wouldn't you?" he asked softly.

Her brows furrowed, but she nodded quickly then took a swallow of her beer. He raked his hair then shook his head in resignation. She didn't give him much choice but to accept her answer. It was plausible, but something didn't ring true. He'd keep an eye on her, just to make certain.

"You look exhausted yourself," she said, eyeing him carefully. "Everything okay up there?" She jerked her head in the direction of the mountain.

"No." Then, because he had to tell someone, he said, "Laurel's boyfriend arrived. He's up there with her now."

"Damn. Why'd she invite him here? I thought things were getting pretty good between you two."

"He works with her father. They're both coming."

"Double damn. Whew, that's a lot to deal with all at once. No wonder you've been a bear. There's nothing you can do if Maybelle invites them. But as for that Colin character, I don't get it. If he's up there, what the hell are you doing down here?"

"The last thing I want to do is hang around them. She's where she wants to be. With the man she wants to be with."

"You don't know that."

"I do." His spoke softly, his fingers tapping the glass in thought. "I overheard them in the garden, talking about all the plants and the papers they could write. They can't wait to get their hands on my plants and examine them under the microscopes. They talk like their plans for the future are all set." He sighed and shrugged in defeat. "I know her. She loves that academic stuff, doing research."

"She loves it here, too. Working in the garden. And she's painting now. Maybelle says she's really good. That she's having her agent arrange for a viewing of her work."

"It's all new and exciting for her. A summer's fling. Like me." He met Daphne's gaze, his own resigned. "You should've seen her today with Colin. It's clear what she really wants. Maybe even what she needs."

"Did you ever think she might need you?" Her frustration was bubbling.

He shook his head, crestfallen. "I'm not her type. She wants the bookish kind of guy, someone with brains." Dane's face pinched. "Not a drifter, like me."

"Dane, you're driving me crazy!" Daphne exploded, her patience with his depression at an end. She slammed her bottle on the counter and came at him like a bantam rooster. "What are you talking about? You're the smartest guy I know. When are you going to get over your feeling that you're not smart? You're a friggin' genius, everyone knows that but you. The problem is you won't own up to it. And you're lazy."

"Lazy? Me?" he thundered. "I work harder than any man, any at all."

"Sure, in the fields and the gardens. But you're lazy about your papers. You've got a treasure trove hidden in that room," she said, pointing her finger toward his study. "Laurel told me all about it. But you won't work on it, won't get it together to publish. You say you don't want the fame or to have the species exploited. I say bullshit! You're afraid to let anyone see it. Afraid that they'll laugh at you like they did when you were a kid. That they'll call you *Dumb Dane* again. You're so ter-rified that the world will say your work isn't good enough that you won't even put it out there for them to see."

Her words were like bullets, riddling him with holes and exposing hurts and truths that he kept pushed deep in his gut. He closed his eyes tight against the pain, clenching his jaw to hold back the roar of anguish.

Daphne came to his side slowly, tentatively reaching out to touch his arm. He flinched when she touched him, like a wounded animal.

"Dane," she said softly, coming closer. "You're my brother. I love you more than anyone else in the world, so I've got to say these things to you. When are you going to see that you're not dumb? That you're smarter than Colin, or guys like that? You have a gift to see things that most people miss or are just too blind to see."

He wanted to believe her, but a lifetime of doubt and anguish clouded his thinking. He knew only one thing for certain: that Laurel was with Colin now.

"She knows where I live. Let her make the choice."

"Oh, that's just great," Daphne spat out. "You're the mountain and everyone has to come to you."

"Mountains don't move," he replied wearily. "It's a fact of nature."

"Wrong, bro. A good quake shakes mountains up." She shrugged off her jacket and tossed it on the kitchen chair with disgust. "If you ask me, I think you're sitting on a fault line and are due for at least an eight on the

Richter scale." She yawned noisily. "That's it for me. I'm bushed. Good-night."

"Good-night," he replied, watching her leave in a sleepy shuffle. He rose to return to his office, back to his desk cluttered with his drawings and notes. He picked one up and studied it dispassionately, wondering if it was indeed as good as Laurel and Daphne said it was. Outside, he heard the sound of a car pulling up in the drive. Dane sighed, looked at the hour on the clock, and let the drawing slip from his fingers to join the others piled in disarray on his desk. He stood quietly, hands on hips, listening to the car door slam and a minute later, Colin's footfall on the front porch.

Dane felt the quake begin to rumble in his gut already, knowing in his heart that this quake had the power to bring a mountain down to rubble.

The following morning Laurel came down to the barn to fetch the eggs at the usual time. She rounded the barn and suddenly there he was, tossing grain while a dozen hens picked near his boots. She came closer and smiled. He did not.

"I wanted to thank you for allowing Colin to stay at your house. It was very generous of you."

Dane tossed out the corn with an angry flip of his wrist, sending the chickens scurrying to the far side of the barn. "Generosity had nothing to do with it."

"You needn't be so surly. You did me and Maybelle a favor, and pulled me out of an awkward situation. So I thank you." His face pinched as he tossed the remaining feed into a bunker. He wasn't going to make this easy for her, she realized. "Couldn't you at least try to be civil?"

He gave the feeder a rigorous shake. "I'd have thought Colin Whitmore had all the civility anyone could tolerate in a morning."

So he's jealous, she thought, both pleased and relieved. It gave her hope. "Actually, I had my fill of Colin's civility last night."

He stopped feeding and turned his head, his eyebrows raised.

"Let me guess," she said, a smile twitching at her lips. "He's still sleeping." She was pleased to see a smile crack his face. "I wouldn't expect him to rise much before nine. And he'll probably be looking for coffee."

"I'll be damned if I'll serve him breakfast," Dane said with disgust. Then with a crooked smile he said, "I'll let Daphne make him breakfast. That'll fix him."

It was wonderful to share a laugh with him again, to feel the tension dissipate. He started toward her.

Her hand darted up to nervously tuck her hair behind her ear.

Then he was beside her, looking down at her from his great height. It was a bold, handsome face. It was the face she wanted to see every morning.

He thought she looked especially beautiful this morning in her torn jeans and white T-shirt with the Longfield Gardens emblem on the pocket.

They began to walk to the ladder, each careful not to break this tenuous peace. "How's Maybelle today?" he asked.

"She's much better, up and about. But I'm still worried about her."

"She's not ill?" His worry sharpened his tone.

"Not exactly. She's more clumsy of late. She blames it on her eyesight, and if that's true, I'm concerned that it's getting worse."

"She won't see a doctor. Never has, never will." They reached the ladder and he rested his arm against it. "I think it's the company. She doesn't tolerate strangers well, and she hasn't had a visitor in years."

"But that's what makes it so odd. I admit I was worried last night that I'd made a terrible mistake allowing my father to stay at Fallingstar. It was at Maybelle's insistence, Dane, really it was. I suggested he stay at the inn, but she wouldn't have it. And this morning, well, I believe she wants him to visit. She's happy nervous."

He raised his brows. "*Happy* nervous?"

"Yes. Not worried nervous, but excited, like she was

before the summer solstice. She's preening before the mirror, like a young girl before prom." Seeing his widening eyes, she nodded. "She's trying on dress after dress. You should see her bed, there's a mountain of discards. And when she's not fiddling with her hair, she's whirling about the kitchen, cooking up a storm. Dropping things, true, but not the least upset about it. Oh I just remembered, I'm supposed to invite you and Daphne for dinner, seven o'clock sharp."

He frowned and shook his head. "Don't set a place for me. I won't be coming."

"Dane, please."

He silenced her with his look. She didn't pursue it, knowing his refusal was fixed and she could not change his mind.

"I best be getting my eggs," she said with disappointment, turning to place a foot on the bottom rung of the ladder. "There'll be cakes tonight."

He held her back gently. "You smell good," he said, bringing his nose to her hair.

She paused to relish his nearness. It was as near to an apology as he could offer. "I'm not wearing any perfume."

"I know," he replied.

She held her breath, felt his closeness as a palpable thing. His soulful eyes revealed his dilemma: his feelings for her and his feelings about the roses, about Colin, about Fallingstar, and something deeper still.

"Keep an eye on Maybelle," he said, stepping back. "It isn't at all like her to be fussing about in front of a mirror. Something's not right. Maybelle doesn't care a whit how she looks or what people think of her."

Maybelle sat before her mirror, staring at her reflection in agony. What would Arthur think of her? When did she grow so old? When did her skin loose its elasticity and become so soft? she wondered. Leaning closer to the mirror, she brought her hand to her face and let her fingertips trace the lines at her eyes, her forehead, and at the base of her cheeks. Smile lines, they called them.

Well, they were nothing to smile about . . .

Oh, this punishment was too much to bear. How could she face him like this? He would see that she was no longer young and beautiful. Her skin was no longer as dewy as the fresh morning, nor was her hair as lustrous as the moonlight. How she'd taken her beauty for granted when she had it, how she'd taunted mortal men for the sake of her own vanity.

Her small hands formed fists as she tapped them in pique on her dressing table. If she could only have her powers back, just for a little while. She wouldn't abuse them again. She would be careful, oh, so careful. Please, Mab! Never did she need her glamour more!

But that was the test. To see if his love was true. Arthur had to be the classic fairy-tale hero who could see past the disfigurement to the real beauty beneath. Her hand trembled as she cupped her face and stared at her reflection. Could he see her as she was today—an older, human woman—and still recognize her as his love? Without the glamour?

Her lips trembled and her eyes moistened. She reached out to grab a tissue. Oh, bother with these tears! Once they started, she didn't know how to turn the water off! The least little thing set the tears flowing, and when she cried torrents, like last night, she soaked her pillow with them. The frightening aspect was that they seemed to be washing away her eyesight in the same way a hard rain washes away the topsoil. It was a signal that her time was running out. Queen Mab was growing impatient.

She leaned toward the mirror and dabbed the tears from her cheek, pinching them to pinken them. "Oh please, Arthur, hurry," she said aloud. "Please see *me*. Please love *me*."

Twenty

Laurel stood at her favorite ledge overlooking the drive, her long gauzy skirt catching the wind. She wrung her hands and moved from foot to foot in a little dance of excitement. She could hear the whine of an engine on the hill. Colin had volunteered to pick up her father from the airport. They'd be here any moment.

Suddenly bursting through the foliage came the hood of Colin's sleek, black BMW. Laurel arched on her toes to wave, then grabbed her skirts to race to the front of the hedge row to greet them, shouting, "They're here! They're here!"

Farther out in the garden, Dane drove the prongs of his fork into the ground and leaned against it, pensively watching. He glanced up at Maybelle's window. He saw her shadowed reflection lean close for a better look.

The car came to a stop on the gravel, the car door opened, and she saw her father rise out to face the mountain and breathe deeply of the crisp, fresh air. Her heart beat happily at seeing him again, here, where she felt so at home and so happy.

"Dad!" she called out, then rushed toward him without the least reserve or inhibition. He had just enough time to open his arms before she barreled into them, delivering a heartfelt hug.

"My goodness, child," Arthur exclaimed, momentarily surprised by her emotional welcome. But soon enough she felt his arms wrap around her and the affectionate pat on her back that she didn't know until this moment that she had missed. "Here now, stand back and let me look at you."

He beamed with both pride and astonishment as he surveyed his only child. She'd dressed especially carefully in the gauzy, rose-colored dress that Maybelle had sewn for the summer solstice. She'd plaited the sides of her hair and pinned them back with multiple-colored clasps of amethyst, fluorite, peridot, and apatite, letting the back hang loose, almost to her waist now.

"The mountain air has been good for you," he exclaimed, his eyes sparkling with appreciation. "You've filled out and there's a bloom in your cheek I like to see." He reached out to touch her hair, amazement etched on his face, soon replaced by a poignant expression that she recognized. "You look so much like your mother."

She heard no recrimination or criticism in his voice. Rather, the words were spoken as a compliment. She shuddered, having waited so long to hear it.

"I told you, sir," Colin said, stepping forward to place his arm around her waist again, taking claim. "She's more beautiful than ever. Come inside the house," he volunteered, stepping forward. "You'll find it terribly primitive, but quaint in its own way. You're probably thirsty and Laurel's prepared a fine tea. Thank God for that. I had the most ghastly breakfast cooked by that young woman down the road. You go on in while I bring in your suitcase."

Laurel thought his behavior presumptuous but allowed that he was just trying to make her father feel comfortable.

"Hang tea. I want to see the roses," exclaimed Arthur impatiently. "Twenty-one years is long enough to wait to see La Belle Rose! Where is it?"

"It's not here," Laurel replied, patting his arm. "It's in a fissure, found deep in the woods. It will take a day's trip to get there. Don't worry, we'll go first thing in the morning. In the meantime, Colin was right, I've made a lovely tea. And I want you to meet Maybelle. She's wonderful, Dad. You've never met anyone like her."

A thrashing about in the shrubs drew their attention. Before they finished turning in its direction, Vincit came tearing out, making good his escape and racing straight for his beloved Laurel. Colin shrieked and began running, which naturally sent the curious cub detouring straight for him. The chase was on with Laurel running after them, clapping her hands and calling for Vincit to stop.

The cub did stop, but only once he'd caught up to Colin and had him standing, frozen in fear, as the cub pawed at his legs.

"Get him away," he ground out, his eyes closed tight. "Before he bites me."

"Colin, relax!" she called out, running up. "He's harmless, just a baby. He only wants to play."

"Get that filthy animal off of me!"

"He's not a filthy animal. He's just a bit over-affectionate. Come on, baby," she crooned, tugging at Vincit's collar. "Mama says no." Eventually the cub's attention returned to Laurel and he began to nudge her for play.

Colin visibly relaxed, brushing the dirt from his slacks with angry swipes of his hand. "You shouldn't have a wild animal like that so near the house. He ought to be in the woods. Or a zoo. Or shot."

"Don't say that," Laurel said crossly. "His mother was killed, which is why we're taking care of him until he's old enough to survive on his own. Right now he thinks I'm his mother, don't you, sweetie?" She reached into her pocket and offered him a biscuit.

"He seems perfectly harmless," Arthur said, walking up. He had a look of amused amazement on his face. "You know, it's fascinating that he's formed an attachment to you, Laurel. Your mother was the only other woman I ever knew who attracted the attention of wildlife. You must have inherited that from her."

Laurel looked at her father with wonder, never having known that about her mother. The knowledge filled her mind with a thousand questions she was eager to ask him.

"Let me put this fellow into his pen, and Colin, you can wash up in the kitchen. I think you've had quite a welcoming, don't you, Father? Come on then," she called out, bending down to get a firm hold on Vincit's collar. "Tea is waiting."

She didn't know how much she sounded like Maybelle just then, nor did she see the curious expression on her father's face at her new attitude, or the scowl on Colin's face as he watched her walk away from him.

She put Vincit securely in his pen, then led the way through the winding path, past the fairy carvings, statues, and windchimes to the charming berm house with its lacy thatch roof while listening to her father mumble, "Amazing, absolutely incredible," as he followed.

Maybelle had not yet emerged from her room to greet her guests. It was a bit awkward, serving refreshments in Maybelle's kitchen without her. Laurel frequently cast worried glances toward the stairs that led to her room, wondering when Maybelle would make her appearance— or if she would. Her father was completely distracted. While she served Arthur his favorite poppyseed cake he leaned over in his chair, craning his neck to look out the greenhouse window for a better view of Maybelle's wondrous garden.

"It's really the most superb design," he said, his eyes gleaming. "I've only seen one other similar garden, years back. In England." He tugged at his ears while his eyes grew misty. After a moment he shook his head, seemingly to clear it. Turning, he faced his cake without his usual relish. "I don't know what it is about this place. It stirs up so many memories."

"It's the magic of the place," Laurel said, her eyes shining into his.

"There you go again," Colin admonished, buttering his roll. "Magic. That's all she talks about anymore. We need to bring this girl home." His voice was teasing but there was an underlying criticism that set Laurel's teeth on edge. "It's the magnificence of the garden, to be sure," he answered Arthur with authority. "There are dozens or more species and varieties out there that I haven't yet placed and my head is spinning with possibilities. It's a gold mine out there! We'll have to catalogue her inventory. You realize that, too, sir. I'm sure that's it."

He crossed his legs and popped a bit of roll into his mouth with a flick of his wrist. Suddenly his elbow jerked, sending the roll flying, landing buttered-side-down on his trousers. Colin's mouth fell open with a look of horror on his face. "I don't know what happened. It just flew out of my hand!"

Arthur frowned, displeased that his private ruminations should be so summarily dismissed by this popinjay. He looked down at Colin's trousers as he busily dabbed at the greasy slick of butter and said with his face aghast, "Good God, man. You're socks don't match."

Colin sat up abruptly, dropping his roll again and stared down at his socks. It was true; one was a blue argyle and the other was solid green. Colin sputtered, aghast, "What? I never . . . But I thought . . . I'll go change them. And my pants."

Laurel laughed lightly, bending to pick up the roll and thinking he was making an awful fuss for such a trifling matter. "Whatever for, Colin? Who's to see them, and who even cares? We certainly don't."

Colin's face mottled, revealing that *he* certainly cared and that he'd be nettled for the afternoon unless he rectified the matter.

"Oh, go on then. Change them if you must. You can meet us in the garden when you return," she told him.

"I'll just be a minute," he replied, hurrying to his feet and out of the kitchen.

In the resulting peace, her father moved his plate away and folded his hands on the table. He looked at her searchingly. "How *are* you?" he wanted to know. "You seem so different. You even sound different."

She reached out to place her hand over his folded ones. "I'm good," she replied, then more truthfully, "though a bit confused. I'm learning so much about myself. But it's not all easy to digest. All these new thoughts and feelings are swirling around in my head, getting mixed up with what I used to feel and think and I can't make sense of it all. I have so many decisions to make, and instead of being my usual, decisive self, I feel totally incapable of making any decision at all. I don't know what to do."

He smiled in understanding. "You will, in good time."

"I don't know, Dad." She lifted her slim shoulders, thinking of Colin's pressure for an immediate answer, of Dane's demands, of Maybelle's expectations for her to take over her art career. "So many decisions and so little time."

Arthur withdrew his hands and reached into his coat pocket to pull out a long, thick white envelope with a flair of ceremony and secret. "I've a little surprise for you. It was in the mail when I returned home, just waiting for you. I think," he said with a lilt in his voice, handing the envelope to her, "that this might just make your decision easy."

Laurel took the envelope and read the return address. Her heart started pounding in double time as her eyes widened. "Cornell?" she said, the hope rising in her voice. With trembling fingers she tore open the envelope, tugging out its contents and reading it voraciously.

Dear Miss Carrington,
We are pleased to welcome you . . .

"I can't believe it! I'm accepted. I'm in! Dad, I got in!" Her cheeks were flushed, and when she looked into her father's eyes she saw the pride that she'd yearned to see for so long. Suddenly she didn't feel like a failure. She'd achieved her goal at last!

Except . . . Laurel's breath slowed as the reality of her acceptance into Cornell began to seep inside her brain. She shifted in her seat, suddenly uneasy, like she was a square peg being forced into the proverbial round hole. She couldn't believe she was even thinking this, but . . . did she want to go to Cornell? Was it still her goal in life to become a biogeneticist? She thought that this had been her dream, and it had come true. But was it really *her* dream?

Her elation slipped, looking out the window at the mountains she'd come to love. Since her arrival at Fallingstar, she'd had so many dreams . . .

She spread the letter out on the table, smoothed it, then folded it neatly into thirds and tucked the letter into her pocket.

"I think," she said, looking up at her father's expectant face, "it's time to see the garden."

Predictably, Arthur spent over an hour perusing the rare plants, bringing his nose within inches to examine them with exacting detail. He'd removed his jacket and rolled up his sleeves, eventually calling Dane over to chat with him about methods of propagation, pH levels, and strategies to produce varieties with specific traits. She was proud of the way her father engaged Dane and listened to his comments with the respect she knew Dane deserved. Arthur didn't care whether Dane's jeans were stained or his hands callused. He saw only a man with a storehouse of knowledge and skill.

She also watched as Dane loosened his shoulders from a rigid stance to one more relaxed as his wariness fled and his ideas were shared. She loved to see his eyes sparkle with enthusiasm and his hands gesture as he vigorously made a point. For his part, he was seeing beyond Arthur's suit and tie to a man that could understand his theories. It was gratifying, too, to see the eagerness in her father's eyes as he listened, nodding, appreciating the brilliance and originality of Dane's thoughts. This confirmed her own belief that Dane was very, very special. They had their heads bent close together and were having a heated discussion when Colin called out in greeting.

He strolled into the garden, immaculate in gabardine slacks and a collared polo shirt—his socks evenly matched—swinging his arms as though he owned the place.

"Back again," he announced as he arrived, smiling fixedly at Laurel. He linked arms with her in the familiar manner of a man who is assured of his claim. "Miss me?"

Her father chortled, pleased at Colin's show of affection for his daughter. Dane stood quietly by, expressionless.

"I've been having the most fascinating discussion," her father told Colin, gesturing toward Dane. "This is the most remarkable young man."

Colin's eyes flickered over Dane. "I'm sure I'm interested in hearing it myself," he replied, with a half smile. "You know, I often think it's a shame I don't get out to speak to our field hands more often at Longfield. I'm just so busy in the lab with my microgenetic research, I don't get out to see the plants *au natural*, you might say. So tell me, Dan. What about the compost you use? Is it mostly rotted leaves?"

Laurel cast Colin a warning look, embarrassed for his rudeness.

Dane merely shrugged and stared out at the enormous pile of compost a few yards away just waiting for him to lay it thick in the gardens. His eyes took on that look she knew so well—one that lay somewhere between mockery and disdain.

"Nope," he replied in a thick drawl. "I reckon it's mostly shit."

She bit her lip to keep from laughing. She caught her father's eye and they shared their amusement.

Colin's smile went hard. "Very enlightening," he replied in a clipped manner. "Well. We don't want to keep you from your . . . work any longer."

"You won't," Dane replied.

"Let's continue our tour of the garden," Colin said, directing his comments to Laurel and Arthur. "There's the most interesting species of Verbascum I want to point out. I'd love to get a cutting."

"Are you sure you won't come for dinner?" Laurel asked Dane, eyes entreating.

"Yep," he replied in a tone that brooked no discussion, then turned and walked away to his compost pile, digging his heels into the path.

Colin led them on a tour through Maybelle's garden with a sense of proprietorship that was as embarrassing as it was inappropriate. While he droned on and on about various specimens, Laurel kept swinging her head to look at Dane. He stood tall in the sun, heaving fork after fork full of compost onto the beds at a fevered pace. She watched as he tore off his shirt in the hot midday sun, wiping his brow and tossing it without thought onto the grass. She held back a 'sigh as she admired the way his chest muscles bunched as he lifted, extending those bulging biceps, tanned and sleek with sweat. *My, my, my*, she thought, releasing the sigh, *he is a handsome specimen indeed*.

She felt a tug on her arm and turned to see Colin glaring at her through narrowed eyes. The blue-gray looked turbulent. "Coming?" he asked, taking hold and moving her forward.

She felt herself being dragged along in so many ways, slipping along the path of obedience that she'd followed all of her life. When Colin and her father had arrived at Fallingstar, she'd felt a singular sense of duty and lost her ground, sliding right back into the role they expected of her. Focused, competent, yet docile and accommodating Laurel. Most disconcerting of all, she had awakened this morning not able to recall her dream.

When they walked back into the house they found the rooms adorned with bouquets of fresh flowers, cultivars and wildflowers. Every corner, tabletop and empty space was covered, filling the house with scent.

"How perfectly marvelous," Arthur exclaimed, enchanted. "Whenever did you find the time?"

"I didn't. This is all Maybelle's doing," Laurel replied, casting her glance around in search of her.

"Ah, the mysterious Maybelle Starr. I must say, after viewing her fabulous garden I'm most eager to meet her. But most especially to talk to her about La Belle Rose." He clasped his hands together, as a man in prayer. "La Belle Rose," he repeated with reverence.

"I can't imagine what's keeping her. She's prepared

the most wonderful meal and I'm sure she's expecting to serve soon. Excuse me while I try to find out where she is. Make yourself at home."

While the two men fell into conversation, Laurel hurried up the stairs to Maybelle's room and knocked gently on the door. "Maybelle? Are you in there?"

"I'll be out soon, dear," came her voice behind the door.

"Is everything all right? You've been in there all day. Have you eaten?"

"I'm fine. Everything is as it should be. Not to worry. Go entertain your guests. I'll be down presently."

Her behavior was all very odd, but Laurel returned downstairs and engaged her father and Colin in conversation, looking from time to time in the direction of the staircase. She could tell that her father was growing restless but Colin talked on, oblivious to the minutes that ticked on and on. Outside, the sun was a fireball in the pink sky.

"Come look at the sunset," she said, waving them to the window facing west. They clustered around her, each praising the beauty of the sky. For it was surreal, with hues of azure streaked with pinks and wispy clouds of white. Venus was dazzling beside the slender moon, high above the tips of spruces at the crest of the mountaintops. They watched the sun's graceful descent in awe till the room was bathed in the dim gray light of dusk. The silence was broken by a rustling and the clear, melodic sound of Maybelle's voice.

"Welcome to Fallingstar."

Laurel spun on her heel to gasp at the sight of Maybelle, resplendent in a long, flowing gown of a red every bit as brilliant and spectacular as that of the setting sun. The crimson set off her silvery hair, worn wound her head in multiple, intricate braids adorned here and there with the sparkle of diamonds. She stood still and pensive in the doorway, rivaling the sunset. Laurel had never seen Maybelle look more lovely.

"My dear Ms. Starr," Arthur said, turning to face her.

He gave her his full attention. "It's a pleasure to meet you at last."

Laurel saw Maybelle physically quiver under her father's regard. During an awkward lull during which everyone seemed to be staring at her, Maybelle's hands clenched her skirt and she took one step back, as though to turn into the hall and escape again into her room. Laurel thought it was her shyness with strangers that spooked her and stepped forward to come to her side. But Maybelle recovered, straightened, and stepped forward into the room as regally as a queen.

"The pleasure is mine, Dr. Carrington," she replied.

Arthur's head tilted to one side, as though he was hearing something he was trying to recognize.

"A pleasure to see you again, Ms. Starr," Colin said, coming forward without hesitation.

Maybelle spared him a quick, assessing glance. Then she returned her full attention to Arthur. "Laurel," she said, "it is quite dark in this room. Could you light the lamps, please?"

"Of course," she replied, and quickly went to do so.

"Quaint, aren't they?" remarked Colin on the oil lamps. "Saves on electricity, I'll bet."

Maybelle's nose rose a tad. "I assure you, young man, that cost is no concern of mine," she replied with an enviable cool. "I choose to live my life in a natural manner. Such a lifestyle requires a fortitude of spirit and a gift for nature that is all too rare. Your daughter," she added, directing her comment to Arthur, "is one of the rare ones." Maybelle's face softened as she smiled warmly at Laurel. "The rarest."

"Don't I know it," Arthur said, his pride audible.

Soon the small living room was bathed in the soft, golden light of the oil lamps. Maybelle remained still and quiet, her eyes fixed on Arthur with an expression of expectancy. He returned the study in earnest with a puzzled expression on his face. It was the most awkward meeting, Laurel thought, with none of the exuberance and warmth she had hoped for. Instead, everyone seemed to be on tenterhooks, awash in uncertainty.

"Let's sit down, shall we?" she said, hoping to get them moving at least. "Then I'll see to dinner. You've done enough already, Maybelle."

"If you insist," she replied, stunning Laurel. Maybelle usually brushed away suggestions that she sit in one place. Something very strange was going on.

Maybelle took a few steps across the room toward the sofa when she tripped over something on the floor. Laurel gasped, and reached for her.

Arthur was faster. He lunged and caught a stumbling Maybelle in his arms before she hit the floor. There was a moment of flustered embarrassment and exclamations of surprise and concern.

"Are you all right?"

"Yes, yes, I'm fine. How clumsy of me. I didn't see it."

Arthur righted her to her feet with the care and gentleness he would a fragile butterfly. When Maybelle was standing again, his hands remained on her arms a moment longer while they stood, inches from one another, searching each other's eyes. For a moment in time, neither of them spoke. Neither of them moved apart.

"Are you all right?" Colin asked, rushing forward to assist.

Arthur blinked heavily, as one coming out of a trance, and clearing his throat, dropped his hands from Maybelle, stepping back to a polite distance.

"What? No, I'm fine," said Maybelle, her hands fluttering in the air to chase away Colin at her elbow. "I said I was fine." Looking hopefully into Arthur's face, she asked, "And you?"

"Oh, fine, fine," he blustered in a distracted manner, patting his pockets as though looking for something. "It's just . . ."

"Yes?" Maybelle held her breath.

He stilled and thought for a moment. "It's the damnedest thing. For a moment there I thought . . ." He paused to tug at his ear. "It's ridiculous, I know, but I could have sworn I knew you." He looked at her again, searchingly, before shaking his head and chortling. "But of course that's wrong. I would have remembered meeting someone as lovely as you," he said gallantly.

Maybelle seemed to wilt on the spot. Her shoulders slumped, her face paled and she faltered in her step. Alarmed, Laurel rushed to her side.

"Maybelle, you aren't well. It's all too much. I never should have . . ."

"Nonsense," she gently scolded, tapping Laurel's hand.

Laurel escorted her to the open window where she held on to Maybelle while she breathed a bit of fresh air. When color returned to her cheeks, Maybelle turned to Laurel and said in a motherly way, "Don't live in a world of *I never should have*. Regret is a terrible burden to carry through life. It stoops your shoulders and keeps you looking down at the ground rather than up at the stars." She sighed and patted Laurel's cheek. "Not to worry. I'm just under the weather. It happens to the best of humans, you know. I shall just go to my room and rest awhile longer." She glanced over her shoulder but did not face Arthur or Colin. "I do hope you'll forgive me for not joining you at the table."

Assurances were hastily made and Laurel escorted Maybelle back up the stairs into her room. Maybelle appeared older and weaker, and even more disheartened as she took mincing steps. Laurel helped her change from her elaborate attire into a simple, white nightgown with ribbons and lace high at the neck. She unwound the many braids and brushed her magnificent hair, then helped her into her bed and covered her with the airy down coverlet. How small and childlike Maybelle appeared in the large bed made of trees, with her silvery hair spread out in waves across the pillow. Up close, her eyes appeared more cloudy than ever and Laurel shuddered, wondering how much time Maybelle would have before she was completely blind.

She closed the door behind her, pausing on the landing to wipe her eyes and straighten her skirt before joining the others. Despite Maybelle's warning, Laurel felt a storm of regret in her chest. She should never have invited her father and Colin to Fallingstar. Dane had been right. It was clear Maybelle could not tolerate the presence of strangers. Nothing had been the same since they'd arrived. She regretted ever having seen La Belle Rose.

Arthur rejoiced at first sight of La Belle Rose. He slipped to his knees into the soft ferns and grass of the fissure before the rose he'd sought for twenty-one years. Sunlight poured through the aperture directly onto the small, thronelike bed and the single rosebush it held.

He stared in awe. Such delicacy of color, the soft, artless purity of the virginal white, tinged with a maiden's blush . . . Arthur's breath exhaled in a long, whistling plume. He did not even remember how beautiful the rose was. How could his mind conjure up such perfection? His hands shook as he reached out to touch the delicate petals of one rose blossom.

"She's exquisite," breathed Colin, coming closer.

"I've spent a quarter of a century devoting myself to the preservation of old roses," Arthur said. "I've searched all over the world for rare cultivars. I've amassed the nation's largest collection of rosebushes, spending thousands upon thousands every year in maintenance, research, and development." He waved his hands in front of the rose, searching for the words, so caught up in the sight his mind stumbled. "But none of them, not a one, compares to La Belle Rose. She is unparalleled. The reward of a lifetime of dedication."

Laurel came to his side to rest her hand on his shoulder. He turned to face her and she was surprised to see tears in his eyes. He smiled tremulously and patted her hand. "I had begun to doubt that she really existed," he said in a low voice. "I thought perhaps it was all a trick of my memory. As was your mother. But today, I see that it was true. She exists. And it's all thanks to you, my dear. You found La Belle Rose for me. You've restored my faith." He rolled his eyes. "And to think I tried to stop you from coming here. What a foolish, stubborn old man I can be at times, eh?" He squeezed her hand fervently and his eyes shone. "This was your destiny, you see that, don't you? Your birthright. To find La Belle Rose."

"Sure, Dad," she said, shaken not only by his rare show of emotion but by his assertions.

He averted his eyes, catching sight of Colin looking at him askance and Dane not far away, looking on with compassion. "Oh, don't mind me," he said, seemingly embarrassed. "I was merely unprepared for the power the memories would have on me by the sight of La Belle Rose again. I'm quite all right, just a tad emotional."

Embarrassed, he rose to his feet and walked around the small, tropical enclosure, collecting his composure. It didn't take long for him to become completely enthralled, not only by the collection of roses but by the fissure itself. He sought Dane out, who was standing off to the side.

"I don't understand. How can you grow these rare roses here, in Vermont?"

"It's a natural microclimate. The pools are underground water systems and the sun streams in like a funnel. They work together to create this oasis of protection in a zone too harsh for roses."

"But where did Maybelle find them?"

"I can't answer that question. You'll have to ask her yourself."

He shook his head, incredulous. "The whole thing is absolutely fascinating. Miraculous."

"If you want to see miraculous, look at this," Colin said excitedly, waving over Arthur. "Am I nuts, or am I seeing a true blue rose? Blue! Unbelievable. Calgon Labs has been developing the technology to engineer this color for years but the color has always been more violet." He turned to Dane. "What did you do? Remove the genes from something else, a petunia, say? Then splice it into the rose?"

Dane snorted with disgust and shook his head. "We don't splice roses here. We don't cut them at all."

Arthur was confounded. "Are you saying the color is genetically coded?"

"But there is no genetic coding for the pigment that gives blue flowers their hue," Colin argued.

"There is with this rose," Dane replied. He was unable to keep the smugness from his tone. "What you're looking at, gentlemen, is an ancient species. Virtually unknown."

Colin's mouth dropped open as he stared at the blue rose. "Impossible! A natural blue?" His voice rose and his chest heaved as the implications hit gale force. "Why, if this is true, it . . . it would be worth millions." His gaze swept the collection of roses in the fissure with the hungry intensity of a hawk's soaring for prey. "Why, they all would be."

"Forget it," Dane snapped, stepping forward in a threatening manner. He didn't like the look in Colin's eyes or the greed in his slack-jawed expression. "Nothing here is for sale, public knowledge, or so much as idle gossip. You've come to see La Belle Rose, and now you've seen it. Pack up your gear," he said, his voice loud with authority. "We have to go. It's a long way back and the rocks are very dangerous in the dark. You could fall to your death in a hundred different places." He lowered his voice in warning and pointed his index finger at the two men. "There are forces at work in these woods that will not allow trespassing. You'll never find the fissure again, so don't even try."

Arthur and Colin no doubt thought this a personal threat from Dane. Laurel understood exactly what forces Dane was referring to.

"Wait!" Arthur called out as Dane started to leave. His tone and demeanor were frantic as he swung his head for a last glimpse of La Belle Rose. "Will *she* let me come again?"

"You'll have to ask Maybelle." Dane's brows lowered with suspicion as the two men exchanged glances. "Hurry up now," he said, impatient to get them out and away from his roses. "There's no time to lose."

Laurel's heart broke when she saw Arthur turn once again toward La Belle Rose, adoration in his eyes. She knew what it meant for him to see the rose again and the memories it invoked. She knew, too, how it would pain him to leave it behind and lose it once again.

A single petal fell from La Belle Rose, dropping like a tear drop to the fertile soil. Arthur hurried to kneel before it, his fingers flexing pensively.

"May I?" he asked Dane.

Dane's face softened at the obvious sincerity in Arthur's voice and nodded.

Arthur reached into his vest pocket and tugged out his handkerchief. Unfolding it, he gingerly picked up the delicate petal and carefully set it inside the cloth. He wrapped it with reverence and tucked it back into his pocket.

Laurel's breath hitched and she turned her head, lest he see the tears. She knew that he had tucked safely away his memories of his long-lost love along with that single rose petal.

Dane walked to Laurel's side to take her backpack from her back and hoist it over his own shoulder. Then he took her hand, cast a challenging look at Colin, and led the party out from the fissure on the long, arduous journey home.

The debate continued later that night. Maybelle joined them for dinner, though she remained unusually reserved and distant. It was as if the glow within her that Laurel had come to expect was sputtering and growing dim. Even Amor remained puffed and huddled on his perch. Dane had noticed it too and was extremely alarmed, so much so that he agreed to stay for the torture of dinner. Laurel didn't flatter herself that he stayed for her benefit. She knew that he wanted to be there for Maybelle's sake, to protect her from the inquisition sure to come.

Dane was right. As soon as the angel cake and strawberries were served, Colin launched into his campaign for the roses.

"I have to say again just how extraordinary the roses we saw today are."

Maybelle smiled politely.

"I hope you don't think I'm too bold to discuss such

things, but I implore you to consider allowing me to introduce your roses to the world."

There was a stunned silence, during which Dane's brow lowered threateningly and Maybelle lips pinched.

Even Arthur seemed taken aback at the suddenness of the question. "You'll forgive my assistant," he said, "but he is young and impetuous."

"Miss Starr," Colin boldly continued, "I feel compelled, for the sake of mankind to make this request. And yours! You must know your roses are priceless. If brought to the public's attention, not only would you bring the world the pleasure of their beauty, but . . . do you know how much they're worth?"

Dane's mouth tightened with annoyance and Laurel could feel her own shoulders stiffen. Maybelle, however, merely picked up her spoon and lazily scooped out a strawberry.

"I know exactly what they're worth, young man. To me."

"Well, of course," Colin said with a self-deprecating chuckle. "I'm not disregarding the emotional price." He placed elbows on the table and leaned forward with a speculative look. "What would you say if I told you that I could arrange it that you could make millions from your roses. Many millions." He sat back in his chair with the air of a man who'd just placed four aces on the table. "Just think of what you could do with all that money. You could update your house. Get real plumbing. Electricity. A car—many cars!"

"Imagine that," Maybelle replied with a straight face, popping a strawberry into her mouth. Laurel choked back a laugh and caught Dane's eye. His face was lit and it was clear he was enjoying this immensely. Arthur shifted in his seat uncomfortably and cleared his throat, muttering, "Damn fool."

Colin cast a victorious glance at Dane. "I'm especially interested in the blue rose. The quest for a blue rose has already taken centuries. And I'm your man to end the search, just in time for the new millennium. Cuttings from that one plant could be made, genes cloned. Rosebushes could be reproduced in the thousands, millions, and sold throughout the world. We'll all be rich. Famous!"

"Forget it," Dane fired out with contempt. "The roses can't be cut."

Laurel saw clearly the greed and ambition in Colin's eyes and the conviction in Dane's. Colin couldn't have used any argument that would have solidified Dane's position more. To think, a few short months ago she would have shared Colin's excitement. A treasure trove such as this would guarantee one's career and fortune. Now, however, she saw that reasoning as worthless in light of what was at risk.

"It's not your decision, farm boy," Colin fired back.

"You don't understand," Laurel said, jumping into the conversation. "This isn't just another science versus nature discussion, or a cocktail debate on whether genetic engineering is helpful or harmful. Dane means these roses in particular can't be cut. Literally. If they are, they'll die."

"But that's ridiculous," Colin exclaimed, slicing his hand through the air. "All roses can be cut."

"Not necessarily," Arthur interrupted, his palm up in the air. "Not everything in nature is so cut and dried . . . you'll pardon my pun," he added with a deferential bow toward Maybelle.

Her eyes crinkled with delight.

"I've heard of such roses," Arthur continued, tugging at his earlobe. "In clubs or while having drinks with old cronies. I'd thought they were rumors, but now I'm not so sure. And I never got a cutting from La Belle Rose, of course. Meant to, but . . ."

His voice trailed off but Laurel knew that that was the precise moment her mother had appeared and distracted him.

Maybelle set her spoon down and sat very straight in her chair, her pale, opaque eyes only on Arthur.

"If this young man states that the roses can't be cut," Arthur said with decision, "I for one would be inclined to believe him."

"Well, even if the particular plant did die," Colin argued, "the genes would live on for future propagation."

"You don't know that for sure. Or if you can genetically reproduce the rose without flaws," Dane fired back. "Then there's the risk of contamination by bacteria, molds, yeasts, and the death of the plant. Genetic experiments are being conducted at random today, without thought to risk or accountability."

"I know your type. You're just too ignorant to understand the technology and are afraid of progress," Colin snarled. "Well, welcome to the new millennium and move out of our way."

"He's not that type at all," Laurel fired back in defense. She was furious at Colin, not for his stance as much as his nasty, personal swipes in the debate and in the garden. In fact, she realized it was his style to make nasty remarks to a lot of people. "Dane doesn't trust the technology, and with good cause. We all recognize that plants and animals, and indirectly, humans, are all becoming mere research tools."

"Taking his side now, are we?" Colin said in a low, calculating voice.

"Now, now ... It seems we've slipped into a heated debate anyway," Arthur said in a placating manner. "I assure you, we won't settle these weighty issues. Laurel was right. This debate can go on for hours and we're all much too tired after our exhausting trek today. And besides," he said in summation, "all our points are moot without the consent of Ms. Starr. We must remember, they are *her* roses."

"Roses can't belong to any one person," Colin said indignantly. "They belong to the world."

Dane set his hands on the table so firmly the silverware rattled. "I'd be happy to explain that fact to you in no uncertain terms. Outside," he said in a deadly calm, but his eyes were glittering dangerously.

Colin snorted derisively but his eyes appeared hunted.

"What makes you think you have the right to these roses?" Laurel asked Colin. "What makes these roses any different from a few paintings by Michelangelo hung in some single collector's private collection, or a handful of uncut diamonds sequestered in a vault? Or perhaps a young colt with incredible speed left by its owner to grow and breed in peace without running a single race? They're all treasures, privately held, unknown to the public. Do you think you have the right to go into their homes and simply take what you will by virtue of being a human being? Maybelle is such a collector. Dane and my father are quite correct in stating that it is her decision whether or not to share her treasures."

She dabbed at her mouth with her napkin and set it neatly on the table. "And I can assure you, Colin, I will encourage her not to share them. Not with the public or the scientific community. And least of all with you."

Colin's face flushed furiously, taking her stand as a personal betrayal. "So you're taking his side again?" he said, jerking his head in Dane's direction. "You? Someone who has just been accepted into Cornell's graduate program for genetic engineering? Doesn't that strike you as a bit two-faced?"

Dane's head swung around to stare at her searchingly.

Laurel could have killed Colin. She had wanted to tell Dane and Maybelle in her own way, in her own time. She pushed back her chair and rose to stand, the flush of fury staining her cheeks. All she could think was that she was an idiot to have waited so long to have come to her current decision and that she would burst if she had to wait one moment longer.

"Colin, I'd like to speak with you, alone," she said. She spoke calmly, civilly, but the trembling in her voice betrayed her. "Excuse us, please," she said to Maybelle, then with a curt nod to Colin, led him from the kitchen to the garden outside with her chin in the air.

"How dare you call me two-faced?" she hissed, spinning on her heel as soon as they reached the outdoors. "In front of my father? In front of Maybelle. In front of . . ." she bit off Dane's name, but she knew by the way Colin's eyes ignited he understood anyway. What she didn't know was that inside the kitchen, three adults sat quietly in an awkward silence as they listened to the argument through the open windows.

"I'm simply calling it as I see it, my dear. You wax and wane in there in front of your hostess, who is a first-class nut case, by the way. You put on this show in front of them, pretending you're against technology and progress, and all the while you're planning a career in genetic engineering. That makes a rather interesting ethical dilemma, wouldn't you say?"

"Not at all," she replied coolly, though the trembling in her voice gave her away. "Genetic engineering is not wrong in itself, nor is the technology of cloning. In the end it boils down to two things. Personal accountability and a sense of responsibility to nature." She drew herself up and crossed her arms across her chest. "Neither of which, I'm sad to discover, do I feel you possess."

She heard him suck in his breath, saw the gray storms forming in his eyes.

"I suppose your farmer in there does?"

"As a matter of fact, he does."

"Aha, now we're getting to the truth of it. Let's not pretend any longer that you've not been having your cake and eating it too. Talk about two-faced! You're fooling around with both me and that farmer in there. I've seen the sparks fly whenever you two are together."

In the kitchen, Arthur's brows rose and he turned his head to look at Dane as only a father could under such circumstances.

Laurel laughed, infuriating Colin all the more.

"What's so funny?"

"It's the cake thing. You wouldn't understand."

Colin's anger deflated and he took a step closer to her. "Why are we fighting, Laurel? We both want the same things. Darling, this is the big break we've been waiting for! If we can pull off this deal we'll be set for life. So will your father. I can reproduce thousands of those blue roses, and the same goes for all the others, even that La Belle Rose that you and your father are so fond of. All we have to do is sneak back in that fissure and take a few clippings. No one need know. Just a snip here and a snip there . . ." He clicked his fingers. "And we're rich. I'll buy you a diamond that will be so heavy you won't be able to lift your hand."

Laurel was so appalled she couldn't speak. She took a long breath, stuffing her hands in her pockets to prevent herself from strangling him. Her fingertips brushed against something hard in her pocket . . . a piece of jewelry. A ring.

Her eyes lit up with recognition. How did it get in there? Did she leave it? What did it matter? Feeling a huge relief, she raised her chin to look at Colin in the eyes.

"I'm sorry, Colin, but your total lack of concern not only for the roses but for Maybelle Starr, a person I happen to love very much, reveals a side to you I've never seen before. I always had my doubts about our relationship, but now that I've seen the blatant disregard with which you pursue your own greed and ambition in the name of science, I'm only ashamed that I even considered your proposal of marriage."

Inside the kitchen, no one took a breath. Maybelle looked at Arthur with a secret smile. He looked totally nonplused. Dane sat with his hands folded on the table and a look of utter focus on his face.

Outside, Colin stiffened and looked as though he'd just sucked a lemon. "Is that your answer?"

"Yes, you have my answer," she replied. Then, pulling out the diamond, she held it out to him and said, "And you have your ring."

Colin's face mottled as he stared at the ring with eyes ablaze. "You're mine!" he shouted, slapping her hand and sending the diamond ring hurtling into the lily bed. In a move much quicker than she expected, he lunged and grabbed her shoulders, dragging her to his lips for a hard, punishing kiss.

Her whimpers sounded in the kitchen, sending Dane leaping to his feet. His chair went flying behind him as he tore off out the door, with Arthur right behind him. When Dane saw Laurel struggling in Colin's arms, batting her hands against him, his world colored red. He lunged forward, ripping Colin away from her and holding him up by the collar while his meaty hand formed a fist. He was about to swing when Arthur jumped forward to grab his arm.

"Hold!" he shouted with authority. "Drop your fist!"

Out of respect for Laurel's father, Dane managed to restrain his wrath—barely. He had to take a deep breath first, then he released Colin with an angry shake of the collar and a low growl.

"Thank you," Arthur said with dignity, straightening his shoulders and facing Colin, who was smiling weakly in relief. "I'm her father," he said. "It's my right."

With that he hauled back his fist and socked an unsuspecting Colin squarely in the nose.

Maybelle stood at the kitchen window, looking out at the unfolding scene in her garden. Tears flowed again down her face and hope stirred in her breast. She had just caught a shadowy glimpse of the hero she had fallen in love with, once upon a time.

Twenty-one

"Careful with that step now. Mind the stump!"

Maybelle allowed Arthur to take her arm in his and lift the hem of her skirt a few inches so as not to trip her. They had taken a walk together every evening that week, and another in the morning after breakfast. During the day, they often worked together in the garden, chatting over plants. Oh, he had so many questions! She had always enjoyed that about him—his boundless curiosity. His mind was always seeking answers. Not for the sake of self-aggrandizement or to figure out what he could gain from such knowledge, like that horrid Colin fellow. Arthur was more like Dane, she thought. They pursued knowledge simply for the pleasure of knowing.

Thank heaven that Colin fellow left immediately after the incident, she thought with a shudder. He certainly was not a part of her plan.

"Are you comfortable, my dear?" Arthur asked her. "You aren't too chilled? Too tired?" He lifted her shawl a notch higher up her shoulder.

"I'm perfectly fine, Arthur," she replied, leaning into him. "I'm happy just to be with you."

His cheeks pinkened with pleasure and he muttered, "Good, good," as he led her at a snail's pace along the garden path, mindful lest she trip.

Her eyesight was failing rapidly, making her world dim and precarious. She would be more dismayed, except that Arthur was so solicitous, staying by her side and seeing to every detail. Arthur had always been attentive, Maybelle recalled, but even more so as an older man. When he was younger, his attentions were so . . . physical. She could hardly keep up with his desire for her! This gentlemanly restraint and attention to her comfort was most pleasing, she decided. Every moment they spent together was pure ecstasy for her. If only . . .

No, she wouldn't think about that, she decided, shooing away the glumness and raising her face toward the sunset. As painful as it was, she had to accept that he didn't recognize her as his lost love. That he found Maybelle Starr attractive was flattering. She should not be selfish and hope for more. Her fate was sealed. But she would cherish every moment she had left with him and her daughter! For during the past week she realized she loved Arthur more now than ever. And she thought he was growing fond of her as well.

"Look at that sunset," he said, slowing to a stop at the ledge that faced westward. "I'll wager it makes you want to paint it."

"Perhaps once upon a time, Arthur," she said on a sigh. "But I don't paint much anymore."

"Oh my dear, I'm sorry. I didn't mean to imply . . ."

"Not at all. I've seen many sunsets, so I'm reconciled to the idea that I can't paint them any longer." She tapped his sleeve lightly. "I have Laurel to paint them for me now."

She looked over toward the studio, perched on the other side of the plateau. She couldn't see the details, but she was able to just make out the blurry form of Laurel through the large window, at work in front of an easel.

"Look at her," she said to Arthur. "So dedicated. She's been in there every day, all day. She is so very talented, isn't she? More than I'd ever dreamed."

"I hate to admit it, but she is," he replied somberly. "It's not what I'd hoped for her."

"She must make her own decisions. Have faith in her. I do."

"I try. But it's hard for me. I'm her father. I'm all she has. It's my duty to worry about her."

Maybelle's heart pinged and she kept her lips tight lest she release a cry. Here they were, for the first time since Laurel's birth, standing together and discussing their daughter. And yet she couldn't tell him who she was, could not share this moment with him. She closed her eyes tight lest she say the words and break her vow of silence.

"I don't see much of that Walden fellow lately," Arthur said. "I thought he'd be up here all the time, now that the coast is clear, so to speak."

"It is strange, isn't it?" Maybelle said, tapping her lips. "Both he and Laurel are keeping themselves mightily busy. Too busy, if you ask me. What could be more important than love?"

Arthur's eyes gleamed. "I couldn't agree with you more, my dear."

Maybelle's heart tripped lightly in her chest as she gazed back at him.

"But you know these young ones," he continued. "They have to spin their wheels a bit, see what catches before they zoom off again. I suspect they're both trying to figure a few things out." He looked at her with none of the sheepishness he had exhibited earlier. Each day he seemed a bit more self-assured with her, as though he were no longer afraid of the fire, after having been severely burned. "Isn't it nice that at our age, everything seems so simple? So very straightforward."

Maybelle returned a weak smile that was interpreted as coy agreement. In her mind, however, she was wondering how at their age everything was so twisted with the past. Nothing was straight at all.

"When is that agent fellow coming up? To see her paintings?" he wanted to know.

"On Friday. There's no question that he'll want to sign her. He'll be cool and reserved, it's his manner. But I know he'll be busting his buttons to get her signature. Laurel's paintings of fairies are a step beyond even mine. She just completed one of a fairy contemplating her reflection in the pond, and it is translucent. And poignant. I can see a glimpse of her in the painting.

She's trying so hard to see herself. Laurel has an insight into the fairies that is a gift, I'm sure. For the fairies love innocence more than any other human trait, you know." She turned to Arthur. "You've done a wonderful job raising her. She has a good and open heart."

"As do you," Arthur said, turning to face Maybelle, his hand over hers. "Have I told you yet today how lovely you look?"

Maybelle's face blushed as pink as the sky overhead. When he stood so close, she could catch glimpses of his beloved face between the shadows. After twenty-one years of dreaming, it was enough.

"You've told me at least a dozen times," she replied. Then lifting her eyes coyly she added, "But I wouldn't complain if I heard it again."

Later than same evening, Laurel lay on top of her bed linens reading for the hundredth time the letter from Cornell. *We are pleased to welcome you . . .*

Laurel sighed in disgust and threw the letter on the floor. Why couldn't they have been so jolly well pleased last May? Back then she was so sure of what she wanted. She wouldn't be in this torture of indecision she found herself in now, when she didn't have a clue what she wanted. Her life used to be so easy, her course had been set. All she had to do was follow the path of decisions made for her way back when she was a little girl. It seemed fate had deliberately thrown landmines onto the path to veer her way off course.

And the biggest landmine of all was Dane Walden. A damn big explosion, she groaned, flipping over to her stomach and burying her face in her pillow. Where was he lately? He did his work, then headed straight back down the mountain with hardly a word. She'd been equally busy finishing her series of fairy paintings in time for the agent's visit, but she certainly wasn't deliberately avoiding him—as he was her.

Outside her window she heard a high-pitched, feminine giggling, followed by a low masculine murmur. Laurel groaned and plopped her pillow over her head.

Maybelle and her father were at it again. They were like a couple of lovesick teenagers. She'd never seen her father moon about a lady like he did with Maybelle Starr. He followed her wherever she went, guiding her lest she fall, handing her tools in the garden, helping her bake in the kitchen. And Maybelle! Who'd have guessed she was such a bodacious flirt! They tittered and giggled so much in each other's company that it was hard to be around them.

And yet . . . she thought, tugging off the pillow and tucking it under her chin to stare out at the moon. It was very sweet. She was happy for them, really she was. It was just that her own love life was in such a shambles that hearing the sounds of happiness only reminded her of her own unhappiness.

And how selfish is that? she scolded herself. She had to act on her feelings, not moan and groan. Lying on this bed moping on a beautiful summer night was certainly no solution.

The summer breeze was soft and warm, and it seemed to kiss her cheeks and play with her hair as it swirled around the room. Her lids lowered heavily as she breathed in the sweet scent of roses. Omni hooted in the trees not far from her window. Three low, persistent hoots.

"Uh-uh, no way," she said loudly to the bird, snapping her eyes wide open. "I'm not going to sleep." If she wanted happiness, then she'd have to go find it! She lifted her head from her pillow, swung her legs around and rose to a stand. In front of the mirror she hurriedly coiled her long blond hair up on her head and hastily fastened it with a clip. "No more escaping to my dreams. I'm tired of only being happy in my dreams. I want to find happiness in my real world for a change."

Slipping her feet into her sandals, she opened the door that led outdoors and slipped past the two adults spooning under the nearly full moon. She knew where she might find that elusive happiness, and she quickened her pace down the winding road to a certain Victorian house, and Dane.

She didn't feel the uneasiness she used to feel walking alone in the woods at night. She still sensed the presence of many pairs of eyes watching her from the trees. But she didn't feel they looked on with wariness any longer—rather, in welcome. Laurel felt she belonged here now. The self-bored stone felt warm against her chest as she walked and she touched it briefly, feeling her own inner warmth imbued in the stone.

In a short time she came through the foliage to arrive at Dane's house. The fresh white paint gleamed incandescent in the moonlight. She thought again how much she loved the round tower topped with a weather vane that depicted a long line of dancing fairies, from tall to short. The weather vane was pointing to the north, a sure sign of a coming storm.

Laurel hurried to the front door and knocked. When it swung open, she was surprised to see Daphne's face, not Dane's.

"Well, look who's here," she said, opening the door wide and smiling with welcome. "I was beginning to wonder if you'd ever pay us another visit."

Laurel's gaze searched the room, from the TV flashing in the corner to the empty chairs and sofa, to the dining room. The place was as quiet as the grave.

"Is Dane around? I . . . I had a question for him," she stammered. "About the eggs."

A small smile played on Daphne's lips and her eyes sparkled. "Oh yeah, the eggs. Sure. I'm sure he'd love to talk to you about eggs. You go right on in his office. He's been holed up in there for days. Go on now, don't be shy. Just duck if he throws something. Oh, not at you, darlin'. He's been throwing things in there all day. I warn you, he's in a terrible mood," she said, releasing the smile. It bloomed across her face. "But I think you're just the tonic he needs right now."

"Sure, um, okay," Laurel said, embarrassed to be looked on by Daphne with the same humor that she'd just looked at Maybelle and Arthur. What was so funny about love? she wanted to know.

She walked with a cautious step down the hall to the

closed door of his office. She paused, looking over her shoulder. Daphne stood watching her, still smiling that teasing smile and waving her hand, *go, go*.

Cringing inside but determined, Laurel pushed on the door. It creaked open little by little. When she got it open enough for her to stick her head through, she caught her breath in surprise to find Dane hunched over his desk, his hand tugging at his hair in utter misery as he pored over pages and pages of his copious notes.

The door betrayed her by releasing a loud, aching screech on its hinges as she pushed it fully open. Dane swung his head around to face her, his brows high.

She melted just seeing his face again, with his high cheekbones, his dominant nose, and his forehead so broad and high that his wild, uncombed hair resembled the mane of a noble lion. Except that this lion seemed wounded, or trapped in a cage looking for an escape.

He sprang to his feet to stand awkwardly before his desk, almost as though he wished he could hide the sight of his papers from her.

"I'm sorry to barge in like this," she said, self-consciously. "Daphne told me to come right in. Should I go?"

"No. No problem. Come in, come in," he said, stepping aside to make room.

The room was so crowded she had to squeeze in past him, making certain she didn't brush against him. Her head barely reached the top of his shoulder and she felt the urge to stop a minute just to lay her head upon it in the way she saw Maybelle rest her head on her father's. She moved to stand across from him.

"I haven't seen much of you this week," she said, feeling a bit embarrassed for coming down on the spur of the moment. It wasn't her style to be spontaneous. She usually called first. "I thought I'd come by and see how you are."

"I've been busy." He briefly indicated the desk.

Laurel peeked over his broad shoulders and her eyes widened with surprise. "You're working on your rain forest notes?"

He nodded, looking at the cluttered mess. Then, with a pained expression, he reached up to scratch his head in exasperation. "I'm trying to. It's a damn mess as you can tell and I can't make head nor tails of it."

Laurel felt a tremor of excitement to discover him at work on his notes. If she said "good for you," he'd take it as condescending. If she offered to help, he might take it as an intrusion. He could be so touchy, and he was showing his teeth tonight. She stepped forward tentatively. "What seems to be the problem?"

He turned toward the papers with a look of utter defeat mingled with angst. "There's so damn many scribbles and drawings and descriptions . . . it's overwhelming. I don't know where to begin. Organization has never been my strong suit."

"But it is one of mine," she said, with a touch of pride. "I could help you, if you like. Tell me, what are you trying to accomplish?"

She was shocked to see a faint blush tinge the tip of his ears. His mouth worked but the words didn't come. She waited patiently.

"I thought I'd . . ." He cleared his throat. "Well, you know . . ." He shrugged his shoulders. "I thought maybe I'd . . . write that book." He flipped his hands in a self-deprecating manner, as if to say, *can you imagine that?*

Laurel could imagine, and her heart soared. She was deeply moved and impressed that he'd even try, knowing what a breakthrough this was for him. "Dane, that's wonderful," she said, stepping close to him, her voice enthusiastic. "You *should* do this. It's such a contribution. I'm so proud of you."

Dane turned toward her in degrees, his face a mask of deep emotions. He looked down at her from his great height, and the contrast between his physical power and his inner vulnerability moved her.

"Are you?" he asked.

"Yes. Not just for this, but for everything about you. Your honesty, your goodness. The way you take care of those you love."

His smile came quick and was devastating.

"May I see what you've got so far?" she asked.

"Of course," he replied, lifting a pile of papers from a chair. Once they were settled side by side, he began explaining how he'd tried to catalogue his collection of work, showing her his limited progress on the drawings and notes she'd seen before. "I haven't a clue what's to be done," he muttered, shaking his head in his palm.

"But I know exactly what has to be done." With an alacrity that Dane was astounded by, she began to tear through the papers like a whirling dervish. He could barely keep up with her questions.

They worked at the desk for a long while, heads together, going through enormous piles of his papers. Dane's anxiety eased as he saw order begin to emerge from the chaos. After an hour, he stretched out his arms and legs and mopped his face, emerging from his palms with an ear-to-ear grin at seeing Laurel still with her nose close to a paper and writing with furious intensity. He reached out to whisk the pencil from her fingers. She snapped her head up, blinking her lids over those mesmerizing green eyes.

"That's enough for one night," he said. "I'm sure you didn't come down here to work. Though I have to confess, I never thought it could be done. You're a miracle worker, Laura Carrington."

"No," she said with characteristic modesty. "Chalk it up to experience. You're just like my father," she told him. "You both have an eye for detail, you're both patient, not to mention brilliant. But neither of you have one sliver of ability to organize your thoughts or present your ideas clearly. I suppose if I can help my father I can help you, too. I may not be a genius but I'm good at collaborating."

"I'm like your father?" he asked, pleased by the notion. "Do you really think so?" Idly, he began to twiddle the pencil between his fingers. "Imagine me, being compared to a scholar like your father."

"Dane," she said, leaning back in her chair and searching his face, "that's very easy for me to imagine. Why does that come as such a surprise to you?"

His face clouded as the pencil stilled in his hand. The confidence she had seen in his eyes a moment ago dimmed. She was tempted to say something, anything, to bring it back but kept silent, waiting, giving him the moment to say what it was he needed to.

"I told you I'd try to open up to you, Laurel, and I suppose now's as good a time as any to start." He laughed in pain and shook his head. "Except my thoughts are as jumbled and confused as the papers on that desk."

"I'll help you sort them out too," she said softly, gently urging him on.

He registered that somewhere deep inside. Then he nodded, placing his hand on hers and began speaking.

"Growing up, I wasn't like most other boys around here," he said, his eyes glazing over as he tried to conjure up the memory. When the memory came, it always hit hard and sharp, like a slap from Joe Flannery's hand. "When you're a kid you don't think things through to realize that being different isn't a bad thing. That maybe it's even a good thing. You only know you want to be like the other kids. You only care if you're accepted. And it hurts if you aren't.

"I struck out on all counts. Part of it was our isolation, I know that now. My mother and I lived alone up here in the mountains till I was five. Life wasn't easy, I can tell you. We might've been dirt poor and hungry but we were never unhappy. Rosalind had a gift for living, a rare ability to love everyone and see past their faults to the goodness inside. She met Maybelle, and being a mountain woman, she helped Maybelle survive. Maybelle was having a hard time of it before her paintings took off. But she had a natural gift for growing and she knew all about herbs and flowers." He grinned in memory. "They bonded instantly."

"Did your mother believe in fairies?"

"Not at first. But she was open to the concept, I guess you could say." He glanced up and almost smiled. "It was a fine life for a while. It was hard for us not to get sucked right into Maybelle's magical world. The idea of fairies and gnomes are like candy treats to a lonely boy."

He glanced out the window and she admired the nobility of his profile as he looked out at the mountains he loved. "These mountains were my backyard," he continued, gesturing. "The woods were my playground. I felt more at home in them than I did indoors. The things I used to see!" He laughed shortly, remembering.

"You saw fairies, didn't you?"

The laugh in his eyes died as his glance turned wary. "I was just a lonely kid with a vivid imagination. Hell, I thought I saw a lot of things. Faces in trees, sprites in the pond, elves in the woods. The place was teeming with the Good People. Of course, the problem came when I tried to tell other kids about them. My teachers too."

"I can imagine their reaction."

"The bigger kids beat me up and it was *explained* to me—repeatedly—by teachers and counselors that I was just lonely and had created these imaginary beings as my companions." He paused to add with a tone of defense, "Many children do this."

"I know," she replied seriously. "I did too."

"You saw fairies?"

"No, though I wish I did. I don't know, maybe fairies don't hang out in cities. But I had an imaginary friend who was every bit as real to me as any girl in the school."

Dane smiled again, his gaze sweeping over her with appreciation. "So you were a little bit odd yourself, were you? You know what it's like, to be alone. To be . . . different."

She nodded, thinking to herself that she'd never felt this connected to another person, not even Maybelle. She wasn't even aware that she'd linked fingers with him, knotting them tightly together. "Except I wasn't really all that lonely."

"Me neither! I was pretty damn happy, too, if you want to know the truth." They laughed together with the joy of discovering this secret about each other. Then his smile faltered and gradually fell.

"Then my mother married Joe Flannery and everything changed. We didn't see much of Maybelle anymore. After Daphne was born, Joe really had it out for me. Beat me whenever he had a drink, which was often. I'll never know why he hated me so much. I was just a little kid. I used to think it was because he was jealous of my mother's love for me, something Freudian like that. Bastard that he was, he truly loved my mother, but it became an obsession over the years. It turned mean and ugly. It drove her to become more and more involved with Maybelle's fairy world."

"What happened to her? No one ever talks about Rosalind. There's this shroud of secrecy around her death."

He frowned and considered his words. "We don't talk about it because there was a lot of idle speculation and gossip." A sigh rumbled in his chest and when he spoke, she heard hints of his old obstinacy. "She got sick with cancer. Nothing strange about that. Maybelle gave her tonics, to help ease her pain. Nothing strange about that either. And they worked. But Rosalind became even more disconnected from us. She was still there physically, but her thoughts were elsewhere. Every night at sunset, my mother would walk into the woods alone. Always alone—always at sunset. She'd come back hours later with this look of utter peace on her face. When she wasn't in the woods, she'd sit at the window and stare at them. We all knew she was dying and didn't want to stop her from doing anything that brought her peace, but it was like she was yearning for them, and her visits to the woods grew longer and longer.

"One night, she just didn't come back. We looked everywhere for her." His face was bereft when he lifted his face to hers. "Laurel, I know these woods and I searched every square inch, but I never found her. Not even a clue."

"Never? You still don't know?"

He shook his head. "No, other than she died somewhere, of course."

"So that's when the rumors started?"

"Her disappearance got people claiming that weird

things were happening at Fallingstar. Everyone got in on it. Some local folk started claiming how they'd seen fairies and elves. I write it off as mass hysteria, of course. The next thing you know a story got printed in the newspaper and then all hell broke loose. The article was printed in another city paper, and people from all over started coming. Real believers, not just in the Good People but in all kinds of metaphysical stuff like crystals and extraterrestials, witches and angels, you name it. They believed in everything but the right to privacy. They trampled the woods with their cameras, electronic 'fairy finders,' books, and chants. Kids came with butterfly nets. Worst of all, they hounded Maybelle. Then, after my father disappeared in the woods a short time later, the general idea was that there was some evil lurking deep in the woods."

He snorted and tossed the pencil down on the table. "Bunch of bull, but it kept the trespassers away."

She listened to his story and heard one clear, though unspoken, reality. Placing her hand on his, she leaned forward and asked, "When did you stop believing? In the fairies?"

He appeared troubled, even sad. He looked at her hand, so small on his, as though he could read his answer written upon her pale skin.

"At about twelve," he replied in the manner of an admission. "I guess you could say it was beaten out of me. Not just the physical poundings, but the verbal ones." He clamped his big hands together, fisting one in his palm as he spoke. "Joe told me again and again how worthless I was. How I was dumber than dirt. Not worth the food he put in my belly." His voice turned bitter. " 'Dumb Dane' he used to call me, and the name stuck. Bullies have radar for things that hurt. The bigger I got, the boys didn't dare hit me. So they figured out they could hurt me with words. *Dumb Dane,*" he repeated, staring off. "If a kid hears that enough, he begins to believe it."

She understood so much more about him now. Why he doubted himself. Laurel could picture him, a big, strapping boy with fists like shovels and those vulnerable eyes. She wished she could have been there, to hold him. She reached out to cup his chin and turned his head so that he faced her and looked directly into her eyes.

"Look at me, because I'm going to tell you something true. I find you to be one of the most brilliant men I've ever met," she said with as much conviction as she could place in her voice. "Dane Walden, who are you going to believe? Joe Flannery or me?"

He looked into her eyes, stunned by the stark clarity of her question. What a fool he'd been to waste years believing as true what Joe or bullies or narrow-minded people told him was true. The truth was simple, found in his own heart. And in hers.

"I believe you," he replied, feeling the weight of years of doubt fade into oblivion.

Laurel's face bloomed into a smile and, encouraged, she confessed her own story. "My father always told me that only logic and rational thought had value. I strove to be sensible. Unemotional. These were traits admired by him and the people I grew up with. It was a compliment to be told that I had no spontaneity, no creativity. No spirit. After awhile, I believed him."

"I see the fairy in you, Laurel Carrington. I have since the moment I laid eyes on you. I've never known such a beautiful spirit."

Looking into his eyes, she believed him.

They both laughed then with that unique joy that comes from finding someone who sees you the way you've always dreamed of being seen.

"You know what this means, don't you?" he asked. "We're either crazy or in love."

"Either way," she replied, beaming, "it's magic. We see the best in each other."

His eyes smoldered with emotion as he leaned slowly forward to kiss her forehead, her eyes, her cheeks, her chin, with an excruciating tenderness and restraint. When his lips touched hers she sighed high in her throat that yearned to sing out loud with happiness. The sigh traveled lower into her chest, where it made her heart dance joyously, and lower still, to where a fire sparked and burned for him, only for him.

"Make love to me, Dane," she whispered urgently along his neck near his ear. "No more dreams. I want you to love me now. Make it real, Dane. Please."

She could feel his shudder as he bolted from his seat to draw her up beside him with a suddenness swift and fierce, like a wild creature of the forest. Her breath caught in her throat as she thought he would take her right then and there in the study, against the desk. Instead he reached up to undo the clasp in her hair, catapulting her hair down her shoulders. He coiled the hair in his hand like a skein of silk and with a steady determination typical of him, he pinned her head as he stared long and deeply into her eyes, considering, deciding. Then he kissed her, devouring her mouth, plundering with a responding urgency that told her, in no uncertain terms, that he would make his love known to her as something very physical, very real indeed.

Releasing her, he let her hair tumble down her back again and led her from the room. The hall was dimly lit by a single lamp. The TV was dark and the room still. She peeked around his shoulder for Daphne and was relieved to find she had already left for bed. Dane turned and squeezed her hand, his eyes lit like lamps themselves, then led her up the spindled staircase to the first room on the left.

It was a large room, neat and sparsely furnished. Moonlight poured in through open windows. A single bureau stood against the opposite wall and a single rocking chair sat before the rosy brick fireplace. The room was dominated by a heavy, oak four-poster bed that looked rooted to the floor and scraped the ten-foot ceiling. It was a bed big enough for a man Dane's size to stretch out in, his one indulgence in an otherwise spartan room. The only decoration was the painting over the squared headboard: her painting of the bear cub. That single, moving gesture chased away the tremors she felt stepping into this powerful man's bedroom, of being led by his large hand toward his enormous bed.

This was so different from her dreams. In them she was always ethereal, ensconced in a secluded forest, dancing in moonlight, swirling in a twinkling mist. Here, the floor she crossed was of varnished wood, the bed she approached was bold, square cut, and covered with practical, white, crumpled sheets. The man holding her hand was not an illusion. He was flesh and blood. He smelled of cherry smoke and leather. He was hard boned, and under his skin, his blood ran hot.

She released his hand and began unbuttoning the row of buttons on her cotton blouse. This was what she wanted, she was not too shy to show it. He turned his head to look down at her with a flashing of fierce desire. She thrilled to it, amazed that even the hint of seeing her body was enough to spark such passion in this man. He tore off his own clothes, throwing them carelessly to the floor. His body was more magnificent in reality than in any dream. She wanted to tell him he was beautiful, but the words were all jumbled in her mind. All she could do was reach out to gently touch the glorious expanse of muscle, as smooth as marble.

Her touch ignited him and he delighted in seeing her body too, for real this time. She was pale as the moonlight, a luminous creature of soft curves and flowing gold hair that curled around her shoulders to cup the curve of her breast and the bone of her hips. She appeared so lovely as to be otherworldly, but he didn't want a dream. He wanted his hands on her, to feel the softness of her skin against his coarse palms. His large hands moved to her shoulders, trembling as they gently slid down her flesh, lowering the slender bra straps. They caressed her as they traveled down her back to the clasp and with a flick of his fingers, the clasp was undone. In one smooth sweep his hands moved to her breasts, sampling their fullness. Another sigh escaped her lips and her head tilted back, exposing her long, pale neck. He lowered his lips to it, bringing goosebumps of pleasure to her skin. Then lower to graze the gentle swell of her breasts.

Laurel arched against his hold while her hands raked

his hair. Her knees weakened and he caught her, lifting her in his arms, thinking she weighed little more than a feather pillow.

He lowered her to his bed, arching over her to study her face in the shifting light. She lay there, her hair spilled upon his sheets, totally vulnerable and open beneath him. Yet it wasn't fear or lust he saw shining in her eyes. In those green orbs that were wide open, he saw a love that was as deep as it was true.

His breath caught in his throat as a memory triggered and he recognized those eyes. Fairy eyes, he'd called them, and they were. He'd seen eyes like these before— peeking out from behind leaves as a boy, luring him to play. The eyes of a sprite, his friend in the forest. His best friend. How he'd loved that pixie! When he'd looked into those fairy eyes as a boy he saw himself as anything he wanted to be: an Indian warrior, a pirate, an astronaut, an explorer. No dream was too big!

He never thought he'd feel that way again. He'd thought he had lost that exhilaration and confidence along with his youth. Yet, that was how he felt now, looking into Laurel's eyes. In her eyes he felt he could be anything he wanted to be, do anything he wanted to do. He was a conqueror. He felt invincible.

This was the magic he'd sought all his life, he realized with a glorious rush. And it was right here before him, real and without illusions. It was here all the time, all he had to do was see it. The magic was love.

"I love you," he said, giving voice at last to the sentiment that had played in his heart for so long.

Laurel heard the words and felt she'd sprouted wings and taken flight. Looking into his eyes, shimmering like dark woodland pools, she saw her true reflection at last. In his eyes, she was revealed as both fairy and human, lightness and dark, sun and moon, spontaneity and reserve, capriciousness and honesty. In his eyes she was a woman in all her glory. All that she was now, and all that she could ever be. Suddenly her dreams shimmered into crystalline reality.

"I love you," she said.

They both felt a sudden, desperate need to join together, to become one. He lowered himself, bringing his lips to hers, relishing the sweetness of her lips, enveloped again by the scent of mountain laurel that seemed to permeate her skin.

Laurel reached up to wrap slender arms around his neck, clinging tight to his body as it lowered into hers. She arched again in welcome, closing her eyes as she felt the blade of a two-edged sword, forged by love and honed by honesty, obliterate the division between dream world and reality. As he plunged deeper within her, she felt him cut through to a simple truth. She couldn't analyze or rationalize—she couldn't think at all. She could only feel, captured in the moment. Her senses overwhelmed her, victorious, as she reveled in the taste of him, the smell of him, the feel of him.

She felt her two worlds spinning within her, the outer and the inner, faster and faster until they skidded out of control. They collided, exploding in a burst of blinding light. She cried out, holding him tight as the light transformed her. Then it trailed off into a flurry of tiny, sparkling lights that danced in her veins, behind her eyelids, and in her chest, tickling her and making her smile, aglow in happiness. She never knew she could feel such happiness.

Dane was shattered, blown to bits. His breath heaved and sweat pooled on his brow as he slumped beside her, bringing her up onto his shoulder, cleaving her close to him. He felt her cheek nestle in the crook of his arm, felt her shoulders nudge against his side, and her fingers come to rest on his chest.

He'd never known he could allow anyone to touch him in this way, to reach far down into the deepest corner of his soul where some remnant of the joy he'd experienced as a boy could be found again. She'd pulled it out, shaken the ragged scrap in the moonlight to whisk away the dust of doubt and neglect that had obscured its light over the years.

How long he lay there with her in his arms he didn't know. Time had no meaning. He felt exposed. Newborn.

Empowered. So he simply watched her, stroking her hair gently, as her breathing gradually grew slow and steady. He didn't dare sleep, wouldn't take his gaze from her as he held her close in his arms. A love like this came once in a lifetime, maybe. It was a gift promised in dreams and only occasionally, given in reality. He held tight to Laurel, to the love he felt for her, lest this slip of magic in his arms dissipate then disappear like another of his dreams.

Twenty-two

Laurel stood in a shroud of silence between her father and Dane, wishing her heart would stop pounding so loudly. Across the room, Maybelle was chatting amiably with the distinguished art agent, catching up on old times. The portly man in the well-cut suit and highly polished shoes spoke softly, making it almost impossible to catch the conversation.

It was clear by Mr. Silverman's bright eyes and animated hand gestures, however, that he was terribly excited. It had been five years since Maybelle Starr had released a painting to the public. When Maybelle had called to inform him that she had an apprentice ready to show her work, Mr. Silverman begged to drive up immediately from Boston and had to be persuaded to wait the two weeks Maybelle had requested. Laurel could hear Maybelle describing her paintings to Mr. Silverman as "positively inspired."

Such praise whittled Laurel's confidence rather than build it. Maybelle had spared no energy to make this event special. The front room was overflowing with a bounty of freshly picked flowers from her garden. In the corner, Maybelle had set up a delectable tea on snowy white linen that included buttery scones, poppy-seed and angel cakes, and a bowl of fresh fruit. And all this was but a shadow of the preparations she'd made for that evening. Maybelle was all aflutter for a grand celebration in honor of the blue moon due to rise.

"Why does Maybelle praise my work so to him?" she

348

whispered, leaning close to her father. In her shoes, her toes were curling. "I'll only have to live up to it."

"You're just being modest," he replied, squeezing her hand in a fatherly manner.

"You have to say that, you're my father."

"No one is more surprised than I am to discover your talent!" he replied. "I am your worst critic, Laurel. I didn't want to see you do anything but fail as an artist. You know that to be true. So when I tell you that your work is marvelous, you have to believe me. I couldn't be prouder of you."

When she saw Maybelle coming her way with Mr. Silverman in tow, however, she straightened upright, unable to catch her breath. She might have darted from the room but she felt Dane's arm firmly around her waist.

"You'll do fine, love," he whispered in her ear.

She might have come up with some clever retort but her mouth was busy forming a gracious smile as Mr. Silverman extended his hand. Maybelle was right behind him with her brows high in anticipation over glittering eyes.

"This has been such a lovely afternoon, visiting again with my dear friend Maybelle," Mr. Silverman said. "But I haven't forgotten the purpose of my visit. If you're quite ready, may we progress to the studio?"

Laurel swallowed her stomach that had just jumped into her throat. With her smile in place, she led the way across the gravel path to the small studio that perched on the mountain ledge like a summer house. Taking a deep breath, she pushed open the door and stepped aside for the rest of the party to pass. Dane's eyes signaled a quick and meaningful message of support as he walked in, but he kept a respectful distance, aloof with his hands deep in his pockets, allowing Laurel to focus solely on the business at hand.

It was a working studio, with pots of paint, empty canvases, and boxes of fairy costumes stored neatly on wooden shelves. Yet it, too, was dressed up for the day. The wood floors were polished and it was filled with flowers she had chosen this morning. Their sweet fragrance diluted the pungent odor of oil paint and turpentine that permeated the space. Sunlight poured in through the sparkling clean windows, expertly illuminating the four paintings hanging on the pristine white wall. Laurel clutched the self-bored stone she always wore around her neck and squeezed it, seeking courage from this small touchstone.

The paintings depicted four fairies, each in a different pose, one more exquisite than the other. They appeared otherworldly, glimmers of light and transparent shapes that transcended physical form. Though the surroundings were expertly rendered: a woodland pond, a fairy bower, the canopy of trees, an old graveyard—the fairies drew the eyes, then held them mesmerized.

She watched Mr. Silverman walk as one transfixed toward the farthest one on the left. He studied it with his hands clasped behind his back for some time before moving on to the second, then the third and the fourth in the same manner. Maybelle, Dane, and Arthur clustered together with their heads bent, looking at the paintings, then at Mr. Silverman in turn.

Laurel could only look at her paintings. Each fairy represented some part of herself that she had discovered this summer. As this stranger scrutinized the paintings Laurel felt so exposed, as though he were reading bits of her diary.

As one would look through a telescope, Laurel lifted the self-bored stone and squinted through the opening to better examine a painting. Suddenly, she saw the fairy's eye wink, directly at her, and her translucent, dragonfly-like wings fluttered delicately at her back.

Laurel gasped and dropped the self-bored stone from her fingers, feeling it thud against her chest on the leather strap. Stunned, she took several deep breaths, trying to calm herself, trying to convince herself that she hadn't seen what she thought she'd just seen. It was her nervousness, her imagination, her . . .

"Marvelous, Miss Carrington. Simply marvelous!" Mr. Silverman was rushing to her side, his face suffused with excitement. He turned to Maybelle, clasping her hands, shaking them, muttering more exclamations of praise. Maybelle's eyes were as round as her teacups, never before having seen her agent so enthused.

"I must confess," he gushed on, "that I was concerned that anyone could capture the style of Maybelle Starr. But you managed it, you absolutely did! And I'm delighted to offer you a contract right here on the spot. There is a tremendous interest now in anything remotely connected to fairies. They're the height of fashion, bringing visitors to exhibitions of fairy paintings in droves. I can't imagine what's spurring it on, but Miss Carrington, your timing is impeccable. I'd love to take these with me, upon reaching terms, of course, then perhaps we can discuss a timetable for your next canvases?"

Laurel felt a choking sensation, strangling off her reply. Of course she was pleased, delighted! Yet she wasn't prepared for it, never really thought she'd succeed. Now it was like she was boxed into a corner with only one avenue of action. She put her hand into her pocket to finger the envelope from Cornell University. She'd brought it with her today to remind her that she had other options to consider, as she had brought another envelope with her one May afternoon. How long ago that day felt now.

Her gaze darted to Dane for an answer. He stood apart, watching her intently with his dark eyes, like an animal in the brush. He gave her no sign of encouragement or any indication of what it was he would have her do. She knew he would want her to make her own decision.

Her father stood beside Maybelle, his chin up and rocking on his heels. He said nothing, but she could see his pride in the sheen on his face and gleam in his eye. He would accept any decision she made.

Finally, she sought out Maybelle. She stood beside Mr. Silverman, somber. Her opaque eyes seemed to look inward. Laurel expected a delighted expression, but instead, it was concern she saw on Maybelle's face as she tilted her head and studied Laurel.

Mr. Silverman cleared his throat with impatience, his brows raised in question.

"That is quite an exciting offer, Seymour," Maybelle replied, graciously ending the awkward silence. "But sudden. Would you mind allowing Miss Carrington time to consider it?"

"Of course, of course," he replied, anxious to comply. "Take all the time you need, Miss Carrington. I've some important calls to make. Why don't I return to the Inn? You can reach me there when you're ready."

"Thank you," Laurel replied, relieved. "I have the number of the Inn."

"Do you need help finding your way out, sir?" Dane asked.

"No, no, I can find my own way. A lovely drive," he murmured, hurrying to the door.

After the door closed behind Mr. Silverman, Maybelle turned to face them with solemnity. "There is one more painting that we should see. Privately. Dane, would you come with me, please? I could use your assistance. This one is quite large."

Laurel held her breath, bringing her fingers to her lips to stifle her whimper of protest. Arthur swung his head to face her, his own brows raised in question. Laurel could only shrug as she saw Dane carefully carrying in a large five-foot draped canvas.

"Set it right here, please," Maybelle directed, centering the painting against the wall. Everyone moved nearer, drawn close by their curiosity, which was heightened by Maybelle's obvious nervousness. Her hands trembled as they smoothed out the large swath of blue velvet that draped the canvas, seemingly delaying the moment of unveiling. If she were a professional auctioneer, she couldn't have worked up their excitement any higher.

She turned away from the painting slowly, her face unusually pale against the brilliant blue. Her eyes sought out Laurel's and in that gaze Laurel felt an overpowering surge of love and a plea of some sort. Understanding? Forgiveness? If so, Laurel couldn't imagine for what.

She assumed it was simply that Maybelle hadn't discussed with her the showing of this particular painting. It was of no matter, so Laurel nodded and returned Maybelle's smile, indicating she should go ahead.

Instead of elation, she was disturbed to see Maybelle's anxiety deepen. Next she turned her gaze to Arthur and settled it on him. She drew her shoulders back and lifted her chin in the regal stance that came so naturally to her.

Arthur stilled, returning Maybelle's pensive gaze, sensing something imminent approaching.

Dane and Laurel exchanged concerned glances.

Maybelle turned swiftly, swirling her long skirt around her legs. With a graceful sweep of her arm, she lifted the blue velvet with a snap. The fabric rose high in the air, off the canvas, then floated soundlessly to the floor.

There was a collective gasp in the room. Under the brilliant light of the sun, the magnificent blues and silver colors of Laurel's painting seemed to pulse, breathing life into the portrait of two young and beautiful fairy women holding hands, both with shimmering hair, dancing in all their natural glory together in a moonlit meadow.

Dane stood ramrod-straight, his hands bunched at his thighs as he stared in shock at the portrait. His mind whirled, asking again and again one frenzied question: *How could Laurel have painted his dream?* He stared at the painting, then swung his head to stare at the artist. What was reality and what was a dream blurred.

Arthur staggered forward, his mouth agape, his hand uplifted, his finger pointing at the painting like a man possessed. His face had gone pale and his eyes were wide and bulging.

"It's you!" he cried, staring at the painting. He swung around, directing his pointing finger at Maybelle, screaming accusingly. "You!"

Maybelle remained motionless, saying nothing, meeting his wide-eyed stare with anguish.

"What madness is this?" Arthur cried, stepping to within inches of Maybelle's face and searching it frantically. His was reddened with passion. Hers was as pale as death. "You lured me here, lured our daughter, under false pretenses, never once divulging who you really are? How inhuman can you be?"

"I'm . . ."

His eyes were wild with grief and he cut off her reply with a sharp swing of his hand. "What possible pleasure could you gain from watching me, watching our only child, endure heartbreak again? You can't know how I suffered when you left me. Have you any idea what pain your abandonment has caused Laurel? What kind of creature are you?" he shouted.

"A fairy!" she cried back, tears streaming down her face.

Arthur stepped back, his arms splayed out as he stared back at her with disbelief.

Laurel stifled her cry with her palms, too stunned to make sense of the scene unfolding before her. Beside her, Dane remained motionless. Everyone stared at Maybelle as though she had just sprouted fairy wings on her back.

Arthur moved first, rising to his full height, straightening his suitcoat and smoothing back his hair from his face with quiet dignity, though his hands trembled. Then he faced Maybelle with the cool reserve that Laurel was accustomed to.

"How dare you?" he asked with cold civility. "You show up in our lives once again, after twenty-one years, and the only explanation you have is that you are a fairy? And you expect us to believe this? You're mad, woman."

"I am a fairy. I know it sounds incredible, but it's true. Arthur, think!" she cried in a panic, holding out her hand to arrest him from stomping away in a fury. "Remember back to when we first met. It was in the rocky glen. In Danbyshire. You were about to cut into the rose you had just discovered, do you recall?"

He half turned, not looking at her directly, but listening.

"I stayed your hand then. I knew one cut would kill

the rose. And I was particularly fond of that blossom. I should have left you then, should have conjured up some trickery that would have led you away from the rose and me. But you asked my name, do you recall? And I answered you. *Belle*, I replied. And you said that you would call this rose, La Belle Rose, in my honor, for you had never seen the equal in beauty or grace. I will never forget those words, if I live to be another century." She stepped forward, closer to him, and said plaintively, "Arthur, you must remember!"

His shoulders slumped and he turned to fully face her, tears shining in his eyes. "I remember," he replied, his voice husky. "You were the most beautiful thing I had ever seen, before or since. I've never loved anyone as I loved you."

Maybelle's own eyes were overflowing and she nodded tremulously. "I used my glamour to entice you, Arthur, as I had so many before. Please, forgive me. I admit, at first it was all a lark. But you . . ." She tilted her head in a girlish manner. "You were different. You enticed me right back, making me fall in love with you. What I felt for you—still feel for you—is unlike any other emotion I've ever known. It is true and abiding. I loved you, Arthur. I always have and I always will."

"Then why?" Arthur exclaimed, pain and regret tearing at his throat as he gave voice to the question that had tortured him for over two decades. "Why did you leave us?"

"I had to," she replied in a broken voice. "I had no choice." When his eyes clouded with frustration she stepped closer, her own eyes appealing. "Arthur, try to understand. A love between fairy and mortal is forbidden. I knew this but I risked everything, so much in love was I. When we were discovered, I was punished. Exiled. But worse, I had to give you up, to give up my child. And I was condemned to live as a mortal until the child of my love became an adult." She turned to face her daughter. "My Laurel. I waited for you both for twenty-one years, each day living with the hope that someday I might see you again. And now that I have . . ." She buried her face in her hands, unable to continue.

Arthur stood staring at her, speechless, as the years melted between them.

The silence was rent by the sound of laughter. It was too high, too hysterical for humor. Laurel's laughter ended abruptly with a pained cry.

"You're not my mother!" She stepped back from the hurt that welled in Maybelle's eyes. "You're just some insane woman who believes she's a fairy. As I was insane to have fallen under your spell these past several months. What a fool I was to have believed all that nonsense about lights and dreams and magic. I was like some little kid, lapping it all up, playing dress-up and make believe. Well, I'm not a child! I'm grown up and I know that there is no such thing as magic or fairies. There is only common sense and reason and purpose— and I thank God I came back to my senses in time to stop this madness and get a grip on my life again."

"Laurel." Maybelle reached out to her daughter. "No matter what happens between you and me, don't say that. Magic exists. You must believe."

Laurel recoiled from her touch. "Don't!" she cried back, loud and bitterly, turning her shoulder against Maybelle. "Don't pretend that you care. You are not my mother. A mother is someone who is there to tend to the hurts, there when her child cries. I never had that. Not one morning, afternoon, or night of my life. You're just some woman who abandoned me at birth. You mean nothing to me. It's only your guilt that causes you to blather out such a ridiculous story, such utter nonsense, such garbage." Her voice rose in a hurt rage that betrayed all the years she'd told herself that it didn't matter that she didn't have a mother.

Shaking away the memory of that heartache, she straightened and said in a calmer voice, "I refuse to listen to this anymore. I'm leaving this place. Going back home where I belong. You can keep these paintings or burn them, I couldn't care less. Donate the money they earn to an orphanage to help other abandoned children.

But I won't be signing any contracts. I'm not an artist. Frankly, I don't care if I ever paint again." Turning to her father she announced, "I'm going to Cornell."

Maybelle darted a quick, worried glance at Dane. He remained still as death in the corner of the room.

Arthur stepped forward to take Laurel's hand, the hard, angry angles of his face softened by a new, boyish wonder.

"Child, don't be so hasty," he said gently. "I know this might be hard for you to understand, or accept. But . . . I believe her."

Laurel heard Maybelle's soft intake of breath beside her, but she could only stare at her father, stunned. She thought he'd be delighted with her rejection of Maybelle Starr, that he would compliment her on her ability to bypass this clearly emotional scene with level-headed, logical thinking.

"You can't be serious," she sputtered, withdrawing her hand as though she were touching fire.

"I'm absolutely serious. It all makes sense for the first time. You see, I never really understood what had happened to me when I met your mother. She was lovely, yes, of course, but there was some otherworldly quality to her, to our whole relationship. I saw . . ." His eyes took on a faraway look. "I saw the strangest things. I attributed it years later to my being out of my mind in love. Or possibly LSD." He cleared his throat and said offhandedly, "There was quite a bit of scientific exploration with that substance back then. The point is that I've never really accepted those rationalizations. Not in my heart. Now, when I look at Maybelle, when I look at your paintings . . ." He lifted his hands, grasping for the right words. "I know it was magic all along."

He moved to take Maybelle's hand. "I lost the magic once. I don't ever intend to lose it again."

Laurel gaped at him, unsure of what she'd heard. As his words seeped into her mind, she was blinded by a red haze of betrayal. Looking at her father and her mother wrapped in each other's arms, all she could see was a web of lies and deceit. With a strangled sound in her throat, Laurel lurched out from the studio, racing away as fast as she could.

Maybelle released a mother's cry of anguish and started after her, stumbling across a pile of paint supplies. Only Arthur's quick step stopped her from hurtling to the floor. Dane swiftly moved to halt her from continuing on out the door.

"Maybelle, let her go," he said, his voice brooking no argument. "She needs time."

"Time is the one thing I don't have to give!" she cried back. Her eyesight was dimming rapidly, shadowing her world in a shroud of black. She shuddered, feeling a strong cloud of evil blanketing Fallingstar. Thunder rumbled low and angrily in the mountains. "Dane, I sense a danger. I must get to her. To make her understand."

"You'll never catch her. I'll go. I know the woods better than anyone. And I think I know where to find her." He was almost out the door, when he turned and came back, this time to confront Arthur. He felt none of the wariness with the older man that he'd felt earlier. Dr. Arthur Carrington, the scholar, the academic, the rose rustler was simply the father of the woman he loved.

Dane had seen himself clearly in Laurel's eyes and he was never letting go of that image. Just as he was never letting go of her. He was not going to slink off to the mountains to lick his wounds in solitude like some great, hulking bear. He was a man, and he was going to fight for the woman he loved.

"Do you have something you want to say to me, young man?" Arthur asked, his tone defensive.

"Yes sir, I do. I want to ask for your daughter's hand in marriage."

Arthur's frown changed to a smile of relief and surprise. He grinned widely, extending his hand and grasping Dane's shoulder. "You have it, my boy," he said with enthusiasm. "And my blessing. Now go find her—and be quick about it!"

Twenty-three

Daphne entered the north meadow with a sense of utter devastation. A pall of heat and humidity that preceded a storm lay over the entire valley, wilting the tall grasses and wildflowers. She walked with a heavy tread, ignoring the gnats that clouded her head and the bits of green and burrs clinging to her jeans. The meadow was still and sorrowful.

Her bees were gone. Row after row of white wooden boxes lay broken and trashed on the ground. Gone, along with the best season of honey she'd ever had. All lay strewn on the ground in the dirt, ruined. Whoever did this knew what he was doing. A smoker had been used, a club or an ax, and poison. A face net and heavy leather gloves lay tossed in the dirt amid the dead carcasses of thousands of bees. She looked up to search the horizon, hoping against hope she'd spy a few scouts in the air, a clue to where her swarm might have landed. For thousands more of her bees would have taken flight.

There wasn't a bee in the sky, only the sight of countless wildflowers in peak bloom in the soft grassy meadow.

The angry, thrumming of countless, spiteful mental hornets teased to a fury in her mind. Only one person in the world would have done this horrible deed. Only a man so foul that he could hurt his own child in the worst way possible. Joe Flannery. The man she was cursed to say was her father.

You'll be sorry. Those were his words.

And it stung, most deeply of all, to realize that he was right.

She stuck out her chin at a stubborn angle. She was resolved not to lose what bees remained. She'd have to hurry. The hunt was on. A swarm was hers only if she could catch it.

Laurel climbed down into the fissure, retracing the steps she'd made with Dane. Several times she hesitated at a juncture; should she turn left? Where was the secret passage? A flash of light would catch her eye, a single pulse that guided her as crumbs of bread guided Gretel through the forest. She didn't question and took her time, remembering Dane's warning: *You could fall to your death in a hundred different places.* Onward she journeyed, feeling a desperate need to see La Belle Rose, to see if it was really there or if it was just another fantasy spun at Fallingstar.

Down she climbed, deeper into the fissure. She made her way through the musty, dank caves, around the rocky obstacles, and through the dark tunnels, following the flashes of light. At last she pushed through to Maybelle's natural greenhouse of rock and spring baths, where funneled sunlight poured onto the roses. Laurel crossed directly to the small raised bed bordered by quartz.

La Belle Rose was here! She stood as regally as Maybelle had in the studio, alone and upright, graceful yet thorny. La Belle Rose was real; she wasn't some dream. The comfort of seeing the beautiful rose wilted Laurel's anger, leaving her instead with a sadness that ached in her chest.

Her rose . . . that was how she felt about it. Perhaps because growing up she had held its image in her mind every night—a kind of kiss before sleep to comfort her in the dark. Laurel reached out to touch the velvety petals, then bent low to inhale her heady, sweet perfume. La Belle Rose . . . there was no other like her in the world.

She sank to her knees in the soft earth, lowered by

the thought that many children felt that way about their mother: *There was no other like her in the world.*

"Maybelle, how could you?" she cried, releasing the flow of tears for the first time that day. She sobbed bitterly, not knowing what hurt her more: the concept that Maybelle Starr, a woman she'd come to love, was in fact the mother she'd spent a lifetime hating. Or that the happiness she'd known here at Fallingstar was all just a fairy tale after all.

Weeping, she did not hear the man enter the garden. He crept on soft soles past the large flower bed of ancient roses, reaching in his pocket as he walked to pull out a small army knife. The soft click and whir of the steel blade as it sprung from the shaft was lost in the trickle and gurgle of the hot-water pond. He came to a stop a few yards away.

"I suppose I should thank you for leading me here, little lady."

Laurel's cry caught in her throat as she turned on the ground to follow the sound of the man's voice. She had expected to see Colin, but it wasn't him. This was a wiry man, thin and hungry looking, with heavy bones that protruded from dirty, worn jeans and a faded T-shirt. His grimy red hair clung close to his scalp and he oozed malevolence. It was his smile that frightened her, a sinister, ear-to-ear grin that revealed teeth the color of corn.

"Who are you?" she asked, leaning back against her arms.

"You can call me Lazarus," he replied, then broke into a hideous chuckle.

Laurel started rising to her feet, gauging the distance to the portal of the fissure. But the man thrust out his arm, revealing the glint of steel pointed directly at her.

"Don't you go running off in any hurry. I need to get clear of here well before I can let you go. Can't have you tellin' folks I'm here, can I?"

"What are you doing here? What do you want?"

He pointed his blade in the direction of La Belle Rose. "I want this rose." He jerked his head in the direction of the larger bed. "And the others."

Laurel paled and unconsciously held her arms out in a protective gesture. "You have no right. They're not yours."

"I ain't going to take them. I'm just going to help myself to a few cuttings."

"You can't. She'll die if she's cut!"

"That's not what that young scientist guy told me. I met him in the bar down in town. He was mighty upset, I can tell you, drunk as a skunk. Couldn't stop talking about some roses that were worth a fortune. Millions, he said. All he'd need were some cuttings. Well, I decided right then and there to get me some. Make your own opportunities, that's my motto. I had a big disappointment recently, but this'll make up for it and then some. We made a little deal, but damn! I've been searching in this godforsaken fissure for hours getting nowhere. I was just about to give up when you came along and led me right to them. So I'll thank you, and ask you to move aside."

"No, I won't. I know that man you're talking about. He's an ass. He didn't tell you the roses will die if you cut them."

"That's no concern of mine," he said, picking his nails with the blade of his knife. "Or his. He says he only needs cuttings." His eyes turned suddenly hard and his smile dropped. "So move—or the roses won't be the only thing I'll be cutting."

Laurel blanched but stood her ground. "If it's money you want, I'll get you some. I'll . . ."

The man was as quick as a ferret. In a flash he grabbed hold of her arm and wrenched her to her feet, shoving her out of his way. She fell against the wall of rock, slamming her palms, but was unhurt. Looking over her shoulder she saw the man step nearer to the rose-bush. It all happened in seconds. Sunlight reflected from the knife. She felt her body tense. She reached out into the empty air, grabbing at nothing, her scream stuck in her throat.

The sharp edge of the steel blade cut and pierced the rose's woody cane.

A shudder of revulsion and despair ripped through her. Laurel thrust herself from the rock and hurtled herself against his shoulder.

"No!" she screamed in heartfelt fury.

Dane heard the scream as he climbed down the fissure and his blood ran cold. With a thrust he lunged down, tearing his clothes and skin as he ripped past through the maze of rock and scrubby brush, then sprinted through the tunnel toward the light. He burst through the veil of green in time to see Laurel caught in a desperate struggle with a man. In that instant he caught a glimpse of his nose and chin, but it was enough. The realization of who the man was slammed home. Dane's blood ran hot, and fury pumped through his veins. With the ferocious roar of a lion he tore across the garden straight for them.

Joe Flannery looked up with horror. He spun around, pushing Laurel in front of him with one hand and pointing the blade of the knife toward Dane with the other.

Dane saw the dangerous intent in Joe's face, saw the fear and shock in Laurel's, saw the knife in Joe's hand, and came to a dead halt. The sight of Laurel in the grip of this vicious beater caused him to grind his teeth. He never knew he could feel such hate or the lust for murder as he did at that moment.

"I should've known it was you," he ground out. "I could smell your evil stench for miles."

"Well, well, well," spat out Joe Flannery. "Look who shows up to help another lady in distress. That's a role you just can't seem to shake, isn't it? You sure were a pain in the butt stickin' your nose in my business when you were a kid, and here you are doing it again." He jabbed the knife in his direction. "Boy, what am I gonna have to do to teach you a lesson?" He looked at Laurel then slid his glance back at Dane with a sinister grin. "I might just have an idea."

Dane saw a trickle of saliva at the side of Joe's mouth, saw the treachery in his gaze. His body coiled, ready to pounce. "Don't touch her," he ground out. "I'll kill you if you do."

The man cackled in glee, delighting in causing Dane

any pain. "Mr. Tough Guy, huh? Where were you the other day when I was *explaining* things to your sister? She didn't want to hear what I had to say neither."

"Daphne," Dane hissed as he took a step forward, his fists bunched.

Joe tightened his grip on Laurel with a fierce jerk. She released a soft cry that brought Dane to an abrupt halt.

"Ah, just figuring it out now, are ya? *Dumb Dane.*" He chuckled again, that high, self-serving cackle. "Got that one right, didn't I? Your sister, she deserved it. She turned on her own father when I needed her. She's got a hard head, that one does." He spat out a bitter laugh. "Hard head, get it?"

Dane felt an unbearable heat of fury scorch his pride that he wasn't there for his sister when she needed him. His mother, his sister, and now Laurel. He ground his teeth and readied his fists. No one would ever hurt Laurel, he vowed.

Laurel looked at Dane and saw the same dangerous glint in his eyes, the same intent to kill that she saw with the bear. Only this time, Joe Flannery had the knife. She had less than a minute. Dane would attack at any time. She had to act. Without warning she twisted in Joe's arms, whipping her arm up under his and knocking the knife from Joe's hand. In a blur of speed, he swung his hand down in a fist, connecting with the side of her head and knocking her down against the rocks.

Dane felt the blow himself, and releasing a savage cry from his lungs, he lunged forward, out for blood. Joe was smaller, but quicker. He jumped out of Dane's reach and began running toward the exit. Dane wanted his hands on him, wanted to pummel years of rage into that man's body. He took a step after him, but the sight of Laurel lying on the ground, not moving, changed his course. He hated Joe Flannery—but he loved Laurel Carrington more.

He crouched beside her while his gaze wandered over her head. Her long golden hair had fallen from its clasp and lay in a tumbled heap over her face. With extreme tenderness, his large hands lifted the hair from her face.

Her eyes were closed and blood trickled down from a gash on the side of her head, but she was breathing at a regular pace. His own breath returned and he gathered her in his arms, resting her head against his shoulder. With a smooth sweep, he lifted her and rose to a stand. His one thought was that she was hurt and he had to take her home to Maybelle for care. Laurel needed her mother.

Dane carried Laurel through the tunnel and the caves with utmost care, then began climbing up the rocky face of the fissure with the sure-footedness of a mountain goat. He took his time, careful not to take any risks. She still hadn't regained consciousness and each moment, each step was a torture of worry. A quarter of the way up he heard a whimper and felt her stir in his arms. With a surge of relief he moved to a grassy knoll to cradle her in his arms while he watched her face intently.

"Laurel," he called to her. "Open your eyes, Laurel. Come on, wake up."

Her long, spiky lashes fluttered. He held his breath. Then they opened to reveal those green eyes that he wanted to see every day for the rest of his life. Dane felt such love and relief he could have wept.

Laurel blinked heavily. Through the blur of pain and sun she saw Dane's brown eyes and furrowed brow, and in a rush it all came back to her—the man, the fight, the rose. Oh, the rose . . . But she was in Dane's arms and felt a wave of relief, knowing that she was safe. She whispered his name, "Dane."

"I'm here. I have you. Don't ever run from me again."

"I won't," she replied, nestling against his chest, suddenly very tired and sleepy.

"Oh, no you don't. I can't have you falling asleep on me now. You might have a concussion and it's a long way to the top." He gently guided her into a sitting position.

Laurel's head was spinning and she put her hand to her gash, swallowing thickly. "I don't think I can make it. My head feels woozy and my stomach is tumbling. I think I should rest awhile first."

Dane looked up at the threatening clouds that darkened the sky. "There's a storm coming. We could be stuck here all night, but I think you're right. Better to be safe and dry. Are you sure you're all right?"

She started to reply but a small rock came tumbling down the slope, narrowly missing them. She followed the line of fall, craning her neck back and squinting.

"Dane, look!" she cried with alarm, pointing to the top of the fissure. "It's him! Joe. He's reaching the top. Stop him. Don't let him get away!"

Dane followed her pointed finger to see Joe scrambling to reach the top of the fissure. He was too far to catch now, and even if he could, he wouldn't leave Laurel. "He can't get far and I'll find him. Don't worry, Laurel. I'll never let him hurt you again. I promise."

"He cut La Belle Rose," Laurel said, her voice catching. "I saw him do it. He cut right into her and I tried to stop him."

"Shhh . . ." Dane crooned, holding her close, grateful that only the rose was cut. "Fate has a way of meting out justice."

They watched in silence as Joe tackled the final few feet of the climb to stand at the precipice. He paused with his hands on his back, catching his breath and staring down into the fissure. She knew when he spotted them. His back went up, he paused, then he pulled out a narrow twig from his pocket and waved it in a wide, mocking arc over his head. She couldn't hear, but she was sure he was laughing. Laurel knew it was the cutting from La Belle Rose. She clutched Dane's hand, wishing that someone, something would stop him from getting away.

The clouds overhead shifted, casting a blinding ray of sunshine directly onto Joe, bathing him in a dazzling light. Suddenly he was enveloped in a dark swarm that darted and zigzagged around his body. They watched as Joe began batting at them, swinging and ducking at first, then waving his arms in a fury as the swarm thickened mercilessly around him. Laurel ignored the pain in her head and sat upright, clutching Dane's arm tightly as Joe lost his footing.

"No, stop!" she cried out.

Joe teetered at the edge. The swarm advanced, then he fell.

Laurel screamed and buried her face against Dane's chest as he tightened his hold around her.

Daphne stood on an open ledge looking up in the direction of her bees' flight. She could've sworn they'd veered to the left toward the line of spruces. But she heard a man's screaming and shouting directly to the right. She followed the shouts at a run, her heart pounding in fear as much as from the exertion. She rounded a bend just in time to see a man off in the distance, swatting and shouting at what looked to her like a swarm of bees. Those had to be her bees! She was about to take off on a run to help him when she saw him lose his balance, sway backwards with his arms flailing wildly, then disappear over the edge.

Maybelle squelched her cry of distress when she found Amor huddled in his feathers on the bottom of his cage, his little body heaving in erratic breaths. Taking faltering steps to the cage, she crooned and cajoled a tender song, but the little bird did not move from his one-legged isolation. Maybelle's eyes filled with pity and understanding. With shaky hands, she unhinged the cage's gate and turned it toward the open window.

"Fly away, dear faithful friend," she said in a weak voice to the small bird. "No use lingering on. Your work here is done. Go on home now, where you belong." She opened the gate fully. "I'll be along presently."

"What do you mean by that?" Arthur asked with alarm. He was standing at her side, distraught at seeing how pale and weak she'd become since the sun had lowered into the mountains. She'd fretted all afternoon, pacing back and forth at the window, wringing her hands, but still Dane and Laurel had not returned. At some point in the afternoon, however, her worry for their welfare deepened to physical illness. The storm that threatened in the mountains had passed quickly, leaving in its wake a remarkable sunset of hallucinatory glory. But as the sun set, Maybelle's eyesight dimmed and her health fell precipitously. She would neither eat nor drink, wanting only to sit with Arthur by the window and look out at the woods on a vigil for Laurel and Dane.

Now, as night settled, Arthur hovered around her in a nervous fret, watching uselessly. It seemed to him that he was watching her life slip away.

"You mustn't talk like that," he said to her, taking her in his arms. "You're not going anywhere. You're staying here, with me. And Laurel. You'll see. Just wait."

"I cannot wait much longer," she replied, looking sadly into his eyes. "Some destinies cannot be changed. I tried, but it was beyond me. I must accept my fate, Arthur. As you must accept yours." She looked into his eyes with the most profound sadness. "Please, take me into the garden to sit in the moonlight. There is a blue moon, did you know that? I've waited ever so long, longer than you can know, to sit under such a moon with you. Just being in your arms will be enough."

He wrapped her slim shoulders in a shawl and, slipping his arm around her waist, helped her as she took slow faltering steps out to the garden that she so adored. The moon was exceptionally high and bright, as round as a white plate hovering in the sky.

They sat together on a wooden bench, shoulder to shoulder, holding hands, staring out at the moon as a history of lovers had done before them. After awhile, Maybelle sighed heavily and rested her head against his shoulder.

Arthur, alarmed, patted her hand and said with bluster, "Don't fade away on me. You must rally, old girl."

"Old girl," Maybelle repeated weakly with a bittersweet smile. "Oh Arthur, I'm sorry you see me as such an old girl. I was a fool to believe all these years that you would see me as you once did."

Arthur turned to face her, lifting her head from his

shoulder so he could look into her eyes. He gave her a gentle, loving shake. "But I *do* see you as I did years ago," he replied, his voice ringing with emotion. "You can't think that a few lines on the face or the color of your hair would diminish the beauty I always saw in you. It was never the glamour that enticed me in the first place. It was always the magic I saw in your eyes. I saw that magic again when I met you again, after all these years. But I couldn't trust myself to give into it once again. I was afraid. A coward to take the chance again. Oh Maybelle, don't you know? Beauty has nothing at all to do with it. I love you! As much now—even more—than I loved you then."

Overhead, a sparkling falling star streaked across the dark blue sky, its silvery plume disappearing into the blue moon. Seeing it, Maybelle's eyes lit up and she kissed Arthur with all the love that was in her heart, holding tight to him, holding tight to the moment, knowing that the curse was lifted. It was a kiss that sprang from their youth, stretched to the present, and would linger well into their future.

When they drew back, Arthur looked at her with joy and surprise. "Maybelle, the bloom is back in your cheeks! I told you that you would rally. And the children will return, I know it. And when they do we'll tell them—well, what will we tell them?" He took her hand, his own hands shaking in eagerness. "I'm asking you, Maybelle, once again, to be my wife. Will you say yes? Will you stay with me this time, forever?"

Maybelle's fingers went to her lips, uncertain, as her heart warred with her reply. She turned her head toward the woods, trembling in indecision, while Arthur waited beside her in a tense silence. In the distance she saw her beloved fairy troop assembled at the woodland border, beckoning. They shone like stars in the Milky Way. In the forefront was Amor, her friend and mentor, resplendent in his translucent gold cloth and Omni, in white. Her heart yearned to end this painful exile and rejoin her own kind in her own world.

Yet before her was Arthur.

Meeting his gaze, her heart had her answer. "I have all the magic I will ever need sitting before me," she replied to him. To them. "I'd rather spend the remainder of my mortal lifetime with you, my love, even in darkness, than live without you in immortality. Yes, Arthur, I will marry you. At last."

In a gush of wind they found themselves engulfed in a cloud of small, dancing lights.

"Fireflies!" Arthur called out, laughing in boyish wonder. "There are so many!"

Maybelle smiled with happiness and lifted her face to the lights, accepting the vibrations of energy as gentle kisses into her heart. Then, as quickly as they came, the dancing lights flew off into the woods in a streak of sparkling stars.

Arthur removed his handkerchief from his pocket and held it in his palm between himself and Maybelle. He unwrapped it with precision and care, first one side of cloth, then another. Inside, laying on the crisp cotton, was a single rose petal of the purest white, tinged with blush.

"Ma belle rose," he said.

Maybelle reached up to pick up the single petal with two dainty fingers. With sparkling eyes, she pursed her lips and kissed it gently, then with a puff of air, blew the petal to the moon. Arthur smiled into her eyes, took her hand, and guided her back into the house.

Behind them, the rose petal caught a breeze, arced and somersaulted, then floated in the blue moonlight to the ground.

Deep in the fissure, Laurel knelt beside La Belle Rose, her heart as broken as the wooden cane of the slender rosebush. In the blue light of the moon and stars, she could see the magnificent blossoms, once so fresh and full of life, drooped on the stem, withering. Their scent had dissipated and the vibrant green leaves, once so glossy and firm, were already curling at the edges.

"There's nothing we can do," Dane told her, taking

her hand and leading her away. "Nothing short of a miracle can help the rose now."

"Maybelle will be brokenhearted," she said.

"I think she will be much more concerned about the loss of your love than the loss of a rosebush," he replied soberly. "Besides," he said, bringing her to a makeshift bed he'd created out of soft grass. "I suspect Maybelle knew that something like this might happen. She knew the risk when she allowed your father to see the rose. And Colin. It was inevitable that others intrude." He shook his head. "But it rankles to think that clod told that scum, Joe, about the roses. He'll tell the world next."

"It won't matter," Laurel replied, lowering herself to enter his waiting arms in the soft grass. "Without proof, no one will believe him. Just as no one will believe the existence of fairies, or elves, or angels. Or anything else that exists outside the realm of reason. Because there is no proof."

He cradled her in his arms and kissed the soft hairs of her head.

She sighed and nestled closer, deeper in his arms, feeling a security she'd never known possible. He'd already ripped his shirt and cleaned her wound with warm spring water from the pond. It was a surface cut, she knew. Nothing to fret about.

Nonetheless, Dane worried, gently placing her head in the crook of her arm and holding her close, keeping her warm with his body.

They lay together in a long, comfortable silence, listening to the sound of each other's breaths in the quiet night. Each lost in their own reflections, each comforted by each other's presence.

"Dane?" she asked in time, afraid to ask the question uppermost in her mind, yet compelled to do so. "What should we do? About Joe? I mean, who do we tell?"

"No one. He designed it so the world would believe that he disappeared in the woods seven years ago. Let the world keep on believing that. And let yourself forget."

"I need to talk to you first. I need to get things straight in my mind. When Joe was on the precipice . . ." She licked her dry lips, hesitant. "What did you see?"

There was a pause. "It was far, I couldn't see much, but it was clear he was attacked by a swarm. I don't know where they came from. Divine justice, I call it."

"A swarm. Of what, bees?"

"Yes, of course. Why? Did you see something else?"

Laurel chewed her lip and played with the buttons of Dane's shirt. She was relieved that he couldn't see her face. The garden was dark and the only illumination was the dim light of the stars and the magnificent moon overhead. What did she dare tell him?

She writhed in bleak anxiety, recalling the moment she looked up to see Joe standing on the precipice in a blazing glow of light. She did not see a swarm of bees. What she saw in the dazzling light was an army of fairies. Small beings armed with crystallike spears.

She tightened her mouth and clenched her fingers in the fabric of his shirt. She couldn't tell Dane this; he would think she was crazy. As insane as her mother who went one step further and claimed she was a fairy herself!

"Laurel, what's troubling you?" he asked, gently stroking her hair.

His low voice rumbled in his chest in a soothing cadence. Encouraged by his perspicacity, secure in his arms, she gave voice to the rambling thoughts and questions that were plaguing her.

"I'm so confused," she began in grand understatement. "And unsure. All I once held true is shaken. For the past several months, Maybelle inspired me to trust my intuition more than the facts in front of me. I questioned my understanding of time, space, and matter. And now I feel like I'm floating."

She felt his lips move into a smile against her scalp. "I know what's troubling you. You're trying to equate what you perceive as real and acceptable with the incredible things you've seen or experienced here at Fallingstar. I know, because I've gone through that struggle myself, many times, since I was a boy. I've studied long and hard, and all I can tell you, quite simply, my love, is that there is no answer I can give you with any certainty that will concretely satisfy you. To understand, you must drastically change the way you comprehend the physical world. You must open up to possibilities, not close or reject them because it doesn't make sense."

"That's too simplistic," she argued. "It diminishes generations of research and scholarship to simply say *believe*."

"Not at all! Belief doesn't deny the importance of science. Rather, an open mind provides a window through which new ideas can enter and help us grow. Remember back to when you were a child. You must have been open-minded because you admitted you listened to the trees. You didn't question it, or think yourself crazy. You just listened and *knew* at some level you heard. And it happened again here, didn't it? With the bear? And the butterflies and the bees?"

She nodded, feeling the excitement that always came to her when she was catching the tail end of a concept that she didn't fully grasp yet.

"I don't pretend to understand the physical universe," he continued in a far-off voice. "But I'm excited by a new theory that describes strings of microscopic particles that vibrate in a well choreographed dance. I know they're on to the truth. Think of it Laurel! While they dance, they surely glow."

"Fairies?" she breathed.

Dane laughed, shaking his head. "Who knows? Primitive people have long given common names and built stories around natural principles they did not fully understand. We still don't understand them, but the chase is on."

"But the fairies," she said, opening up, trusting him. "I saw them, Dane. Not only in my dreams or imagination. I caught glimpses of them before but today, on the precipice . . . they were there." She raised herself up to her elbow and looked at him, her eyes fearful. "Didn't you see them?"

He shook his head. "No, I didn't. I'm sorry, I only wish I did." When she turned away in dismay he nudged her back, urging her to face him again.

"No, I'm crazy," she said in distress. "Loony. I'm seeing things. I knew it."

"Laurel, it doesn't matter if I actually saw them or not. Some people are given gifts. They are able to perceive things at a different level. Yet that doesn't mean I can't believe. I study the science and play with the ideas, then I go into the garden to put my hands in the earth and walk through the forests where the sun dapples and I hear a whispering in the trees and I know magic is occurring in my universe. I can only rejoice at the wonder of it all and attempt to understand the truths at an intuitive level." He looked in her eyes, satisfied to have her attention. "That, Laurel, is faith."

Laurel wept then, not in sorrow but release. She didn't know for certain how she would resolve the deep-rooted conflicts with her mother. It would take time, certainly. But in Dane's arms, while his hands cradled her head, she believed that she was not crazy. And if she were not crazy, then she had to come to grips with the reality that she had seen fairies. Taking it to the next step, then, if she could accept this truth for herself, then she had to accept that what her mother told her was true as well.

It was a frightening concept, every bit as overwhelming and intimidating in her mind as goblins under the bed at night.

Suddenly she wanted to go home, to the charming little berm house with a thatched roof and crooked stovepipe that nestled against the mountaintop. To where countless whimsical fairies danced, carved in wood, etched in metal, or painted in murals. She wanted to live a simple life, close to nature so that she would never lose touch with the magic the lay in the drops of dew in the morning grass, or the soft whistling of the wind in the trees or smell of green grass and brown earth in the deep woods.

Most of all, she wanted to go home to her mother, to be held in her arms, to kiss her cheek, to smell the sweet perfume of her mother's skin, to whisper in her ear about all the things she'd seen and heard just to tell her—knowing she would understand, sure of her love.

"Dane," she whispered, bringing her lips to his. "Thank you."

"For what?" he asked.

"For being you. For being here. For loving me."

"It's I who should thank you."

A small smile curved her lips. "For what?"

"For inspiring me to believe once again."

Dane kissed her soundly, blanketing her with his body as the velvety night blanketed the earth. His kisses were as fiery as the stars overhead, his love as warm and full as the moon. She returned his kiss with all that was good and light and loving within her. Like the blustery wind and the refreshing rain, the tiniest atom and the magnificent, swirling galaxy, they joined together in a wondrous, exhilarating waltz in the universe.

Above them, the stars twinkled.

Around them, the fairies danced.

Epilogue

The meadow was a riot of spring colors. Marsh marigolds spread across the earth like softened butter, coltsfoot raised its tiny crowned heads, the catkins of willow bushes waved in a golden haze, ferns stood knee high with their heads still curled, and countless violets scattered the fields with their infinitesimal blue blossoms.

Most beautiful of all, however, were the small spring green canes of a single rosebush, La Belle Rose, Maybelle had claimed. No one knew for certain how it sprouted there in the meadow beside the bench. No one, perhaps, but Maybelle, who remembered one magical night and a single petal that floated gracefully to the ground. She doted on the small bush and was already making plans to transplant it to the fissure.

It was a sweet-smelling morning; the world felt fresh and new. Dane and Laurel stood at the edge of the forest, holding hands, watching as their bear cub, Vincit, grown large, fat, and strong over the winter, ambled into the woods where he belonged.

"He didn't even look back to say good-bye," Laurel said, her lip quivering in disappointment.

"He's a young male and it's spring. The last thing on his mind is his mother."

She laughed and cradled her hand on the swell of her abdomen, where, nestled inside, another baby slept and grew and would someday leave his mother behind.

"I was just thinking.," she said with a wistful note in her voice. "He's the last of them. They're all gone:

Omni, Vincit, and Amor. My first friends at Fallingstar. I guess you could say they were the harbingers of my future."

Dane turned to looked at her, surprise mingled with delight on his handsome face. "But of course! It all makes sense."

"What does?" she replied with another laugh at his expression.

"*Omni a vincit amor*! That's Latin for 'love conquers all.' "

Laurel's face registered the surprise she felt that she hadn't put the names together herself in all this time. "But what . . . how?"

"Don't try to understand it," he said with a roll of his eyes.

Laurel shook her head and leaned against him, relishing the feel of his arm as it slipped around her shoulder to press her nearer. "I won't," she replied. "It's serendipity."

"Come, wife," Dane said, taking her hand. "Maybelle is waiting lunch for us and I don't trust your father not to make mincemeat of my notes. The deadline for the book is looming and I've more work to do today than I can shake a stick at. We'd better head back."

Laurel whimpered her protest. She dragged her foot, tugged at his arm, and cast him a sloe-eyed glance that spoke of magic and miracles to be found in the shadows of the woods. Drawing him near, her delicate fingers played at the buttons of his shirt, toying with the plastic discs until one popped free.

"Whatever happened to spontaneity, hmmm? To experiencing the moment?"

A soft, sweet-scented wind whistled between them, whisking the tips of their hair, tingling their skin. Dane looked into her eyes and groaned with mock resignation. "I'm done for. It's the fairy in your eyes, you know they bewitch me. I'm powerless against it. And you're shameless, you know that? You use your powers to lure me to no good. Well, it'll be your fault if your child has a mindless father, worn out by fairy magic."

Laurel laughed with delight and tugged at his arm, luring him to follow her into the cool, welcoming shadows of the woodland she loved. As they crossed the threshold of betwixt and between, she heard a soft twittering and the gentle, vibrating strings of a violin. Dane heard it too; she could tell by the gleam of wonder in his eyes.

"*Omni a vincit amor,*" she said again, believing it, enjoying the sound of the beloved names as they echoed in the trees.

"Love conquers all."

Dear Reader,

Whether I finish a book, I love I begin to look for another that I'll enjoy just as much. And now that you've turned the last page of the book you have in your hands, I know you'll be keeping an eye out for another story to fall in love with.

Historical romance readers need look no further than next month's Avon Treasure by Connie Mason, *A Taste Of Sin*. Set in romantic Scotland, Lady Christy has been claimed as a bride—but in name only. Now, it's up to her to seduce the dashing rogue who has taken her as is wife . . . and to have her wedding night at last!

Patti Berg has charmed contemporary readers with her dynamic heroines, sexy heroes, and sassy humor. Now, the bestselling author of *Wife for a Day* brings us another rollicking love story, *Bride for a Night*. Cairo McKnight never wants to see her husband-for-one-night, Duncan Kincaid, again. But now he's back in her life . . . and just as irresistible as ever.

Ana Leigh's *The McKenzies* are some of the best-known characters of our time. Now, they make a spectacular return in *The MacKenzies: Josh*. Josh MacKenzie is hot on the trail of Emily Lawrence, who has fled her stuffy, wealthy home for the freedom of the west and life as a Harvey Girl. His mission is to get Emily back to Boston, but the beautiful spitfire fights him at every turn . . .

Susan Sizemore is a rising star of historical romance and the author of *The Price of Innocence*. Now, don't miss her latest sensuous page-turner *On a Long Ago Night*. Years ago, Honoria Pyne was forced to make a bargain with a mysterious rogue, and now he's come to claim her . . . as his bride. She has sworn to hate James Marbury forever . . . but some promises are meant to be broken.

Enjoy!

Lucia Macro

Lucia Macro
Senior Editor